Praise
of J

Temple of a Thousand Faces

"An epic, extraordinary novel about love, beauty, and war, *Temple of a Thousand Faces* is sure to please."—Sandra Gulland, bestselling author of *Mistress of the Sun*

"A gripping love story with a mystical quality that is utterly beguiling. John Shors vividly re-creates the world of twelfth-century Angkor Wat with his breathtaking descriptions, and packs it with a powerful tale of danger and revenge that had me hooked. I was there. I lived it. Riding a war elephant or gliding naked through a pool of water lilies. Full of fascinating characters and impressive storytelling."
—Kate Furnivall, *New York Times* bestselling author of
The Russian Concubine

Beneath a Marble Sky

"[A] spirited debut novel. . . . With infectious enthusiasm and just enough careful attention to detail, Shors gives a real sense of the times, bringing the world of imperial Hindustan and its royal inhabitants to vivid life." —*Publishers Weekly*

"Jahanara is a beguiling heroine whom readers will come to love; none of today's chick-lit heroines can match her dignity, fortitude, and cunning. . . . Elegant, often lyrical writing distinguishes this literary fiction from the genre known as historical romance. It is truly a work of art, rare in a debut novel."
—*The Des Moines Register*

"An exceptional work of fiction . . . a gripping account." —*India Post*

"Highly recommended . . . a thrilling tale [that] will appeal to a wide audience." —*Library Journal*

"Evocative of the fantastical stories and sensual descriptions of *One Thousand and One Nights*, *Beneath a Marble Sky* is the story of Jahanara, the daughter of the seventeenth-century Mughal emperor who built India's Taj Mahal. What sets this novel apart is its description of Muslim-Hindu politics, which continue to plague the subcontinent today." —*National Geographic Traveler*

"[A] story of romance and passion . . . a wonderful book if you want to escape to a foreign land while relaxing in your porch swing." —*St. Petersburg Times*

"It is difficult to effectively bring the twenty-first-century reader into a seventeenth-century world. Shors accomplishes this nicely, taking the armchair traveler into some of the intricacies involved in creating a monument that remains one of the architectural and artistic wonders of the world."
—*The Denver Post*

"[Shors] writes compellingly [and] does a lovely job of bringing an era to life . . . an author to anticipate." —*Omaha World-Herald*

Cross Currents

"Shors re-creates the devastating, life-overturning tsunami in prose that is stunning and profoundly moving. . . . It is testament to the power of his depiction that I felt my own world wrenched apart in these pages—and that I finished the last two chapters, portraying the tragedy's physical and emotional aftermath, more deeply desirous than ever to visit this rich and resilient place."
—National Geographic

"*Cross Currents* is about the power of nature and the power of love—romantic, brotherly, and parental. You are held in suspense, watching the love between characters grow, knowing that this love is going to be tested severely when the tsunami hits. And when it does, you are carried away by the clash of both forces in a maelstrom of riveting action. I loved this book."
—Karl Marlantes, *New York Times* bestselling author of *Matterhorn*

"John Shors has a great feeling for Thailand. The beauty of its geography and the pliant strength of its people are in every word of his novel *Cross Currents*, which is set in the days just before the tsunami. The suspense around what will happen to his characters (each with a vivid history and set of troubles) makes for a supremely readable tale." —Joan Silber, author of *The Size of the World*

"Gripping, moving, and ravishingly written, Shors's latest is a stunning story of family, connection, and the astonishing power of nature."
—Caroline Leavitt, *New York Times* bestselling author of *Pictures of You*

The Wishing Trees

"An affecting and sensitively rendered study of grief and loss, the healing power of artistic expression, and the life-altering rewards of travel to distant lands. I was deeply moved by this poignant and life-affirming novel."
—Wally Lamb, *New York Times* bestselling author of *She's Come Undone*

"Shors's fourth novel is a moving, emotional story about coping and coming to terms with loss. Anyone who has lost a loved one will relate to this poignant novel." *—Booklist*

"John Shors has made himself a reputation for re-creating exotic landscapes that surround heartwarming stories with captivating details. *The Wishing Trees* is no exception, as he replaces what might be a standard tale of recovery from loss with an alluring travelogue filled with colorful details of these chromatic countries." *—BookPage*

"Poignant. . . . Country by country, their odyssey transforms into a journey of worldly healing and renewal, nurtured by the wisdom and compassion they discover in the cultures they pass through and by the realization of the commonalities—hope, death, love—that bind all fathers, mothers, and children." *—National Geographic Traveler*

Dragon House

"A touching story about, among other things, the lingering impacts of the last generation's war on the contemporary landscape and people of Vietnam. In a large cast of appealing characters, the street children are the heart of this book; their talents, friendships, and perils keep you turning the pages."
—Karen Joy Fowler, *New York Times* bestselling author of *Wit's End*

"A wonderful novel. . . . Shors transcends politics and headlines and finds the timeless and deeply human stories that are the essence of enduring fiction. This is strong, important work from a gifted writer."
—Robert Olen Butler, Pulitzer Prize–winning author of
A Good Scent from a Strange Mountain

Beside a Burning Sea

"A master storyteller. . . . *Beside a Burning Sea* confirms again that Shors is an immense talent. . . . This novel has the aura of the mythic, the magical, and that which is grounded in history. Shors weaves psychological intrigue by looking at his characters' competing desires: love, revenge, and meaning. Both lyrical and deeply imaginative."
—Amy Tan, *New York Times* bestselling author of *The Joy Luck Club*

"Features achingly lyrical prose, even in depicting the horrors of war. . . . Shors pays satisfying attention to class and race dynamics, as well as the tension between wartime enemies. The survivors' dignity, quiet strength, and fellowship make this a magical read."
—*Publishers Weekly*

"An astounding work. Poetic and cinematic as it illuminates the dark corners of human behavior, it is destined to be this decade's *The English Patient*."
—*Booklist*

"Shors has re-created a tragic place in time, when love for another was a person's sole companion. He uses lyrical prose throughout the novel, especially in his series of haiku poems, [which] plays an integral role in the love story, and develops accessible, sympathetic characters. . . . A book that spans two and a half weeks, set on a deserted island, easily could become dull and redundant. But Shors avoids those turns by delving into the effects of war on each character, causing readers to attach themselves to the individuals yearning for home and the ones they love."
—*Rocky Mountain News*

Also by John Shors

Beneath a Marble Sky

Beside a Burning Sea

Dragon House

The Wishing Trees

Cross Currents

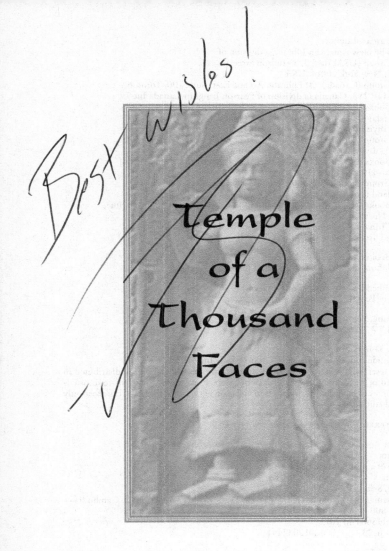

Temple
of a
Thousand
Faces

John Shors

NEW AMERICAN LIBRARY

New American Library
Published by New American Library, a division of
Penguin Group (USA) Inc., 375 Hudson Street,
New York, New York 10014, USA
Penguin Group (Canada), 90 Eglinton Avenue East, Suite 700, Toronto,
Ontario M4P 2Y3, Canada (a division of Pearson Penguin Canada Inc.)
Penguin Books Ltd., 80 Strand, London WC2R 0RL, England
Penguin Ireland, 25 St. Stephen's Green, Dublin 2,
Ireland (a division of Penguin Books Ltd)
Penguin Group (Australia), 707 Collins Street, Melbourne, Victoria 3008,
Australia (a division of Pearson Australia Group Pty. Ltd.)
Penguin Books India Pvt. Ltd., 11 Community Centre, Panchsheel Park,
New Delhi–110 017, India
Penguin Group (NZ), 67 Apollo Drive, Rosedale, Auckland 0632,
New Zealand (a division of Pearson New Zealand Ltd.)
Penguin Books (South Africa), Rosebank Office Park, 181 Jan Smuts Avenue,
Parktown North 2193, South Africa
Penguin China, B7 Jiaming Center, 27 East Third Ring Road North,
Chaoyang District, Beijing 100020, China

Penguin Books Ltd., Registered Offices:
80 Strand, London WC2R 0RL, England

First published by New American Library,
a division of Penguin Group (USA) Inc.

First Printing, February 2013
10 9 8 7 6 5 4 3 2

REGISTERED TRADEMARK—MARCA REGISTRADA

LIBRARY OF CONGRESS CATALOGING-IN-PUBLICATION DATA:
Shors, John.
  Temple of a thousand faces/John Shors.
    p. cm.
  ISBN 978-0-451-23917-4 (pbk.)
  1. Jayvarman VII, King of Cambodia, ca. 1120–ca. 1215—Fiction. 2. Cambodia—
History—800–1444—Fiction. I. Title.
  PS3619.H668T46 2013
  813'.6—dc23   2012032441

Set in Adobe Garamond
Designed by Alissa Amell
Title page photo courtesy of Alex Castellino and Andrew Ambraziejus

Printed in the United States of America

For Allison

Author's Preface

One of the architectural and spiritual wonders of the world, Angkor Wat is a legendary temple located in Cambodia. At the time it was built almost a thousand years ago, Angkor Wat dominated the city of Angkor, which was populated by as many as a million people and was one of the largest and most advanced cities on earth. The local people, known as the Khmers, were skilled artisans, warriors, and scholars.

For centuries, the Khmers fought the Chams, who flourished in what is now central Vietnam, for the spoils of Southeast Asia. Forces from both sides crossed borders, plundered treasuries, and captured slaves. In 1177, the Cham king, Jaya Indravarman IV, sailed up the Mekong River with a massive army and sacked Angkor, destroying much of the city and subjugating its citizens. A Khmer prince and his beloved wife avoided capture, vowing to retake Angkor.

The events surrounding *Temple of a Thousand Faces* are based on historical fact. However, most details of this remarkable clash of civilizations have been lost through the trials of time. Only one surviving eyewitness account of the Khmer Empire exists, written by a Chinese envoy in the thirteenth century. Therefore, through necessity, I've created many elements of this novel. For the sake of the modern-day reader, I've also simplified the names of the people who fought and loved so long ago.

Angkor Wat is believed by most scholars to be the largest religious structure in the world, a sprawling complex built by fifty thousand Khmer artisans and laborers with the help of four thousand elephants over a forty-year period. The temple, which was fashioned from five million tons of gray sandstone, is something I'll never forget—seemingly too wondrous and immense to have been conjured by human minds and hands.

What is known about Angkor Wat's history is as remarkable as the sight of the temple itself. More than three hundred years before Columbus set sail, a series of betrayals and battles, deeds and sacrifices, decided the fate of one of the world's greatest empires—an empire that was lost, but found again.

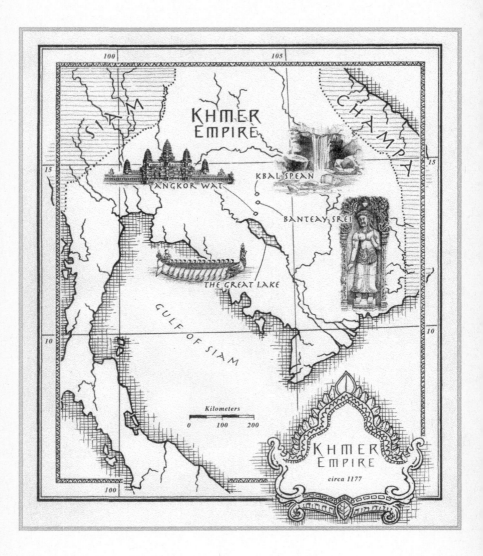

SIAM

KHMER EMPIRE

CHAMPA

KBAL SPEAN

ANGKOR WAT

BANTEAY SREI

THE GREAT LAKE

GULF OF SIAM

Kilometers
0   100   200

KHMER EMPIRE

circa 1177

One can live in a cluttered house. One cannot live with a cluttered heart.

—KHMER SAYING

Part One

One

The Fallen

The temple of Angkor Wat had been designed to house the Hindu Gods but looked as if it had been built by them. Rising from the top of the massive, terraced temple were five towers shaped like lotus buds, the central and tallest of which stretched upward for two hundred feet. These towers symbolized the peaks of Mount Meru, the core of the Hindu universe, where the Gods resided and from where all creation sprang. The wide, square moat surrounding Angkor Wat represented the cosmic ocean, and the walls near the moat were meant to remind Hindus of the mountain ranges at the distant edges of the world.

Dedicated to the God Vishnu, Angkor Wat could hardly have been more imposing. Each tower was tiered and tapered, coming to a point at the top and as wide as a tree's canopy at the base. The towers were situated on the highest of three rectangular terraces, each stacked on top of another. Though visible from miles away, the towers weren't the only element of Angkor Wat to inspire visitors. Large swaths of the temple were rich in carvings depicting heroic images of Vishnu and Shiva, as well as of the king who had ordered the temple built and everyday Khmer people. Many of these bas-reliefs were painted. Others were covered in gold.

Though Prince Jayavar was Buddhist, the sight of Angkor Wat filled him with pride. At fifty years of age, he was old enough to remember the temple's creation. Many of his early memories were dominated by the sights and sounds of sandstone being carted and chiseled. Now, as he stood on the causeway leading to the main entrance of the complex, he watched Hindu priests sweep the slabs of sandstone with thatched brooms.

Jayavar's gaze drifted to his chief wife, Ajadevi, who stood beside him. In the fashion followed by most Khmers of either sex, her hair was pulled back and wound in a knot atop her head. Like everyone else, she was naked to the waist. A silk skirt cloth was wrapped around her hips and tied in the front below her belly button. The skirt cloth, which fell to her shins, featured a floral design of white irises against a blue background. Encircling her fingers, wrists, biceps, and ankles were golden hoops and rings. A chain of jasmine flowers hung from her neck, resting between her full breasts and infusing the air with a sweet scent. Both the soles of her feet and the palms of her hands had been dyed red. As was customary among her people, she went barefoot.

Almost a decade younger than Jayavar, Ajadevi still retained some features from her youth. Her skin was mostly unlined and the color of teak. Her eyes, wide and dark, remained sharp and restless. Her angular, proud face reminded Jayavar of a boat's bow. Like most Khmer women, Ajadevi's body was thin, the result of a diet of rice, fruit, vegetables, and fish.

Husband and wife leaned against a balustrade of the sandstone causeway. The stonework was rounded at the top—the midsection of a *naga*, a seven-headed snake, which formed the balustrade and was thought by Hindus to be a deity of the ocean and mountains.

Though Jayavar and Ajadevi did not know it, they would be fleeing for their lives before the morning ended.

"Your father is weakening," Ajadevi said, lifting the jasmine flowers to her nose. "No one dares to say it, but everyone sees it."

Jayavar nodded, still watching the priests. Nearby, four slaves carried a high-ranking official past them on a palanquin held aloft with gold-plated poles. "Can no one find the strength to walk?" he asked softly, his right hand on the hilt of a sheathed sword that hung from his side. He was dressed like his wife, though his hip cloth fell only to his upper thighs. His face was round and pleasant, made memorable by full lips and a broad nose. The softness of his features contrasted with the rest of his body, which was dominated by muscles and scars. His hair, also gathered in a topknot, was streaked with gray.

"Last night," Ajadevi said, "a vision came to me."

"What sort of vision?"

"The river was red. The red of both birth and death."

Jayavar turned away from Angkor Wat, looking to the north-east, toward the land of their enemy, the Chams. "Father shall stay strong enough," he replied. "He's always been of stout mind and sound body."

"Always is an assuming, imperfect word."

"But nothing of war looms. Our spies are as silent as stones. And our army is ready."

"You should take care to be even better prepared. The visions tell me that we're not alone. When the river runs red, it can mean only that war descends upon us, as it has so many times before. We don't want it, but like the wind, it cares nothing of what we want."

He thought about his father, who rarely emerged from the

Royal Palace. Jayavar's mind then shifted to the whereabouts of his army. Many of his men were helping to strengthen levees outside the city, as the monsoon rains had been stronger than normal and increased the chances of catastrophic flooding. "What else do your visions tell you?"

"That you love me."

"You need no visions to tell you what you already know."

"True enough," she answered, then closed her eyes.

He wondered whether she was praying. Though most Khmers were Hindus, she was a Mahayana Buddhist, more devout than anyone he had ever met—a seeker of signs. As he watched her, an elephant trumpeted somewhere in the distance. Because of the depth of its voice, Jayavar knew that it was a war elephant, not a working elephant; only the largest of elephants could make such a sound. Somewhere a group of his men was training for battle.

Only when she opened her eyes did he speak again. "I would rather tend to our people than wage war."

"How shall you tend to them?"

"By building hospitals. Roads. Way stations for travelers. Our city has grown too big. And the needs of our people are too numerous."

A peacock, bright and billowing with color, wandered down the causeway. Ajadevi studied the bird, wondering what its presence portended. "Your sword is heavy, I know. You tire from carrying it, and your arms sag and crack with the passage of time as a tree's limbs do. But you mustn't rest yet, Jayavar. Do what your father should—destroy our foe. Then build your hospitals and roads. Then tend to your people."

Jayavar turned, looking again to the northeast. Unseen in the distance, past countless homes and the magnificent Royal Palace, stretched a field where warriors trained. The prince imagined the sight of his men, of spearheads striking shields. "We should use our strength against famine. Against leprosy. Such strength shouldn't be wasted on Chams."

"The path you walk isn't yours to choose."

"What if we ran? If we left here, just you and I?"

"You wouldn't leave the fate of our people in the hands of others. Nor would you flee your wives and children."

"True enough. I could never leave my children. But I want you in my hands. That should be my fate."

She reached for him, her fingers caressing his calloused palms. "Tell me what you'd do with these hands of yours. These instruments."

"They'd celebrate the softness of you. The hills and valleys that comprise the world that is you."

"I shall show you this world," she replied. "Find me tonight, when the moon reaches its zenith."

He smiled and said good-bye, then walked toward three of his waiting officers, toward where he needed to be, but away from where he wished to be.

Ten miles downstream, an army swept forward. This army rode neither war elephants nor horses, but barges carried by the swollen Tonle Sap River, which, because of the monsoon season, had reversed its normal flow toward the sea and now headed in the direction of Angkor. The barges were stout and long, steered by rudimentary rudders and a variety of handheld poles. Each vessel held anywhere from fifty to one hundred Cham warriors who wore short-sleeved, quilted armor and carried circular shields made of wood, metal, and leather. The Chams had no helmets. Instead, they all wore green and pink headdresses designed to resemble overturned lotus flowers—symbols of enlightenment.

Most of the men carried spears, though some had opted for swords, daggers, axes, or bows and arrows.

The Tonle Sap River was part of a confluence of waterways that comprised the Mekong Delta and was constantly intersected by various streams and lakes, a watery maze that had confounded intruders for centuries. The Chams would not have found this route to Angkor if not for the one-handed traitor who stood at the bow of the royal barge and passed along instructions. Though his father was a high-ranking official in Angkor, the traitor cared little for the fate of those who shared his blood. His allegiance had been bought with a bag of Cham silver.

The royal barge was the largest of all the vessels. It carried ten stallions and nearly a hundred men. While the horses neighed nervously, the men laughed and fingered the hilts of their weapons. Almost all were eager for battle, for with battle came plunder. The quickest way to get rich was to conquer, and these warriors craved wealth.

On a dais covered in tapestries and shaded by several silk umbrellas sat the Cham king, Indravarman, who had been born into privilege but had come to power through the sword, and sought to do the same in Angkor. He was clad in decorative armor and gripped a spear made of teak and silver. An oblong pearl the size of a child's fist dangled from his neck. Gold bracelets and rings adorned his wrists and fingers. A small piece of iron, purposely buried beneath the skin of his belly, brought him good luck. An unusually large man, he had spilled blood before and longed to do so again.

Surrounding Indravarman were dozens of his most decorated officers. These men kept cool under umbrellas held by nearly naked slaves who had been taken from the mountains in the north. As their king spoke of strategy and the future, the officers listened attentively, only the most experienced and brave among them offering suggestions. One such officer, Asal, was younger than all the rest and had been in the army long before he'd become a man. His parents and siblings had died of cholera when he was a child. Somehow he had survived the illness and, in the years that followed, he had stolen vegetables from farms and fish from bamboo traps. He'd been hunted, beaten, and twice left for dead. But each scar had only made him stronger. And once his muscles began to thicken, he had made a spear and sold his services, ultimately protecting the very fields that he'd once plundered. Life had been tolerable until one day when he'd let a starving girl leave with two mangos and, having failed in his duty, quit the very next dawn to join the army.

Though Asal cared little for Indravarman, he respected the king and the way he had come to power. The high rank of the king's father had provided him with opportunities, but he'd taken more than he had been given. And while Asal didn't seek to gain through the suffering of others, he coveted power, prestige, and all other trappings made possible by war.

Long ago, Asal had decided that his future lay with ascension in the army, and he had trained himself for such a journey. Not only had he practiced with spears, swords, and shields until his palms bled; he'd also studied military strategy and heeded the counsel of older warriors while other young fighters rushed blindly into battle.

Years of training had hardened his body. Though nearly a head shorter than his king, he was still a large man with broad shoulders and thickly muscled arms and legs. He wore his hair pulled back and bound in a topknot like other Chams, though his locks were slightly longer and swayed when he ran or fought. An inverted lotus-flower headdress partially shaded his eyes. It had been made to provide him with solace on the battlefield, announcing his spiritual enlightenment to friend and foe. Time had not yet imprinted itself on his face, which remained youthful. His smile, when he shared it, was wide and pleasant. His eyes were bright, his skin the color of honey. Unlike most officers, he wore no jewelry. Instead of using plunder to purchase rings and necklaces, he acquired the best weapons and shields.

Daring to shift his attention away from the king, Asal glanced toward the other barges, which seemed as countless as the black hairs bundled together atop his head. Everywhere he looked, steel glistened and men stood in tightly packed groups. The odors of sweat, dung, and vomit hung in the damp air. The sounds of strained voices rose from distant vessels as men dominated other men, exhorting them to fight, to make their ancestors proud.

Several small, fast boats advanced ahead of the royal barge. These boats were filled with archers and strong warriors. When they spotted a Khmer fisherman or hunter, the boats sped forward, and the Cham warriors tinted the water with the blood of their enemies. In that way the army was like a virulent disease, spreading out and killing everything in its path.

Asal looked back at Indravarman. The barges had been Asal's idea, and he worried that something would go wrong. Perhaps the Khmers had returned from reinforcing the levees and would be alerted and awaiting them on their dreaded war elephants. Perhaps too many of the Chams were sick or ill trained for the ferocity of combat. If his plan succeeded, Asal knew that power and wealth would be bestowed upon him and his unborn children. If it failed, he would be wise to die in battle rather than find himself at his king's mercy.

As Indravarman spoke of plunder and pillage, Asal reminded himself to avoid such temptations. He wanted to capture the Khmer king or prince. Such an act would grant him further honor, would ensure that his children would never know hunger or shame. While other officers fought over jewels or women, he would forge ahead with a few men he trusted, fighting his way deep into the Khmer stronghold.

Weary of his own thoughts and the constant movement of the barge, Asal focused on Indravarman, noting the way men listened to the king, striving to catch his eye.

"Our struggle against the Khmers has raged too long," Indravarman said, standing up as he made his point. He thrust the butt of his spear against the deck. Other men repeated this action with their own weapons. "So we shall end that struggle today," he continued, and then rubbed the piece of iron in his belly for good luck. "Leave their temples for me. But slay their priests, their bureaucrats, their men, their hopes. Let them fear us so much that they shall never wage war on us again. I want their women, their old, their children to be as submissive as a dog that's been kicked since birth. If a Khmer warrior asks for mercy, spear him like a boar. If a boy sees his father die, then kill the boy also, for revenge is the sharpest of blades."

Indravarman found Asal's eyes, held them for a moment with his own, and then nodded. "Once we land outside Angkor, find your men and spread my words. Then follow me into the city, a city that knows no equal, which has cast a shadow on our land for far too long." Again, Indravarman slammed his spear butt into the deck. "This city that mocks us shall soon be ours. Let me repeat those words in case the blood of battle already fills your ears. Everything that is theirs will be ours. Temples, farms, silks, gems, women—all of these things shall be yours once the men are dead. But wait until every Khmer warrior lies broken at your feet. Wait until this moment, and then enjoy the spoils of victory. Enjoy them as a king would, for on this day you shall all be kings!"

As the officers around him beat their weapons together and echoed Indravarman's words, Asal looked ahead, toward the city that would soon be torched. Indravarman would watch him, he knew, and he would have to take the battle to his foe. If he was ever to live free and proud, he must be a lion this day.

Closing his eyes, ears, and mind to the clamor around him, Asal gripped the shaft of his spear so tightly that his knuckles whitened. He thought of his unmet wife, his unborn children. The knowledge that their fates rested upon this day gave him a profound sense of strength and determination. Khmers would die on his spear, he knew. They would die in great numbers. But would he create a name for himself? Would his deeds make his future wife and children proud and ensure that they never knew the pain of hunger and fear?

Ahead, his countrymen overtook a trio of Khmer fishing boats. Bodies soon drifted among the barges. The Chams mocked the dead, filling them with arrows and scorn.

Asal tested the sharpness of his spear point against his thumbnail and watched a shaving fall to the deck.

My time has come, he thought. The time of me, of my ancestors, of my family—it is now.

Not far upstream, in a branch off the main river, a father and his two sons sat in their boat and hauled in a long fishing net. Though not even forty years of age, the father looked as worn as his boat, which was nothing more than the trunk of a tree that had been hollowed out. Once, it had been smooth and scar free, but those days were long past. Though still strong and worthy, the boat was marred with wounds. The father was much the same—his face prematurely wrinkled by too much sun, his skin as dark as the muddy waters upon which he plied his trade. And while his body was still muscled and powerful, three decades of hauling carp and catfish from the river had worn him down. The thumb of his left hand was missing. His legs and arms were battered and gouged from countless encounters with knives, snapping turtles, hooks, and crocodiles.

In the front of the boat, the man's two sons, fourteen-year-old twins, hauled in the coarse net. Like their father, the sons were naked but for the smallest of hip cloths. None of them wore any ornamentation—such trappings were reserved for the wealthy, and even a heavy load of catfish had never put silver in the father's hands.

The sons bantered back and forth as they worked. Though they looked and acted alike in many ways, there was a stark difference between them—one could see and one was nearly blind. The son with the gift of sight was known as Vibol. His brother was called Prak. Though the father was proud of both of them, he had a deep, secret adoration for Prak, who had never been slowed by his condition. In many ways, Prak was the rope that bound their family together, prompting them to laugh when their nets were empty, to find sources of solace when mosquitoes and misery descended upon them.

Prak called out to his brother. An immense green and yellow eel was caught in the folds of their net. The size of a man's arm, the eel flopped and twisted, seeking a way out of its entanglement. Though to Prak the eel appeared as only a blurred shadow, he reached down with practiced motions, grabbed its head, and dug his thumbs into its gill openings. Vibol bent over and jammed a short knife into the eel's neck. It writhed for a moment and then was still.

Grunting, Prak lifted the heavy eel toward the boat, dropping it in a bamboo basket filled with the rest of their catch. "We should leave soon," he said, dipping his hands in the river. "The market will be open by now."

"Once the rest of our net is in, we will," the father replied, pleased with their catch. Known as Boran, the fisherman paddled forward so that the bow of his boat drew nearer to the submerged part of the net.

"We should keep that one for ourselves," Prak said, nodding toward the eel. "Smoke it tonight and save what we don't eat."

Vibol shook his head, drumming his fingers on the gunwale. "I'm weary of fishing. Let's leave for the city."

"You're weary of everything," Prak answered. "Maybe that says more about you than anything else."

With the back of his hand, Vibol whacked his brother's head.

Prak was undaunted. "You just want to bathe with the pretty girls. To pretend that you're not watching them when even I can see how you stare."

"We should bathe. After stinking of so many fish, why not bathe like everyone else?"

"Why not wash here? Right now? Why wait until we reach Angkor?"

"Because he doesn't want to look at our ugly backsides when the view is so much better in Angkor," Boran answered, smiling.

Vibol splashed his father and brother, who were both laughing. He turned his attention forward once again, reaching for the net, pausing as a group of starlings rose suddenly from a distant tree's canopy, filling the sky with their dark bodies.

Boran and Prak stopped laughing. While the father peered into the distance, the son closed his eyes and listened.

"A tiger?" Vibol asked.

Boran shook his head. "Birds have no fear of tigers."

"A leopard, then? A leopard that climbed into a tree?"

"No."

"Be silent," Prak said, his eyes still closed. He was almost immediately aware that the jungle had grown unusually quiet. The day was still—too still. At first he thought that other fishermen were encroaching upon their water, but the wind soon brought unusual scents to him. He smelled cooking fires and dung. A few heartbeats later, he heard the faint neigh of what sounded like a horse. The voices of men found his ears next, only these voices were foreign. "Father," he said, "I hear men. But . . . but they aren't Khmers."

Boran strained to listen, but heard nothing. "Are you certain?"

"Yes. And they draw closer."

Staring ahead to where the river they'd been fishing intersected with the much larger waterway, Boran heard a horse's neigh. The skin on his back tingled. "Cut the net," he whispered. "Cut it now."

Vibol drew his knife. "But, Father, we—"

"Do it."

The net was severed and dropped into the water. Boran quietly paddled their boat toward a massive ficus tree that had toppled into the river, almost cutting it in half. He positioned their craft in the midst of the thickest branches, which lay between them and the main waterway. "Be still," he said softly.

"Why?" Vibol asked.

"Because I fear we're no longer the hunters here."

Time passed slowly, lingering like clouds on a windless day. The voices drew nearer. And yet the larger river remained unburdened, shimmering in the heat. A carp flopped in their basket and Vibol drove his knife into its spine. The father and sons hunched lower as other birds, much closer than the starlings had been, took flight.

Several small boats came into view. They were manned by warriors dressed for battle, and Boran felt as if he had tumbled from a high perch. The royal barge came next, immense and brimming with men and stallions. Even in Angkor, Boran had never seen such a craft. He glanced toward their distant home, where his wife would be mending nets, unaware of the impending attack.

Barge after barge passed within their view. There seemed to be no end to the Chams, and the image of the royal barge began to feel like an old memory. Though Boran was used to seeing formations of warriors in Angkor, these thousands of Chams struck fear into his heart. They seemed more numerous than all the fish he'd ever caught, than all the dawns he'd seen.

"We have to warn them," Vibol whispered. "We can do it. The streams will take us to Angkor faster than—"

"And your mother?" Boran asked. "What are we to do about your mother?"

Vibol closed his eyes, only then realizing that their home lay in the path of the Chams. "No," he muttered. "They wouldn't—"

"They would," Boran replied, his voice still low. "And we must go to her. Now."

"Put me ashore. I can run ahead. I can reach Angkor faster than the Chams. Those barges are slow."

"Not slow enough. So we stay as one."

"I can outrace them. And I'll find you. After I've—"

"After you've been killed?"

"But the city! We have to warn them."

Boran clenched his fists, knowing that his son was right, that somehow his countrymen must be warned. But doing so would leave his wife alone and unaware. And he understood what fate would befall her when the Chams reached their home. She would be killed, raped, or enslaved, and no such fate could he endure.

"Let me go," Vibol persisted.

"No."

"Put me ashore and let me run."

"You'll stay with me. I need you."

"My people need me!"

Boran placed his hand over Vibol's mouth, fearing that his words had carried. A pair of Cham barges passed. Sunlight glinted on their armor and weapons. The men appeared to look in their direction, but eyes did not meet eyes. The barges disappeared.

Cursing himself for wasting too much time, Boran picked up his paddle and carefully maneuvered them out of the sagging branches. He turned their boat away from the Chams, heading for a maze of streams that would carry them home. Though they tried to keep as low a profile as possible, a shout went up in the distance. Boran didn't turn, didn't falter. His paddle fell deep into the water and he yelled at his sons to throw their catch and supplies overboard. Vibol and Prak did as he demanded, then began to paddle. An arrow splashed into the water beside them, followed by another. Boran imagined his sons impaled by the shafts, and this image gave him great strength. He began to shout, warning his countrymen of the invaders, hoping that his voice would travel.

More arrows bit into the water, and he turned down another stream, trying to put trees between them and their pursuers. Glancing back, he saw that one Cham boat was still after them—a fast boat captained by strong men. Though he was tempted to paddle to shore, the thick jungle would slow their flight. They would be overrun. No, wiser to stay in the boat, to live or die on the water that he knew better than the Chams did.

Though still far from home, Boran began to call out to his wife. He told her to hide, to wait for him. An arrow hummed through the air, nicked his leg, and slammed into his boat.

Prak shouted an insult at the Chams, and Vibol followed his lead. His sons' defiance resonated within Boran, and his love for them seemed to double. He couldn't watch his sons—or his wife—die. Better to cast himself against his enemies and let them hack him to pieces.

The skin of his palms splitting, Boran paddled as he never had. He smelled smoke. He heard distant screams. And he wondered if this was the moment when his world would collapse.

The third and final day of her wedding had been Voisanne's favorite. Already her family and friends had celebrated some of the most important parts of the ceremony—the groom's processional, the call to ancestors, the priests' blessings, and the cleansing rites. Now, as the sun climbed higher in the sky, Voisanne and her husband-to-be, Nimith, were in the midst of a ritual that honored their parents, as without parents neither could have been brought into the world, could have favored the Gods, or could one day produce children of their own.

Voisanne held a silk umbrella over her mother, and Nimith did the same for his mother. The umbrellas meant that after years of being sheltered by their parents, now the bride and groom became their protectors. Married couples formed a circle around Voisanne, Nimith, and their parents. Anyone not married stood outside this circle. As a woman sang about parental duty and the sacrifices necessary to raise honorable children, three candles were passed around the circle, and each time a candle came to a person, he or she pointed it at the bride and groom and silently sent a blessing their way.

Voisanne was naked but for an elaborate silk skirt cloth. One end of the cloth was pleated and tucked in at the waist. Her skirt cloth depicted jasmine flowers set against a red background. The same flowers hung from her neck. Like the other women present, she wore her black hair up, tied in a tight knot atop her head. Silver armbands, bracelets, and rings encircled her arms and fingers. The soles of her feet and the palms of her hands had been dyed red. To onlookers her beauty had never been so pronounced. Her face appeared soft and feminine, her body lean and sculpted. Women were happy for her, jealous of her. Men were happy as well, though their jealousy was directed toward Nimith, who was only a middle-ranking officer in the Khmer army but had managed to attract Voisanne. He stood, muscled and proud, a sword falling from his waist, holding himself so that his shadow fell upon her.

She glanced up, appreciating his intention, adoring him. Like most Khmer couples who entered into marriage, they had already savored the delights of each other's bodies. They'd shared an intimacy of the mind as well. She knew of his desires, strengths, and fears, just as he understood her innermost thoughts.

As the woman continued to sing about their parental duties and the candles went from hand to hand, Voisanne wondered if and when she would become pregnant. Many Khmer couples never experienced this blessing. In fact, Prince Jayavar and his chief wife had not brought a child into the world, though he'd fathered sons and daughters with his other wives. Voisanne knew that Nimith wanted a boy to train as he had been trained, and she yearned to give him such a gift, yearned so much that every day she went to stand inside Angkor Wat and pray that she would be as fertile as the river, as the nearby fields.

Throughout her life, Voisanne had known more happiness than not, more comfort than most. And yet today she felt enveloped by a sense of bliss that she had never experienced. She was marrying a good man who loved her. Her parents and siblings were nearby, all watching with smiles on their faces. After almost three days of festivities, they were still with her, as much a part of the ceremony as she was. And their commitment to her, to this union, seemed to strengthen her own belief in the sanctity of what was unfolding.

The woman stopped singing. A priest began to speak as Vois-anne's mother and father brought colorful ribbons into view. The ribbons would soon be tied around the bride's and groom's wrists, another symbol of their approaching union.

As Voisanne watched her father, delighting in the pride etched in his face, a dog barked in the distance. Such noises were not uncommon, but soon other, odder sounds drifted across the land. Voisanne glanced up, noting the distant but still-magnificent pres-ence of Angkor Wat. Smoke rose from near the temple—the thick billowing smoke of burning wood. It was every Khmer's duty to help put out fires, and despite the importance of the moment, Voisanne touched Nimith's arm and gestured toward the temple. His brow furrowed. He shook his head. And then the nearby jungle exploded into horror as warriors poured forth, shrieking in a strange tongue, sunlight glinting off their shields and weapons.

Nimith thrust Voisanne behind him, drew his sword, and called to his men. They quickly formed a circle around the wed-ding party, but they were a force of ten, and hundreds of Chams burst into the open like bees erupting from a hive. The Chams swept forward, raising their axes, aiming their spears. Voisanne screamed Nimith's name as he stepped ahead, toward his foes. He ducked beneath the sweep of an axe, thrust his weapon into the belly of a Cham, and was knocked backward by a shield's iron edge. He rallied though, twisting and thrusting and killing two more Chams.

A spear flew through the air. Voisanne saw it coming and screamed a warning. But the weapon was faster than her words, and buried itself in Nimith's chest. He toppled backward. She tried to run to him, shouting his name as her father held her back. Before she knew what had happened her father was dead, then her mother. Her siblings began to fall and Voisanne reached for a younger brother, pulling him against her chest. She tried to shield him with her arms, but another spear darted forward and he went limp in her grasp, like a water pouch pierced by steel. An image flashed in her mind of him holding her hand at night when he was ill. She screamed, still clutching him, telling him that he was safe, that she was with him, and that he would never be alone.

Rough hands tried to pull her from him, but she continued to cling to his small body even as the Chams kicked and beat her. She called his name, again and again, fighting as she never had, desperate to hold him as his soul traveled forward, believing that if he was thinking of her, of his parents, he would be born again into their same family. She shouted out her love for him and said the names of their family members, still trying to direct his soul, knowing it could go in so many directions at the moment of his death.

The shaft of a spear struck her forehead. She seemed to choke on her words, to stumble over them. Still holding her brother's hand, she fell on top of him, her body pressing against his, her thoughts going dim.

She saw him then. She imagined his smile.

Then the Chams carried her away.

For generations, the city of Angkor had flourished. Its temples and palaces stretched from east to west, as if inspired by the path of the sun. Glorious and gold-covered bas-reliefs adorned the sides of the grandest structures while imposing statues lined roads, bridges, moats, and parks. Equally impressive, Angkor's citizens had populated the landscape with abundance and grace—praying, bathing, and working together.

Neither the passage of time nor the often inclement weather had ever diminished the wonders of Angkor. And yet now, as stretches of the city burned, the Gods that had protected Angkor seemed to have abandoned it. While remnants of the Khmer army battled the invaders and horsemen galloped away for help, ordinary citizens fled into the jungle—some escaping, others finding only death or despair. Screams rose above even the tumult of warfare— the striking of axes against shields, the trumpeting of the few Khmer war elephants properly mounted and capable of battle. The Chams in their strange, inverted-flower headgear appeared to be everywhere, swarming forward in massive packs. For each Khmer there seemed to be two or three Chams. And while the Khmers fought ferociously for their homes and their families, most were unprepared for conflict. Few wore armor and even fewer had found their officers and formed into proper battle groups. Despite the enormous size of the Cham army, its presence had remained un- detected until it was too late to save the city.

Not far from Angkor Wat and the Royal Palace, at a temple called Bakheng, Jayavar and Ajadevi fought for their survival alongside several hundred Khmer warriors, citizens, servants, and slaves. Though Bakheng stood atop a hill, rising like a stepped pyramid and lined with immense sandstone lions that snarled and stood proud, it was the Khmer warriors who were driven back. Jayavar, naked but for his hip cloth, held a Cham axe in one hand and a Khmer shield in the other. While some of his men had fled to save their families, Jayavar had stood his ground, fighting in front of Ajadevi, struggling to protect his wife as Cham after Cham, goaded forward by the sight of her silver and gold bracelets, lunged in her direction. Ajadevi had since removed her valuables, but the Chams knew that she was highborn and still sought to capture her.

Jayavar's axe shattered a Cham's wooden shield, then bit deeply into the man's side. Even though the warrior still lived,

Jayavar wrenched a spear from his hands and tossed it to Ajadevi. She caught it and then lunged toward a Cham. He deflected her blow with a sword, but her attack had left him vulnerable, and a Khmer warrior cut him down from behind.

Coughing from the dense smoke that poured out of the barracks near the Royal Palace, Jayavar tried to calm his raging emotions and make sense of the assault. The Chams had obviously come from the river but must have then spread out and attacked Angkor from multiple directions, creating the greatest possible fear and chaos. There were no lines of attackers and defenders, only pockets of struggling warriors. Several dozen Khmer warriors mounted on elephants and horse-drawn chariots were running rampant against their enemies in open fields, but Jayavar saw too few of them.

"We must leave!" Ajadevi shouted.

Jayavar realized that she was covered in blood. He looked for a wound, then grimaced as a Cham spear glanced off his shield and impaled a Khmer beside him.

"It's not my blood!" Ajadevi yelled.

"But—"

"Lead us, Jayavar! Lead us!"

He glanced at the Royal Palace, the site of the fiercest fighting, surrounded by thousands of Chams. A sudden despair gripped him. He wanted to fight toward his parents, his other wives, and his children, knowing that they would likely be killed in an effort to sever all links to the throne. But he could not get through to them, not with so few warriors beside him. His family was doomed.

Though Jayavar had never felt the joy of battle, as some men did, he excelled at warfare, and his axe rose and fell in murderous arcs. Seeing their prince take the fight to his foes, other Khmer warriors mirrored his efforts, driving the Chams back.

But the battle was lost. To confirm his fears, Jayavar forced his way to the edge of the temple. Shouting at his men to protect Ajadevi, he climbed up one of the structure's main staircases, his bloody hands slipping on the feet of the carved lions as he dragged himself up the steep steps. He made it to the top, looked down, and pounded his fist against the stonework as he watched his city burn. Everywhere buildings were aflame and Chams were cutting down the remnants of the once-mighty Khmer army. Some of his countrymen were fleeing into the jungle. Few were pursued, as most Chams were intent on either crushing the opposition or plundering the city.

Jayavar hurried down the steps. Rather than seeking the advice of one of his junior officers, he strode to his wife.

"Angkor is lost!" she shouted.

"My father—"

"Would want you to live. So live!"

"But my children! I have to find them!"

"They're dead. I am so sorry, my love, but they're dead."

"No!"

"You must flee!"

Horns sounded nearby. The noise was foreign, and Jayavar realized that Cham reinforcements were arriving. He thought about his children, fearing that Ajadevi was right but trying to deny the possibility of such a fate. He closed his eyes, his world spinning. Ajadevi tugged on his arm, shouting at him to think of his empire, his people. Stumbling, he took a step in the direction of the Royal Palace, wanting to be with his loved ones even in death. But Ajadevi must have understood his intent, because she said that perhaps some of his children had escaped and that he could never help them if he was slain.

Jayavar looked at those who fought with him—perhaps ninety warriors and an equal number of slaves and citizens—and realized that she was right. If he ran toward his children, he would die, and would not be able to save them if they had managed to survive. But neither could he stay here; to linger longer would ensure his demise. Surrounding his people was a single line of Chams, men already anticipating their victory, not the blades of their foes.

"To me!" Jayavar shouted at his warriors; then he ran toward a weak point in the Cham force. The jungle lay behind that line, and Jayavar knew that the trees might be their salvation. His despair turning to rage, he parried the spear thrust of a young Cham warrior, beat an axe strike aside with his shield, and burst into the open. Rather than run ahead, he turned, attacking another warrior, fighting and killing until Ajadevi appeared beside him. Her spear was bloody, and she thrust its point into a Cham's belly. Dropping the weapon, she headed toward the tree line, her skirt cloth impeding her movements. Jayavar caught up to her and with one stroke of his dagger he cut a slit in the garment from her thighs downward.

Now she could run, and she did, less fearful of her own death than of his. They entered the jungle—a towering assortment of banyan, ficus, and teak trees that snuffed out most of the sunlight. Jayavar hadn't expected the Chams to pursue them, but they may have known that the heir to the throne and his wife were among the small group of survivors, and perhaps they were under orders to kill or capture any member of the Khmer royalty.

Ajadevi had spent countless mornings praying in the jungle and knew which trails to follow. She led the group forward, skirting away from Cham war parties, heading west toward the land of another enemy—the Siamese. She heard fighting behind her and knew that Jayavar would be with the rear guard, struggling against their pursuers. An arrow pierced the arm of a servant beside her, and Ajadevi hauled up the shrieking woman and helped her continue. Though Ajadevi's feet were as calloused as any, they began to bleed. Smoke thickened the jungle with its ominous presence. Distant screams resonated. Looking for signs of where to go, Ajadevi forged onward, glad for the first time in her life that she didn't have children, that she wouldn't bear the burden of loss that her husband must.

Several hundred paces behind her, Jayavar and his men were fighting a running battle with the Chams. As he thought about his family and people, he was nearly overwhelmed with grief. But he forced his mind to shift to Ajadevi, forced himself to imagine her being raped by the Chams. The image gave him enormous will to fight back, and his men drew inspiration from the fierceness of his assaults. He attacked, retreated, and attacked again. And though he lost men with each onslaught, the Chams were now leery of his blade. They sought to flank his warriors on both sides, and he shouted at Ajadevi to hurry. Then he split his force in two so that each group of Chams could be attacked. Arrows whistled past him, thudding into dirt, wood, and flesh. Men and women fell and didn't rise. A spear thrown by a distant Cham sliced into the side of his hip, cutting him deeply enough to affect his gait. Still he kept fighting, pausing when he came to a seven- or eight-year-old slave boy who had fallen. Jayavar looked for the boy's mother, saw that no one claimed him, and so he dropped his shield, threw the child over his left shoulder, and ran forward. The Chams knew that Jayavar was vulnerable and two attacked him at once. Rather than flee, he charged them, swinging his axe so hard that it cleaved through a spear shaft, killing one foe. The other notched and aimed an arrow, and Jayavar turned away, shielding the boy with his own body.

The arrow never flew. Since childhood, Jayavar had piled stones atop one another in the jungle, marking his favorite places. Ajadevi had run past one of his piles, interpreted it as a sign, and hurried back in his direction. She had seen the Cham aiming his arrow and had leapt onto his back, gouging his eyes with her fingernails.

Jayavar heard her voice, saw her struggling, and killed the Cham. Still holding the boy, he helped his wife to her feet. They started running again, darting like deer through the jungle, following drops of blood left by fellow Khmers.

At some point the cries of their pursuers faded and disappeared. The Khmers continued on, running in streams to hide their passage, leaving their dead where they fell, urging one another forward even as their strength waned. Other escapees joined their ranks. The sun dropped and they followed its flight toward Siam.

The boy wept on Jayavar's shoulder, and for the first time since they had left Angkor, Jayavar thought about stopping. In the distance a pyramidlike structure rose from the jungle floor. Crudely cut laterite bricks had been stacked upon one another, and though parts of the ancient structure had fallen, a pair of large banyan trees jutted out from its base, appearing to hold the remaining assembly of bricks in place. Jayavar had never before come across these ruins. He paused, gently setting the boy down. A woman ran forward, shouted a name, and picked up the child, tears wetting both their cheeks.

Jayavar limped forward a few steps and embraced Ajadevi. He then turned to their people and told them to expect only a short rest. After Ajadevi bound his wound with a strip of silk from her skirt cloth, he climbed one of the banyan trees. Two of his officers wanted to join him, but he needed Ajadevi's counsel and asked that only she follow him.

The base of the banyan tree was so full of branches that it almost looked as if the tree had been turned upside down and that the canopy jutted from the jungle floor. Despite wincing from his wound, Jayavar climbed quickly. His heart was still pounding, and he knew that the Chams would regroup and come again. As the heir to the throne, he was a threat, and threats must be destroyed.

When he finally reached the topmost branches, which placed him higher than most of the surrounding trees, Jayavar paused to help Ajadevi move to a perch beside him. Though other treetops obscured some of their view, they could make out Angkor Wat and smaller structures in the distance. The city was still burning, vast plumes of smoke rising into the sky. Jayavar thought of how his children were likely dead, and the fortress he'd thrust up around his emotions crumbled. He wept, still staring at his home, his blood-splattered shoulders shuddering.

Ajadevi saw his tears but did not cry with him. She would weep later, she knew, after he was asleep. Now he needed her strength. With her love and her fortitude he could lead again. Without them, he would be lost.

She placed her hand above his wound, thankful that the spear hadn't skewered him. She looked for Chams, saw none, and then closed her eyes and prayed.

"Prayers . . . shall not help us," he whispered, though he was almost as devout as she. "They shall not save . . . my sons and daughters. Nor my mother and father."

Ajadevi shook her head. "Your parents were old and in pain. Now they're reborn. If you were them, which fate would you prefer?"

"And what of my children? What of their journey?"

"The young don't have time to pollute themselves with hate, with crime, with jealousy. Your sons and daughters were all good, and they're now reborn into better lives. Better lives, my love. They've taken one more step toward Nirvana, and no one should lament that."

"I do. I will."

Ajadevi nodded, placing her hand against his wound and holding it there. "I know, and I am full of sorrow, so full of it that the beauty seems to have faded from the world. But . . . but remember what we believe. And trust that your sons and daughters are reborn. As the sun will rise tomorrow, so will they. They are not gone. Someday you'll be reunited with them."

He turned to her. "I can't . . . lose them like this. Not today. Not ever. So please . . . ignore my earlier words and pray with me. Pray with me that they still live."

"I shall."

Husband and wife prayed together, prayed that a miracle would befall them. Without the hope brought by his prayers, Jayavar knew that he would lack the strength to endure.

"A child should never die," Ajadevi said. "Remember that. Remember that so when you defeat the Chams you'll let their young go free."

"Defeat them?" he asked, watching the distant fires. "My army is gone."

"An army is nothing more than a collection of believers. Build another."

"With what?"

"With your will. With what remains of our people, who surely hide in these woods. Live in exile, raise an army, and then return to claim your father's golden sword. Just as you saved that slave boy, you can save your kingdom."

"He is but one."

"A kingdom starts with one."

"I cannot do what must be done. I cannot—"

Ajadevi pulled her hand away from him. "Before you tell me what you cannot do, think of the Cham king in your father's bed. Think of those you saw die today, of the women we left behind, of the children who are now slaves, of the hospitals you wanted to build. Every Khmer is counting on you, Jayavar. Your children, whether alive or dead, are counting on you, either for this life or the next."

"But I've already failed them. My little ones . . . I've failed them all."

"You can still help them. Indeed, the river runs red today, full of our people's blood as well as with sorrow, pain, and anguish. But that Cham spear missed you for a reason. You were meant to return to Angkor."

"I should have—"

"You've never doubted me, Jayavar. Please, please, don't begin to do so now. I need you to trust me. For my sake, please trust me."

Jayavar was about to respond when he heard faint voices to the east. The voices belonged to his foes, and now that he had rested, a part of him wanted to gather his men and attack the attackers. He wanted revenge.

"We need to leave," Ajadevi said, tugging on his arm.

"I long to kill them."

"Later. There's been enough killing today."

He closed his eyes, thinking of his sons and daughters, shuddering as he imagined their deaths.

"Come and follow me," she said. "This is a world of infinite dawns and today is just one day. Tomorrow shall be another."

"Tomorrow is too far away."

"Hurry, Jayavar. They draw near!"

"Let them."

"Stop this foolishness! We run or we die. We run or our city is lost forever. So run. Run now!"

Shouts erupted in the distance. Their trail had been discovered. Jayavar forced himself to push his rage and sorrow aside. He hurried down the tree, told his people to follow him, and was soon on the move again. His wound opened up, and blood trickled down his leg and fell to the dirt. His dirt, he reminded himself. The dirt of his ancestors. The Chams had come to make it their own. They had killed and pillaged. They had won the day. But the soil was rich from the blood of the Khmers, not the Chams. And someday, Jayavar promised himself, he and Ajadevi would return to reclaim it. They would free those enslaved; they would walk again in the footsteps of their ancestors.

Jayavar continued onward, leading now, helping the weak and wounded. Though on that day little luck had befallen him, he was fortunate that he ran to the west, away from his home. If he had seen what was happening to his people, seen the horrors that they now endured, he would have turned back and stepped into the flood of Chams. He would have fought them until they danced in his blood and even Ajadevi would not have been able to save him.

Two

From Shadow to Shadow

hough nearly three weeks had passed since she had seen her loved ones perish, Voisanne was unaware of the daily wax and wane of the sun's rays or of the changing colors in the sky. Time had lost all meaning. She cared not if she lived or died, rested or suffered. Food was of no consequence, nor were her enemies, her thoughts, her dreams. She had been blessed for so many years, but now those blessings were gone, and it seemed that she lived a new life, one bereft of joy and meaning. If only she had been killed along with everyone else. A spear through her heart would have let her travel with those she held dearest, emerging into life again like a butterfly leaving its cocoon.

But Voisanne had not been killed. Instead, the Chams had gagged and bound her and locked her underground for many days. She was not alone. Several dozen other Khmer women, all beautiful and young, shared her fate. Each morning the door would open and the Chams would drag a shrieking woman into the light. The woman never returned.

When the Chams finally came for her, Voisanne made no protest. She walked with them, her head held high, believing that she would die soon and rejoicing in that belief. Her misery was almost at an end. Whatever waited after death could be no worse than the present.

To Voisanne's surprise, she was led to the vast moat that surrounded the city of Angkor. She was told to bathe and given a fresh skirt cloth. Though she had never been ashamed of her nakedness, she turned away from the Cham warrior, covered her privates with a cupped hand, walked down the steps leading into the moat, and waded until the water was up to her neck. She didn't emerge until he called to her several times in his strange tongue.

The warrior then led her into the immense and bustling Royal Palace, which was located just to the north of Angkor Wat and had hardly been damaged during the attack. Since it was built to house mortals and not the Hindu Gods, the Royal Palace was made of impermanent materials—namely, various hardwoods. The building had been home to the Khmer king, his wives, and his five thousand concubines. Though the Royal Palace didn't rival Angkor Wat in terms of its beauty, it featured carved lintels, enormous wooden columns, courtyards, and bathing pools. Its most striking feature was its size, for the Royal Palace was two thousand feet long and half as wide.

Deep within the structure, Voisanne was turned over to a trio of Cham women. She didn't understand their words, but they made it clear that any effort to disobey them would result in a beating. Voisanne only shrugged. When the women anointed her with perfume and gave her a necklace of flowers, she expected the worst. But no Cham warlord appeared. No one ravaged her.

That same evening she was brought to an elaborate feast. Seated before the foreign dancers and harpists were the Cham king and his confidants. Standing without thought or purpose, Voisanne simply waited for her fate to unfold. From somewhere in the distance, screams drifted to her, usurping the voices of a troupe of Cham singers. Voisanne listened to the screams, not the music. The sounds came from men, from Khmer men. One after another they shrieked, moaned, and went silent.

Nothing happened to Voisanne that night or the night after. She was locked in a small room, but left alone. Several times throughout the subsequent days she was close to the Cham king and felt his gaze on her. He was a brute of a man, a head taller than most of his officers and seemingly as wide as a horse. She never saw him hurt anyone, but he spoke at length with Khmer prisoners, and when they didn't tell him what he wanted to hear, they disappeared and the screams began anew.

For almost a week, Voisanne lived in such a way, a witness to her masters' doings but called on neither to speak nor act. She was being saved for something or someone, she decided. She was a gift that had not been opened. At some point this pattern would change and she would suffer. But that day had not yet dawned.

Now, as the sun climbed high, Voisanne stood on the east side of Angkor Wat. She didn't watch the nearby Cham warriors or their prisoners but turned to look at one of the most spectacular bas-reliefs in all of Angkor, which graced the lower portion of this side of the massive temple. She was unsure why the Cham king liked to interrogate his prisoners here, within sight of such beauty. The sandstone carving was called *The Churning of the Sea of Milk* and was almost two hundred feet long. Taller than Voisanne might reach, the bas-relief depicted the Hindu myth of creation. One side was dominated by ninety-two demons that pulled on the end of a giant snake. Eighty-eight Gods pulled on the other end of the snake, which was wrapped around a mountain set in the cosmic sea. The tug-of-war twisted the mountain, which churned the sea and created life—dragons, fish, turtles, and crocodiles.

Had she known the Cham king's plans for her, Voisanne might have listened to the voices of her captors. She might have tried to understand what was happening to her countrymen. But she only looked at the demons and Gods, remembering how she'd talked about them with her father and, later, her lover. Her father had told her the story of creation. Her lover had wondered how anyone could fashion such beauty from stone.

Fifty feet away from the fabled bas-relief, several hundred Cham warriors stood behind their king and his closest advisers. Now that the invasion was over, none of the men wore their lotus-flower headdresses. The group was gathered in a courtyard that sprawled to the east of Angkor Wat. A sheathed sword hung from Indravarman's hip, as usual. Weapons were cumbersome, and he believed that only by carrying them as often as possible would they become a part of him, no more aggravating or heavy than his hands or feet. Then, when battle came to him, as it inevitably would, his instruments of war would be readily available and easy to wield. Indravarman's soldiers were required to carry their weapons everywhere outside their private quarters. Anyone forgetting to do so would be put to death without trial or defense.

The Chams were gathered in the shadow of Angkor Wat, a shadow that mimicked the rises and falls of the temple mountain above. As distant screams rose, Indravarman leaned toward a high-ranking Khmer official and a stout Khmer warrior. Both men were bound and on their knees. Asal stood beside Indravarman, his hand gripping the hilt of his sheathed sword. On Indravarman's opposite side was Po Rame, his personal assassin and the most feared of all Cham killers. Po Rame and Asal were old adversaries, and Indravarman enjoyed their close proximity.

Because Indravarman demanded that all his officers learn to

speak the language of their enemy, he had no need for a translator. He studied the Khmer official, saw fear in the man's eyes, and then glanced at Angkor Wat. Six beautiful Khmer women stood at the base of the temple mountain, and he considered each of them, thinking that they looked stronger than their men. The women showed less fear and more resolve. He admired them.

Indravarman stepped closer to his prisoners. "The screams, do they disconcert you?" he asked in Khmer. "You seek a seamless rebirth, but if you fail to tell me what I long to hear, you too shall produce such screams before you leave this body for the next."

The Khmer official nodded but said nothing. He trembled. His hip cloth was dark and moist around his groin.

"The work of your ancestors inspires me," Indravarman said, pointing to the bas-relief that depicted the tug-of-war between the forces of good and evil. "It's why your countrymen scream. Only I use two elephants. A man is tied between them, and they move in opposite directions. You see, the Gods make life. I destroy it."

"I . . . know nothing, lord," the Khmer muttered, his eyes darting again to the bas-relief. "I know nothing of where he's gone."

Indravarman felt his temper rising and let his emotions be known. He clenched his fists. "Jayavar left you," he said. "He abandoned you. And yet you protect him."

"I don't pro—"

"You expect me to believe that no fallback plan existed? No staging point for a rally?"

"I . . . I am not a warrior, lord."

"You had access to the king! To the prince! The false king is dead, but his son is not, and I want him!"

"I swear, lord. I don't know where he is. I beg you, please, please believe me. I'd tell you if—"

"Tell me something now, of value, or the elephants are next."

"I—"

"Tell me!"

The prisoner leaned forward, beating his bound fists against his brow. He wailed and closed his eyes, flailing at himself until he suddenly straightened. "Stones," he said. "You must look for piles of stones."

"What?"

"The prince makes piles of stones in the jungle. I've heard that he does it to teach himself patience. If your men see one of them, lord, far from here, then you should look for him in that area."

Indravarman cursed in his native tongue. "I want locations and you give me stones."

"It's all I have, lord. It—"

"Would you kill me, if you had the chance? Would your countryman, the warrior beside you, kill me?"

"What?"

"Would you kill me, coward, if you could?"

"No."

Indravarman spat toward the prisoner. He then shifted his attention to the Khmer warrior, knowing that the man had slain five Chams before he was captured. Indravarman admired such strength and resolve. His own man, Asal, had killed an equal number of Khmers, and suddenly Indravarman was bored with interrogations and lies and whimpering. He wanted to take the measure of his man, to test his loyalty and prowess against the best that the Khmers had to offer.

Turning to his left, Indravarman took a shield and a sword from one of his officers and tossed the instruments toward the Khmer warrior. "Free him," Indravarman commanded to no one in particular.

A Cham untied the leather straps that bound the prisoner's

hands and feet. The Khmer remained almost motionless, though Indravarman saw him unclench his fists. Somewhere an elephant trumpeted and a man screamed. The scent of sweat hung in the still air.

"The prisoner has escaped," Indravarman said, turning to Asal. "Kill him."

Asal stiffened. Indravarman had tested him often over the past few months, tested his courage and his devotion. And after the successful completion of each test, Asal had been promoted higher in the ranks, finally becoming one of Indravarman's most trusted officers. Asal had pleased his king many times over. He was where he wanted to be. He had made his ancestors proud. But suddenly now everything had changed.

To ignore the order would be to die; Asal was certain of that. He closed his eyes and tried to hear songbirds over the surge of his heartbeat, forcing his fear downward, as if it were an enemy that he could crush beneath his feet. Opening his eyes, he pulled his sword free, raised his shield, and stepped forward.

The Khmer stood up, unsteadily at first, and Asal gave his foe time to adjust to his freedom, so that no one could say the fight was unfair. Asal wondered if he would soon be reborn. He bit his lip, resigned to his fate and yet disappointed that he had climbed to such a high peak only to stare at an abyss. His wife was still unmet, his children yet unborn. Though he had been alone for most of his life, he didn't want to die alone.

The Khmer warrior seized the sword and shield, screamed a battle cry, and ran at Asal. Their weapons met, and Asal felt the strength of his adversary's blow. He pulled back, raising his shield, spinning away. The hum of a sword cutting the air filled his ears, and he knew that the Khmer's blade had passed a handsbreadth from his neck.

Though Asal didn't realize it, his countrymen had gathered in a circle around them. Everyone but Indravarman and Po Rame encouraged him. Indravarman wanted to witness Asal's skill with a blade again and to study his tendencies in combat. Po Rame longed to see him die.

The swords rose and fell in curving arcs, clanging rhythmically. The combatants appeared well matched, and Asal took a blow on his shield, a strike so powerful that the iron edge and teak interior were split like a giant leaf. Asal threw his ruined shield at the Khmer, attacking without pause, parrying another swipe of his opponent's sword and then smashing his fist into the man's jaw. The warrior absorbed the blow with only a grunt, but his eyes watered, and Asal kept up his attack, swinging and lunging. His sword seemed to come alive, an extension of his arm, a bridge that would lead him to the future he coveted. Though the Khmer was large and skilled, though he carried a shield and a sword, a moment came and went when every onlooker knew that he would soon die. Asal was simply too quick. He was like a mongoose that danced around a cobra, darting and circling, feigning and attacking, probing for an opening. His sword finally pierced the Khmer's defenses and the man fell, mortally wounded. Still filled with the fever of battle, Asal spun around, looking for another enemy. He saw none and so he took the life of the Khmer. He took it swiftly, giving the man a noble death.

Asal's chest heaved and his throat felt dry. He didn't care to speak, and simply stood his ground, wanting the crowd to disperse, to be free of their eyes. He felt weak, yet no one could see this weakness; no one could sense his fear. Indravarman was watching him, he knew, and though deceptive, Asal's stance was wide and strong.

When Voisanne saw the Cham king turn and motion her forward, she remained still, certain that she must have misunderstood his intentions. He shouted and suddenly warriors ran toward her, pulled her ahead, and threw her at the feet of the Cham who had just killed her countryman. She saw blood on his hands and arms. She hoped that he would kill her too. But he made no move, remaining as motionless as the Gods and demons on the bas-relief.

"You are his," the king said in her own tongue. "His and his alone. Please him or perish."

Voisanne stared at the warrior's feet. She sensed a blow coming from the king, so she nodded.

Indravarman said something to the Cham warrior and then walked away, calling out loudly to his other men. The Khmer official was carried, screaming, toward the unseen elephants. The remaining Chams began to disperse. They left as one, walking on the land of Voisanne's ancestors, where the footsteps of her loved ones should have fallen. Voisanne longed to hate the Chams; she longed to plan her revenge. But such a profound weariness gripped her that she could not even hate.

Soon no one remained in the courtyard but Voisanne and the warrior. She expected him to move swiftly, as he had in combat. But he merely stood there, looking up, his face revealing no hint of emotion. For the first time she noticed that he was wounded— a dark bruise was appearing on his neck, left perhaps by the strike of a sword hilt.

Finally, he looked down at her. He did not grimace or mock or smile but simply stared. When she could endure his gaze no longer, she stood up, keeping her head bowed. "Follow me," he said in her language, his accent less thick than the king's.

Voisanne glanced toward the distant jungle. She thought about running, about how much it would hurt when his sword pierced her body. She was no longer afraid of death, but she didn't want to shame her ancestors. Better to die another way, in a manner worthy of the blood in her veins.

So she went with the warrior, wondering if he had killed her lover or her mother, if he'd been there when the light of her world went out. She would never know, but at that moment, as she stepped where he had stepped, she decided that she would kill him. When he came for her, as he would, she would kill him and then end her own life.

Voisanne would make her ancestors proud. There was nothing else left for her to do.

Far from Angkor, deep within the maze of waterways and lakes that led to the city, the fisherman and his family sat on a log and studied their surroundings. Though they had seen no Chams during the three weeks since the invasion, they remained vigilant— listening to the forest, smelling the air, looking for signs of intruders. Boran and his wife, Soriya, took this task even more seriously than did their sons, who had spent much of the past few days arguing about what to do. Vibol wanted to avenge the atrocities they'd seen. He couldn't forget the stench of disfigured Khmers floating down the river, the sight of their burning homes, or the whimpers of a dying boy. For once, Vibol had been jealous of Prak's poor vision, though he knew that his brother smelled and heard sufferings that he did not.

While Vibol was angry at his father for not letting him warn their countrymen, he felt grateful that his mother had escaped the Chams. She'd heard their approach and disappeared into the jungle, hiding beneath clumps of giant ferns. As she had listened, the Chams had burned their family's home and stolen their few valuable possessions.

Vibol, Prak, and Boran had been equally lucky. The Cham boat had drawn close to them, but in their haste the invaders had tipped over their vessel. Though Vibol had wanted to turn around and kill them, Boran had paddled on, desperate to reach Soriya. Their reunion had been silent out of necessity, but they had held each other as their home was reduced to embers.

In the days that followed, the family had paddled their boat westward and lived off the waterways. One morning they came across a Khmer soldier atop a war elephant. The blade of a spear was lodged in his belly and he was dying. They gave him comfort, told him that his loved ones were safe, and watched his eyes go blank. As the man died, Prak played his bamboo flute, trying to put him at ease. Once he was gone, the family burned his body, as he'd requested.

Boran and his sons had experience handling elephants, since most every Khmer who farmed or labored in the outdoors had some need of the beasts. Farmers counted on them to clear fields. Fishermen used them to drag new boats to waterways. And so once the family had burned the warrior to ashes, they left with his elephant, Vibol sitting on its neck and using an iron hook to tug its ears in one direction or another. The elephant was a danger because of its bulk and inability to blend into the jungle, and Boran was relieved when two days later they discovered a group of Khmer warriors and turned over the beast. Vibol wanted to go with the other men, to regroup and fight. But after much discussion and argument, Boran forbade it.

Now, as the family sat on a log and ate smoked eel, they debated whether they were better off on their own or with a larger group of survivors. Because he knew the waterways so well and possessed a fast boat, Boran felt that they should stay by themselves. Soriya shared his views, which were opposed by their sons.

As Soriya reminded her boys that they were fishermen, not fighters, Boran watched her with pride. Though she was only two years younger than he, she looked half his age. Her face was wide, pleasant, and bore no scars. A dark mole sprouted next to her nose. Certain bends of the rivers held sand the same color as Soriya's skin. Like all Khmer women, she wore only a skirt cloth, and her black hair was bound in a tight knot on top of her head. She wasn't as lean as she'd once been, but Boran was glad that she had put on weight, for it meant that he was feeding her well.

"Do you seek death?" she asked, gazing at Vibol.

Her son took a bite of the smoked eel. "No. But neither will I run from it."

Soriya paused, and Boran wondered if she would speak again. His wife used words as a bowman used arrows—carefully and only when needed. Most of the time she listened to her husband and sons in silence, often on edge, concerned about a diseased neighbor or Prak's worsening eyesight. Since her sons didn't worry enough, she fretted on their behalf—cleaning their cuts, whispering that they should consider marriage.

When Soriya didn't respond, Boran turned to Vibol. "Maybe you should remember how that warrior looked with the Cham steel in his belly. Remember how he suffered? How his eyes filled with tears?"

"He said nothing of regrets," Vibol replied. "So I can't find fault in his death. At least he died fighting, not running."

"Why can't a warrior run one day and fight the next?" Prak asked, repeating an old argument.

Vibol stood up and kicked at a fallen branch. "They burned our home, killed our people, and the time to fight was then. Instead we hid like frightened children. We heard screams and did nothing!"

Soriya wished her son were as wise as he was headstrong. In the past his rashness had been something to smile at, to jest over, but now she feared it would cost him his life. "Think of me," she said quietly. "Please, please, think of me before you run off to your death."

"I do think of you. That's why I'm still here."

She nodded. "Thank you. Because I . . . I'd shrivel up like an uprooted plant if you were killed."

"But we should have fought," Vibol insisted, bending down to pick up the branch, which he broke in half and tossed into the jungle. "We should have at least killed those Chams who chased us and ended up in the water. Killing them would have been easy."

Boran pointed to the half-healed wound on his leg, which Soriya had stitched up with silk thread. "You see this, Vibol? Don't you think I wanted to kill the Cham who did this, who tried to put an arrow through your heart? Of course I did. Of course I was tempted. But sometimes being a man means taking the more difficult path—a path that leads to a better tomorrow, not a better today."

"How can running from an enemy be a better path? An enemy who destroyed our home? Who killed our people?"

"Because—"

"You were afraid, Father! You won't admit it, but I know you were afraid. That's why we ran! We ran like three cowards, not like three Khmers!"

Boran's nostrils flared and he stood up. He started to speak, but his son turned and hurried away from the stream, toward the jungle. Though he wanted to shout at Vibol to stop, Boran dared not raise his voice. He watched his son get smaller and smaller until the jungle seemed to swallow him up.

"I'll find him," Prak said, looking from his mother to his father. "I won't see him, but I'll hear him."

"Are you sure?" Soriya asked. "Maybe your father should be by your side."

Prak smiled. "It would be better if I spoke with him alone. He'll listen to me. He'll see me coming and let me find him. Then I'll bring him back."

"Why is he acting like this? He should be grateful that we all live."

The smile faded from Prak's face. "A girl, Mother. A girl he liked is dead. The Chams . . . they hurt her. They left her body tied to a tree."

"Who was she?"

"He kissed her once, while bathing in the moat. He laughed with her. He dreamed about her, I think. And the Chams took her from him. He found her body and he hasn't been the same since."

Soriya rubbed her brow, wondering whom her son had favored. The knowledge of the girl's death made her feel tired. She was weary of running, of hearing so many stories of suffering. "Please be careful, Prak," she said, grasping his hand.

"I will, Mother. I promise."

"You can't ever leave us."

"I know. And I won't."

She watched him make his way into the jungle. He could never run as his brother had, so he took a few steps, then paused and listened. Cicadas buzzed. The calls of birds seemed to echo. Monkeys scurried in the treetops, causing large leaves to fall. The leaves were green and thick but would quickly turn brown on the ground, as the monsoon season was ending.

Prak moved on. Soriya thought about asking Boran to follow him but knew that Prak would hear him. And she wouldn't let her son lose face, not when he had worked so hard to gain it.

When Prak had finally disappeared, Soriya turned to her husband. "What will we do?" she asked. "We have to do something or Vibol will burst."

"He thinks I'm a coward."

"He said that . . . but he doesn't really believe it."

"Maybe I am. Maybe I should have killed those Chams."

"You chose life over death."

"As a coward would. And now, to make up for his father's cowardice, Vibol will do something foolish."

A monkey screeched from somewhere above them. As she thought about her sons alone in the jungle, Soriya started to sweat. She remembered them at her breast and couldn't imagine the world without them in it. "But what will we do?" she asked again, then rubbed her brow.

Boran glanced at the axe he'd taken from the dead Khmer warrior. "The Chams will come into the jungle. They won't lie idle in the city like a tiger next to its kill."

"Shouldn't we go, then? Shouldn't we flee?"

"If we flee, then Vibol will leave us. He won't run from the Chams again."

Soriya closed her eyes, knowing that Boran was right. "But we can't stay."

"Maybe . . . maybe somehow he can have his revenge. Let him wet the blade of that axe with Cham blood, and then he'll have no need to prove himself again."

"How?"

"I don't know. But the war found us, and now we'll have to find it. We'll find it in a time and place of our choosing, and our son will have to get blood on his hands."

"Your blood? His blood? What you speak of carries too much risk. You're just a fisherman, Boran. You're no warrior."

"I know. But he's a boy yearning to be a man. And if we treat him only as a boy, he'll leave us, and he'll die alone and afraid. At least this way, if we aren't strong enough, aren't wise enough, we'll die together, as one. We'll die together and we'll be reborn together, and it's better to die together than to live alone."

Soriya shook her head, tears welling in her eyes. She squeezed his hand and then walked into the jungle, searching for her sons amid the endless trees and bushes, needing to reach them before they drew too far away.

A five-day journey to the west of Angkor, Jayavar and Ajadevi sat before one of the many fires that illuminated the night. Though the presence of so many fires worried Jayavar, the jungle was so thick that the light didn't travel far. Rain fell, silent and fine, hissing on embers, soaking each of the eight hundred and sixty survivors who had gathered together. They were a varied mix of warriors, slaves, officials, women, and children. Many of them huddled in groups, each as wet as the next, sitting as close as possible to the weakened flames. A few Khmers had propped giant leaves above their heads, which kept them somewhat dry. Most had endured far worse hardships than the rain, however, and made no effort to keep it from themselves.

Jayavar studied their location, wishing it was more defensible, aware that they needed to find some sort of natural fortification in case the Chams came. Some of the nearby lakes and rivers contained islands, which might make suitable places of refuge. There were a few caves and crags too, places where several hundred warriors might hold off ten times their number. But any such place could also be surrounded. And to be surrounded would be to die.

Wondering if he should move his people from location to location or build defenses in one place, Jayavar threw a branch into the fire. Somewhere a child laughed, prompting the prince's thoughts to slide to a darker place. He saw the faces of his sons and daughters, smiling faces that he had loved from first sight. Longing to see his children again, but fearing that he never would, he bit his lower lip, his tears mingling with the rain. He silently called out to them, telling them each, one by one, that he loved them. Thinking about how he had taught them all to stack stones and to move with care into the world, he picked up two rocks and then tried to balance the smaller one on top of the larger one.

Ajadevi reached through the darkness, her hand coming to rest on his knee. "Do you miss them most at night?"

Jayavar shrugged, the rocks falling. He missed his children constantly. "I yearn for them."

Nodding, she looked above him, her gaze lingering on an immense teak tree that flickered with the light of the fire. She thought about his loved ones and searched for signs. The tree seemed barren and she feared that his sons and daughters were all gone. But perhaps, she thought, she should find a sapling and study it. This tree was too ancient to speak of children. "A king may hope but a king must do," she finally replied, looking again at his face.

"What do you mean?"

"You may hope that your children live, but you must act as if they do not. Please forgive me, my love, for saying such things. But if your people are to survive, you must act like a king."

"What would you have me do?"

"You must produce an heir."

Thunder rumbled, and Jayavar's face tightened. "No."

"I cannot give you that heir, and so you must wed a woman whose loins are fertile."

"I shall do no such thing. Not while my sons may live. Not while you're at my side."

Ajadevi's gaze swept from right to left as she looked for a young teak tree that stood in the shadow of its ancestor. She saw none, which further convinced her that all Jayavar's children had been put to the sword. "I . . . I would willingly sacrifice my life to give you a son. But since I cannot give you this gift, you must lie with another. For the sake of your people you must."

Thunder came and went again, and the rain seemed to strengthen. "What I must do is return to Angkor," Jayavar said, pulling up his soaking-wet hip cloth.

"Why?"

"To discover if my sons and daughters live."

"Send a spy. A hundred men would gladly go."

"While I sit here and hide? You know me better than that, Ajadevi. If my children escaped, if they're hiding somewhere in the city, I must go to them."

She looked at the tree again. "Better to send another man. If you were caught, all hope for our people would vanish. You're now our king, remember?"

"Better, I think, to let our people know that their king lives. I shall return in secret to Angkor, ask about my children, and then, if necessary, disappear into the jungle like a shadow at dusk. Our people will know that I live, that I mean to retake Angkor. And that's how I shall give them hope, how I shall make an army—by showing my face and spreading my words." Jayavar nodded to himself, thinking about how he would travel to Angkor with a dozen warriors. He'd find Khmers outside the city and would let them know that he lived, that he was raising an army to reclaim their kingdom. He would learn the fates of his children and either plan their escape or escape himself into sorrow.

"I shall go with you," Ajadevi replied.

"You should stay here, where our army will grow."

"The people should know that I'm still at your side."

Jayavar started to speak but reconsidered. She was right. The people would want to know that she still lived. The path to retake the throne would seem more clear with her beside him. "I worry," he said, "of our fate if we're captured. If—"

"If we're surrounded, we shall use poison to take our own lives. Better to be dead than to have the Chams as masters."

"You would risk the good standing of your karma? Wouldn't Buddha frown upon such a fate?"

"Buddha never condemned suicide. But, yes, he saw it as a negative form of action, at odds with his belief in a path toward Nirvana."

"Yet you seek Nirvana."

"Yes, but that path is not one to be walked quickly. I have suffered in past lives and can do so again if my karma is tainted. The Chams must never capture us alive, Jayavar. If they do, they'll use us against our people." She closed her eyes, smelling the damp air, connecting to the earth. "And so we will carry poison."

Something moved in the darkness. Jayavar did not sense it, but Ajadevi did. An animal, perhaps? A shift in the wind? Or something more sinister? She asked herself these questions as he cast more branches onto the fire, which crackled and popped, as if protesting the damp wood.

Whatever presence had neared, it now receded. She thought about telling him, about calling to the guard, but she remained quiet. The presence was gone, and they would not find it. Not this night, amid the darkness and the rain. Still, she reached for a curved knife the length of her forearm and placed it by her feet.

"Will we retake the throne?" she asked.

"Yes."

She made Jayavar repeat his answer, but it was clear to her that he did not believe it. How could he? They had fewer than four hundred warriors, and many thousands of Chams awaited them in Angkor. "Is not life a miracle?" she asked, reaching for his hand.

"What do you mean?"

"We live. We breathe. We drink water that falls from the sky. These things are all miracles. We're surrounded by miracles, and because of that, your faith must never waiver. Believe that your father's throne will be yours."

"How? How can you say such words?"

"Because I feel warmth from a light in the sky. Because I met you amid all the faces that I've seen. I believe in these miracles. They're noble and good and we're not finished with them."

He sighed. "You've always believed."

"And that's why you must find another wife. You must start to train your heir. Start to train him as soon as possible."

Lightning flashed, followed by thunder. One of their few war elephants trumpeted nervously. "A woman . . . here in camp?" he finally asked.

"Yes."

"Are you sure?"

"I have doubts about many things, but not about this."

He nodded, and in his silence the night came alive. A child coughed. The scent of steaming rice lingered in the air. She saw him nod again and was suddenly glad for the rain, glad that he could not see her tears. She pulled him closer, leaning against him, letting his presence carry her away to a place where he would forever be hers and hers alone.

As one of Indravarman's highest-ranking officers, Asal had a private room in the Royal Palace not far from the king's chambers. The room, about seven paces across and ten paces long, was far too ornate for Asal's liking. The floor of dark lead tiles contrasted with the yellow clay tiles that made up the walls and ceiling. Teak beams ran across the ceiling, bearing intricate carvings of elephants, serpents, and fish. Part of the floor was covered by a thick mat woven from bamboo. A cotton blanket lay on the mat, as did a silk mosquito net that could be hung from the nearby wall. Asal's shield and weapons occupied one corner of the room. Another corner held a dais upon which rested sheets of stretched deerskin that had been dyed black. A wooden bowl contained sticks of white chalk that were used for writing on the deerskins, which Asal did more than he would have liked, as Indravarman demanded daily reports. Like all Cham officers, Asal was required to read and write—skills he had developed as a young man under the tutelage of a Hindu priest.

The most unusual sight in Asal's room was not made of wood, lead, or clay, but of flesh and blood. Voisanne sat in the far corner, her face blank, her eyes unfocused. She was aware of Asal as he stood near the dais and sharpened his sword, but her gaze didn't follow his movements. Instead, she tried to prepare herself for whatever he would do to her. As the Cham king had said, she was his. She had seen him slay the Khmer warrior and knew that he was strong and ruthless. He would take from her what he wanted, and though a part of her felt as if she had nothing left to lose, she was frightened. The thought of him ravaging her caused her hands to tremble like those of an old woman. She tried to still her fingers by sitting on them, but then the surging of her heart seemed to become even more pronounced. Her chest rose and fell with increasing speed. Sweat ran down her back. She wished once again that she'd died with the rest of her family. Better to have died with them than to be the Cham's plaything.

Voisanne still planned to slay him, and then to end her own life. Later, after she had endured whatever he'd done to her, after he was asleep, she would kill him with his sword. And then she would cut her own throat. As her life bled away, she'd think about her loved ones, letting them know that she was hurrying to reach them.

The Cham stopped sharpening his sword and turned to look at her. He was large and muscled, and she felt his eyes on her body as if they were his hands. She started to breathe even faster, and the room seemed to sway back and forth as if she'd arisen too quickly. Though she wanted to be strong, to honor her ancestors, she began to cry. Would it be better, she wondered, to please him so that he would sleep and then die? Or should she resist as her lover had? Should she fight until she could fight no more?

He walked toward her and then dropped to his knees with the grace of someone much smaller. "Why do you weep?" he asked softly, his accent barely noticeable.

She made no effort to reply but wiped her eyes and looked away.

"Why?" he repeated.

As if to make up for her continued silence, thunder boomed in the distance.

His brow furrowed. "Did you lose someone . . . in the attack?"

Though she didn't want to answer him, she found herself nodding. She thought about her lover, her parents, and her siblings. "Everyone," she whispered.

Asal watched her cry, her tears and shudders reminding him of his youth, of witnessing his loved ones succumb to cholera. Their deaths had not come quickly, and though he had been young, he remembered much. As he watched the Khmer woman, he began to pity her. He didn't see her beauty or even her face but only her suffering. Having known suffering as intimately as a farmer knows dirt, Asal wanted the woman's shudders to cease.

He leaned closer to her. "My king," he whispered, "has given you to me. And he shall . . . he shall expect certain things of me."

Voisanne shrugged.

"But I'll not do these things," Asal added in a low voice. "I'll not hurt you. I may carry a sword and I may kill, but I shall never hurt you."

She looked up at him. "Why?"

"Because that's not my way." Someone shouted outside the teak door leading to Asal's room. He stiffened, his jaw tightening and relaxing, and he leaned even closer to her. "But you must act as if I've hurt you. You must give my king and his men what they expect."

"What . . . do they expect?"

"You must whimper now. You must cry. You must fool them."

"I cannot."

"You can. And you must never speak of what I've said. If you do, I shall hear of it and my mercy will vanish."

Voisanne nodded.

"Now cry," he whispered. "Let them hear your tears."

She did as he asked, whimpering at first, drawing on her true sorrow. In her mind's eye, she saw the Cham spear fly and kill her lover. She felt her brother die in her arms, felt life flowing from him as she desperately tried to keep him whole. Her tears and sobs intensified as her emotions, caged for so long, ran rampant. She thought of her loneliness, of how she should have been wed and in bliss, and her world began to crumble.

Asal yelled at her to be silent. He smashed his shoulder into the nearby wall. He slapped his own thigh, hitting it hard. She knew he was doing these things for her benefit, and yet his rage seemed so real. Such anger had killed her family, had shattered her city. She pleaded with him to stop, and he shouted in reply, demanding that she be still. He picked up the wooden dais, raised it above his head, and slammed it into the tile floor. Again he slapped his thigh, then yelled at her, and the ferocity of his voice made her draw back in fear.

Outside the room's eastern wall, thunder boomed. A storm rose up, obscuring her cries. Once the thunder became regular, he stopped shouting. She could see that his thigh was red from where he'd hit it, and she closed her eyes, fearing him even though he hadn't touched her.

His chest heaving, he lowered himself in front of her, his lips drawing close to her ear. "Do you wish to live?" he whispered.

"No."

"You should."

"Better . . . to die."

He shook his head. "Once I was all alone. I sought death. But now I seek life."

She drew away from him.

"On the outside," he whispered, "you must look as if you want to die, as if my beatings pull you toward death. But on the inside, you must stand tall; you must seek life. And know that despite whatever I do on the outside, for the sake of others, I also want you to live."

Voisanne shuddered, trying to hold back a sob.

"So tomorrow, when you leave this room, leave it as if I've broken you. Always leave it as if I've broken you."

"Why?" she said, her voice quiet but ragged. "Why do you help me?"

"Because you've suffered enough. I am a Cham. The blood of your people is on my sword, on my hands. But I say you've suffered enough and there's time yet for you to live."

A tiring but manageable walk to the northwest of Angkor Wat, the ancient, elegant temple of Baksei Chamkrong rose into the dark night. The temple was similar to a stepped pyramid except for the top, which was dominated by a brick tower encased in stucco and carved with inscriptions that praised previous Khmer kings.

Baksei Chamkrong meant "the bird who shelters under its

wings" and referred to the legend of a Khmer king who was forced to flee a siege. As he made his way from the battle, an immense bird landed next to him and spread its wings, protecting him. He was then able to stay and fight his foes. Indeed, the temple seemed to have been created to celebrate such protection, because inside the tower a golden statue of the Hindu God Shiva, and his consort, Devi, stood on a raised platform.

The golden statue appeared to sway in the candlelight, and Indravarman studied it carefully. Though he had already plundered Angkor of some of its riches, he wasn't certain what to do with this statue. He admired it greatly and, now that he was the ruler of Angkor, he was in no rush to destroy its beauty.

Standing next to Indravarman was his chief assassin, Po Rame, who was tall, lean, and well muscled. Though Po Rame carried a spear, his weapons of choice were poison, knives, and a braided cord that he used to strangle his enemies from behind. Hanging from Po Rame's neck was a tiger's claw that came from a beast he had stalked and killed. The man's regal face reminded Indravarman of those of the countless stone statues around Angkor—with mouths fixed permanently in half smiles and eyes that seemed to see all. The assassin's skin was lighter in color than most of his countrymen's, which pleased him.

Indravarman looked down into the courtyard that surrounded the temple. Several colossal ficus trees sheltered his men from a steady rain. Standing next to one of the trees was Thida, who had been captured after the invasion and was the most beautiful woman Indravarman had ever seen. Even Angkor Wat, he thought, replete in all its splendor, could not duplicate her exquisiteness. It was as if the sun had never touched her skin, which appeared as smooth as Siamese silk. Her body was sculpted and perfect. Her eyes were wider than those of most Khmers, and her voluptuous lips seemed to celebrate the virtues of her femininity.

Her name meant "full moon" and Indravarman thought her parents had been wise to select it for her.

During the past several weeks, the Cham king had reveled in the company of many Khmer women. But earlier that day, once he'd seen Thida, the other women had been sent away. He hadn't spoken to her yet, however, and now, as he watched her stand in the rain, he wanted to touch those lips.

Suddenly impatient, Indravarman turned to Po Rame. "Jayavar remains a threat," he whispered. "He may be far from here, but a storm may also be far from a sailor. And as a sailor must watch the sky, I must watch the jungle."

"We—"

"As long as a claim to the throne exists, I'm in danger, which places you in danger."

Po Rame nodded, listening to the wind. "My spies, King of Kings, are in the jungle. They search as we speak." Though Po Rame was vicious, his voice was soft, almost feminine. "Jayavar—"

"Men are not enough. You should send women and children also. He'll be more suspicious of a man than of a child. And a woman will have more guile than a man would."

"Yes, Lord King."

"His chief wife is with him. From what the prisoners say, we should fear her as much as him." Indravarman paused to rub the lucky piece of iron that lay beneath the skin of his belly. "I want them both dead, gutted like fish. Mount their heads on spears and plant those spears at Angkor Wat for all to see."

"It will take time, Lord King. Those rats have burrowed deep."

Indravarman glanced again at Thida, who was now leaning against a tree. She appeared to sway with the wind, as if she might topple. "Take ten Khmer prisoners, the best of their warriors, to the river. Have your men torture one, and let the others escape. They'll need to kill our fighters for the ruse to work."

"But we'll never see them again."

"You're no fool, Po Rame, so don't speak like one," Indravarman replied. He stepped forward to touch the golden statue of Shiva, wondering if he should have it brought to his sleeping chambers. "Before going to the river, interrogate one of the Khmers, one with a family who lives. Let him know that his family will be burned alive unless he helps us, unless he discovers the whereabouts of Jayavar. When he tells us these whereabouts, he and his family shall go free. Tell him that I'm a man of my word. If he helps us, his loved ones shall live. And they shall leave Angkor carrying gold."

Po Rame pursed his full lips. "Better to have two such men, Lord King. In case illness or circumstance strikes one down."

"So be it. And plan it so that all our men die. Otherwise the Khmers will expect treachery. They must believe that we blundered. Convinced of our folly, the group shall find Jayavar for us. And then we shall go to him, with swords in our hands and malice in our hearts."

Po Rame began to speak again, but Indravarman dismissed him. Lightning flashed, illuminating a massive Khmer war elephant that stood outside the gathering of Chams. Indravarman shouted at one of his men to bring Thida forward. She moved grudgingly, climbing the slick sandstone steps that led to the temple's covered summit. Glistening from the rain, she appeared more desirable than ever. Once she entered the tower, Indravarman touched her chin and smiled when she leaned away.

"You would do well to return my gaze," he said in Khmer.

"Please . . . forgive me."

"Please forgive me, Lord King. That is what you should say. That is what you shall say if you wish to avoid an unfortunate fate."

Lightning flashed again, illuminating the golden statue.

When Thida made no reply, Indravarman moved closer to her, his calloused fingers tracing the contours of her neck, her shoulder, her arm. "Do you think me cruel?" he asked, still touching her.

"Yes . . . Lord King."

He saw wetness beneath her eyes and wondered if it was rain or tears. "I'm only cruel so that I can obtain what I desire. Ambition begets cruelty."

She looked away, trembling now.

"I desire you," he said. "Must I be cruel to fulfill my desire?"

"No."

"A pity so many of your countrymen didn't share your wisdom. Their fates could have been much more pleasant."

Thida glanced up at these words, and Indravarman rejoiced at the fullness of her eyes. Even in the darkness he saw that they were red and inflamed. Grunting, he stepped outside, curious if she would stay or follow. After only a heartbeat's hesitation she stepped into the rain, trailing his footsteps.

So quick to break, he thought. Too bad all Khmer women aren't like you. If all Khmer women were like you, my enemies would be naught.

Far to the west, back at Jayavar's camp, a shadow seemed to float through the night. The shadow avoided the prince's sentries, circumventing anything that might betray its presence, whether a restless elephant or a fallen twig. Every few feet, the shadow paused, studying the darkness. The rain had finally stopped, and the wet ground made for silent steps. The voices of insects had replaced the splatter of water, their chirps and cries punctuating the air. Most of the cooking fires had gone out, though embers glowed near sleeping warriors, women, and children.

The shadow crept closer to where the prince and princess resided. A simple shelter of bamboo and deerskin had been erected, and the couple must be sleeping under this roof, since they weren't near what remained of their fire. Pausing once again, the shadow surveyed the immediate surroundings. The moon and stars were hidden by clouds and it was exceedingly dark.

A muffled cough emerged from the shelter, and the shadow crept forward, holding a spear with small yet hardened hands. Though the spear had once been of simple design, its shaft was now carved with temples and Gods. The weapon was unique, while its iron blade remained sharp and deadly.

More tentative steps were taken. The cough came again and the shadow's heartbeat quickened, seeming to race forward like that of a runaway horse. The shadow moved past the dying fire, heat emanating into the darkness. Two figures could be seen faintly within the shelter. The prince lay next to the princess, her head on his chest.

Whispers infiltrated the night. Three figures moved through the trees, all carrying weapons. Instinctively, the shadow lowered itself to the ground. As the guards neared, the shadow took a final look at Jayavar, then receded into the blackness, backtracking, moving swiftly yet silently.

The shadow circumvented warriors and elephants, hurrying to the opposite side of the camp, setting the spear down, then lying in an empty space and watching with patience as the clouds slowly parted to reveal a sea of stars.

Three

Searching for Yesterday

he horses were restless. Even Ajadevi, who had never ridden before, sensed their disquiet. Back in Angkor, she'd either walked or been carried on a jeweled palanquin. Now, as she sat behind Jayavar on a silk pad tied to the animal, she rested her hand on their mount's broad back. She closed her eyes, felt heat emanating from the firm flesh, and was reminded of a distant time and place. The catalyst of the memory, one from a former life, was the heat. Something had burned and blackened. Wood? Straw? She shook her head, patterns emerging, fabric smoldering beneath a flame.

Their horse neighed and the vision was gone. Ajadevi opened her eyes. The jungle through which they traveled was thick with towering ficus and teak trees. Many of these behemoths were limbless for the first two hundred feet and then topped with rich canopies. Smaller trees, shrubs, ferns, and flowers competed for the early-morning light that managed to penetrate the leafy ceiling. Black squirrels, gray monkeys, and colorful birds traveled in the dangerous heights, causing leaves and twigs to fall. The dry season was about to start, but for now dampness hung in the air. Scents of decay and new growth lingered from bend to bend, from hill to valley.

Ten horses and an equal number of warriors accompanied Jayavar and Ajadevi. They rode in the middle of the group, which stretched in single file as far as one might throw a rock. The warriors were the strongest of the remaining Khmers. Each would gladly give his life for the prince or princess, and each was bent on revenge against the Chams.

"I saw a moment," Ajadevi said softly.

Jayavar turned, his gaze meeting hers. "What moment?"

"Burning silk."

He nodded, accustomed to her visions. "And why did the fire start?"

"Passion, I think."

"Passion?"

"The flames . . . rose from passion."

"Did you see anything else? Anything that might aid us?"

Ajadevi thought about the Chams, about how the heat of a former life might provide insight into what they faced. "The Chams . . . covet our beauty, but may destroy it."

"I know this."

"They destroy our future."

"Our children? My children?"

Sunlight filtered down from a gap in the tree canopy, warming Ajadevi's shoulders. "The Chams are like shadows, but a few . . . a few are like light. A few can be trusted."

"The only Cham I trust is a dead Cham."

"Don't talk like that, Jayavar. The world isn't a place of black and white, but of color. Some Chams deserve your blade and some do not."

"If my children live, I shall be merciful."

She reached around his waist, her hand finding his. "I love your children too. I've always loved them as if they were born from me."

"I know."

"And I've had my own children," she said, aware of warmth within her belly. "Long before I came upon this body, I was a mother."

"So you understand how I feel. The ache. The emptiness."

"I do."

Jayavar nodded. "A part of me wishes to rush to Angkor, to see if they live. The other part of me wants to proceed slowly, for I fear what we shall discover and I cling to hope."

"Hope clings to you."

"How?"

"The hope of your people. Of your unborn sons and daughters. Of me."

He studied the men in front of him, thinking that most of them also had children, that their burdens were as great as his. "I fear . . . that I'm not strong enough," he whispered. "Men will die for me, but I'm the same flesh and blood as they."

"Men will die for a belief. Not for you, but for the belief that you stand for something noble. Angkor Wat was built on such beliefs. The Hindus created the temple to house their Gods, their faith. Though Buddhism leads me on a different path, I still like to look at the Hindus' statues, to see the faces of their Gods."

"Why?"

Ajadevi thought about Angkor Wat, remembering the steepness of the steps that led toward its summit, which served to remind Hindus that the ascent into a supreme soul was a challenging task. "When I climb the steps of the temple," she said, "I feel as the old Hindus wanted me to feel, as if I'm climbing a mountain, climbing toward something beautiful."

"Maybe you helped them build it, in an earlier life."

"I think so. I have memories . . . of carving. Of blistered hands and an aching back."

Jayavar's gaze swept through the jungle. "Do you think me reckless to split up our forces? To take our ten best men, to steal them from the women and children we left behind?"

"They have enough warriors to protect them."

"What should I do once we reach Angkor? How shall I discover the fate of my children? I have considered entering the city dressed as a priest, but perhaps there is a better way."

Ajadevi glanced at an immense web that hung between a pair of narrow tree trunks. A black and yellow spider, nearly the span of her fist, waited in the center of the web. "Last night I dreamed I was a beggar," she replied. "I was seen but unseen."

He pursed his lips. "Yes, that might be better, even more inconspicuous. We could soil ourselves and beg outside the city walls. We could look humble, but talk to Khmers, let them know who we are, and inquire about my children."

"We should."

"And if . . . if they were slain?"

"Then wherever we sit you shall promise your children to build them a temple in their honor. You shall think of them, pray for them, love them. And then we shall leave."

He shook his head. "A hospital. If they're gone, I shall one day build a hospital on that site. A hospital for children."

Her hand tightened around his. "You see? That's why men will die for you."

"Whatever I've learned, I've learned from them. And you."

She looked away. "And yet I still fail you."

"How?"

"You need an heir and I cannot give you one. Perhaps another of your wives should have lived instead of me. Perhaps I—"

He twisted around, placing his fingertips under her chin and gently lifting it. "Without you I'm nothing. Without you the Chams would prevail."

She kissed his wrist. "I don't wish you to be nothing."

"Then stay beside me, Ajadevi. Always stay beside me."

The faintest of smiles graced her lips. "I'm a part of you. Not beside you, but within you. Like your children. As they remain within you, as they always have and always will, I am within you."

"I feel you."

"Please remember my words in the days ahead. They will be days that will test you as you've never been tested. And so you must believe that you do not walk alone."

Morning light bathed the towers and stairways of Angkor Wat in amber. Before the Chams had arrived, the temple had been mostly filled with Hindu priests and pilgrims. A few Khmer warriors and administrators had walked its great chambers, but the majority of those who entered the complex came to pray. Since the invasion, everything was different. Cham warriors were posted throughout Angkor Wat, and Khmer priests had dwindled to a fraction of their usual numbers.

As Voisanne strode beside Thida, she avoided the eyes of the Chams. Yet she felt their gaze on her and increased her pace, wanting to be free of them, wondering why the enemy warrior had protected her. She'd thought about killing him throughout much of the night but had finally succumbed to exhaustion and slept as far from him as his room allowed.

Voisanne proceeded down the long corridor on the southwest side of Angkor Wat. To her left ran a series of square, sandstone pillars that framed her view to the west, through the open side of the walkway. On the opposite side stretched an enormous bas-relief that depicted hundreds if not thousands of warriors in battle. Horse-drawn chariots charged at formations of foot soldiers carrying spears, swords, shields, and flags. The bas-relief depicted the Hindu legend of the Battle of Kurukshetra, and though Voisanne had always enjoyed the story, she turned away from the scene, not wanting to see spears and death. She glanced at the high ceiling, which bore painted carvings of red lotus flowers, and then turned to her left, passed through Angkor Wat's main entrance, and stepped onto the causeway that led to the moat.

Thida kept a few paces behind Voisanne, and their Cham watchdog stayed farther back, the shaft of an axe resting on his shoulder. Thida's eyes were downcast, her hands held in front of her. She might have been the most beautiful woman Voisanne had ever seen, but she seemed to drift ahead without purpose, like a cloud on a windless day.

The causeway, wider and straighter than any road, was inundated with people of all backgrounds, though the majority were Chams. Voisanne passed a pair of statues of *nagas*—seven-headed serpents. Between the statues, sandstone steps led to a street that teemed with more of the enemy. Nearby, Khmer homes, built on stilts so as to protect residents from tigers and snakes, were occupied by Chams. Khmers were also present, though they often huddled under trees, cooking rice and fish over makeshift fires.

After a short walk to the west, Voisanne passed through a gateway that was part of the stout wall surrounding all of Angkor. Another few dozen paces brought her to the moat, which was nearly six hundred feet wide. She smiled for the first time since the attack, because the water, as usual, was filled with her people.

Each side of the moat was lined with steps made out of laterite blocks, and Voisanne proceeded to the water, the black blocks warm against her feet. She removed her skirt cloth, covered her privates with a cupped hand, and stepped into the moat. As Thida repeated these actions, Voisanne moved away from the shoreline and into cooler water. She studied her people. Thousands of Khmers bathed to the north. Her view to the south was blocked by the causeway, which led across the moat toward towering trees. Though a few Khmer children laughed and played in the water, the adults were somber. Usually couples could be seen clinging to each other or washing off after intimacy, but Voisanne saw no lovers. People simply sat in the shallows or swam far from shore.

Voisanne splashed water on her face, then rubbed the dust and grit from her features. She repeatedly dropped underwater to scrub her hair and body. Like most Khmers, she bathed several times a day in an attempt to stay clean and to keep the heat at bay.

When she finished washing herself, Voisanne turned to Thida, who had hardly moved. Voisanne studied her companion, wondering why they had been ordered to bathe together. Why, when there were thousands of concubines in the Royal Palace, had Indravarman arranged their pairing?

"What brings us together?" Voisanne asked, then glanced at their guard, who remained at the moat's edge.

Thida didn't seem to hear her.

Voisanne stepped closer to the other woman. When Thida still made no effort to speak, Voisanne thought about the Cham warrior. If he'd ravaged her, as she had expected, she would have killed him and then herself. She would be on the path toward rebirth, toward her loved ones. Instead she stood in the shallows and felt the wounds of her memories. Her brother died again and again in her arms. Her lover perished without a final, gentle word between them.

Her tears came then, as swiftly as pain. Somehow, even as her vision blurred, she noticed that Thida also wept. Voisanne reached for her companion and their fingers met and clutched.

"What happened to you?" Voisanne asked.

Thida slowly shook her head, as if waking from an unpleasant dream. "Indravarman."

Voisanne understood. The fate that she had predicted for herself had befallen Thida. The Cham king had used her as he pleased. Thida's beauty, which most would have seen as a blessing, had become a curse.

Thida leaned forward, collapsing into Voisanne's arms. Voisanne supported her as best she could, weeping also, wondering if they should somehow drown each other.

A deep laugh caused Voisanne's heart to skip. She turned and saw that the Cham guard was smiling. Two other warriors had joined him.

Suddenly Voisanne wished she were a man. If she were, she would pick up a weapon and kill the Chams. She would avenge her loved ones. For so long she'd wanted to create life, to witness her child emerging into the world. But as the Chams gawked at her, she longed to take life, to send the demons back to the underworld from which they had come.

But Voisanne could do no such thing. And so she held Thida as upright as possible, their teardrops forming ripples on the water, their bodies and minds clinging together, searching for solace when none could be found.

The giant catfish was proving to be a good distraction. Boran had thought about cutting it loose, but decided that his sons could benefit from the challenge of catching it. They'd spent the night beside a large river, risking a fire to ward off mosquitoes and flies. Boran had set out three lines, leaving a dead frog on each hook. He hadn't expected to catch anything, but now, as Vibol and Prak allowed the thin rope to be pulled through their hands, he could tell by the movement of the water that they'd hooked a beast. Worried that his boys would run out of rope, Boran hurried into the jungle, found a vine as thick as his remaining thumb, and yanked it from the branches above. He tied the end of the rope to the vine. "Be patient," he said to his sons. "Fight too hard and you'll lose him."

"Too bad he's not a Cham," Vibol replied. "Then you'd really see a fight."

Prak turned to his left, stepping into the shallows. He could feel the catfish trying to make its way downstream. "He's smarter than a Cham. Look where he's headed."

"So follow him downstream," Boran advised. "You'll never pull in such weight against the current."

His sons did as he suggested, moving with the water. Prak tripped twice over unseen logs. He regained his footing on both occasions, trying to outmaneuver the catfish.

As Vibol and Prak pulled on the rope, Boran asked Soriya to hand him a weapon. She gave him the Cham axe and he held it ready. The river widened, becoming slow and lazy. "Your chance is at hand," Boran said. "Put your backs into it."

The twins heaved on the rope. Seconds later, the dorsal fin of the catfish appeared, then its arched back. Boran could tell that the fish outweighed any of them and he was suddenly as excited as his sons. Seldom did anyone catch a giant Mekong catfish. Had they tried to pull it in from their boat, they would have foundered.

As the catfish entered the shallows, it headed toward a sunken tree. Boran shouted a warning, but Vibol and Prak could do nothing as the line snagged on an unseen branch. Though now tied to the tree, with its next burst of strength the catfish would likely break the thin rope. Before Boran could utter a word of advice, Vibol grabbed the axe from him and ran into the water, lifting his legs high as he charged forward. He struck a hidden branch, stumbled, but managed to bring the axe down hard on the catfish's broad snout. The water erupted in spray as the creature thrashed against its attacker. Vibol swung again and again until Boran shouted at him to stop. The fish was dead.

They hauled their catch to shore and marveled at its size. At five feet long and as thick as a pig, the gray, spotted catfish could have fed fifty people. Soriya wondered aloud how many hungry Khmers were hiding in the jungle, and Boran decided to cut the meat into thin strips so that it could be smoked and preserved. As Boran and Soriya started to make a drying rack, their boys went to work with knives. Soon they were covered in blood and entrails.

The jungle was full of tigers and other predators, so Boran built a fire at the base of an acacia tree. He also cut a groove in the tree's trunk and set a burning branch inside the groove. Soon tar would seep from the wound, which he'd use to patch a crack in his boat.

"We could stay in these waters forever," he said. "Just the four of us."

Vibol stopped working and looked up. "But—"

"But we cannot do what I'd like to do," Boran added.

After Soriya positioned their drying rack near the fire, she stepped toward her husband. She had created a necklace of jasmine flowers for herself, and the petals trembled as she moved. "What would you have us do?" she asked.

Boran eyed his sons. "The Chams traveled to Angkor using their boats. They're a kingdom of seafarers. More boats will surely sail from their homeland, bringing men and supplies. The most sensible route would take them across the Great Lake. So it would seem that they must have a base there, near Angkor."

Prak set down his knife. "You think we should spy on them?"

"What do you think?"

"We could track them from afar," Prak suggested. "And report their doings to our Khmer brothers."

"Yes," Vibol added, standing up. "And if we happen to meet a few Chams, we can—"

"There will be no killing," Boran interjected. "Killing puts us at risk of discovery. Better to watch and report. That task is much more valuable than the blood of a few Chams." He pointed a gnarled finger at Vibol. "Agreed?"

Prak and then Vibol nodded.

"So we'll spy on them," Boran concluded. "We know how to find and study fish. It can't be so different to study men. Only we'll let others catch them."

The brothers reconfirmed their agreement, then went back to work. They hauled the catfish's carcass into the water, leery of crocodiles and snapping turtles. As the current swept away the carcass, the siblings washed themselves.

Soriya beckoned Boran to her side. "The spying worries me," she whispered. "I can lose anything but my loved ones. Please, please, don't take us to a place where I might lose one of you."

Boran nodded. "I'm worried too, but if we go nowhere, if we do nothing, Vibol will leave us. And we can't guide him if we're not near him."

A monkey or squirrel must have passed overhead because leaves started to fall. Soriya bit her lower lip. "If they were younger, I'd want to run."

"I know."

"I'd do the opposite of what we're doing."

"And leave your homeland to die?"

"Better to lose my homeland than my loved ones." She pointed at him. "Please, Boran, please move with care. One wrong step and everything we've built will crumble. And what we've built is as precious as any temple."

"We won't crumble."

"My heart tells me to run. To run and not look back. So please swear to me, Boran, that if the danger becomes too great we'll turn around. We'll flee rather than fight."

More leaves fell from the canopy above them. Boran nodded again, then rubbed his aching neck, which often troubled him from dawn to dusk. He thought about his children, wishing that they were younger and that Vibol didn't yet understand the concept of revenge.

Boran continued to massage his neck, feeling increasingly torn between the desire to support his sons and the need to protect them. "If the danger seems too much," he finally replied, "we'll run like deer and won't look back. Vibol will just have to become a man another day."

The battle had been brief, but ferocious.

Po Rame had discovered the presence of a sizable force of Khmer warriors to the west of Angkor. The Khmers had been camped at the far end of the West Baray—an enormous, rectangular reservoir that was four miles long, a mile wide, and reached a depth of twenty feet. Years earlier, Khmers had built the reservoir to trap rainwater. In the dry season, water could be released from it into the surrounding fields, allowing farmers to grow rice and other crops throughout the year. The West Baray was the largest of the Khmer reservoirs and ensured that the kingdom could feed its multitudes of people.

Through his network of spies, Po Rame had learned that

nearly three thousand Khmer warriors had taken refuge on the far side of the reservoir. Convinced that they'd discovered the whereabouts of Jayavar, Indravarman had led a force of five thousand Chams around the vast body of water. He'd come at the Khmers from behind, trapping them against the shoreline. Though his surprise hadn't been complete, the Khmers had been forced to fight. A few had escaped, others had been captured, and many had fought, killed, and died.

After the battle, Indravarman had interrogated the prisoners, learning much to his dismay that no one knew the whereabouts of Jayavar. An old general had led the Khmers, and once his corpse had been thrown into the water, Indravarman had called for Asal. Now, as Indravarman sat on his war elephant and watched his young officer approach on a similar beast, he recalled how Asal had charged into a thicket of Khmer warriors at the shoreline, using a long spear to impale them like fish. Asal's elephant had trampled several Khmers, and would have done more harm, but the *mahout*—the small man who sat on its neck and controlled the beast—had been slain, and Asal had been forced to leap down from his elevated platform so that the creature could be managed. Several Khmers had attacked him at once, pulling him into the shallow water. Somehow Asal had landed on his feet, lashing out at his attackers, killing two before other Chams came to his aid.

Indravarman had also engaged the enemy while on his elephant and had been slightly wounded by an arrow that had grazed his shoulder. The wound pleased him, for blood trickled down his arm for everyone to see. Many had witnessed how he'd fought in single combat against a Khmer atop a massive war elephant. The two warriors had exchanged blows until Indravarman slipped his spear under the Khmer's shield.

The immense war elephant was now his. Indravarman told

his *mahout* to let it bathe in the shallows. The slight man pushed a knee into the base of its right ear, clucking with his tongue. The beast lurched forward, stepping farther into the water, continuing ahead until the bottoms of its tusks were wet.

Asal's new *mahout* moved their elephant alongside Indravarman's. The king dismissed both *mahouts*, who bowed to him, jumped into the water, and waded back to shore. As usual, Asal made no effort to break the silence, and Indravarman studied him, noting that blood oozed from his knuckles.

"You had to hit them?" Indravarman asked.

Asal nodded.

"Unforgivable to lose your weapon in battle." The king swiped at a fly that had found his wound. "When you lose your blade, you give a man hope."

"He's dead, Lord King. Whatever hope I gave him, I reclaimed it swiftly."

Indravarman laughed. "A lion among cubs, that's what you were."

"As were you, Lord King."

"Because Jayavar wasn't here. Without Jayavar, the Khmers will always be cubs."

A snake swam across the murky water, not twenty paces in front of Asal's elephant. He felt the giant beast tense, and he leaned forward, running his hand upon its back through the hard and thick hairs that marked its age.

"Po Rame's information was sound," Indravarman said. "Once again, I find myself indebted to him."

Asal remembered how the assassin had once murdered a senior Cham officer and his family. The officer had been an adversary of Indravarman's but a friend of Asal's. Poison was Po Rame's weapon of choice, and Asal had come upon the children writhing in pain, their bellies swollen and hot. He'd tried to save them but was forced to watch them suffer and die, reminded of the distant cries of his own siblings. Days later, Asal had learned who had killed his friends and he'd been filled with rage. He'd sought out Po Rame and called him a coward, but, leery of Indravarman, had not lifted his sword. Neither had Po Rame retaliated, likely out of the same concern.

"What should I do with the prisoners?" Indravarman asked, pointing with his thumb toward a group of Khmers who stood in water up to their necks.

Asal knew that his king would kill the Khmers, but he didn't want to give Indravarman motives to try and become less predictable. "Put them to work, Lord King," he replied. "As farmers and blacksmiths. We have thousands of men to feed and arm. They'll fight better with full bellies and sharp swords."

Indravarman frowned. "True enough. But these Khmers won't break so easily. They'll rise up again. And I tell you, it's better to have an empty belly as you fight one man than a full belly as you fight two."

"If you believe so, Lord King."

"You're too forgiving, Asal. That's your great weakness. On a field of battle, you're nearly unrivaled. But off that field, you're as dangerous as a child."

"I—"

"Enemies are everywhere. They don't always hold swords, but often parchment, hoes, or silks. Every Khmer is my enemy and I'll treat them as such. I take no joy in it, but that's how you break an enemy, how you rule a defeated kingdom. You steal their pride, their comfort, their ambitions. You show them that death can come at any time, and in this way they'll be grateful for life." Indravarman wiped away blood that continued to trickle from the wound on his shoulder. "I see the doubt in your face, Asal. It's true that the Khmers are fellow Hindus. I admire their temples. I believe that there's much that binds us to them. But our people live on the seas. We trade. We pirate. We endure, but don't flourish. To our north, the Vietnamese grow stronger by the day. Here in the south, the Khmers build cities that surpass anything we create. And the Siamese encroach on our territory from the west. We're squeezed from all directions. If we don't strike out, as we do now, our people will cease to exist."

Asal nodded, though he believed that Indravarman took joy in his military campaigns, that his philosophical musings were attempts to justify, even ennoble, choices he'd already made. "Then why not strike the Vietnamese, Lord King?" Asal asked. "They seem weaker than the Khmers."

"Because the Khmers have gold and silver. Because they've grown soft in their pursuit of pleasing the Gods. It took fifty thousand Khmers and thousands of their elephants to build Angkor Wat. Imagine that. They could have scattered us with such a force, and instead they built a temple. Po Rame was right—the time to conquer them is now. Better to strike an enemy, to crush an enemy, before the chance has come and gone."

"And what of the prisoners, Lord King?"

The muscles of Indravarman's jaw tightened. "Prisoners or enemies? They were gathering an army to attack us. And so I'll bury them up to their chins in the dirt, in their precious dirt. Let their people see what happens when I'm opposed."

Asal glanced at the men who remained in the water. Some must have just died of their wounds, for there seemed to be fewer of them. Asal saw defiance in the faces of those who still lived. They would do better, he thought, to hide their hatred.

"Tell me of your woman," Indravarman said, removing his

inverted lotus-flower headdress, which he always wore for battle, as did the men beneath him. Though most of the shoulder-length headdresses were highlighted by colorful silk and painted beads, the king's also contained a single row of small, gold spheres.

"What of her, Lord King?"

"Does my gift please you?"

"She does."

"An unlucky Khmer, that woman. We attacked as she was about to be wed. Her man was killed."

Asal shook his head. "I didn't know."

"Does our timing make you her husband?" Indravarman asked, laughing.

"She—"

"Did you ever think that you'd have a Khmer wife? And such a pretty one at that?" Indravarman slapped his thigh, continuing to chuckle. He called to his *mahout*, telling the man to lead his elephant ashore. "That's why power is good, Asal," Indravarman said. "We saw something beautiful, and we took it. A kingdom and a woman."

"Yes, Lord King."

"Keep me happy as she keeps you happy. Do that and you shall have a blessed life."

Asal watched as Indravarman returned to shore and began shouting orders. As the prisoners were dragged from the water, Asal thought about Voisanne. He remembered her tears, how she had feared him even when he meant her no harm. Suddenly he needed to tell her that he was sorry, that he had also suffered and understood her pain. Surely she hated him, but he did not want to be hated, especially by her.

Feeling dirty, as if the taint of injustice had soiled his skin, Asal slid off his elephant and into the cool water. He removed his headdress, tossed it to shore, and then swam away from the beast. After loosening his topknot, he ran his hands through his hair, wishing to rid himself of the foulness that covered him.

Back at Jayavar's base camp deep in the jungle, a small hand held an ornately carved spear. Night had fallen, and free to roam in the darkness, the shadow explored large areas within and around the Khmer perimeter. The terrain was flat, dominated by rivers, lakes, trees, and wild animals. Back in Angkor, humanity had seemed all powerful. But here the jungle was so thick that even during the day it was impossible to see twenty paces ahead. Animals were the lords of this domain, and gibbons, langurs, tigers, leopards, deer, boars, elephants, crocodiles, cobras, hornbills, and kingfishers dwelled in the dense foliage, their calls permeating the night.

The shadow wished that Jayavar and Ajadevi hadn't left. They had departed without warning, vanishing with a select group of warriors. No one seemed to know when the prince would return, though people said that it would take many days to journey to Angkor and back. If rumors could be believed, Jayavar would reappear in the same manner he'd departed, though with a much larger force.

Voices drifted through the darkness, and the shadow stepped into a bamboo thicket, disappearing from sight. The voices strengthened, and soon two Khmer warriors became visible as they patrolled. The sentries were stout and muscled, but far too loud. They didn't know how to become a part of the jungle, which the shadow had been born into and then taken from; only recently had he returned. Though many of Angkor's slaves could buy back their freedom, the shadow had been captured in the eastern highlands and been cursed with a cruel master. Freedom had seemed to be an impossibility—at least until the Chams had attacked.

The Khmers passed, talking as if they were back in Angkor watching a cockfight. They walked within five paces of the shadow without realizing it. How could these fools be free? the shadow wondered. How am I a slave when I could be so much more?

As the moon set and the jungle grew darker, the shadow remained in the thicket, wondering when Jayavar would return. The prince may have left with ten warriors beside him, but he might as well have been alone. Ten men, if they were like the sentries, would be more a curse than a blessing.

The prince was alone, thought the shadow, and if he wasn't careful the jungle would swallow him up.

Four

Seeds of Discontent

The highest vantage point at Angkor Wat could be reached only by four steep sets of sandstone stairs. Located on the east, west, south, and north faces of the pyramidlike tower, the stairs were narrow and treacherous. A slip could send someone falling to his death.

Voisanne had climbed to the terrace several times before, but she'd never been as preoccupied with the danger as she was now. When she reached the midway point, she thought about just leaning backward and falling, letting her head strike the stone and welcoming whatever fate came her way. But when she paused, Asal stopped as well, looking down at her. His eyes found hers and with the slightest of movements, he nodded. Only then did Voisanne realize that he was encouraging her, but doing so secretly, as if fearful of the Cham king who led them, followed by Thida, toward the summit. For a reason Voisanne didn't understand, this realization prompted her to nod in return, and she continued on.

At the top of the stairs was an elaborate entrance that led to a corridor. At the sides of the entrance several three-feet-high *apsaras* were carved into wide pillars. Hindus believed that *apsaras* were female spirits of the clouds and water. Voisanne had always been fascinated by *apsaras* and remembered when her father had told her how they danced in the palaces of the Gods, entertaining them as well as fallen heroes. Her father had also said that Angkor Wat contained almost two thousand *apsaras*, each of which was different, though all tended to look happy, to be dressed ornately, and to be dancing. The *apsaras* at the top of the steps resembled women found in the Royal Palace who had entertained the Khmer kings and now, she suspected, amused the Cham king.

Though Voisanne had sometimes felt powerless as a woman, she had long been comforted by the knowledge that the creators of Angkor Wat had placed such an emphasis on women. In addition to the numerous *apsaras*, there were carvings of *devatas* throughout the complex. As female guardians, *devatas* tended to face the viewer and appear as if they were standing still. They seemed reflective, sometimes leaning forward or with a falcon perched atop a shoulder. At the summit of Angkor Wat, as in many other places throughout the temple, women seemed to be celebrated.

Voisanne walked through the entrance, following Asal down a long corridor. To her right, through a series of ornate openings, she could see the city of Angkor far below. She felt as if she were atop a mountain, as the temple's architects had intended. Nothing within sight rivaled the height from which she stared. Everything else was below her, further removed from the realm of the supreme soul.

The group stepped past a massive set of teak doors, turned to the left, and walked into a large chamber at the base of the lotus-shaped tower that rose from the middle of the terrace. The cham-

ber was open on all sides and held an immense bronze statue of
Vishnu, to whom all of Angkor Wat was dedicated.

A devout Hindu, Indravarman walked up to the statue and
knelt before it. So did Thida and Asal. Voisanne remained standing, not because she didn't believe in the God, but because she
felt defiant. While the men bowed their heads and prayed, Thida
studied Vishnu's face and Voisanne looked out into the countryside. From so high, she could see what had long been a great empire. The terraced platforms of Angkor Wat fell away like steps
that a giant might climb. Outside the temple grounds, the city
thrived with innumerable people, horses, and war elephants. The
huge, square moat surrounded the city, and in the distance, older
temples rose from the tops of hills and the crooks of streams. To
the far south, the Great Lake spread out toward infinity. She
could see its beginning, but not its end.

The men continued to pray. Voisanne wondered why Indravarman had summoned her and Thida to accompany him to the
top of the temple. Voisanne had heard stories of past kings enjoying women atop temples, and she knew that if he made such an
intention known, she would run and throw herself to her death.

Indravarman stood up. "Why," he asked, "do the faces of
women dominate this site?"

Asal and Thida also rose, though no one answered.

"Is it because Khmer men are weak?" he continued. "They
chisel their memories and beliefs into stone while their women
toil far below."

The wind whistled through an unseen gap in the sandstone.

Voisanne was tempted to reply, to defend her father and lover.
But she sensed that too much boldness would kindle Indravarman's interest in her, and she would rather have him remain
entranced with Thida's beauty.

Indravarman shook his head. "Your empire cannot be rivaled

when it comes to wonders such as Angkor Wat. You've made the Gods proud, and that's not easy to do. That's why, when many of your men fall so easily and act so meekly, I wonder if they've truly fallen. Could the men who built this place bow to me so quickly? I think not. I think defiance runs in your blood, a defiance toward mortality, toward me. And that's why I've brought you here, to ask you what I should do about such defiance. How do I put out a fire that has yet to burn?"

Thida glanced up. "Why us, Lord King?"

"Because your men celebrate your beauty, your wisdom. They celebrate it in their carvings. They guard their temples with visions of you, and so you must have more merit than it would at first seem."

"We may, Lord King," Thida said, "be of—"

"Ten of my warriors were found dead this morning!" Indravarman suddenly yelled, his voice booming, hurting Voisanne's ears. "Their throats were cut and this is why I speak of defiance! Because when I find ten of my warriors dead, floating in the moat, I know that your men aren't as meek as they appear. And a fire threatens me. A fire that's strong enough to consume my land."

Voisanne thought that he was the fire, burning without control, but, once again, she said nothing. The combination of his bulk and anger seemed to dominate even the large statue of Vishnu. Of the two figures, Indravarman was far more imposing.

"Since our playthings have lost their tongues, what do you advise?" Indravarman asked, turning to Asal.

"Kill ten Khmers, Lord King. Ten of your prisoners. And let their fates be known."

"Ten warriors?"

"Yes."

"You think, fool, that the men who built this place care about the fate of ten warriors?" Indravarman shouted. "Your sword arm may be strong, Asal, but your suggestion invites our foes to rise up against us. If you wish to remain by my side, you'd better learn how to make men fear you."

Asal bowed. "Forgive me, Lord King. I only wish to—"

"Take ten Khmer families out into a courtyard, for everyone to see. Execute them all. The men, the women, the children."

"No!" Voisanne said, dropping to her knees. "Please don't—"

Indravarman reached for the hilt of his sword, but Asal was quicker, kicking her hard in the stomach. "Silence, woman!"

Gasping for breath, Voisanne fell to her side, her eyes tearing. Indravarman laughed. "And so she does speak," he said. "She dares to speak when not asked a question."

"I'll deal with her, Lord King," Asal replied. "And she won't enjoy it."

"Do."

Voisanne started to cry, imagining the fate of the children who would soon be killed. She thought of her siblings, wondering how the beauty of their lives could be extinguished so easily by the cruelty of strangers.

As Voisanne continued to weep, Asal asked himself how he could save the lives of the innocent. "Lord King?"

"Yes?"

"You speak of a fire that's yet to burn."

"It smolders."

"But the death of the young might make it burn more quickly."

"So what would you have me do? Ten of my men are dead! Slain outside my palace!"

Asal bowed. "Kill ten of their priests, Lord King. A public execution. Ten of their highest-ranking priests. The sight of ten dead priests will sap their spirits. The sight of dead children will inflame them."

Indravarman grunted, then rubbed the iron buried within his belly. Though troubled at the thought of offending the Gods by putting priests to death, he suspected that Asal was right—better to kill the old than the young. "But cast the bodies into that moat, Asal, and let the Khmers know that I'll turn its waters red with their blood if there's another attack on my men."

"Yes, Lord King."

"Red with the blood of their children!"

Asal nodded as Indravarman whirled away. Thida followed him. Though Asal wanted to help Voisanne to her feet, to tell her that he had kicked her to save her, he could do nothing of the sort. Instead he shouted at her to follow, and when she hesitated, he dragged her up, pulling her after them. She beat at his side, shrieking.

Indravarman yelled at Asal to hurry, and Asal thrust Voisanne forward. She slapped him hard on the face and would have slapped him again but he caught her wrist. He was pleased that she continued to struggle against him, because Indravarman would not be easily duped, and if Asal's compassion for the Khmer woman were ever known, she would be put to death.

Fearing Indravarman's guile, Asal cursed Voisanne as he dragged her down a long corridor. He passed carving after carving of the smiling women, who looked so at peace. A distant memory unfurled. He saw his mother grin. He wanted to see more, but then Indravarman shouted for him and the memory was gone.

Jayavar could tell that the river had fallen since the peak of the monsoon season. A nearby bamboo thicket, five feet above the water, had once acted as a net of sorts, catching debris that had

floated on the river's surface. The bamboo trunks, so close together, held driftwood, leaves, and an old rope.

Gazing up and down the sandy shoreline, Jayavar looked for a
flat stone about the size of his palm. He soon found what he required, retrieved the object, and carefully placed it atop the pile
of stones that he had already stacked. Needing two smaller stones,
he waded into the water, searching and discovering.

The finished pile was taller than his knee. He touched the
stones, which had been sculpted by the passage of water and time.
Each was beautiful. Jayavar believed that his pile would remain
standing until the monsoon rains came again. Then the river
would rise, lap at the bottom stone, climbing higher until it toppled his creation. The stones would scatter, yet remain near one
another, perhaps unmoving for centuries.

A gibbon screeched overhead. Jayavar glanced up, looking for
the monkey. He saw nothing, but leaves drifted downward, fluttering like feathers. Some of the leaves landed in the water and
were carried downstream, green vessels that might make it to the
sea. Jayavar felt a pang of regret as he realized that his youngest
children had never visited the coast. He'd planned to take them,
to watch them run into the endless swath of blue, to hear their
laughter as they leapt over waves or chased crabs on the beach.

His eyes watered, but no tears fell. Ajadevi and his small band
of warriors were nearby, and he didn't want anyone to see his anguish. They had been riding through the jungle all morning, and
the closer they got to Angkor, the more eager and hopeful everyone seemed to become. Everyone but him, that is. Though Jayavar often spoke to his men about hope, about the future, he felt
further removed from his children, as if he had already said good-
bye to them.

"You used eleven stones."

He turned, surprised to see Ajadevi standing only a few paces away. He'd never met anyone capable of moving with such stealth. She might as well have been a part of the forest. Though his wife had always been talkative with him, she was quiet with everyone else, preferring to dwell within her own thoughts.

"A stone for each of your children?" she asked.

He looked at his pile. "Yes."

"Come. There's something I wish to show you."

Cicadas screeched from unseen places as he followed her upstream along the riverbank. She walked about twenty paces and then pointed to a pool of water that had been separated from the river. Within the pool were six or seven fish the size of Jayavar's hand. They were perch, one of the most delicious fish to be found near Angkor. The pool also contained a large soft-shelled turtle that was almost as big as a shield. Jayavar wondered if the trapped fish knew that freedom was so close. Soon the pool would dry up, and when it did, they would be eaten by the turtle or alligators or ants.

"You should release them," Ajadevi said.

"Why?"

"Because release is good."

He studied the fish, which darted about the pool, seeking escape. "You think I should release my children? That I hold on to them too tightly?"

"I'm sorry, my love. But yes, you should release your past. You should release yourself."

"You think I'm trapped? Like these fish?"

She sighed and then touched the wound on his hip, which, thanks to her care, was healing quickly. "Your bond to the past makes your connection to the present more tenuous. In that way you are trapped."

"The past defines me."

"And the present will define the future of your kingdom."

He turned away from her. "You ask the impossible, as if I have a heart of stone instead of flesh."

"But, Jayavar, your men see your despair. It's etched on your face. And you'll never free your people, never free the memories of your children, if you plant seeds of despair. You have to plant what will grow, not wither."

"You know nothing of what you speak! Of my loss!"

"Because . . . because I'm not a mother?"

"My bond to the past shall always be a part of me. It will define me more than the present, more than the future." A mosquito landed on Jayavar's arm, and he crushed it with the palm of his hand. "You push me too hard, Ajadevi. You want me to abandon hope when I cling to it as if it were a final breath of air that I might draw into my lungs. Until we reach Angkor, until I hear for certain of their fates, I shall cling to hope. And if my men see my despair, then they shall also see how I remain faithful to my duty even in the face of such grief."

Ajadevi bit her bottom lip. "They were my children too. We didn't share the same blood, but I always considered them my children, and my pain is more than you'll ever know. But I hide it, Jayavar. I hide it because I must. No one sees my tears except me. No one hears my whimpers except me. So don't act as if you're the only one among us who has suffered. I've most likely lost my parents, my siblings, and . . . our children. I don't ever expect to hear the voices of my sisters again—voices that made me smile but, because of my station beside you, have surely been silenced. I, like so many, have suffered, and yet we each go forward. Not because we want to but because we must."

Jayavar reached for her, but she spun from him and walked downstream along the shoreline. She stopped at his pile of stones, kneeling beside them, her hands against her face. She seemed to shudder, and he looked past the bamboo thickets, ensuring that his men were not near. He saw no one else, and so he turned back to her, watching her until she regained her composure. To his surprise, she began to construct a pile of stones next to his. She worked with care, never looking in his direction.

Only when she finished her pile did he turn his attention to the fish. In a week or two the pool of water would dry up. Though he would never release his children, never accept their fate, he bent over, scooping away the damp soil between the pool and the river. He worked with determination, glancing at the fish, wanting them to be free. Soon he created a channel between the bodies of water. He deepened the channel, then stood up and walked to the far end of the pool, herding the perch forward. They entered the channel, swam into the river, and disappeared. Though he doubted that the turtle needed his help, he picked it up and placed it also in the river.

Ajadevi remained near the two piles of rocks. For the first time in several days, Jayavar considered her losses. Some of her loved ones might still live, but others had certainly died, and he chastised himself for being selfish. Sometimes her strength was so apparent that he forgot about her grief.

Walking farther upstream, Jayavar headed toward a ficus tree that had fallen over the water. Dozens of purple orchids grew along the rotting trunk. Jayavar removed several of them from the damp wood and then pulled off their petals, dropping them into the water. The petals drifted toward Ajadevi, reminding Jayavar of lotus flowers in the moat around Angkor. Ajadevi saw the petals and looked toward him. He lowered his head, bowing to her, acknowledging her pain. Though he wanted to go to her, he also needed to respect her moment of mourning.

"Forgive me," he whispered.

Then he turned away and headed into the bamboo stand, toward the men who longed for him to lead, to carry them forward with his belief in the future. He would have to find inspiration from his wife and bury his grief, deep down, where others couldn't see it.

In the darkness of night he would honor his loved ones. But in the light of day he would honor those still living, those who rode by his side and who would soon fight for a better tomorrow.

The afternoon had passed quickly for Asal. He'd heard a rumor that Jayavar was raising an army to the north of Angkor and, followed by a hundred good men, Asal had searched a wide area. His force had found several dozen scattered Khmer warriors, and brief skirmishes had ensued. But no one knew the whereabouts of the prince. The Khmers all believed that Jayavar was alive and would return, yet it was as if the jungle had swallowed him up.

Asal had endured Indravarman's displeasure at the failure of the foray. The king was tired of rumors. He wanted facts. And when Asal had had no facts to give him, Indravarman had smashed his fist onto a dais and waved his advisers away. Asal had bowed and left to find ten Hindu priests to execute—the task that Indravarman had given him.

Though Asal wasn't a deeply religious man, his father had been, and he wished that the priests didn't have to be killed. He consoled himself with the knowledge that his plan spared the lives of children, but he still felt empty as he climbed the steps of Angkor Wat, heading for the summit of the temple where the oldest priests tended to congregate. He paused, gazing toward his homeland in the north. Suddenly he missed the sea. He'd been born in a coastal village and remembered hunting in the shallows for horseshoe crabs with his brothers. His mother had always set the crabs on embers, cooking them whole, making her children eat their pungent eggs for extra nourishment.

Of all his loved ones, her death had pained him most, because she had seen her children die and her misery had seemed without end. She hadn't been able to protect them from the cholera, a failing that killed her with greater swiftness than the disease. She had thought that Asal would die as well and had clutched him against her chest as she took her final breaths, trying to sing a song that he'd always liked.

Asal had lain against her body for two days until he finally recovered. Then he'd dragged the bodies of his family members to a field overlooking the sea. As was customary among his people, he didn't bury or burn them, but left them in the open, so that nothing would impede their path to rebirth.

At the top of Angkor Wat, having reflected on the death of his family, Asal thought about the priests, about their memories and regrets. He didn't want them to be executed and mused over how he might help them while still fulfilling his duty. An answer of sorts came to him, and he found an old priest. They spoke in hushed tones. They nodded and prayed. And then Asal returned to the Royal Palace, where he asked one of his men to bring him Voisanne.

While Asal sat in his room, he looked over the dinner that a slave had prepared for him. Like everyone of high rank within the palace, Asal ate from golden bowls and plates. The bowls contained rice, slices of mango, and fish sauce. The plates held eight sets of skewered frog legs that had been grilled. To protect the food from flies, squares of red silk had been draped over everything.

Waiting for Voisanne, Asal used a narrow bamboo tube to sip rice wine from a silver flask. He didn't drink often, but alcohol soothed the aches of battle, the memories of seeing a foe die on his blade, and let him sleep for at least half of any night. After he had taken another man's life, he always settled down and asked for rice wine. He wasn't alone in this practice.

Asal had made certain that there was ample food and drink for Voisanne. Though he was hungry, he neglected his food, continuing to wait patiently for her return. He wanted to apologize for kicking her, for dragging her down the long corridor. His man must have struggled to find her from amid the five thousand concubines in the Royal Palace, for by the time she arrived, the meal was cold. She glared at him as he thanked the warrior, who shut the teak door behind him.

The food had been placed on a rattan mat, and Asal motioned for Voisanne to sit. She stood for a few heartbeats, then moved as far from him as possible, kneeling at the opposite end of the mat. He asked if she was hungry. He encouraged her to eat. But she didn't move, not even after he whispered an apology, explaining that he'd been afraid of what Indravarman might do to her when she so openly disagreed with him.

She ignored his words, and he began to eat, using his right hand. Several times he washed his fingers in a golden water bowl. He had always been a slow eater, but in her presence, he moved like smoke, fluid and graceful. Placing the bamboo tube to his mouth, he sipped from the flask of rice wine.

"You're a kingdom of murderers," she said, her brow furrowed, her knuckles white in her clenched fists. "None of you can do anything other than kill! You sit here in our palace, using our bowls and plates and silks. You pray in our temples. You use our women! You're nothing more than a pack of wild dogs!"

Asal washed his hand. "Not all of us are—"

"Yes, you are! All of you! You killed my family, and you took everything in the world from me. And it matters not that you sit here and eat like a prince. You're nothing like a prince. And your king is no more a king than a fly on a pile of dung!"

"Keep your voice low."

"You don't rule me!"

"No, but I shall muzzle you if necessary."

Voisanne glared at him, a drop of perspiration running from her brow to her nose. "I'm not afraid of you. I don't tremble before you like you do before your king."

"Because I'm not wicked," Asal replied softly.

"Yet you kill. Ten priests, each as innocent as the day he was born, will be executed."

"Better ten priests than ten families. I was trying to protect—"

"Better no one!"

Asal took another sip of his wine, grateful for its calming effect. "You assail me, and yet you don't know me."

"I know that you're a coward! That you understand right from wrong and do nothing to prevent the latter."

"Listen," Asal whispered, leaning toward her. "Listen to me."

"Why should I listen to a coward?"

"Please."

"Tell me why!"

"Because I tried today, tried to do something good." When she made no reply, Asal set down his flask. "I went to your temple. I found an old priest and we prayed together. I told him about the ten lives I needed, about how those ten lives would quench Indravarman's rage."

"So?"

"So I asked him to help me, to select ten priests who are sick, who are close to passing from one body to the next. He agreed. Later, he volunteered to be among the ten."

Voisanne nodded. "A lesser evil . . . is still an evil."

"True enough. So I asked the priest to spread the word, to let the ten lives be the end of it. If Chams aren't attacked within Angkor, if we aren't killed, then there shall be no further reprisals against Khmers. I asked Indravarman to promise as much. And he did."

"A promise means nothing to a king. Especially to that demon who wears your crown."

"Please . . . lower your voice."

"A thousand promises were broken when you Chams arrived. Promises made between wives and husbands, mothers and daughters."

"Yes. And I am sorry for those failings. But there is always tomorrow. Promises may be fulfilled tomorrow."

She started to speak, but stopped. "Then what do you promise? What do you promise to me?"

"I would rather wait to make such an oath."

"Why?"

"Because I don't know you. How can I promise you something of importance when I don't know what matters most to you?"

Voisanne shifted on the mat. Asal studied her face, her beauty reminding him of the female guardians carved into Angkor Wat. But most of the guardians smiled. He had never seen her smile.

"Did you kill my family?" she asked.

"What?"

"I have to know if you killed my family."

"I'm a warrior, not a murderer. The day Angkor fell, I was outside these walls, fighting your king's men."

She nodded, and he was surprised at the swiftness with which her eyes filled with tears. "They . . . shouldn't have died," she whispered. "Your words mean nothing to me because they shouldn't have died."

"I'm sorry."

"May I go? Please, let me go."

Asal glanced at the door, then at her face. Tears descended her cheeks, dropping to her breasts. She seemed so young and vulnerable, as if she were a child rather than a woman. He stilled a desire to reach for her, to comfort her. Though he longed to let her know that she was not alone, he knew she didn't want his touch and so he made no effort to offer it.

"You may leave," he said quietly.

She hurried from him. In her absence his room was too still, too empty. He reached for his sword, then stepped through his door into a wide corridor. Though the ceiling towered above him, even the grandness of the Royal Palace seemed stifling. He needed to get outside.

His countrymen bowed to him, but he paid them no heed. Instead he followed a well-traveled road that led from the Royal Palace to Angkor Wat. He thought about Voisanne, about how tears seemed to connect them. His many sufferings, which he had buried so deep, seemed to rise to the surface whenever she spoke about her family. Her pain rekindled his.

Later, after his emotions had settled, Asal stepped into Angkor Wat. He wanted to find the old priest, to ask why the Gods allowed such pain and to wish him well on his journey.

At the far north end of Angkor, night fell quickly as massive ficus, banyan, and teak trees blocked out the fading light. The imposing square wall that surrounded the city was about fifteen feet high and four feet wide on the north side. Cham guards were stationed every fifty paces atop the wall. The warriors held spears, but no lanterns, as it was easier to peer across the moat within a cloak of darkness. The distant shore was illuminated by sporadic fires that marked concentrations of Cham warriors. Though there seemed to be only a scant chance that the Khmers would try so soon to reclaim the city, Indravarman wasn't one to take risks.

Dressed as a guard, Po Rame studied his surroundings from his position atop the wall. The body of a Cham warrior was hid-

den below in a clump of bushes. Even under the light of a full
moon, the corpse was barely visible. Po Rame had climbed the
wall, slit the man's throat from behind, and carefully lowered the
body into the bushes. He'd been waiting ever since, watching a
nearby building that held twenty Khmer prisoners. Earlier in the
day, Po Rame had interrogated four prisoners separately, promising that their families would be burned to death if the Khmers
didn't escape, discover Jayavar's whereabouts, and return with the
information. Po Rame showed each man five golden coins, saying
that they came from Indravarman and that the Khmers would be
given the coins and their families would be freed once Jayavar
was dead. Two of the men had agreed to the plan. Two others
were defiant, and Po Rame had killed them slowly.

Now, as Po Rame waited on the wall and cleaned his teeth
with a silver pick, he wondered when the Khmers would make
their escape. The two Khmers had been told to convince their
fellow prisoners to break out in the dead of night. Po Rame had
ensured that only six Chams guarded the Khmers. And twenty
men, though they were fools, ought to be able to overpower six
unsuspecting guards.

The building where the prisoners were being held was set
apart from the rest of Angkor's structures and surrounded by
trees. Yet it was possible that another Cham might see an escape.
To mitigate such a risk, Po Rame had given the two Khmers detailed instructions on how to flee and which route to follow. He
was confident of his plan, which he hadn't shared with Indravarman. It was better that the king remain unaware of his meth-
ods of deception.

Most men wouldn't have noticed the melee when it finally
came, but Po Rame heard the faint splintering of wood, a stran-
gled cry, and several grunts. He saw shadows struggling against
one another. Some fell and stood up. Some did not move again.

Voices drifted to him. Khmer voices. Po Rame raised his spear and stepped to his right, away from the Khmers. He walked along the wall, pretending to investigate, creating a bigger gap in the city's defenses. His back was to the Khmers, and he felt a moment of acute vulnerability. But he didn't turn. The Khmers would be climbing the wall by now, and he had to give them more time to escape.

Po Rame counted to fifty, then turned around, gazing into the darkness. Amid the croaks of countless frogs he heard faint splashes. But he didn't look toward the moat. Instead he gazed at the prison building, pretended to notice something, and climbed down the wall.

As silent as an animal that spends its life being hunted, Po Rame made his way to the building. The bodies of six Chams mingled with those of several Khmers. Po Rame listened for approaching footsteps, heard none, and inspected the dead. No witnesses could be left alive, as an injured man could still raise an alarm. Beneath the prison's entrance, Po Rame rolled a Cham over and was surprised to see the man's eyes flutter.

"Call . . . call for help," the guard said, his voice barely audible.

Po Rame inspected his wound, which was a jagged thing, a cut above his collarbone. "You were to guard them," Po Rame replied. "You failed in your duty."

"There is . . . still time."

"Tell the Gods I wish them well."

"The Gods?"

A blade appeared almost magically in Po Rame's hand. He slit the man's throat in one motion, then watched as the guard tried to breathe. The man clutched at Po Rame's arms, and he enjoyed feeling the other's desperate strength, which flowed like a swollen river at first but quickly began to weaken, soon becoming a mere trickle of life. Po Rame grabbed the man's head and lifted it upward, forcing their eyes to meet. As cicadas called out in the canopy above, Po Rame studied how death overcame the other. Terror never seemed to consume the guard, as it did so many. He was simply there one moment and gone the next.

Po Rame regretted killing him so swiftly, but he'd had no choice. He set the man's head on the ground, checked the other dead, and then moved away from the building, blending into the night. By the time the escape was discovered, the Khmers would be far from Angkor, on their way to discovering Jayavar's whereabouts. If Po Rame could uncover the prince's location, he was certain that Indravarman would continue to reward him. Not that Po Rame coveted wealth or women or power in a traditional sense. What he coveted was the opportunity to do what he had just done, to steal a life, and to sense that life as it passed through him, leaving a part of its essence within him, giving him power and knowledge.

Po Rame had been weak until he killed his first man. As a young slave, he had feared the strong, feared the Gods. But when he found the courage to fight back against those who assailed him, to kill his master in the dead of night, strength seemed to flow into him, strength stolen, he believed, from his former tormentor. Ever since that day Po Rame had been addicted to killing. Taking life made him feel invincible, made him a man to be feared and respected. And that was why, more than anything else, Po Rame wanted to kill Jayavar. To kill the Khmer prince, whom some might now consider a king, would be better than the conquest of a civilization.

Indravarman wanted to rule far and wide. But Po Rame had no such ambitions. He longed only to feel Jayavar's blood on his hands, a man he'd never met, but who might have led a kingdom. To kill Jayavar would be to fill himself with a power and a peace that he had never known.

Po Rame had always believed in the Hindu Gods, in their battles and their deeds. They had fought, struggled, and now were worshipped. He hoped that one day he'd be seen in such a light—because as much as they were loved, the Gods were also feared. If enough people feared Po Rame, if they knew of his reputation and cowered as he passed by, then he would live forever.

Five

Incursions

Khmers were accustomed to the swiftness with which the weather changed from wet to dry. After months of daily rains and overcast skies, winds seemed to blow out the moisture, to reveal the land so that the sun could once again beat down. The sandstone temples warmed in the light. Mud turned to dust. Rivers shrank. Mosquitoes dwindled in number.

Though in some ways the heat was a welcome relief, the only means Khmers had to stay cool was to bathe often. Slaves and servants, high priests and warriors took dips in the moat or in one of the many bathing pools within the city. On particularly hot days, Khmers sought out the waters every few hours, lounging in the shallows, swimming where possible. The shorelines were filled with Chinese traders who took fewer baths and were much more modest about nudity. While Khmers swam naked and sometimes found pleasure in one another's bodies within the waters, the Chinese sat in the shade and stared. The foreigners, who were present in large numbers, wore silk tunics and maintained many of their own customs. They cremated their dead, used lavatory paper, and slept in beds. Because Chinese goods were in high demand, the foreigners were generally well respected. Many of the most successful traders took up residence with Khmer women, who advised them on local customs.

Voisanne was used to the Chinese staring at her naked body when she bathed and she thought nothing of it as she made her way down the steps leading into the moat. Thida was beside her. The two women had spent more time together in recent days. They had continued to live in the Royal Palace alongside five thousand other concubines who were on constant call for Indravarman's demands. Though most of the other women never saw the Cham king, he often sought out Thida's company, which put him in close proximity to Voisanne.

The moat was filled with many of the royal concubines, and Voisanne nodded to several as she waded into deeper water. She didn't like to be near their Cham guard. He pretended not to speak Khmer, but Voisanne suspected differently. She had watched his face while she and Thida chatted, and once her suspicions were aroused, she told Thida within his earshot that she thought he was handsome. He had been kinder to her from that moment forward, and later, in secret, she'd advised Thida to watch her tongue.

Voisanne waded to a clump of floating lotus flowers. The sacred flowers with pink petals and yellow stamens sprouted upward from wide green leaves that rested on the water's surface. Voisanne remembered her father telling her how the spreading leaves of lotus flowers symbolized the expansion of the soul. He'd also explained how the lotus flower is untouched by water, as a pure being is untouched by sin.

"I was his lotus," she said softly, continuing to study the flowers.

Thida moved beside her, only her shoulders and head above water. "Whose?"

"My father's. He said that I was his little lotus. That I always bloomed."

"You do."

Voisanne reached for Thida's hand and squeezed it tightly. "Maybe when I was a girl. But as a woman . . . I don't feel as if I'm in bloom. Not now at least."

Cries erupted from the distant shore. A group of Khmers had gathered close together, cheering as they watched a cockfight. Bets would have been wagered and boasts exchanged. Though Voisanne had never liked such spectacles, she was glad that her countrymen were enjoying themselves, even if just for a moment.

"Do you fear your Cham?" Thida asked.

Voisanne thought about Asal. He had never made any move to harm her, nor did she think that he ever would. "He's cruel," she lied, unsure whether she could trust Thida.

"How?"

"He takes . . . what he wants."

"And you don't fight him?"

"I tried once. But it made things worse."

On the opposite side of the moat, two Cham warriors atop a large war elephant maneuvered their beast toward the group of Khmers, breaking them up. The roosters continued to fight until their owners scooped them up and stuffed them into bamboo baskets. The Chams yelled something at the Khmers, then turned the elephant so that it began to lumber across the immense causeway that spanned the moat toward Angkor Wat. Khmer priests and pilgrims scurried away.

"Is nothing sacred to them?" Voisanne asked. "They kill. They enslave. They pollute our very existence."

Thida made no reply. She bit her bottom lip as if trying not to cry.

Voisanne turned to focus on her new friend. "Is Indravarman hurting you?"

"He . . . uses me, but no, he's never hit me."

"And yet?"

"And yet he frightens me. His temper is so great."

"How do you know that? What has he done?"

Thida shook her head, then splashed some water on her face. "When people fail him, they suffer terribly. If I failed him, I'd share their fate."

Voisanne wondered how she would endure if she belonged to Indravarman. "Can you avoid him? There are so many concubines. Why not try to hide among them?"

"His men find me."

"Try harder."

"But then I risk failing him. And that would mean a beating."

"I'd rather have a beating . . . than a certain encounter with him. And maybe if he beats you he'll find you undesirable."

A tear dropped from Thida's right eye. "No. I have to please him. I'm afraid of not pleasing him."

Voisanne tried to put herself into Thida's position, to imagine her terror. "The Buddhists believe that suffering is a part of life," she said. "I don't agree with them, because I don't want to suffer. But maybe . . . if you accept your suffering, accept it for now, you'll be able to escape it."

"What do you mean?"

"If that snake trusts you, he'll let down his guard. And when that happens, you can escape."

"Me?"

"We . . . we can escape together."

Thida shook her head. "But where would we go? What would we do?"

"I don't know. I haven't thought about escape until just now. Until just now, I've wanted to die."

"What changed?"

Voisanne looked again at the lotus flowers, envisioning her father as he compared them to the expansion of the soul, and to her. "Because my father wouldn't want me dead. Because I want to bloom again . . . for him. For everyone I loved."

"And you're not afraid?"

"I have nothing to lose, so how can I be afraid?"

A long walk to the northwest of Angkor Wat, Phimeanakas Temple still shone like the sun, though it was more than a hundred years old. The three-leveled temple had steep stairs leading up each side. The stairs were flanked by statues of lions, while the corner of each level held a massive stone elephant. On the upper level, the central tower, which was square at the bottom and tapered at the top, was covered in gold. The sparkling gold seemed to give life to Phimeanakas, which was visible from great distances.

The grounds near Phimeanakas had been cleared of the giant trees that would otherwise have obscured the temple. A sandstone courtyard was warm against Indravarman's feet as he studied his opponent, Asal. Both men held shields and wooden practice swords. Indravarman liked to spar with his officers, and Asal gave him a better fight than any other man. More than a hundred other Cham warriors and officers were gathered around the combatants, heads bowed but eyes staring up. Beyond this group, war elephants and horses were held in check by slaves. Several Cham philosophers with whom Indravarman liked to debate stood at the periphery of the group.

The fight would begin only when the king was ready, and for now he was content to study the temple. He wondered how the Khmers had mined such a vast amount of gold and if he should have it removed, melted down, and brought to his homeland. The gold on Phimeanakas alone represented an almost infinite wealth—money that could have been spent expanding the Khmer army and bringing ruin to the kingdom's enemies. Instead the Khmers had decorated a temple.

Indravarman wasn't sure what to think of the golden tower. As a Hindu, he was pleased that the Gods were so honored, but he also believed that the Khmers had been weakened by their wealth. A people once bent on conquest had grown soft with their own success, creating mountains and heavens as if they had become the very Gods they wished to commemorate.

From the corner of his eye, Indravarman also studied Asal, who seemed as still as the golden tower. Many warriors would have spent time adjusting their armor or wiping their sweating brows. But Asal did nothing of the sort. He simply stood, facing Indravarman, his sword extended and his shield held high.

Indravarman attacked without warning, moving quickly, but not quite as fast as he might have. He had never shown anyone whom he hadn't killed his true skill, and Asal was no different. Still, Indravarman's wooden blade blurred as it swept through the air, and Asal was barely able to raise his shield in time to ward off the blow. Asal stepped backward as Indravarman pressed on with his attack, his great strength allowing him to reverse the direction of his blade and to bring it upward, toward Asal's groin. This time Asal parried the stroke with his own weapon—sword struck against sword, and shield met shield. Both men grunted. Indravarman pivoted his wrist, simultaneously thrusting his weapon forward as if it were a giant dagger. His blade slid past Asal's. The younger warrior dropped to avoid the blow, but Indravarman had expected such a maneuver and brought the edge of his shield up, slamming it into the bottom of Asal's chin. The impact opened a wound that immediately bled. For an instant, something flashed across Asal's face. Rage, perhaps. But then the look was gone as he counterattacked, forcing Indravarman to use nearly his full strength to defend himself.

The combatants attacked and retreated for several minutes. Finally, when both had received minor wounds, Indravarman lowered his weapon. He laughed. Had it been a real fight, he was certain he would have killed Asal, and this knowledge gave him enormous joy. Battle, even with its pain and injuries, always made him feel young, and his bout with Asal was no different.

"Walk with me," Indravarman said, and then headed toward Phimeanakas.

As they climbed the temple's northern stairs, Indravarman studied the guardian lions. Defiance had been etched into their faces, and he once again wondered where Jayavar was. Surely the exiled prince was building an army and planning to retake the city. Po Rame's spies had heard such whispers, though no one knew Jayavar's location.

After reaching the temple's top level, Indravarman walked to the central tower and placed his hand against the warm gold. Asal's chin still bled, and red drops fell onto the gray sandstone. "Now you're a part of their temple," Indravarman said.

"I—"

"Were the priests executed this morning?"

"Yes, Lord King."

"How did they die?"

"With grace."

Indravarman nodded. "Why were they all old and feeble?"

"Because, Lord King, they were held in the highest regard. Your message was heard."

An elephant trumpeted below. Indravarman looked to the west, eyeing a swath of empty space and wondering if the Khmers had planned to build another temple nearby. "Where is he hiding, Asal? Where would you hide?"

Asal scanned the horizon, shielding his eyes from the sun. "He's near."

"Why do you say that?"

"I'm not certain, but—"

"Tell me."

"Because he can defeat us only if he knows what to expect, Lord King. And the only way to learn about us is to study us."

"So how do we trap him?"

Asal shifted his weight. "We invite an attack. We appear to spread ourselves thin when in truth we're as hard as teak."

Indravarman moved his hand along the gold, marveling at its uniformity. "Po Rame plans to bring me Jayavar's head."

"Po Rame can try. But it's easier to boast than to do."

"I boast and I do."

"Yes, Lord. But that's why you're king. Po Rame is nothing but a plague."

Indravarman remembered the rage that had flashed on Asal's face. He would have to be careful of this one. Asal was valuable, but at some point his importance would diminish, and when that day arrived, he would have to die. "Find me Jayavar," Indravarman said. "Find me Jayavar and you shall know wealth beyond your boldest dreams."

"My dreams are humble, Lord King. I only wish to serve you."

"Why? Why do you only wish to serve me?"

"To fulfill my duty. To ensure the station of my unborn sons."

Indravarman patted the gold. "You're wise to keep secrets, Asal. Some men hide gold. Others cover a mountain with it. You,

I think, would conceal such treasure, though I'm unsure what you covet. Someday I shall know. You shall tell me, and whatever you seek I shall provide."

"I'll hope for that day, Lord King."

"Leave me."

Asal nodded and walked back down the stairs. Indravarman watched him depart, wondering how long it would take to discover his desires. Every man had desires, and through those wants he could be exploited. Indravarman sensed that behind Asal's stoicism lay a dangerous unpredictability, which made him potent on a field of battle and the most valuable of all Cham officers. But Indravarman had come to power by understanding his friends and his foes. Asal remained a mystery, which was both troubling and fascinating.

You're worth a thousand men, Indravarman thought, still watching Asal. And that's why, once Jayavar is dead, you shall join him. Because a king doesn't surround himself with the mighty, but with the meek. And you're mighty, Asal. You hide secrets from me, and that's why I shall have to kill you.

The Great Lake was everything that its name boasted. During the monsoon season, the lake swelled to about a hundred miles long and twenty miles wide and was so large that it could have been mistaken for an inland sea. For generations, Khmers had fished the lake, pulling immense catfish, carp, and perch from its brown water, which connected with the Mekong River. Small fishing villages built on stilts dotted the shoreline—a verdant stretch of land that was often flooded.

As far as Boran could tell, the nearby settlement was abandoned. Its thatch and bamboo homes, hardly big enough to accommodate a sleeping family, were empty. Boran had been to the

Great Lake before and knew that the Khmers who lived here spent more time on their boats than in their homes. They must have seen the Cham army approach and fled to a different area.

Boran paddled his boat beneath the homes, the stilts providing ample clearance, since with the end of the monsoon season the water had already started to recede. The homes reminded him of skeletons—lifeless and vacant. Behind him, Prak and Vibol whispered. Soriya sat at the rear of the boat, where she pretended to mend a net, just in case they were spotted by a Cham patrol. Their knives and axe were hidden beneath strips of dried catfish.

They had discovered the Cham encampment the previous evening. Scores of Cham boats were beached and docked on the northern edge of the lake, which was just a day's walk from Angkor. The Chams had obviously sailed to the site from their homeland, bringing supplies necessary for war and occupation. Trees had been felled and crude shelters built throughout the camp, which Boran guessed held several thousand warriors. He'd been afraid to venture near their enemies and had not moved beyond the fishing village, which provided good cover.

Telling his sons to be silent, Boran continued to paddle his boat beneath the Khmer homes. Though he was used to the smell of dead fish, the stench beneath the homes was nearly overwhelming. Bamboo pens built in the water held the carcasses of turtles, alligators, and catfish. During normal times, the animals would have been fed and then either sold or eaten. But the Khmers had obviously fled in haste because no one had released the animals, or returned to feed them. Bloated carcasses floated on the surface, teeming with flies and maggots.

Trying not to gag, Boran steered clear of a pen and maneuvered his boat toward the biggest dwelling. It must have been some sort of communal fishing outpost, as it was far too large for a single family. The structure rose from immense bamboo stilts.

Boran was surprised to see a sleek boat moored at the bottom of a ladder and wondered why such a fine craft had been left behind. The boat would be useful, and Boran decided to take it, paddling with efficient, practiced motions. He was about to ask Vibol to grab it when voices rang out above. There were Chams inside the structure, and Boran immediately ceased all movement. His boat drifted through the water, scraping against one of the stilts. Someone was laughing. Boran's heart began to thump with such strength that he feared the Chams would hear it. He silently cursed his stupidity, appalled that he'd placed his family in danger. More laughter erupted from above, and it was apparent that at least two men occupied the structure. The Chams began to talk. Footsteps sounded. Vibol reached under the dried catfish and removed the axe. Boran shook his head, but Vibol paid him no heed, instead pointing to the other boat, which they could now see was full of weapons, food, and supplies. The Chams must have been scouts of some kind, perhaps about to leave for a long journey. Vibol gestured toward the weapons, indicating that the Chams were defenseless. Boran shook his head again and carefully back paddled. To his dismay, Vibol grabbed a stilt and held the boat in place.

The laughter came and went like the wind. Vibol started to pull them toward the ladder, but Boran grabbed onto another stilt, holding the boat still. He shook his head, silently pleading with his son. Soriya left her position at the boat's rear, moving over the mounds of dried fish, placing her hands on Vibol's shoulders. She pulled herself against him, whispering into his ear.

The Chams stopped laughing. They moved about the room above.

Soriya's brow pressed against her son's as she continued to plead quietly. At first he only yanked harder on the stilt, but as she persisted, his determination waivered. He finally let go. Boran pulled back on his paddle, drawing them away from the Chams. His strokes were silent, strong, and steady. To bump against a stilt would betray them, and he moved with care, maneuvering his boat beneath the neighboring home and then the next.

Feet suddenly appeared on the ladder and Boran froze. His boat continued to drift as the Chams emerged. There were three of them, and though they carried no weapons, they were obviously warriors, as their bodies bulged with muscles. The Chams settled into their boat. They must have been drunk on rice wine. Their laughter came in great bursts and their movements were clumsy. One of them retched over the side of their boat, prompting the others to mimic his movements.

As the Chams paddled away, Boran thought about reversing his direction and attacking them. Perhaps this was the time for Vibol to wet his blade with Cham blood. But a drunk enemy could also be a fearless and terrible enemy. Moreover, the Chams were likely skilled at killing. Vibol was strong but untested. Prak could hardly see. And if they were to lose, Soriya would be ravished.

Boran paddled backward, creating distance between his family and the Chams. The enemy warriors headed toward the vast Cham encampment. With each of their oar strokes the figures grew smaller until they were little more than dots on the horizon. Boran finally stopped paddling and let his boat thump into the stilts of a dilapidated home. "If you ever do that again, Vibol—"

"You're a coward," Vibol interrupted, turning to face him. "You're nothing but a coward! They were drunk and we could have killed them!"

"We came here to spy, not to kill! That means finding the biggest fish, not butchering the little ones."

"Then we came for the wrong reasons! Don't you understand that? They attacked us! They killed our friends!"

Prak put his hand on his brother's arm. "If we learn about them, if we study them, we can kill a thousand of them with our information. We can lead our brothers here. We can have our revenge."

"So now you're against me too? The three of you against me?"

"I'm with you, Vibol. I've always been with you."

Vibol shook off Prak's hand. "They killed her for no reason. They . . . they did things to her. And if you're all too afraid to get revenge, then I'll get it alone. Do you hear me? I'll do what needs to be done!"

"I'll help you, Vibol," Prak replied. "I will. Just give me time. Let me—"

"No!"

Soriya started to speak but stopped, instead reaching for her son's hands.

"Leave me be!" he shouted.

"I love you."

"If you love me, Mother, if you really do, you'll let me go. I'll find my own boat and chase down those Chams."

"You ask the impossible."

He turned away from her. "Then you don't love me. Because you won't give me what I need."

Monkeys leapt from branch to branch, chasing one another, causing leaves and twigs to tumble from great heights. Though sometimes a monkey would drop a few feet, strike a thin branch, and appear destined to fall to its death, no brown blurs plummeted from the canopy. In all her years of watching the playful creatures, Ajadevi had seen only one such demise. She'd certainly come across injured monkeys, but most of those wounds were from teeth and claws. Sometimes the monkeys got carried away with their antics, fighting savagely in the treetops.

As usual, Ajadevi rode in the middle of the column. She had been talking with a young officer who seemed in awe of her husband, and after a while she grew weary of his fawning and let her horse fall back. During the past few days of travel, Jayavar had done better at dealing with his men, and Ajadevi no longer felt pressure to keep up their spirits. Jayavar rode, spoke, and schemed with his officers, filling them with confidence. Ajadevi had always found such interaction tedious. She pursued it when necessary but much preferred to talk with Jayavar, study the jungle, or pray.

Earlier in the day, they had come across a ruined and deserted temple, decorated with carvings of dozens of female dancers. The cheerful *asparas* held flowers and musical instruments. Large ficus trees had grown on top of the temple, their roots wrapping around stone walls and towers. Ajadevi was certain that many decades had passed since anyone had cared for the sacred place. As she'd studied its intricacies, she was reminded of a distant time and place. And that reminder gave her an idea that she wanted to share with Jayavar.

He finally finished strategizing with his officers and directed his horse toward hers. She watched him approach, eyeing him both critically and with affection. Though his shoulders and face were lined with grime, it seemed that his strength had returned. He no longer perpetually studied the ground, but examined the jungle instead. At least some of the time, rather than searching for the spirits of his loved ones, he appeared to look for his enemies.

"You seem better," she said softly, wanting their conversation to remain private.

He pulled his horse alongside hers. "The closer we draw to Angkor . . . the better I feel."

"Why?"

"Because it's home. And the men are filled with hope."

"And you?"

"I'm filled with uncertainty—though I'd rather possess uncertainty than despair."

A monkey screeched and she glanced above. "I've seen something."

"What?"

"When I was a child, I traveled to Kbal Spean. The setting . . . moved me. In a way, I think it's even grander than Angkor Wat."

Jayavar's horse stumbled over a log and the prince lurched forward, then righted himself on the silk pad that comforted both him and his mount. "I've never been to Kbal Spean. Tell me about it."

"At Kbal Spean a narrow river runs over beds of sandstone. Long ago, Hindu priests carved images of Vishnu, of Shiva, and of sacred animals into these beds. In the monsoon season the river covers the carvings. In the dry season they are revealed. The place is sacred. But best for us . . . it lies within a valley that is thick with bamboo. There's game, fresh water, and vantage points from which to view an enemy. We could hide an army there and never be found."

"How high are the rises?"

"They tower over everything. A handful of sentries could watch in all directions."

"And the valley . . . it's deep?"

"Deep enough to cloak our fires, to mask the sound of our mounts. The priests are all gone, I believe. And even though Kbal Spean is only several days' march from Angkor, few people know of its existence. Khmers have forgotten about it. Chams won't even know of it. The jungle is so thick that few dare to wander within it."

"And—"

"And less than a day's march away lies Banteay Srei, the Citadel of Women. This small temple, which I visited as a girl, inspired me in many ways. It could serve as a meeting point. We could spread the word that it's where we shall gather our forces. But when groups of Khmers arrive, they could be led to Kbal Spean. This way we will have a buffer between our first encounter with strangers and our true base."

Jayavar smiled. "You should be king, not I."

"Women will rule one day. But that day hasn't yet come."

"Perhaps it should come tomorrow."

"Perhaps."

Sunlight filtered through the canopy, warming Jayavar. "How many people could live in this valley? Could live in secret?"

"Thousands."

"And the jungle is thick?"

"It would be easier to see through a herd of elephants."

His brow furrowed. "We could send two men back to begin the arrangements."

"They should go soon."

"And what of this thought?" he asked. "I have an idea to send two good men into Siam. We've fought using Siamese mercenaries before. Why not promise them gold and silver? We have plenty."

"Siam is our enemy."

"But its warriors are not. The lure of gold would be hard to resist."

She nodded, thinking about the Siamese, recalling her encounters with them. "There will be spies and traitors among them," she said. "For every ten warriors you receive, one will seek to betray you."

"I know. We'd have to be careful. We could tell them to come in small groups, to arrive at, as you suggest, the Citadel of Women. A few thousand Siamese, fighting for us, could balance the scale."

"Then add them to the scale. But move with care, Jayavar. They're not to be trusted."

An animal's snarl sounded up ahead. The jungle was full of tigers and leopards, and Jayavar put his hand on the hilt of his sword. His horse trotted ahead in silence, and he relaxed as several of his men shouted to scare off the beast. A ray of light fell from a hole in the jungle canopy, and he reached for it, watching as it illuminated his hand and then his arm.

"Do you know what you are to me?" he asked.

"What?"

"My most trusted adviser, the woman I love, and my friend. How can one person be so many things?"

"Because I'm a collection of people. I've lived many lives, and been beside you during those lives. I've been your wife, your adviser, and your friend before."

He reached for her hand. "I love you," he whispered. "More than Angkor, more than my people. If I'm a river, you're the rain that feeds me."

She squeezed his fingers. Though she knew that pride was a weakness and that her karma depended on being pure, she couldn't help but smile. "We shall go to Kbal Spean, Jayavar. And from there we shall begin anew."

The flickering light of six candles illuminated Asal's room, hinting of the draft that emerged from under his door. A slave had carried away his dinner dishes, and he sat cross-legged on a thatch mat, sipping rice wine through a narrow bamboo tube. Though his parents had been poor, they'd made their own wine, letting him sample it on occasion.

Asal smiled at the memory, then looked at Voisanne. For a reason he didn't understand, her beauty seemed more pronounced than ever. He wanted to touch her, to kiss the contours of her flesh. Instead he sipped more of the wine, wondering when she would speak. Music emerged from beyond his door—the beating of drums accompanied by chanting male voices.

"Did the priests die?" she asked, made uneasy by the drums and needing to break their rumblings.

"Yes."

"How?"

"Swiftly and without pain."

She nodded, adjusting a silver bracelet that clung to her damp skin. "Indravarman has ordered that I move into new quarters."

"He has?"

"His men . . . couldn't find Thida. So he moved both of us, along with some other women, into a house near the moat. We have a guard and aren't to leave, except to bathe or if someone comes to claim us. We're prisoners."

"I'm sorry."

"Why did you come here? Why did you attack us?"

Asal had asked himself that same question. "The nature of men is to wage war," he replied, and then offered her a flask of wine and a bamboo tube, which she took. "Chams. Khmers. Siamese. We all fight."

"Perhaps if you were women, if you created life, you wouldn't be so quick to take it."

"That's—"

"How many men have you killed? How many Khmers?"

He looked away, no longer entranced by her beauty. "If I didn't kill, I'd be destitute. My unborn children would have no future."

"Why not?"

"Because fighting is all I've ever known. It is my surest path to a better life for any family I might have."

"You could know more. Your mind could be as potent as your body."

"Indravarman would . . ." Asal paused, the muscles in his jaws clenching. "My station is fixed," he finally replied.

"My station was fixed too, before you came. So was my father's, my mother's, my lover's." She sipped her wine. "But you Chams changed all that. You sneaked up on us like a pack of cowards and changed everything."

"Our war is an old one. Khmers have attacked Chams just as we attacked you. You have burned our cities, enslaved our citizens. I've seen Khmer arrows in the backs of my people—in the backs of women and children."

Voisanne shook her head. "But we wanted peace! And Indravarman is worse than any Khmer king ever was. He's nothing more than a thief and a murderer."

"Many Chams are different."

"Many? You, perhaps, but not your countrymen."

"People are not defined by their ruler."

She scoffed at his words. "Yes, they are. Because your king takes what he wants; he kills whom he pleases. And if you follow him, you're no better than he is. You may be noble, but if you're his instrument, then you're an instrument of evil, destined to be hated and scorned."

A female servant knocked on the door and Asal sent her away. Though he didn't fear men or blades of steel, Voisanne's words shook him. Yes, he'd killed, but he had done so out of necessity. If he hadn't learned to fight, he would have been killed long ago. Yet this Khmer woman didn't understand what drove him; she didn't realize that he wished his fate had been different.

"Your father's home," he asked quietly, "was it near here?"

"Why?"

"Because I could walk past it and see who is there. Perhaps someone from your family yet lives."

Voisanne started to speak, then stopped. "But . . . I saw them all killed. They're gone."

"During battle, the eye, the memory, can deceive. Such trickery has happened to me on many occasions. With fighting comes fear, and fear does strange things to the mind."

"It does?"

"I could look," he offered. "I could inquire."

"And you would do that . . . for me?"

"Of course."

"But . . ."

"I want to help you."

She bowed low. Then in a rush of words she told him where her home was and described her family members. He had never seen her excited, and her enthusiasm was infectious. Though he was taking a risk in making such a promise, he suddenly forgot about Indravarman's spies and suspicions.

"It may not happen tomorrow," he said, "or the day after. But I shall visit your home. I shall be your eyes and ears."

She bowed again, deep and long. "I'm sorry for . . . assailing you, for being so weak when you've been so strong."

"You needn't—"

"I've done nothing but insult you."

"True enough. And you're quite skilled at it. But fortunately for you, I understand how pain taints everything it touches. How the very air you breathe becomes bitter."

"You're much more . . . than a Cham killer. Please forgive me."

Asal smiled, feeling as if he'd been released from a prison of his own making. "Nothing needs forgiveness, my lady."

She bent back, shaking her head. "My lady? Why . . . why would you call me that? Especially after how I've behaved toward you?"

"Because it suits you."

"I'm a slave."

"You're a lady."

She started to speak and then stopped, wringing her hands. "And what shall I call you? What would please you?"

The concern etched in her face made him smile once again. So many years had passed since anyone had worried about his feelings. "Please call me Asal, my lady. That would please me very much."

Six

The Pain and Joy of Truth

hida pretended to sleep though her eyes were half open, and she gazed toward the far end of Indravarman's chambers. She lay naked in the middle of his teak bed, on pelts of tigers and leopards. Indravarman was nude next to her, lying on his belly with his head cocked to the side. Near his right hand were several scrolls containing the translated writings of Confucius.

The king's room, located in the heart of the Royal Palace, was immense and lined with huge wooden columns. Candles that had burned all night fluttered, their feeble light reflecting off gold and silver treasures that he had plundered from Khmer temples, courtyards, and homes. Statues of Vishnu, Shiva, and Buddha were among his most prized discoveries, though he'd taken only small and elaborate pieces that were easily carried. Bolts of silk, precious gems, parchments of poetry, and carved ivory had been placed in tidy piles. Thida didn't know what Indravarman did with all of his plunder, but she had seen him give out items as rewards to his most valuable officers and advisers. He was generous, sharing his treasures of gold, jewels, and women. And yet Thida sensed that his men feared him. They bowed too quickly and spoke too little. Those who displeased him did not always return.

Though Indravarman had never beaten her, she made certain to satisfy him, to meet his demands and even exceed them. As the days had passed, she had learned to anticipate his needs. He asked for her again and again while other women were sent away. It seemed that she alone knew how to please him, which surprised her, because she had never considered herself to be bright or strong. Of course, she'd recognized her beauty, but she hadn't realized that it could be such a powerful blessing or curse until Indravarman had come into her life. She was terrified of him and let him see her fear since it seemed to entertain him. Though she was Hindu, her faith wasn't unassailable, and she worried that she would never be reincarnated. If he killed her, there might be only blackness.

"Why were you never with another man?" Indravarman asked, his accent thick. "All men must have desired you."

The abrupt sound of his deep voice caused her heart to flutter. After it settled, she thought about how her father had deserted their family and how her mother had struggled to feed them. They'd lived in the countryside, and once she blossomed into a young woman she traveled to Angkor with a group of pilgrims, instructed by her mother to seek out a wealthy man. Though her suitors were many, she had remained unmoved by their proposals, reminded of her father's unkept promises, as untrusting of these men as she had been of him. And yet Indravarman had carried her away like a typhoon, his will impossible to deny.

"Most men bore me, Lord King," she finally replied.

"Most men are fools—lead them to a stream and they will only drink."

"I—"

"But some will do more than drink. They'll find gold on that shoreline. They'll hunt the tiger that comes to quench its thirst." Indravarman rolled over and reached out, tracing the contours of her hip with a calloused finger. "I hear you've become close to your countrywoman Voisanne."

"Yes. Yes, I have, Lord King."

"She is the woman of one of my best officers. A man named Asal."

"I've seen him."

"And what do you hear of him?"

"I think he beats her."

Indravarman grunted, stroking her arm. "I want you to befriend her, to learn her secrets."

Though Thida longed to recoil from his touch, she lay still, hoping the sight of her nakedness would not stir him as it usually did.

"I don't trust Asal," Indravarman said. "And so I wish to learn of his doings. Will you seek them out and share this knowledge with me? Should I dare to trust you?"

"I serve you, Lord King. I'll do as you ask."

"Good. Perform this deed and you shall be rewarded. Fail me and your days of comfort shall cease."

Thida felt the strength of his stare, the ferocity within his eyes, and she unconsciously held her breath. He moved closer. Her heart started to race. She felt his hands on her and began to lie, to tell him about her desire for him, about how she wanted him to fall upon her.

"Give your life to me," he said, his movements quickening, "and I shall not take it."

* * *

The scent of steaming rice gave away the location of the Cham scouting party. Jayavar and his men dismounted, then crawled through the thick jungle, staying as low as possible, moving like shadows. They observed four Chams from a distance, whispered their strategy, and crept even closer. Once Jayavar was certain that they would soon be observed, the seven Khmer warriors stood up and rushed forward. No battle cries were shouted, no warnings given. Instead, the Khmers ran as silently as possible with their weapons held high.

The Chams looked up at the last possible moment. One warrior managed to notch and fire an arrow. The others reached for their spears but were too slow, crying out as Khmer blades pierced their flesh. All but one of the Chams were killed. The last warrior, whom Jayavar had identified earlier as their leader, was captured. As his men bound and gagged the Cham, Jayavar turned to look for Ajadevi, only then realizing that one of his warriors had fallen. The lone arrow had struck him in the neck, and life was flowing quickly from him. Jayavar dropped to his knees and cradled the man's head, aware that the wound was mortal. He thanked the warrior for his service, asked about special requests, and finally wondered if he would like to be cremated or simply left in the jungle. Most Khmers wanted their bodies to be set in a special place and then abandoned. This way the cycle of rebirth could be continued, slowly and naturally, within a land adored by its people.

The warrior asked that his body be left in such a manner, and Jayavar agreed, comforting him as much as possible. When he finally died, the remaining Khmers lifted his body and set it within a patch of light that pierced the canopy. They made a circle of stones around the corpse, put the man's sword in his hands, prayed for his rebirth, and stepped away.

Jayavar glanced at the surviving Cham, knowing that he needed to be interrogated as soon as possible. But then the prince thought about his dead countryman, wondering if the attack should have been done differently. With superior numbers and the element of surprise, no Khmers should have died in the assault, and Jayavar berated himself for the loss of life.

The Cham was bound from head to foot to a dead tree, and Jayavar strode forward, stopping a short distance from his enemy. The man was thickly muscled and kept his face expressionless. Defiance seemed to fill him. Jayavar nodded, then called his men forward, so that they formed a circle around the Cham.

"What are your orders?" Jayavar asked in the warrior's native tongue.

The man said nothing, his jaws clenching, his fingers working at the bonds that held him.

Though normally patience was one of Jayavar's strongest traits, he was frustrated by the loss of his countryman and eager to hear of his loved ones. "Gather dry timber and pile it around him," he said to his men.

Ajadevi shot him an angry stare, but for once he paid her no heed. Instead he walked to the campfire that the Chams had made, emptied their pot of rice, and scooped up some embers. After his men had arranged a pile of wood around the Cham, Jayavar carefully positioned the embers beneath some dried leaves. Flames quickly arose. Twigs crackled. Smoke drifted upward.

"Good-bye," Jayavar said to the Cham.

"You can't go!"

Jayavar started to walk back to his horse. Behind him, the Cham began to scream. The flames hadn't yet touched him but were spreading around him and growing higher.

"Don't leave! I'll talk!"

Whirling around, Jayavar strode to the Cham and used his spear to scatter the burning wood. "A falsehood. A denial. Say either of these things and the fire shall return. But I shall not!"

The Cham nodded, sweat dripping from his brow.

"Why are you here?" Jayavar demanded.

"To . . . to find you."

"How many other scouting parties are searching this area?"

"Many. But no one knows where you are."

"Who advises Indravarman?"

"No one. He's his own man. He—"

"And how many Chams are in Angkor?"

"I don't—"

"Give me their numbers!"

"Nine or ten thousand warriors. Maybe more."

Jayavar saw that Ajadevi had taken a fallen spear and was using it to scatter what remained of the burning wood. He knew that she disapproved of his method, but he wasn't held hostage by his belief in karma, as he sometimes felt she was. He had already killed too many men to have led a pure life. If his soul was reborn at a lower station, so be it.

"What of my family?" he asked. "Tell me what has happened to my family."

"I'm only a—"

"Tell me!"

The Cham looked away, momentarily closing his eyes. "There's . . . a rumor, lord."

"What rumor?"

"They say . . . that you're the only one left of your line. That Indravarman put your family to the sword. I'm sorry, but—"

"Who says this?"

"Everyone, lord. That's why he's set a price on your head. Because only you remain to claim the throne."

Jayavar nodded. Though he had dreaded and expected such news, his legs felt weak. He walked away from the Cham and leaned against a nearby tree, imagining the faces of his children, faces too young and innocent to know the pain brought by steel. How he wanted to trade places with them, to give up his life in return for theirs.

"He could be wrong," Ajadevi whispered in his ear, her hand on his shoulder.

"You know he's not."

"I'm sorry, my love. So very, very sorry."

A cicada buzzed in the treetops. Jayavar looked up, his eyes glistening. "If they're reborn, why don't I feel them?" he whispered. "Why have they not come back to me?"

"They will. Give them time. They're young, and the young always need time to find their way."

Jayavar prayed for their return into his life, asking also for the strength to go forward, to honor them by reclaiming their land. He then stood straight and returned to the Cham. "Release him," he said to his men, who started forward but stopped, unsure of their action. "I said, release him."

The Cham was freed.

Stepping close to the prisoner, so close that their noses almost touched, Jayavar shook his head. "Your king was wrong to murder my children."

"Lord, I—"

"Wait here for five days. Then return to Angkor. Tell Indravarman that I'm coming for his head. And before I take it, I shall take other things from him as well. Things he will not want to part with."

"Yes, lord."

"Five days. Leave any earlier and you risk my wrath."

The Cham bowed low.

Jayavar gripped the man's topknot, pulling him up. "Tell him that my children were better than he shall ever be, that they're bathed in light, while he shall dwell forever in darkness."

"I'll tell him . . . these things."

"And after you do, you should flee to your homeland. Because soon every Cham in Angkor will be dead."

Jayavar released the man and then walked into the jungle. His horse was where he had left it. After mounting and assisting Ajadevi up behind him, he kicked his stallion forward, toward his city.

Please, Buddha, he prayed, please let the journeys of my children be swift and uplifting. Their actions, their minds, were noble and good. Their karma was good. They were stars that could be seen on a stormy night. They were beauty in an ugly world. Please reward them for their beauty.

A tear rolled down Jayavar's dusty cheek. Because he knew that his men were behind him and that for their sake he must remain resolute, he sat tall, resisting the sorrow that came at him like an army.

One step, he told himself. One step followed by another. That's how I shall endure. That's how I shall honor them.

Asal walked past rows of Khmer homes, which were built mainly of thatch and bamboo and supported by tall stilts. Perhaps one structure in four had been burned to the ground during the invasion. Of the undamaged homes, many were now occupied by Chams, though Khmers were also numerous. In the shade beneath the dwellings, slaves labored, dogs rested, and hammocks swayed in the wind. The homes were mostly of one or two rooms, and clustered around communal bathing ponds. To the west, Angkor Wat sprawled in all its glory.

Though Voisanne's directions on how to find her home had been explicit, Asal had become disoriented by the seemingly endless groupings of houses. He followed a wide and well-kept boulevard filled with Cham warriors, horses, and war elephants as well as Khmer priests, farmers, and children. Asal wasn't one to be shocked by his surroundings. In his homeland he'd seen officials carried on jeweled palanquins and live snakes being skinned. But some of the sights in Angkor surprised him. A Chinese trader quietly asked about the availability of a slight male prostitute. Khmer workers chiseled gray sandstone blocks as if no invasion had occurred. Young children ran from him, laughing and hiding behind their unsmiling mothers and fathers.

Stepping off the boulevard, Asal headed north, trying to recall Voisanne's directions. He was expected to report to Indravarman soon and so increased his pace. As usual, he carried a shield and a sword. Most Chams wouldn't dare to wander on Angkor's byways without a companion, but Asal was not worried. A bloody death would likely befall him eventually, but that death would come on a battlefield, not in some alley.

He rounded a corner and paused as an unusually large home caught his sight. The structure with its small balcony was as Voisanne had described. A tidy thicket of bamboo rose from beside a nearby pond. A stone statue of Vishnu stood next to the path leading toward the home. Suddenly certain that he was looking upon her house, Asal slowed his pace. Five slaves labored amid the stilts. Women weaved while men chopped wood. Asal studied the slaves but saw no one who resembled Voisanne. These people were fierce and strong, likely captured from the mountains to the north. None were Khmers.

Feeling that he had failed Voisanne, Asal stopped at the statue of Vishnu. Voisanne had said that her father had helped carve it, and Asal pictured her as a girl watching him work. He could tell by the way she'd spoken about her father that her love for him was strong. Wishing that he'd been older when his parents died, Asal tried to remember them. His father was a serious man who often prayed. His mother had been much more carefree—laughing with Asal, holding him on her lap, and surely adoring him. Yet she seemed so distant, as if part of a dream.

The slaves glanced at Asal, and he started to turn away. Then a girl climbed down the ladder that led from the living quarters. She was thin, long legged, dressed as a Khmer, and he guessed her age to be eleven or twelve. His heartbeat quickened, and he stepped forward, peering at her face. At first she turned her back to him, but he moved closer, ignoring the slaves' stares. The girl's face was fine featured and beautiful. In many ways, she looked like Voisanne. Asal was now several paces from her. He started to speak, to pretend that he was lost. But only a few words had escaped his mouth when he saw a birthmark on her chin—a thumbnail-size mark exactly where Voisanne had said it would be.

The girl bowed to him, avoiding his eyes. She seemed preoccupied, and he wanted to tell her that her older sister was alive, that he could bring them together. But a Cham woman shouted from the home above, and the girl stiffened. She hurried to retrieve a nearby bolt of silk and then started up the ladder.

Asal watched her disappear. He turned to the statue of Vishnu, offering a prayer of gratitude; then he walked quickly away. Though he longed to run to Voisanne's quarters and tell her the news, he couldn't afford to be late for Indravarman, and so he headed toward the Royal Palace, unaware of the sights that had previously engrossed him.

Voisanne's little sister was alive. If he could reunite them, perhaps he could right a wrong that had been done to them, and perhaps Voisanne would no longer see him as a Cham, but as a man whom she might someday consider a friend.

Soriya's dream had a tenuous hold on her, like a spiderweb that has temporarily snared a cicada. She saw herself nursing Vibol, milk dribbling down his fat cheek, gathering in the folds of his neck. Humming, she stroked his head, enjoying his soft black hair. He withdrew from her nipple, and she lifted him up, placed him against her shoulder, and began to pat his back. The warmth generated between their bodies made her smile. Nearby, Prak lay on a deerskin, awaiting his turn, patient for the time being.

Shouts arose in the distance. Smoke drifted upward. She looked for Boran, but he was nowhere to be seen. Suddenly people were running past her. She picked up her two sons and was soon fleeing alongside strangers, calling out for her husband. The jungle was on fire. Men and women fell and writhed. An ominous presence loomed behind her—a darkness. She tripped on an exposed root, still gripping both boys as she stumbled. The darkness descended on her, cold and foreign. She screamed.

Awakening from the dream, Soriya blinked at the midafternoon light. She lay in an abandoned home within a fishing village, a home built on stilts and perched above brown water. Boran and Prak still slept. Vibol had left his position by the ladder, but his axe was still there, so he must be nearby. None of them had slept the previous night, as they'd come upon several Cham scouting parties. The pressure had been too much for her, and she'd pleaded with her sons to flee the Great Lake, to go as far as possible from the Cham stronghold. But Vibol and, to a lesser degree, Prak had resisted her, and in the end, she'd given up try-

ing to convince them that their duty was to stay alive, not to help
their countrymen. Angry at Boran for not siding with her, she
had hardly spoken with him for much of the day.

Soriya closed her eyes, remembering what it was like to be a
young mother, unconsciously humming a song that she used to
share with her boys, a song that Prak had learned to play on his
flute. It seemed that when they were young she was forever tired,
and yet the joy of motherhood had given her a deep sense of fulfillment. All her life she had been poor. But two beautiful boys
now belonged to her. She cared for them with love and delight,
protecting them from the elements, remaining always near them
and reveling in such proximity. Though she'd never been as good
as other women at mending nets or manipulating her husband,
she excelled at being a mother. Her babies thrived, provoking a
secret sense of pride in her abilities. And for this pride she loved
them even more, as they'd given her what no one else ever had or
could.

Something splashed below them, and Soriya opened her eyes.
She called out quietly for Vibol but heard no reply. Sitting up, she
shook Boran's shoulder, whispering that Vibol had been gone for
some time. Prak awoke as well, rubbing his eyes, squinting as the
world came into partial focus.

"Where is he?" Soriya asked, and then moved to the ladder
and looked down.

Boran knelt by her side. "When did he go?"

"I don't know."

They called out to him again in hushed voices.

Prak crawled to them. "His axe . . . it is still here?"

"Yes," Boran answered.

"What about the food?"

Soriya rushed to the corner of the room where they had piled up their dried fish and several fresh mangos. She could tell immediately that some of the food was gone, and her heart seemed to drop like a stone. "No. He . . . he wouldn't leave us. Please, no. Where would he go?"

"The Chams," Boran muttered, biting his lower lip.

Soriya grabbed her husband's arm. "No, that's impossible. He's not that—"

"Foolish?" Prak interrupted. "Yes, he is. I think that's exactly what he's done."

"Why . . . why do you say that?"

"Because last night," Prak explained, "when we saw the Cham fires and were hiding, he was whispering to me, asking me what it was like to have my eyes. I thought it odd that he chose such a time to ask how I walked, how I made my way through the jungle. But you know Vibol—he's always restless, always moving and asking. So I told him as much as I could."

Soriya shook her head. "I don't understand. Why would he ask you such things? Why then?"

"Because, Mother, I think he knew that he couldn't get close to the Chams carrying an axe. I think he went looking for them, and when he's close, he'll pretend to be blind. He'll stumble like I do, but he'll see everything. And somehow . . . somehow he'll get his revenge."

Soriya clutched her arms against herself, as if she were once again holding her baby boy. "No. That can't be. He can't be gone." She started to cry.

"I know my brother," Prak said. "He's gone. He's trying to do what he thinks is right. But he's never been blind and he'll fool no one."

Boran imagined Vibol stumbling toward the Chams. Though his neck had been aching, he no longer felt the pain. Though a fish jumped below, he didn't hear its splash. "Then we'll have to go get him," he said. "Before he finds the Chams we'll have to find him."

"How, Father? How will we do that? He must have swum to shore and is probably walking toward them as we speak."

"We can't follow his tracks and stroll into the Cham stronghold," Boran replied, trying to think clearly even as panic threatened to overwhelm him. "They'd butcher us. But we could paddle close to shore. Perhaps we'll find him before he arrives at their camp. And if we're too late, we'll have to devise a way to meet them and to make them need us. If they need us, if we provide a service they must have, they won't kill us. And we can look for him."

"What about fish, Father? We could catch them fish. We could fill our boat with it and sell it to them. Two poor Khmer fishermen won't be seen as a threat. And if we give them a good price, they'll want us to catch more fish. It must be hard to feed an army, and I don't think they'll harm us."

Nodding, Boran reached for a wall, steadying himself, thinking about what to do if the Chams had captured his boy. Yes, while selling their fish, they might get glimpses of the Cham encampment; they might even locate Vibol. But if they saw him pretending to be blind or in chains, what could they do? How could they rescue him among thousands of their enemies?

"I should go alone," Boran said. "If anything should happen to either of you, I'd never forgive myself. Or Vibol."

"But, Father—"

"I know you could help me, Prak. But for my sake, for your mother's and brother's sakes, please do as I say. Let's fill our boat with fish and I'll go to the Cham encampment. I'll sell fish, find Vibol, and bring him back."

"Mother and I would be no safer here. If the Chams found us alone we'd be at their mercy. Think of that, Father. Wouldn't it be better to have us with you, helping to sell fish? Who would bother us?"

Boran looked at his wife. "What do you think?"

"That we should stay together."

They were about a half day's walk from the Chams, and Boran wondered if they might be able to catch Vibol before he arrived there. He'd had a good start, as they had napped all morning and surely he'd left as soon as they had fallen asleep.

Boran imagined his son captured by Chams, and despair welled up from somewhere deep within him. He pushed the despair down, struggling to think straight, aware that his decisions had led to Vibol's departure.

I'm so sorry, my son, he thought. I've failed you. You're rash and young, but you're a man and I should have treated you as such.

"Boran?" Soriya asked, once again squeezing his arm. "Did you hear me?"

A bird squawked. Their unseen boat thumped against the home's stilts.

"Gather our food," Boran said. "We'll stay close to shore, looking for him as we go. If we can't find him, we'll catch some fresh fish and head into the Cham camp."

They collected their few possessions, leaving the axe where it lay. After situating themselves in their boat, Boran and Prak began to paddle. The waters of the Great Lake were brown and still, hiding whatever lurked below.

As her loved ones paddled, Soriya thought about her dream, wishing that she could once again hold Vibol in her arms. He had been such a happy baby. He'd smiled, laughed, and rarely cried. She had felt as tethered to him as a tree must feel to the earth.

Yet now she felt so far from him. The love between them was tempered by disappointment and conflict. She longed for reconciliation, to look into his eyes and say that she respected him and would support him. He didn't need to run away, to distance himself from her. They had shared too many smiles in the middle of the night, when all the world except the two of them was asleep.

"Come back to me," she whispered, tears obscuring her view of the shoreline. "Please come back and make me whole."

Seven

Discoveries

he Cham encampment was even larger than Vibol had expected. Boats of all kinds had been beached along some mudflats beyond the camp, as well as tied to several bamboo docks that stretched far out into the Great Lake. A half dozen of the biggest vessels were anchored in deeper water. The low, gnarled trees covering the shore had been cleared, but were unsuitable for building. Instead, Chams used elephants to drag heavier timber to the site. While officers sent scouting parties into the jungle or set up patrols, craftsmen built bamboo shelters, kitchens, and latrines. Horses were tied to bundles of teak logs. Prisoners stood in cages too narrow for them to sit.

Vibol had climbed to the summit of a hill dense with foliage after rolling on top of a dead carp at the water's edge. The stench was terrible, but he hoped to convince the Chams that he was a blind beggar. Lying atop the hill, he studied their camp, guessing that at least two thousand Chams were present. Boats were constantly arriving, unloading supplies and then picking up items wrapped in thatch or cloth. Metal, perhaps gold, glimmered, and Vibol wondered if precious Khmer statues were being plundered. Though he'd never spent much time gazing at such works of art, he was enraged that the Chams would steal them. His homeland was being raped. He was a witness to this crime and felt shame rise within him again. These were the men who had savaged his friend, a young woman he'd shared many smiles with while paddling past her home, and recently, whom he had kissed in the moat. She was why he'd liked to travel to Angkor, for her home was along the way, and often their fathers spoke while she and Vibol exchanged glances. In the chaos of the Cham attack, he had forgotten about her and had finally made his way to her home long after the Chams had left. At first he'd run from the sight of her ravaged body, but he had returned later to place her in her father's boat and push it out into the water, too full of grief to even pray.

Now he studied the enemy camp but was still too far away to discern any weakness in its defenses. Picking up his walking stick, he stood up and began to move down the hill, pretending to be blind. Though his eyes were open, he stumbled through the low, thick jungle, cutting himself on thorns. He paused often, cocked his head, and listened. The stench of the carp nauseated him, but he dared not wash it off. Several times he purposely tripped and fell, muddying his legs and arms. Though the Cham camp was hidden by foliage, he could hear men shouting and the strike of steel against steel. His heart began to race. He thought about his parents, regretting any pain he had caused them but hoping they'd be proud of him. Once he returned with information about the camp, they would finally treat him like a man. More important, all of them could then travel deep into the jungle, find the Khmer forces, and describe the Cham camp.

A clearing appeared. Vibol swung his walking stick ahead of

him, as if probing his immediate terrain. The edge of the camp came into view. Chams were digging a defensive trench and lining it with sharpened stakes. The nearly naked laborers were as dirty as he was, fighting against the damp soil. His breath began to come in quick gasps, and before his fear overwhelmed him, he called out in Khmer, then dropped to his knees and bowed low.

The voices of his enemies erupted. With his head so low, he saw no one approach, but he heard footsteps. He started to speak but was kicked on the side of the face and dragged to his feet. Four Cham warriors stood before him, all holding weapons and spears. He pretended not to see them, instead moving his head from side to side while he groped with his free hand. The Chams laughed at him. One pushed him backward and he stumbled. Another smashed his knuckles with the flat of a sword and he grunted in pain.

The Chams tied a rope around Vibol's neck and pulled him forward. He babbled almost incoherently in Khmer, saying that he was looking for Gods but would take food from mortals. The Chams continued to taunt him, leading him into their camp. He saw rows of tethered horses, elephants at work, prisoners, countless warriors, and even a few Cham women and children. The camp stunk of dung, fish, and smoke. Flies buzzed atop piles of dirty nets and traps. Men coughed; horses neighed. Cham banners hung in the stale air.

Vibol made eye contact with no one, yet he took note of everything. The sight that intrigued him most was a large group of Chams who lay on their backs in the shade. Several of them were vomiting, while others were being helped to eat and drink. Vibol wondered if illness was sweeping through the camp. He noticed that his four guards swung wide of the invalids, muttering to themselves.

A discarded section of bamboo lay in their path and Vibol

intentionally stumbled over it, falling on his knees and elbows. One of his guards kicked him in the ribs and he grunted, pleading for mercy. He reached out, searching for something to pull himself up with, and the rope tightened about his neck as he was yanked forward.

Though fear still coursed through him, Vibol was confident in his ploy. He'd watched his brother for many years, and while Prak was able to fend for himself, Vibol understood how his faulty vision made him approach the world. Vibol mimicked Prak's movements, exaggerating them when he thought it prudent. His guards seemed to no longer find him amusing and simply prodded him ahead.

He was brought to a bamboo structure large enough to house an elephant. Seven Cham officers were gathered around the floor, eating rice and fish. One Cham stood in the corner. The man was tall, thin, had a regal face, and seemed to carefully study him. Vibol avoided his stare, babbling incoherently until a guard yanked on his leash. An officer set down his bowl of rice, scowled, and snapped at the guards, who pulled Vibol back outside. One of the men began to untie him. Relief flooded through Vibol. He held back a smile, eager to tell his parents how easily he had fooled their enemies.

The tall Cham emerged silently from the structure, a tiger's claw swinging from his neck. He carried a bow and arrow. Before Vibol knew what was happening, the Cham notched the arrow and in one swift motion raised the bow, pointed the arrow at Vibol's midsection, and let the arrow fly. The shaft flew past his hip, prompting him to flinch. The Cham smiled and lowered the weapon. "You lie," he said in Khmer.

Vibol's breath caught in his throat. He pretended not to understand the Cham, who swung the bow up quickly, striking Vibol on the underside of the chin and splitting the skin. Vibol cried out. He put his hands against his bleeding chin, stumbling away from his attacker. The Cham swung the bow again. This time the weapon hit Vibol on the ear, and he fell to his knees.

The tall man said something in his native tongue and the four guards dragged Vibol toward the lake, where they tied him to a stunted tree. By now Vibol was weeping. He still pretended to be blind, though the thin man only smiled at his antics.

"Share your name, boy," the Cham said. "Introduce yourself or die."

"I . . ."

A dagger appeared as if by magic in the Cham's right hand, and with equal speed he slashed the blade across Vibol's cheek. The cut was shallow but stung. Vibol held his hands to his face, pleading for mercy.

"I say again, Khmer, share your name."

"Vibol."

"They call me Po Rame."

"Please, I—"

"Tell me, whelp, why did you come here? Tell me the truth, or I'll take your eyes and you'll no longer have to pretend."

"I only wanted . . . to see your camp."

Po Rame moved the dagger so that its point was a finger's breadth from Vibol's right eye. "Why?"

"Because someone . . . from here . . . killed my friend," Vibol replied, blood from the wounds on his cheek and chin dripping to his heaving chest. "I wanted revenge."

"You came to spy on us, didn't you?"

"I—"

"Who came with you?"

"No one."

"Did Jayavar send you?"

"Prince Jayavar? He's dead."

The dagger's tip nicked the flesh beneath Vibol's eyebrow. "He's not dead, boy. So tell me what you know of him."

Vibol moaned, his face burning from the cuts.

"Tell me!"

"The prince? He lives in a golden tower. He walks with the Gods and—"

Po Rame straightened. "Walks with the Gods?" he repeated contemptuously. "You foul-smelling fool. If he walks with the Gods, why does he cower in the jungle?"

"Please—"

"You waste my time, peasant, and for that I'll show you blindness. I could take your eyes, but that would be crude and . . . unoriginal. No, I have a better idea."

"Please, please. I won't tell anyone where you are. I promise."

"Shout to the world where we are, whelp. Shout tonight."

"What?"

The dagger disappeared into Po Rame's hip cloth. "Take him out into the lake," he said in his native tongue to the guards. "Tie him to a pole, but leave his head above the water. He'll entertain you when the light's gone, when the crocodiles find him."

The men laughed, pulling Vibol to his feet.

"You won't see them coming, boy," Po Rame said in Khmer. "You'll be blind. But come they will. And you'll never see light again. You hear that, you stinking peasant child?"

Vibol screamed as the guards pulled him away. He tried to fight them, but they beat him, then tossed him into a boat. When they left him tied to a bamboo pole with his bloody chin just touching the water, he began to cry, wishing that his mother held him, as she had so long ago. He whimpered, calling out to her, watching the murky water, all too aware of what it contained and what his fate would be.

* * *

The large home was nondescript but well positioned near an entryway in the wall that surrounded Angkor. Situated between the Royal Palace and the moat, the home offered easy access to bathing and ensured that Indravarman did not have to wait long should he request the presence of one of his favorite concubines. Asal wasn't certain why Voisanne had been sent here, but he suspected that the home also sheltered the concubines of other high-ranking Chams. Indravarman liked to keep track of his officers' whereabouts, and housing their women together was simply another way of monitoring their activities.

Two Cham guards stood under the ladder leading up into the home. Asal greeted them, acknowledged their quick bows, and asked for Voisanne. One of the guards called up to her in Khmer, then resumed his position. Though eager to tell Voisanne about his discovery, Asal forced himself to be patient. He let his eyes wander. Four female slaves labored beneath the home. Two were adding blue dye to a bolt of silk while two others carefully broke apart a honeycomb, collecting the precious honey in a silver bowl. The stench from the dye was unpleasant, and Asal pitied the slaves, thinking that his fate could have been the same. No matter what position he attained, he would never own a slave, unlike almost everyone else in power. For generations Khmers had used Cham slaves and Chams had used Khmer slaves. To the victor went the spoils, and slaves were a part of that plunder.

Asal had begun to wonder if Voisanne was somewhere else when she finally emerged from the home, stepping down on the bamboo ladder. She was dressed as usual, though she wore a golden bracelet that Asal had not seen before. Wanting to continue the pretense of disdain for her, he commanded her to hurry, muttering that he was tired of waiting. She lurched on the rungs and he turned around, moving away without another glance in her direction.

Following a narrow road that led to the gateway, Asal walked quickly, worried that he would be away from Indravarman for too long. He passed through the gateway, then headed north alongside the moat, never turning to see if Voisanne followed. The sun beat down on him, prompting him to gaze with envy at the thousands of Khmers who bathed in the placid water. He could have taken Voisanne into the moat, but he wanted to be alone with her when he shared the news of her sister, so that she could react as she wanted and he could enjoy the moment.

His pace increased as he crossed the causeway spanning the moat. Turning to the north, he walked along a bustling road that was nearly overwhelmed with carts, elephants, horses, and people. To his right a series of large sandstone towers rose to the treetops. Someone had told him that the old towers were built to celebrate a Khmer victory on a field of battle, and he was somewhat surprised that Indravarman hadn't draped them with Cham banners.

Glancing behind him, Asal saw that Voisanne was also sweating heavily. She looked angry, and he wanted to tell her that she would soon be overcome with joy, that he was sorry for having to act toward her with distaste. But he could share no such thoughts and so he proceeded onward, turning to his left so that he followed a path into the jungle. Ruins of a deserted palace dominated the space, and soon silence descended. A cluster of monkeys sat atop a pile of garbage, and Asal avoided the creatures, knowing that their bites could cause illness and death. He headed deeper into the labyrinth of trees, glad to leave the chaos behind, if only for a short time.

Asal had spent much of his life within the jungle, and it didn't take him long to realize they were being followed. He heard two distinct sets of footfalls, but far behind came a third. Though tempted to face whoever was spying on them, he decided to feign ignorance, which would allow him to convey any sort of message to their tracker that he wished.

An old royal bathing pool emerged beside the trail, covered in lotus flowers. Asal moved toward it, sitting down on a sandstone terrace that overlooked the water. The entire area was cloaked in shadows, as the nearby trees were numerous and towering. Cicadas buzzed. Frogs croaked. The scents of dampness and decay lingered in the air.

Voisanne sat down on the terrace an arm's length from him. Though she said nothing, her look was accusatory.

"I apologize, my lady, for my discourtesy," he said quietly. "But we're being watched."

She looked to her right. "But—"

"Please keep your eyes on me. And perhaps . . . you could pretend to serve me. That way, we can deceive the deceiver."

Voisanne started to speak and then stopped. She moved to her knees and began to rub his feet, which were calloused and scarred. "Did you find my house?" she asked. "Or was it burned down?"

Asal nodded, longing to share his news but needing to proceed with care. "Whatever I say, you must continue to rub my feet and remain expressionless. Hide your emotions. Hide them and pretend that you hate me."

"What? What have you learned?"

"I found your home. And later I discovered that a Cham general and his wife live there."

"A Cham—"

"They have slaves. Many slaves. Most of them are from the mountains, but there's a young Khmer girl among them. She has a birthmark on her chin and, from the way you described her, I think she's your sister."

Voisanne's hands stilled. She bit her bottom lip, leaning forward, then backward. "It was . . . on her chin? Right in the middle?"

"The birthmark was where you said it would be. But that's not why I know she is your sister."

"How do you know?"

"Because she looks like you. I saw your beauty in her face."

"Chaya," she whispered. "Was it really you? Please . . . please let it be you."

"Your sister lives. She is a slave, but she seems unharmed."

Voisanne's hands tightened around his feet. She looked up. "I need to see her. Right away. I have to tell her that I'll come for her, that I'll—"

"Wait, my lady. We must be patient. The Cham who owns your sister is powerful. She looks well. To move with haste could change that."

"But I have to see her, to let her know that she's not alone."

"And you will. But wait a few days. The general will be in the field soon enough. Wait until he's gone, until I can bring you and your sister together."

A fish broke the surface of the nearby pool, sending ripples into the lotus flowers. Voisanne wiped away her tears. "And you're certain your eyes didn't trick you? I thought I saw her die."

"I was nearly as close to her as I am to you now."

"And she wasn't hurt?"

"She moved like a cat."

Voisanne bit her lip again, shaking her head. "You have to tell her, tell her that I live."

"I shall."

"And then I must go to her."

Asal smiled. "Have patience, my lady. You need it, though I think that impatience suits you better."

"Why?"

"Because I like to see you so full of life."

Her fingers began to move again on his skin. Only now she caressed him, rubbing the sides of his feet as if she wanted to, not had to. "Please, keep her safe, Asal. Don't let anything happen to her."

"I have been thinking of ways to protect her."

"You're sure that she's well? Truly?"

"I am."

"Thank the Gods."

"I have already."

She smiled and shook her head. "How could I have hated you? When we first met . . . I wanted to kill you. But you've saved me. How shall I ever repay you?"

He watched her fingers move against his feet. "You repay me right now, my lady."

"I can never fully repay you."

A bird squawked in the distance, and he wondered who was spying on them. One of Po Rame's men? Or Indravarman's? "Because someone is watching us," he said, "I was going to pretend to strike you. But now I won't."

"Why not?"

"Because why can't a Cham and a Khmer be close? Why must I beat you? I'm a senior officer in our army. I have power. And though we shall have secrets between us, secrets like your sister, my affection for you is something I'll no longer hide."

The fawn moved with care, edging its way through the jungle, nibbling on green leaves. The creature's ears seemed too large for its body, which was brown with white spots. As Jayavar aimed his arrow, he wondered where its mother was and how they had become separated.

The fawn came closer. Jayavar had hidden downwind from it and rested on one knee within a cluster of ferns. Ajadevi knelt beside him, also holding a bow, a weapon that her brother had taught her to use as a child. Like everyone in their group, she was hungry. One of their two bags of rice had been ruined by water and mold, and the group had been forced to split up to conduct hunting forays.

Jayavar applied pressure to his bowstring, ready to pull it back. The fawn's ears twitched, but it moved toward the humans, unaware of their presence. Jayavar had never seen a fawn so close, and he marveled at its beauty. The fawn dropped its head, sniffed the ground, and stepped forward into Jayavar's direct line of sight. He pulled his bowstring back and prepared to loose his arrow. But the fawn looked up, its large black eyes seeming to fasten onto his. The creature was young and beautiful, and suddenly he didn't want to kill it, regardless of the pangs of his stomach.

"Run free," he whispered, prompting the fawn to leap away, crashing through the underbrush.

Ajadevi stood up beside him, releasing the tension of her own bowstring and then slinging the weapon over her shoulder. He rose as well, his knees creaking. "Why did you let it go?" she asked, reaching for his hand.

"Because . . . it was lost."

"A child separated from its father?"

"From its mother. But yes."

She pulled on his hand. "Come. Let's look for fruit."

They wandered through the jungle, staying on a game trail. Giant cobwebs sometimes blocked their path. Black, poisonous millipedes as long and thick as a finger moved silently over and under fallen leaves. Monkeys screeched from above. The carcass of a scorpion was feasted on by red ants.

Jayavar tried to look for mangos, melons, coconuts, and bananas, but his mind traveled elsewhere. Earlier that day they had passed a lake where he'd once taken his children. Memories had flooded into him, good memories of laughter and joy. He recalled lifting his young daughter Chivy on top of his shoulders and walking into the cool water, listening to her joyous shrieks. She'd begged him to return to shore, and laughing, he had plunged forward, dousing them both.

In the past, such recollections had always made Jayavar smile. But now they ripped at him, stealing the air from his lungs, the strength from his legs. A part of him wanted to end his life so that he could rejoin his children, so that he could once again hear their laughter or tell them stories as candles burned low. If he hadn't been his father's son, or if Ajadevi hadn't been by his side, he would have placed a blade to his throat and commenced his journey. Yet his people and his wife needed him. And so he went forward, day after day, step after step.

"I no longer care to hunt," he said quietly, stopping in a small clearing. "What was once a pleasure is now a task. Now I only want to see Indravarman's head on a spear. I only want revenge."

Ajadevi moved to his side. "Humans lust for love, power, comfort, revenge. Buddha would disagree with me, but I think the lust for revenge is a very human trait. If you were a holy man, you'd overcome this need; you'd worry more about your karma than your enemies. But you're a king and a father of murdered children. Thoughts of revenge are going to occupy your mind."

A gray squirrel scampered up a nearby tree.

Jayavar slung his bow over his shoulder and then rested his hand on his sword hilt. "I want Indravarman to share in my suffering."

"And he shall. But once he's dead, you must move forward;

you must sheath your sword. Otherwise you shall forever be hollow and barren, so unlike your land."

"I shall try."

"Though it goes against my teachings, though I will taint my own karma by doing so, I'll help you dispose of Indravarman. But my help comes with a price."

"What?"

"You have to come back to me. You have to love life and love me."

"I already love you."

"Words not backed by deeds have no meaning, Jayavar. They're like flowers bereft of color."

He shook his head. "And the fawn?"

"What of it?"

"I was thinking of my children when I saw that it was separated from its mother. I felt its pain. But then I saw its face and I thought of you. I knew that setting it free would be a gift to you. And I was loving you, in that moment, in the midst of my grief. I was still loving you."

She smiled, thanked him for his gift, and then stepped closer to him. "No man should return from a hunt empty-handed, with a quiet heart. A man should return from a hunt with a surging heart and with strength flowing through him."

"With a surging heart?"

She leaned toward him, kissing him, pressing herself against him. He hesitated, but then she felt his hands on her and the welcome warmth of his touch.

The Chams had made several bamboo docks that stretched into the brown waters of the Great Lake. A variety of boats came and went, unloading and loading cargo. The goods necessary to keep an army at full readiness were numerous. Weapons, armor, food, clothes, rice wine, women, entertainers, and much more were moved from the end of the docks to the shore. Prak watched all of the activity through the dirty lens of his vision. He smelled more than he saw—scents of horse dung, smoke, illness, damp leather, and boiling rice washing over him.

They had been at the largest dock since the early afternoon, and their supply of fresh and dried fish was growing low. At first the Chams had greeted them with distrust, but once a commander of some sort had inspected their wares and questioned them in broken Khmer, they had been free to sell their goods. Though they had expected low prices, the Cham traders treated them with decency.

Prak had been surprised to see other Khmers arrive in their boats and proceed to sell rice, fruit, vegetables, meat, and fish. At first he had been angered at the thought of his countrymen helping their enemies, but it soon became apparent that the Khmers were poor and struggling. Perhaps their normal trading partners were dead.

Now, as Prak handed a large, still-breathing catfish to a Cham, he glanced at his father, who went through the motions of negotiating but was mainly searching for Vibol. Prak had hoped to find him along the shoreline as they approached the Cham camp, but they hadn't seen him.

The Cham accidentally dropped the slippery catfish, which fell into the water. Prak, who was sitting in their boat, reached down quickly, grabbed the catfish, and again handed it to his enemy. The man thanked him and tossed the flopping fish over his shoulder.

Prak noticed that the Chams were gone for the moment, and he turned to his father. "We're low on fish," he whispered. "We should raise our prices or we'll have to leave."

His father nodded, gazing along the shoreline. "He's not here. Come, let's paddle along the shore."

After pocketing some coins, Prak pushed away from the dock. Positioned at the front of the boat, he paddled on his left and weaker side, which allowed his father to steer. Though he wanted to put all of his weight behind each stroke, to search for his brother with as much haste as possible, he forced himself to appear relaxed. "Where are you?" he whispered. "Show yourself, Vibol. We're here."

The shoreline was a blur to Prak, but he noticed that his father kept close to it. He listened to his mother muttering prayers, which he hadn't heard her do in years, as religion was a substance they did not eat. Still, she prayed to the Hindu Gods, sniffling between her thoughts, pleading that her son be found unharmed. Listening to his mother's suffering deepened Prak's own misery. Their family had always been close, but now it was like a cart with only three wheels. They could barely function.

The blurred shapes of Cham boats came and went. Prak heeded his enemies' distant voices and was reminded of how they had first entered his country. All his life he had listened to his parents and brother, to animals, to the wind as it made its way through the trees. These were the sounds he wanted to hear, not the strange chattering of Chams.

Prak increased his pace, and the boat leaned to the right. He felt his father paddle with more strength, correcting their course. Thinking that perhaps Vibol would recognize his voice, Prak began to sing an old Khmer melody. His mother joined him, and their song carried over the water, louder than it would have been on land.

A huge boat loomed to their right. Someone screamed from within the vessel and Prak stopped singing. The scream came again. Though the voice belonged to a Khmer, it was not his brother, and Prak lowered his head, relieved and saddened. Thinking of the prisoner, he reached for his flute and began to play, wanting his countryman's ears to be filled with a sound other than the taunts of his torturer.

The screams dissipated as his father paddled onward. A second dock grew larger, though it wasn't long and served only one- or two-man boats. Prak set his flute on his knees, preparing to grasp the bamboo.

It was then that his mother shrieked. She called out his brother's name, pointing toward the shore. His father hissed at her to be silent but stopped paddling, and their boat drifted. At first Prak saw nothing but the blurred shoreline, but then he noticed what looked like a black rock sticking out of the water.

"It's him," his mother muttered, weeping. "What have they done to him? Go, Boran! Go to him!"

Prak felt tears stinging his eyes. He pleaded with his father, who started to paddle but stopped when Vibol's head moved.

"He lives," Boran whispered. "Praise Vishnu, he lives."

"Then get him!" Soriya replied. "Go get him!"

Prak glanced toward the shoreline and saw the blurred shapes of countless Chams. He tightened his grip on the paddle.

"No," Boran said. "If we free him now, we'll all die."

"What?"

"He lives. He's strong and he lives. We must wait for darkness. Only then will we be able to save him."

"No!" Soriya protested, turning in the boat, nearly capsizing it. "Now! Help him now!"

Prak dropped his paddle and spun around, grabbing his mother. He pulled her tight against him, knowing that his father was right. She struggled like an animal in his arms but was no match for his strength. Whispering, he tried to calm her as his father paddled away, toward open water. Still, she writhed in his grasp, twisting and kicking and seemingly possessed by demons.

Waves lapped at the sides of their boat in the deeper water. The shoreline receded. His mother finally ceased to fight him, and Prak felt her go limp, praying that the Chams hadn't noticed the commotion. His mother moaned, shuddering against him. She continued to weep. He kissed the back of her head.

In the deep water of the Great Lake, he saw nothing—only a vast white emptiness that added to his misery.

In the growing darkness, Vibol's terror became even more pronounced. Through his swollen eyes he saw scores of large fires that partly illuminated the Cham encampment. The flames were exaggerated through the prisms made by his tears. Blood trickled from the wounds on his chin, cheek, and eyebrow, dropping to the water. Tilting his head forward, he drank the brown water, tried to hold it down, but soon vomited.

Something brushed against his shins and he screamed, struggling against his bonds. But the Chams had driven the stout bamboo pole deep into the mud and tied his arms and legs together behind it. His body was stretched and beaten. His thoughts swirled around his impending doom.

Shaking as if he stood in ice water, he begged for mercy, pleading with the Chams along the shoreline. For the most part, they ignored him, though someone occasionally threw a rock in his direction or mimicked his pleas.

Vibol felt small and helpless. He longed for his family. The blackness beneath him made him think of Prak, and he wondered how his brother could be so brave. Prak had always faced this same darkness, uncertain and alone, without complaint or self-pity.

Again something bumped into his knee and Vibol screamed. He tried to tell himself that it was merely a perch nibbling at his wounds, but he knew that the Great Lake was full of crocodiles and huge snapping turtles that would smell his blood. He was surprised they hadn't found him yet. Throwing himself against his bonds, he twisted and fought and shrieked. For a long time, he had wanted to be a man, but he now felt like a child, desperate to find comfort in another's arms, floundering in loneliness as much as in water.

Time had seemed to stand still for Soriya, Boran, and Prak. After rowing away from the Cham encampment, they had gone ashore, argued, wept, and then devised a plan. Fearful of Cham sentries and the light of their fires, Prak had suggested coating themselves and their boat in mud, which they had done. Now, as they gripped dark paddles and slowly made their way back to Vibol, they looked like a mere shadow on the surface of the Great Lake.

Boran had wanted to wait longer, until the dead of night, when the Chams would be in the depths of sleep. But like Soriya and Prak, he had grown fiercely impatient, deciding to risk the safety of his family rather than let his boy suffer any longer.

The night air was still, bereft of wind. Boran would have preferred a breeze to mask the sound of their boat slicing through the water. He paddled without rhythm, often pausing, trying to sound like a fish breaking the surface. Though he yearned to rush blindly forward and yank his son from the water, he forced himself to remain calm. Had he been alone, he would have hurried, putting his own life at great risk. But he couldn't further endanger Prak and Soriya. If the Chams caught them attempting a rescue, their fates would be dreadful.

Thinking about Vibol suffering put such a weight on Boran's shoulders that he struggled to breathe. His son had counted on him, and he'd failed him. No job was more sacred to Boran than protecting his loved ones. And yet he had allowed Vibol to be captured.

Boran didn't contemplate the notion that Vibol might be dead. To wander into such a dark abyss would have rendered his mind useless, and he needed to be sharp and ready for any contingency.

Cham fires appeared. He whispered to Prak to stop paddling and then leaned forward to squeeze Soriya's hand. He let their boat drift. The huge fires cast light across the water, illuminating elephants, boats, and dwellings. Boran slid his paddle into the water, pulled upon it, and propelled his boat forward. Somewhere a Cham was laughing. A horse neighed. The scent of roasting fish hung in the listless air. Anchored Cham boats began to drift past like black hills. Lanterns hung from the bow and stern of each craft, and he steered as far as possible from these sources of light. He continued to fight the nearly overwhelming urge to rush to his child, instead angling away from danger, often moving with such care that he unconsciously held his breath.

Vibol's head appeared in the distance. He seemed to slump forward, and despite the great need for vigilance, Boran's paddle bit into the water with strength. His boat drifted toward his son. He reached for a dagger and slipped over the side and into the water, praying to Gods he had once forsaken, offering his life in return for that of his boy.

He swam to Vibol, wrapping his arms around him. To his profound relief, Vibol moaned. Without pause or thought, Boran dived underwater, feeling along the pole, finding the rope around Vibol's feet and cutting it with care. He freed his son's hands next, then eased him away from the pole. Prak reached into the water and helped pull his brother into the bow of their boat. Vibol's feet thumped against the wood bottom and a Cham called out. A moment passed. A lantern moved atop a distant boat. Boran froze, but Prak pretended to be his brother, moaning loudly.

The night stilled once again. Boran shuddered at the sight of Vibol's battered face. He held him tight, stroking his cheek, sharing him with Soriya, who cried and kissed him.

Prak paddled them forward, away from the fires and toward a darkness that was welcomed by all.

Eight

Return to Angkor

he bronze tower atop Bapoun Temple glistened in the early-morning light. Though the massive, five-tiered temple was more than a hundred years old, it remained in pristine condition, prompting Indravarman to wonder why the Khmers were better builders than his countrymen. The courtyard in which he sat was guarded by eight bronze elephants, each life-size and showing remarkable attention to detail. Some high-ranking Cham had ordered that his kingdom's colors be draped over the beasts. Indravarman thought the bright swaths of silk looked ridiculous on such works of art, emphasizing the Chams' inferiorities.

On another day, Indravarman would have ensured that the fabric was removed, but thoughts of Jayavar's capture dominated his mind, as they often did. Each morning brought new rumors of the prince's whereabouts and activities, goading Indravarman with their very existence.

A huge slab of cut sandstone lay in front of Indravarman. A detailed map of the entire region had been drawn on the slab, and silver coins marked the locations of Indravarman's scouting parties. Cubes of jade indicated the presence of piles of stones that had been found in the jungle, and it was the gatherings of jade that kept Indravarman's interest. Based on multiple interrogations, Indravarman knew that Jayavar had a habit of creating these piles, and he studied the map hard, looking for patterns. His scouts were finding new piles each day, and he was getting a better sense for what parts of the land his enemy tended to frequent. Jayavar seemed to prefer the north to the south, and lakes to plains.

"His tendencies are obvious," Indravarman said. "But does he know as much and intend to do the opposite?"

Po Rame stepped forward, moving with grace and silence. Though he appeared to carry no weapon, a blade and a garrote were concealed in his hip cloth. As usual, he kept his back to the sun. "I don't think the coward is in the south, King of Kings."

"Why not?"

"Because our numbers there are too great. He'd be discovered."

Indravarman's gaze traveled westward on the map. "Has he gone to the Siamese?"

"My spies would have told me as much, Lord King. No, I believe he cowers in the jungle, likely to the north."

"You believe or you know?"

"It's unclear—"

"Enough!" Indravarman slammed his thick fist atop the sandstone. He was tired of speculation. The future would be determined by knowledge, not conjecture. "He knows where we are," Indravarman said. "That gives him an advantage, despite his weaker numbers."

Po Rame eyed the officers who stood in a distant circle around them. Tired of their excuses, Indravarman had sent them out of earshot. "A pity," Po Rame replied, "that all his sons are dead. If a whelp still lived, we'd have leverage."

"Better to have them all dead."

"But what, King of Kings, if we spread a rumor that one yet lives? Would the coward come to save him? Could a trap be sprung?"

Indravarman stood up from his crouched position. "The youngest son? Who would inspire less confidence in the Khmers?"

"A boy, Lord King. He was just a worthless boy."

Nodding, Indravarman wondered if it had been a mistake to kill all of Jayavar's family. Perhaps the boy should have been spared for such a day. "Walk with me."

The two Chams, followed at a distance by a score of officers and several of Indravarman's favorite philosophers, made their way to the vast temple, then proceeded up its steps until they were able to touch the bronze tower. From such a height, the city of Angkor spread out like a gray and green blanket before them, trails of smoke diffusing into the sky. Indravarman studied the distant formations of his men and their war elephants. He imagined himself as Jayavar, hiding in the jungle, raising an army, bent on revenge.

"What of his woman?" Indravarman asked. "What of her line?"

Po Rame answered, "They're also all dead, Lord King. Gutted like fish the day after our victory."

"Then it will have to be the boy. Spread your rumor. Say that he's ill and kept for my entertainment in a cage right here, atop this temple. Say that in order to live, he must pray out loud every day for his father's death."

Po Rame nodded. "We'll have to find a whelp and put him here."

"Do it. And hide a score of our best men within these walls."

"Consider it—"

"Jayavar is too wise to come himself. But he will send someone. And that someone may lead us to him."

"Yes, Lord King."

Po Rame turned to leave, but Indravarman reached out, putting a hand on his shoulder. "And Po Rame, keep an eye on your old adversary, Asal. I value his services considerably, but he seems to have a softness for the Khmers. He should have executed ten of their most popular priests, not ten invalids. His fate isn't to choose, but to do as he is told, and I question the reason behind his sense of sovereignty."

"He's weak—the stock of peasants."

"No, Po Rame. He's strong. Too strong. And that's why there will come a time when you will have my blessing to kill him. Once we claim Jayavar's head and the threat of attack is gone, you may do with Asal as you wish."

Po Rame bowed. "That day can't arrive soon enough for me."

"Don't test my patience with the tediousness of your own desires."

"Yes, King of Kings."

Indravarman turned away from his assassin and walked toward the center of the temple. He rubbed the iron beneath his skin for luck, wanting the future to unfold quickly, knowing that he would never be the unquestioned ruler of Angkor until Jayavar was dead.

Though he had done so reluctantly, in the end Asal had agreed that Voisanne could walk past her old home and look for her sister. Voisanne had promised him that she would move quickly and, for the time being, keep her identity secret.

Her heart pounding with increasing vigor, Voisanne followed

the familiar streets and alleys leading to her former home. She yearned to run but held her pace in check. She longed to shout for joy but only hummed. The knowledge that her sister lived had kept her up all night, tossing in the darkness, brushing away insects that clung to the outside of her mosquito net. Thida had asked about her strange behavior and Voisanne replied that she wasn't feeling well, a claim belied by her newfound energy.

She saw her father's statue, felt a momentary pause in her gait, looked for Chaya, and then spied her beneath their home as she chopped peppers with a small knife. Voisanne unconsciously muttered her name, then covered her mouth with her hands and stepped behind the large statue. Tears dropped to the dusty ground. She closed her eyes as she offered her repeated thanks to the Gods. Somehow Chaya had been spared; she looked well.

Though Voisanne wanted nothing more than to run to Chaya and hold her tight, she remembered her promise to Asal. She also knew that any rash action would only endanger her little sister. It would be far better to contain her joy, to thrive on it, and to plan for their escape. Once that blissful day arrived their reunion would be without end.

Voisanne wasn't sure if Asal would help them but she believed that he wouldn't betray them. She felt his decency every time they were together, and after peeking around the statue once more to watch her sister, she needed to rush back to him, to tell him of her profound gratitude.

"I'll come for you, Chaya," Voisanne whispered, and then turned, keeping the statue between her sister and herself. She walked quickly, wondering how she could rescue Chaya, how they might flee Angkor and never return.

As Voisanne approached the Royal Palace, the streets became crowded with pedestrians. She brushed past them, moving unusually fast for a woman but uncaring of what others thought.

Again and again, she envisioned Chaya cutting the vegetables, and each memory lifted her spirits higher.

Only at the last moment, as she entered the bustling Royal Palace, did Voisanne slow her pace. She lowered her head, deadened the joy on her face, and walked on. The palace's wide corridors were filled with concubines, slaves, warriors, officials, and servants. Both Chams and Khmers were present, though only the occupiers carried weapons of any sort.

Voisanne neared the living quarters of the Cham officers. The area was quiet, and she passed door after door until finally she arrived at Asal's room. Her knock was unanswered and she respectfully called out his name. When no reply was uttered, she opened the door and stepped inside.

The room had been left tidy and clean, as if no one had lived in it for many years. Voisanne eyed Asal's few possessions. To her surprise, his shield rested against the far wall. Though still buoyed by the thought of being reunited with her sister, she realized that she should soon return to her quarters. She'd told the guards that she was going to bathe and if she took too long they would grow suspicious.

But as she reached for the door, Voisanne considered Asal's position and the risk he was taking by helping her. It had been his idea to search for her sister, and it was he who'd rekindled the flame of life in her. Every feeling of hope and promise that she now experienced had started with him. And she had given him nothing in return, had made no effort to repay his generosity of spirit and action.

Suddenly Voisanne felt an urge to leave him something—a token of her appreciation. But a token, whether a flower or a letter, could be discovered and used against him. Her gaze traveled again to his shield. On several occasions, she had seen him adjust its straps and test its strength and she knew that it was almost a part of him. A note could be hidden within the crevices of the shield, in a place where only he would find it.

His dais held white chalk and various squares of deerskin. She picked up a small piece of hide, glad that her father had let her watch him write and encouraged her to try her hand. Though there was much she wanted to say to Asal, space was finite and precious. The chalk stirred against the hide.

I pray that this shield never fails you, and that one day, in what is to become the best of your days, you set it down and you know the same peace and joy that you have given me.

Voisanne folded up the hide and positioned it on the underside of the shield, in a narrow gap between the iron rim and the teak interior. She then propped the shield up against the wall, so that it stood more proudly than it had before.

She smiled, pleased with her words. As thoughts of her sister flooded into her once again, she stepped from the room and walked ahead, unaware of the throngs of her enemies, gripped only by the promise of an imminent reunion.

Vibol lay silent near the fire. His head rested on Soriya's lap, and she gently stroked his brow, avoiding the cuts and swollen flesh around his eyes. As she tended to him, she hummed a song that she'd sung to him as a child. Occasionally, she placed a small piece of honeycomb on his tongue. Twenty paces away, near the edge of the Great Lake, Boran and Prak were on the lookout for Chams, the soft notes of Prak's flute seemingly a part of the land.

Boran had paddled until dawn, trying to create space between the Cham encampment and his family. In an effort to raise Vibol's spirits, they had taken turns telling him stories about his childhood. Boran spoke about Vibol's first attempts at fishing. Soriya recalled how, when he was a baby, his gums would ache and he liked to gnaw on her knuckles. Prak relived many of their adventures together, smiling when he recollected how a wild boar they were hunting had chased them into the river.

None of the stories had done anything to change Vibol's demeanor, and Boran had simply continued to paddle, grateful that his son was alive. As his palms had blistered against the wooden handle, he had listened to Soriya's tales and Prak's flute, unable to remember the last time his wife had spoken so much.

Now, as Boran and Prak stood on the shoreline, Soriya leaned close to her son, ensuring that the heat of the fire wasn't too strong or too weak. His battered face was hardly recognizable, and she had to bite her lower lip to keep from crying. She had never understood the concept of hate, but as she tried to comfort Vibol, she imagined what she might do, if she could, to the men who had hurt her child.

But my hate won't help him, she thought, still stroking his brow.

Seeing that her herbal pastes had smeared off Vibol's wounds and needed to be reapplied, Soriya reached down for a large leaf that held a mixture of crushed plants with healing properties. Still humming, she rubbed the paste between her fingers, breaking the concoction down as much as possible before carefully dabbing the places where she had stitched together his split skin. He flinched when she touched him, as if fearful of Cham blades and fists.

"I know they hurt you," she whispered. "But you're brave, so very brave to do what you did. And you don't have any reason to feel shame."

He leaned away from her, staring into the fire.

"Remember, Vibol, that osprey you found when you were a boy? It had an injured wing. You rescued that bird, and we fashioned a cage for it out of bamboo and spent the better part of the

dry season nursing it back to health. You fed it fish every morning. You spoke to it constantly. Though Prak had always been
more curious about animals, the osprey was your pet. You loved
it, you healed it, and when it was ready, you stepped back and
watched it fly away."

The fire cracked, prompting Soriya to peer into the jungle.
She wiped the paste from her fingers and then placed a fingernail-
size piece of honeycomb on his tongue. They had always looked
for hives together, as Vibol savored the taste of honey more than
anything else.

"Do you know, my son, why we've argued so often these past
days? It's only because I feared losing you, like you feared losing
that osprey. Not because I thought you were still a boy and
needed my protection, but because I couldn't imagine my world
without you in it."

A tear rolled down her cheek. "I'm not strong like you, Vibol,"
she continued. "I'm not strong enough to endure a world without
you. Do you understand that? I have to go first. Because even
though you're a man, I still look at you and see my baby boy, one
of the two miracles I created in this life. When we go into Angkor, people think of me as a poor woman. They pity me. But they
don't know that I've created two miracles. They don't know that
you make me feel rich."

He sniffed, turning slowly in her direction. She saw that his
eyes were also filled with tears, and she leaned down, pulling him
toward her, feeling the warmth of him and rejoicing that he was
not lost.

When night fell, the city of Angkor came to life. Countless
cooking fires illuminated temples and homes, flickering like stars
in the sky. From atop a banyan tree beyond the great monuments,

Jayavar and Ajadevi studied the scene before them. Angkor had never shimmered with the light of so many fires, and Jayavar could only assume that Cham warriors were gathered about the flames. "Indravarman fears us," he said quietly. "He keeps the night at bay because he knows we shall attack."

Ajadevi nodded but made no reply.

Many of the fires seemed to stretch out in lines, and Jayavar imagined formations of Cham warriors. Or the fires could be a ruse, meant to provoke attacks in other areas that looked undefended, but in reality were not.

Cicadas buzzed in the trees. The scent of horse dung drifted up from below. Now that he was so close to his home, Jayavar felt his feelings cresting like the top of a windswept wave. He wanted to rush forward, run through familiar streets, and look for family members and friends. His emotions demanded action and yet his experience counseled patience. He felt torn in so many ways. He dared to hope but knew that he was deceiving himself. He longed to lead his men to victory but needed Ajadevi to pull him forward.

Of all the sights in front of him, it was the silhouette of Angkor Wat that bothered him the most. The wondrous temple was dotted with fires, which made him believe that Indravarman had turned it into some sort of fortress. His men were in its great halls, his horses and war elephants on its grounds. What had become of its priests and artifacts?

The longer Jayavar stared at the fires, the more foreign they felt, inflaming anguish within him. The city had been taken from his stewardship. Even his memories seemed to have been plundered, for the desecration he beheld tainted the few treasures he still carried—the echoes of his children's laughter, the visions of his people and their creations.

"The Chams . . . have stolen everything from us," he said,

keeping his voice quiet so that his men below could not dwell on his words.

Ajadevi moved closer to him on the branch. "And for that we shall drive them from our land. Tomorrow it shall begin. When it will end, I do not know, but tomorrow we shall act."

"It's strange . . . to hate Indravarman, a man I've never met."

"Hate needs no introduction."

"And what if we fail? He has more men, horses, elephants, and resources. What if he breaks us?"

"Then we shall die together."

"As one?"

She reached for his hand. "And that's why, when we do bring the fight to him, I want you to fight with love in your heart, not hate."

"How can I do that? Hate sustains me . . . more than you know."

"Fight with love, Jayavar. Because if you want to be reunited with your children, with me, how shall we find you in death if we don't recognize you? None of us will recognize a man who dies in an ocean of his own hate. It's like now, as we look on our city. It is before us, but it doesn't beckon to us. We fail to rejoice in its beauty because it has changed. And that's why, Jayavar, if a Cham spear pierces your heart, you must die beholding the joys of your life, not the sorrows. You must celebrate your approaching reunion with your loved ones, not lament your failures. Because if we're to find you, the spirit of who you are must endure. If I die it will be beside you . . . and you will feel the light of me as if all these fires had been swept together."

A shooting star flickered across the sky. Jayavar was certain that Ajadevi would consider it an omen of some sort, but he refrained from asking her about it. "A warrior uses hate," he finally replied, "to give himself strength."

"A weak warrior, perhaps. A reed among a field of reeds. But the stoutest warrior fights using love. He celebrates the gifts of his life as he lifts his sword. He feels pain and is reminded of how acutely beautiful his life has been and how beautiful the next one will be. Fight with love, Jayavar, and you shall win. Fight with hate and you shall die alone."

Asal knelt in the corner of his room, rereading the message that Voisanne had left for him. He'd already traced her words with his fingers and smiled at the thought of her seeking him out. She had wanted to see him, to leave a note meant only for him.

Breathing deeply, he savored her earlier presence, aware of the lingering scent of her perfume. His room must have been brighter and warmer with her in it, as if a window had been opened to let sunlight work its wonders.

After hiding her note within his blanket, he picked up a small piece of deerskin and some chalk.

After much thought, he wrote:

Your words were a gift to me. You are a gift to me. Thank you, my lady, for being a part of my world.

He folded up his message and placed it within his shield, just as she had done. Will she write back? he wondered. Will she have the courage and desire to return to my quarters?

Though the day had been long and arduous, a newfound energy filled Asal. Realizing that he needed to acquire a second shield so that his old one could always remain in his room, he hurried out into the Royal Palace, moving with the sort of eagerness he had known as a child, when discoveries rather than duties had awaited him, when life was the sum total of so many pleasures.

*   *   *

The Chinese section of the marketplace was quiet late at night—though from dawn to midday it was dominated by the well-dressed foreigners who traded gold, silver, silk, lacquer dishes, iron pots, writing paper, umbrellas, fine-toothed combs, needles, and various spices. Usually only the wealthiest of Khmers traded there with their Chinese counterparts, but since the Cham conquest, an equal number of occupiers were also present.

After the sun fell, different sorts of sellers arrived—mostly Khmer women who offered themselves to men of all backgrounds. A bolt of silk would often merit four or five nights of pleasure. A fine needle could be exchanged for a brief encounter. The terms of trades were agreeable to all and disputes rarely arose.

Two of Po Rame's spies, both Khmer women, worked at night in this area of the market, and he often pretended to barter for their services and then disappeared into a nearby room and encouraged them to pass along rumors. The women, when properly rewarded or threatened, showed no loyalty to their countrymen. They saw Po Rame as a means to an end.

Now, as Po Rame followed one of his informants toward a room she rented, he wondered if she had already lain with another man. Such actions revolted him, and he tolerated the woman only because she provided him with useful information.

The Khmer turned into an alley, passed a pair of begging lepers, and entered a long, narrow building frequented by her kind. Her room was at the far end of the corridor, which Po Rame had insisted on. Low groans and grunts emerged from behind closed doors. Po Rame tried to ignore the sounds as well as the smells of sweat and sex.

The room they entered was empty except for a thatch mat, some candles, and a washbasin. The Khmer woman, who was old for her trade and as worn as a horse's hoof, lit one of the candles, turned around, and bowed. "Tell me, master, what you seek."

Po Rame found her disgusting and made no effort to hide his distaste. "You know, flesh trader, what I seek, and you play games with me at your own peril."

She nodded, sweat glistening on her brow. "The Khmer prince. The Cham warrior. Who will we discuss first?"

"Jayavar."

"There are whispers that he's near."

"Who whispers?"

"A priest. A priest who seeks my services is certain Jayavar is close."

Po Rame scowled. "To the north? To the south?"

"North."

"How does this priest know?"

"A group of traveling pilgrims passed Jayavar in the jungle, master. Three days north of Angkor. The priest was their leader."

The woman continued to speak, but Po Rame's mind began to race. He had suspected that Jayavar was to the north but was surprised to hear that he was so close. Perhaps he intended to scout the area and then return to his forces.

Po Rame posed more questions to the Khmer, gave her a silver coin, and then shifted his thoughts to Asal, remembering how, many months ago, the warrior had confronted him after he'd poisoned one of Indravarman's adversaries. Asal had called him a coward—an unforgivable offense—and Po Rame knew that only death would bring finality to their antagonism. The assassin would celebrate Asal's suffering and downfall as he had few other enemies. He'd celebrate them because Asal had never openly feared him, and Po Rame needed to be feared. Asal's renowned prowess on the field of battle allowed him to stand tall in the face of threats, but Po Rame had killed men of equal strength. The back of a formidable adversary was no less vulnerable than that of a weakling.

"What of the Cham officer?" Po Rame asked.

"He has a woman, master. A Khmer woman."

"I know as much."

"She went alone, unbidden, to his quarters today. He wasn't there, but she stayed some time."

Po Rame nodded, wondering how Voisanne could be exploited. "Learn why she lingered," he replied, handing her another coin.

"Thank you, master."

"Keep your forked tongue quiet on these matters. Keep it quiet or you'll lose it. I'll return in two nights." His eyes swept over her, and she straightened.

"Would you care, master, to enjoy me? You did once before. You can again."

Po Rame's shame was instant and overwhelming. "You promised never to speak of it."

"I—"

"Be silent," he said, his voice still quiet and unhurried.

Though the woman was valuable to him, she was just one of many informants. As he saw it, in a moment of great weakness he had polluted himself by sleeping with her. He'd gone from being feared, from following in the footsteps of the Gods, to tainting himself with the stains of her existence. He had acted like an ordinary man when he had no wish to be one.

In one fluid motion, Po Rame pulled his leather garrote from where it was wrapped around his waist. Her lips had barely parted when he whipped it around her neck and wrenched her toward him. Though he could have leaned back and broken her neck with little effort, he let her die slowly, savoring her struggles, prolonging the moment of her passing with skill and cunning. He allowed her to beg, reveling in her terror, in his power over her. Strength rushed into him and he felt himself rising up, as if he were one of the Gods vanquishing a demon.

He left the room. Her body would be found by those nearby, and people would know what he had done to her. Fear of him would spread, moving from Khmer to Cham to Khmer, entrenching his position as someone to be answered, not questioned.

Breathing easier now that she was dead, now that her face was gone from his world, Po Rame washed his hands in a bathing pool before making his way toward the Royal Palace, his thoughts returning to Asal's woman. If she had gone unbidden to his room, then she might care for him. And if she cared for him, she could be used as a weapon.

As adept as he was with blades, Po Rame preferred weapons of flesh to those of steel. They were more satisfying to wield, and could inflict as much pain, as much horror, as any piece of iron.

Nine

The Forging of Alliances

T he cool water of the moat was refreshing in the early-morning heat. Rain had not fallen in Angkor for many days, and dust rose from a distant road as throngs of warriors, traders, commoners, priests, horses, and elephants traveled in either well-maintained columns or small packs. Voisanne watched the mass of her countrymen and the occupiers, though her mind dwelled on her younger sister and how they might soon be reunited. Her impatience had driven her to seek out Asal earlier in the day. His room had been empty but she was surprised and pleased to discover his note. She replaced his letter with another of her own, thanking him and asking when they might meet.

Thida scrubbed herself to Voisanne's right. Though Voisanne was tempted to confide in her, Thida had been unusually interested in Voisanne's lighter mood, and at times her questions had seemed too pointed. Voisanne had so far resisted divulging information about her sister, tempted though she was to place trust in her new friend.

Wading away from the embrace of a Khmer man and woman, Voisanne moved deeper into the moat. Children swam in these waters, and pink lotus flowers bobbed in miniature waves. The sight of the flowers prompted Voisanne to think about her parents and the certainty that they would want her to rescue her sister as soon as possible. Anything could happen to a slave.

I must go to Asal again, she thought. I must convince him to free her.

A fish broke the surface between Voisanne and Thida, consuming a moth that had fallen to the water. Voisanne glanced at Angkor Wat, thinking that she needed to pray, to beseech her Gods for Chaya's safe return.

"Voisanne?"

Turning, Voisanne looked at Thida. "Yes?"

"I . . . I want to tell you something."

"What?"

Thida lowered herself deeper into the moat. She grimaced, then rubbed her temples. An elephant trumpeted. Dragonflies skipped along the water's surface. "I haven't revealed anything to him," she finally replied, her words barely audible. "I swear I haven't."

"Who are you talking about, Thida?"

"You can't say anything. If you do, he'll kill me. He'll hurt me, then kill me."

Voisanne put her hand on Thida's shoulder, squeezing it gently. "You can trust me. We share the same house, the same past, and the same fate. We're sisters in everything but blood."

"Indravarman . . . came to me a few nights ago. He asked about you."

"About me?"

"He ordered me to become your friend, to spy on you. And I started . . . to do what he wanted. But then I stopped."

Voisanne's skin tingled and goose bumps appeared on her arms. "But I'm nothing to him. I'm a face amid a thousand faces. Why would he care about me?"

"Asal. He worries about Asal and wants to learn more about him."

"He gave me to Asal. He threw us together."

Thida shrugged. She started to speak, then stopped. "Please . . . please forgive me. I should have told you right away, but he frightens me. He frightens me so much."

"You mustn't—"

"He has spies, and he uses women as spies too, whether we want to help him or not. He keeps track of everyone—his friends and his foes. His strength is obvious for all to see, yet he grows more paranoid by the day. He wants Jayavar's head but can't find him."

Voisanne thought about Asal, fearful for him. "But Asal has done nothing wrong. How can his loyalty be questioned?"

"I don't know why Indravarman distrusts him. But he does. He watches him as he does everyone else."

"And he told you to get close to me, so that you could report to him?"

Tears gathered in Thida's eyes. "I'm sorry. I've wanted to tell you. But I've been so frightened. No one dares to displease him because if they do . . . they disappear. It doesn't matter if they're Khmers or Chams or women or priests. They just vanish, and people are afraid to even talk about them. And I know he'll hurt me and kill me and I'm so afraid of him."

Voisanne embraced her friend, holding her tight. As Thida wept, Voisanne thought about how best to proceed. It seemed that Thida should tell Indravarman something; otherwise he'd begin to suspect her loyalty. She remembered Asal saying that someone was following them in the jungle, and that he would no longer pretend to beat her.

"You needn't be afraid of him," Voisanne finally said, stroking the back of Thida's head. "He's a prideful man—a prideful snake, I should say. And you're so beautiful. You're like a treasure for him to display day after day."

"I don't want to be a treasure."

"Just keep him happy, Thida. Tell him that . . . that I speak about Asal often, that I care for him. I don't think there's any harm in such knowledge, and his spies must have told him as much already."

Thida looked up. "Is it true?"

"Yes. He's brought me back to life. And he . . ." Voisanne paused, deciding not to reveal the discovery of her sister.

"What?"

"He's no threat to Indravarman. He only wants to serve his king, to fulfill his duty."

"But why . . . why were you handed to him and me to Indravarman? It isn't fair. I've done nothing wrong. Why am I being punished?"

Voisanne used her forefinger to wipe away one of Thida's tears. "After the Chams came," she said quietly, "I wanted to die. Death seemed . . . like a noble end. But now, now I'm glad that I still live. I have hope."

"Indravarman . . . he steals hope."

"Then we'll have to steal you, Thida. We'll steal you from him."

"What?"

Voisanne glanced toward the north. "Don't you hear the whispers about Khmers hiding in the jungle? We only need to escape."

"No. He'll kill us."

"He'll kill us if he catches us. But snakes aren't as smart as they look. A child can thrash one with a long hoe."

Thida shook her head, and Voisanne put her hands on either side of her friend's chin, holding her motionless.

"You must stay strong," Voisanne said. "On the outside, when you're with him, pretend to be beaten, pretend to betray me. But inside, stay strong. And believe in yourself; believe in a future free of him."

"I can't."

"Yes, you can. Yes, you will. You've already endured so much. What will a few more weeks matter?"

"I . . . I just—"

"Listen to me—he grows lax with you. We have no guard as we bathe. We have new freedoms. It seems to me that his vanity, his belief in your fear of him, gives us opportunities. So let me plan. You endure him and I'll plan. And one day this will all seem so very distant."

Thida nodded, then leaned her head on Voisanne's shoulder. Voisanne held her tight, the sudden responsibility for her well-being reminding Voisanne of how her father and mother must have felt. Voisanne had been thrust into the role of a protector because Thida wasn't strong enough to make it on her own; nor would Chaya ever escape her Cham masters without help.

Voisanne would have to lead them. She was untested in so many ways. She was young and unwise. Even during her engagement she had still felt like a girl.

But she was now a woman. And she would have to start acting like one.

Prak sat beside Vibol eating some fresh perch that their mother had cooked over the fire and seasoned with lemongrass that she'd found at the water's edge. The perch was succulent and nourishing. Prak felt as if he were growing stronger with each bite. Though the dish was one of Vibol's favorites, he barely ate. His eyes and face were still swollen from his beating, and his jaw hurt when he moved it.

Rarely had Prak seen Vibol so quiet. He tried to engage his brother through humor, memories, and even talk of revenge. But Vibol remained silent, staring into the dying flames of the fire, twisting a stick over and over.

The flames reminded Vibol of his suffering, of how he had begged for mercy as the Chams tied him to the pole and then pounded it into the lake's bottom. His pleas, uttered between his sobs and the sound of their fists striking him, were mocked. Once he was bound, one of the Chams had urinated on his head, prompting the warriors to howl with laughter.

Though Vibol wanted to banter with Prak as he always had, he felt so small and helpless. He had called his father a coward, but he was the coward. He was the one who had cried in front of their enemies, who had begged to them like a child.

Prak continued to speak to him, but Vibol wasn't listening. He glanced at his parents, who stood at the shoreline and appeared to argue. Only now did he understand why his father had been so reluctant to engage the Chams. His father had been wrong not to defend his homeland, but right in believing that the power of the Chams was unrivaled.

Vibol still wanted to drive them from Angkor but he felt that doing so was impossible. While in their camp he had seen thousands of warriors, infinite supplies, and a never-ending stream of boats arriving and departing from the bay. The Chams were in Angkor to stay. To fight them was to die.

Sitting on a log, Vibol shifted his weight, pain racing through him from the movement. He grimaced, holding back a moan. When Prak asked how he was, he shook his head. "The Chams . . . will never leave."

Prak set down his fish. "Why do you say that?"

"Because . . . of what their boats hold." Vibol stilled his trembling hand, repressing a memory of the dark boats, of his screams. "Women and children are arriving," he said softly. "And they wouldn't bring their families unless they planned to stay."

A breeze gathered strength and tugged at the bushes around them. Smoke drifted into Prak's face and he moved to his left, toward a bouquet of flowers that their mother had arranged in a clay jar. "What did they do to you, Vibol? Tell me what they did."

Vibol turned away, ignoring the smoke that blew over him. "We'll never defeat them."

"But we thought they'd never defeat us. Why can't fate be flipped? Why can't—"

"Because they're strong and we're weak!"

Prak began to scoop handfuls of sand onto the dying fire, causing the smoke to billow outward and then disappear. "Maybe they are strong," he finally replied. "But I think they're fools. And a strong fool is less worrisome than a brilliant weakling."

"So, we're brilliant? Some poor fishermen? They pissed on my head and you can't see. I'm sure they must be terrified of us."

"Seeing didn't get you far, did it? Maybe, Vibol, if you couldn't see, like me, everything would be clear. Maybe you—"

"So it's all clear to you? You know what must be done?"

"Yes."

"You know nothing!"

Prak saw that his parents were moving in their direction but he motioned them away. "I know that the Chams hurt my brother. I know that a mind can be as strong as a sword. And I know how to defeat them at the lake."

Vibol halted his reply. His brother's last words both alarmed and incited him. A part of him cowered at the thought of again facing the Chams, but he was also still consumed with the prospect of driving them from their land. "How?" he finally asked, continuing to twist the stick, a motion that disguised the trembling of his hands. "How do we defeat them?"

"Are you sure you want to hear from me, the boy who can't see?"

"Tell me."

"I'm a weakling, remember?"

"Stop it. Tell me how we can win."

"We earn their trust by selling them fish each day. But one day, the fish we sell will be poisoned. And the next day, we attack."

"How . . . how do we poison the fish?"

"Mother knows ways. A hundred things in the jungle can sicken you. Or we just sell fish that has lain in the sun for a day. The Chams will become too sick to fight. At least some of them will be. Maybe enough to even out our numbers."

"But—"

"And just now, as I was watching the fire, I wondered what would happen if we started a fire opposite the Chams' position. The wind often comes from the north, blowing toward the Great Lake. If a breeze blew flames toward the Chams' camp, they'd be forced into the water. We could attack them from boats, and their elephants and horses would be terrified. The Chams would be trapped between the flames and our army."

Vibol sat straighter, still twisting the stick. "What army?"

"We'd have to travel, Vibol. To go into the jungle and find our Khmer brothers and sisters. We'd join their ranks, then tell them our plans. Of course, I'm sure that most of the Chams are in Angkor, so this would be the smaller battle. I have no idea how to retake the city."

An unseen monkey screeched. Vibol flinched at the noise, then glanced behind him. "What will Father say?"

"He'll agree."

"How do you know?"

"Because I've already told him. Because when they hurt you, they hurt him. And he wants us all to live as we did before, without the threat of such pain. That's what he said to me last night, when Mother was with you. He wants life to return to what it was before, and he thinks we have to drive the Chams from our land to make that happen."

Vibol pointed toward his brother. "And you? What do you think?"

"I want the old Vibol back—the blundering, babbling fool who longed to bathe with pretty girls, who was more concerned about having clean teeth than picking up a sword. And the only way I'll get him back is to drive the Chams from our land. So I'll help Father and I'll help you."

"And Mother?"

"As long as none of us gets hurt, Mother will be fine. Because when she thought you were dead, she seemed to die too. So don't walk down that road again. Just stay safe and by my side. Together we can do things that neither of us can do alone. Together we can make the Chams regret ever coming to Angkor."

The road into Angkor was crowded. Massive teak and ficus trees provided shade for groups of travelers—warriors, commoners, priests, and pilgrims. The dusty road was littered with horse and elephant dung. Slaves carried ornate palanquins upon which sat high-ranking Cham officials. Clusters of monkeys begged for food near roadside stalls, often dodging rocks thrown by annoyed vendors. A listless breeze came and went, doing little to carry away the scents of animals, sweat, urine, and spices.

Sitting beneath the shade of an old banyan tree, Jayavar and

Ajadevi watched the endless procession of travelers. Both were posing as beggars covered in filth, with matted hair and empty bowls. They mumbled to themselves as if mad, uncaring of the flies that landed on them, of the taunts from passing strangers. Every so often someone would drop a coin into one of their bowls, and they would bow deeply.

On several occasions Jayavar was tempted to tell one of his countrymen who he was and what needed to be done, but he decided to wait until the right sort of person came by. It would be easy for someone to betray him, and so he called upon his reserves of patience and continued to beg, pleading for kindness and mercy.

The sun was growing hot, and he often looked across the road toward the moat. Already thousands of Khmers were bathing in its waters. He longed to join them but worried what would happen when his disguise washed away.

"It's good for you to beg," Ajadevi whispered, when no one was near. "One day, when you rule this land, you shall remember the suffering of your people."

"You think I need reminders?"

"Not reminders, but memories."

"And the difference between the two?"

"Reminders are for those who cannot remember. Memories are for those who want to remember."

Jayavar thought about his children, visualizing each of their faces, starting with the youngest. He envisioned them when each had seemed happiest. His little girl, Chivy, laughed as she rode on his shoulders. His eldest son, Kosal, rejoiced at the birth of his own child. He wished them well, as he often did, taking his time with his thoughts, trying to connect with his loved ones.

"I think memories make us human," he finally replied. "They give substance to our spirits."

"They do."

"I'm . . . afraid of how I will remember this day. Of what I will be told. Despite what that Cham said, I still cling to hope."

She reached to him, resting her hand on his dirty knee. "I know. As do I. But whatever we learn, Jayavar, don't give up hope. For as long as you live, new memories can be created. They're not finite, like the days of youth. They can be made forever."

He considered her words, understanding that her belief in a series of rebirths made such a view possible. She had often spoken to him about her vague recollections of past lives, of voices that she heard while drifting to sleep, forgotten voices with which she felt distant attachments. Though he'd tried to open himself to the same experience, it had always seemed that his mind was very much grounded in this time and place. Still, he shared her beliefs. He saw how the world went through rebirth each day and imagined that somehow he would be a part of that process.

A group of Cham warriors marched past, pulling a chain that connected scores of Khmer prisoners in a long line. The Khmers, all men, were tall yet emaciated. Jayavar assumed that they were former warriors who now served as slaves. He wanted to go to them, to free them, but only tightened his fists.

"Look who shadows them," Ajadevi whispered, pointing toward a lone man who walked behind a horse-drawn cart but seemed to be intent on the prisoners. The man was broad shouldered and stout. Though he carried a farmer's hoe, he didn't stoop like a man who'd spent a lifetime in the fields. He walked upright, with pride.

Without a moment's pause, Jayavar stood up and moved toward the road, keeping his head low. He approached the Khmer, dodging the cart's wheels and then looking up. "Help an old fool, my son," he said quietly, "and I shall tell you how to free your friends."

The Khmer's brow furrowed. He glanced at the departing prisoners, then back at Jayavar. His shoulder twitched as he lowered the butt of his hoe to the ground. "I have no friends."

Jayavar nodded. "Kindly follow me and I shall explain."

The man's indecision was obvious, but he finally turned to his left and followed Jayavar to the side of the road. There they sat next to Ajadevi, who smiled at the stranger. No one spoke as a large number of Cham warriors passed by, each holding a shield and a spear.

Jayavar kept his head bowed low until the Chams moved on. Finally he looked up. "Where did you fight against the Chams?" he asked.

"What?"

"I see the warrior in you. So tell me, where did you fight them and how did it go?"

The stranger's eyes narrowed. "What does it matter to you, old man?"

"It matters much."

"If you must know, I was stationed inside Angkor's western wall. I saw them coming, and our line held for a time. But eventually we were overrun."

"Were you an officer?"

"Yes."

"Tell me how you feel about the Chams."

"Better to ask me how I feel about maggots. I'd prefer their company."

Jayavar pursed his lips. "What I share with you now I do at great risk. And when I tell you what I must, act as if I have said nothing unusual. Our lives shall depend on it."

"What are you—"

"I am Prince Jayavar, and this is my wife, Princess Ajadevi."

The warrior's mouth opened, but he did not speak. A passing

elephant trumpeted. A trio of priests walked past, chanting rhythmically.

"We've been hiding in the north," Jayavar continued. "There are nearly a thousand of us, and I wish to raise an army, to drive these maggots from our land."

"My lord . . ."

"What is your name?"

"Phirun, my lord. Please forgive my affronts to you. I failed to recognize you."

"Nothing needs forgiveness. Now tell me, Phirun, what happened to my family, to my other wives and children?"

Phirun lowered his head. "You . . . won't want to hear it. I'm sorry."

"Tell me."

"We tried, my lord, to save them. A few of us heard about the imminent . . . executions and we started to plan. But we moved too slowly. Again, please forgive me."

Jayavar shut his eyes. A ringing filled his ears and he had to place his hand on the ground to keep from falling to the side. Ajadevi said something to him, but her words were as loud as clouds, merely passing above him. "Tell me," he said quietly, "how it happened."

"My lord, hundreds of our people were executed, not just your family members. They weren't beaten, or tortured, but . . . but each was killed from behind, with a blade to the neck."

"You saw?"

"Alas, I did, my lord. Many Khmers did. They killed your kin and then made us bow to their king."

"Even my little ones?"

Phirun nodded. "I saw them die, my lord. There's a rumor that one of your sons still lives, that he's chained atop Bapoun. But it's a lie."

"How do you know?"

"Because three of us went to free him late one night. But whoever was in that cage was no son of yours. He was dressed as a Khmer, but when they fed him I heard him offer thanks in their tongue."

Jayavar rubbed his temples. Though the warrior had only confirmed what he suspected, his hopes had been among his most precious possessions. Still, he forced himself to focus, to set aside his grieving for a later time. "How many . . . of our warriors still live?" he asked, his voice as weak as the breeze.

"Thousands, my lord. A few are scattered in the city. Most are said to be in the jungle—men who were fixing the levees and beyond the reach of the first Cham attack."

"Can you send them to us? In small groups?"

"Yes, my lord. But word is bound to spread, and when it does, Indravarman will come for you."

"Let him come. He'll be deceived when the time is right. But for now, tell men and women you trust to steal away to Banteay Srei. There they will meet us."

Phirun bowed slightly. "My lord, I will serve you here. I'll send our people to you. And then I'll find you and fight for you."

"Thank you."

"Our people are not beaten, my lord. They still believe in Angkor. And when they hear that you were here, in the very shadow of our enemy, they will rejoice."

Jayavar took Phirun's hands within his, holding them tight. "Let them know that my wife and I live, that many of us live. And spread a second tale, Phirun. Let Indravarman know that I shall come for him. That after my army defeats his, I shall use ropes and stakes to bind him to the road leading into Angkor. Any Khmer who wants to can step on him as they enter our city. The days will be long for him, and when his death finally approaches, he'll beg his Gods to give it speed, to bring an end to his suffering."

"Yes . . . my lord."

"His end will be our beginning. Angkor will flourish once again and will be celebrated far and wide. The time for vengeance will be over. Instead we will rise to the light of a new dawn. We'll rise, and we'll build something beautiful, Phirun, so beautiful that the brothers and sisters and children who have died before us will smile from wherever they may be."

Later in the afternoon, storm clouds rolled over Angkor—an unusual sight during the dry season. For a short time, the skies turned dark, opening up, cracking with lightning and thunder. Rain fell in thick sheets, turning dusty streets into muddy quagmires, overwhelming stale smells with fresh, wholesome scents. The rain was celebrated by all.

On the second level of Angkor Wat, there were four square basins, each about eight feet deep and forty feet across. These immense basins were filled with rainwater that rushed down from the temple's vast rooftops. The height of the water in the basins was controlled through an elaborate system of drains managed by the priests, who could reach the bottom of each basin by way of a single sandstone stairway.

Open-air hallways lined on both sides with columns separated the deep pools of water, so that they were barely visible from one another. The basins had been designed to accommodate religious ceremonies and represented the cosmic oceans. Priests used the water for rituals dedicated to purification and creation.

Standing next to one of the thick, square columns bordering a basin, Asal watched an old Khmer priest walk down the sandstone stairway. In his cupped hands he held two lotus flowers, which he set carefully on the water's surface. He chanted, bowed, and then walked away. Other priests also chanted in low voices, lighting candles that surrounded the basin. Asal wasn't sure what the candles symbolized. Perhaps stars. Perhaps life. Entranced, he opened his mind to what was transpiring and looked above to the imposing central tower of Angkor Wat. The ornately carved tower aroused something within him, fueling an unknown desire to take flight, to soar toward the heavens and leave his insignificant existence behind.

"They know how to build, don't they?"

Asal turned toward Indravarman, who leaned against a column that bore carvings of female dancers. "Yes, Lord King," he replied.

"What do you think of this place?"

"I think . . . that compared to the magnitude of this place, my life is but a drop of water in the ocean."

"And my life?"

Asal started to speak but paused, studying the king. Indravarman was dressed elaborately. As usual, he carried a shield and a sheathed sword. But he also wore a golden crown that was designed to mimic a series of connected flowers. A colossal pearl hung from his neck. And his fingers, toes, wrists, and ankles were decorated with golden hoops inset with precious jewels.

Asal wasn't certain why Indravarman seemed increasingly interested in such opulent displays. Maybe he saw the beauty around him and needed to stand brighter in its presence. Whatever the case, Asal was careful with his words when he finally replied. "I believe, Lord King, that your life is much more important than my own, though no life can equal an ocean."

Indravarman smiled. "You're a warrior and a politician, Asal. A dangerous combination."

"Perhaps, Lord King, but my sword will always carry much more weight than my words."

"As my sword, how would you strike Jayavar? We know that he hides to the north, rebuilding his army. Yet we cannot find him. How can we bring him to us?"

"Entice him, Lord King," Asal answered, knowing that Indravarman had placed a boy atop a temple and circulated a rumor that the child was Jayavar's. Though he thought the ploy lacked honor and grace, he found it clever.

"Do not answer me with ambiguity, Asal. Ambiguity is for those with no strength of heart."

"I—"

"I want specifics!"

Asal saw several priests glance over at Indravarman's outburst. They quickly returned their stares to the still water and the reflections upon it. "We have everything he covets, Lord King," Asal answered. "So we have much with which to entice him. But to defeat us on a field of battle, he must neutralize the advantage of our war elephants. He must scatter them or, better yet, capture them."

"Continue."

"I would place a large group of elephants, Lord King, outside the city walls. Let them seem unprotected, and let his spies tell him of their existence. He'll try to capture them, and when he does, we can spring a trap."

Indravarman grunted. "I'm told that you have grown fond of your woman," he said, turning to Asal, eyes meeting eyes. "If she's so desirable, maybe I should claim her for myself. There are plenty of others for you to choose from."

Asal felt his body stiffen but quickly recovered, willing himself to relax. The thought of Voisanne in Indravarman's hands provoked thoughts of betrayal for the first time in his life. If Indravarman came for her, Asal would kill him. He would free her, then die in shame, executed by whoever took the reins of leadership.

"Indeed, she pleases me, Lord King," he replied, meeting Indravarman's stare. "She's as meek as a kitten," he added, knowing that Indravarman savored a challenge. "It took me but two days to break her."

"And how long, Asal, would it take to break you?"

"Longer than two days, Lord King. Though I don't think any man knows until he is tested."

"Do you believe that we shall all be tested?"

"Yes, Lord King. Even you. And when that test comes, it shall not be in a time or place of your choosing."

Indravarman smiled. "That's why I like you, Asal. That's why I seek out your company. For not only do you give me sage advice, but you don't cower before my questions like so many of my men do."

"Cowering men tend to die first. They ask for mercy that never arrives."

"What do you ask for?"

"I only wish to serve you, Lord King."

"Then bring me Jayavar's head. Bring me his head, and whatever you covet shall be yours. Even your woman. But fail to find him, and I'll find another use for her."

"I will find him, Lord King."

"Go then."

Asal bowed, turned, and walked away from the basin. He passed through a vaulted doorway, heading toward the sun. Through windows carved into the sandstone walls he saw the city of Angkor far below. On his way up, the view had been inspiring. It had made him think of Voisanne and how she also provoked thoughts of hope and beauty within him.

Now everything looked tainted. Indravarman had stolen so much from the Khmers. Their statues and temples and people were now a part of his empire. And if Asal wasn't careful, Indravarman would take Voisanne. She'd be ripped away from him just when he was coming to know her, to feel as if a part of himself was absent when he wasn't with her.

The best way to protect Voisanne, Asal decided, was to do what Indravarman wanted.

Jayavar must be found.

Ten

The Passage Back

T he jungle was as thick and unruly as ever, inhabited by boisterous creatures both seen and unseen. Jayavar kicked his mount forward, aware of how Ajadevi pressed against him. Though dawn had just broken, the heat emanating from their bodies was significant, and perspiration rolled down his back. The humidity generated by the previous day's rain had changed the personality of the jungle, which now seemed to steam and sweat. Mosquitoes that had died off with the start of the dry season were reborn, tormenting both horses and humans. In many ways, the journey was intolerable, and yet the spirits of Jayavar and Ajadevi had been lifted. While saddened by the confirmation of the loss of their loved ones, each was filled with hope at the sight of the thirty-eight newly escaped Khmers who traveled with them. The children, women, and men had appeared not far outside Angkor, at first mistaking Jayavar's force for Chams and fleeing into the woods. But Ajadevi had heard their voices and called out in their language.

Seventeen warriors had accompanied the group, and after

being introduced to Jayavar and told of his plans, two of the men had headed back to Angkor with orders to quietly circulate the word of where the Khmer army was being remade. Only trusted men and women would be approached and recruited. Though most such Khmers had been killed or enslaved by Indravarman, pockets of survivors existed within the city, as well as in the surrounding areas. And if enough farmers, seamstresses, healers, fishermen, and warriors could be convinced to travel to Banteay Srei, then perhaps a suitable force could be assembled and trained.

Ajadevi knew that word would spread. The question was how long it would take for Indravarman's spies to learn of Banteay Srei. When they did, a mass of Chams would descend upon the temple. The Khmer scouts would then flee to where their army was really based in Kbal Spean, and the whereabouts of the Khmer force would, with luck, remain unknown. Any additional Khmers arriving at Banteay Srei would no doubt be cut down by Indravarman until word could be spread of a new rendezvous site.

Wishing that they could get Khmers to their secret base sooner rather than later, Ajadevi looked for signs in the jungle, hints that might give her a possible solution. As they often did, monkeys screeched within the treetops. Spiderwebs longer than the width of her reach spanned from branch to branch. Everything seemed greener since the rain, though she wondered if her imagination was playing tricks on her. Had a single rain made the jungle flourish? Could a single moment in time affect an entire world?

"Do you think, Jayavar, that the jungle is greener?" she asked, brushing a mosquito from his shoulder.

He eyed his surroundings. "Perhaps. It certainly feels different."

"Did you ever notice such an immediate change while in Angkor?"

"Not like this. But then, we've been living in the jungle. We're more conscious of its personalities."

Ajadevi nodded, inhaling deeply, aware of the scent of growth and decay. "It shall not take long for Indravarman to learn of Banteay Srei. And while it's not the ultimate destination for our people, once he sends his men there, ours will continue to arrive and will meet their deaths."

"I know. But what can be done?"

She thought again about the rain. It was a sign; she was sure of it. But she wasn't certain how to interpret its transformative effects. Turning around, she studied the Khmers behind them. Most were on horseback. On the nearest mount, two children rode in front of their father. The mother, she knew, was at the rear of their column, walking with some other women. The two children were arguing quietly, which made Ajadevi smile. Though everyone always wanted to hear children laughing, she didn't mind the dispute. It meant that the children still cared about trivial things, that their lives hadn't been ruined by the Cham invasion.

A puddle on the trail caught her attention. She studied the muddy water, which would likely be gone before the day was over. "When the Chams come to Banteay Srei," she said, "we must . . . send a signal. We must warn approaching Khmers of the danger."

"Any signal would need to be visible from far away."

She envisioned the temple, remembering how and why it was called the Citadel of Women. A small and elaborate structure, it was surrounded by a clearing and a circle of immense trees. On a hot day, the conditions at Banteay Srei could be almost unbearable. "It's dry there," she replied. "The trees are too far removed to provide shade."

"And?"

"We could create a pile of dry timber to the south of the temple. Dry in the middle, but with patches of moss on top. When the Chams approach, as they shall one day, our scouts would light the timber and retreat. The flames and smoke would delay the Chams and warn approaching Khmers that our position has been discovered."

"That would buy us time. And save lives."

"Yes. We'd bring change to the jungle—a moment of change—but for those who are saved, a lifetime of opportunities."

He reached back, took her hand within his, and kissed her fingers one by one. "How many lives have you saved, my love?"

"One can never save enough lives."

"Yes, but one can try. And you've done just that."

"What I do, I do for our people, and for you."

"And what may I do for you? What would make you happy?"

She briefly closed her eyes, willing herself to be strong. "Did you see . . . the young woman who joined us today?"

"Who?"

"Nuon. Her name is Nuon and we spoke earlier. Her father served yours. He was loyal, as is she. And she is of an age to marry, to bear fine sons. She is wise beyond her years and you should take her as a wife."

Jayavar turned away. "I needn't—"

"I know that you miss your other wives. More than you claim to. Perhaps Nuon would help you overcome that grief."

"My other wives were my companions. You are my love."

"Still, you need an heir, Jayavar. If you don't have one, then all of our struggles, all of our suffering, shall amount to nothing. Even if we're so blessed as to drive the Chams from Angkor, without a strong heir they will return one day. Is that what you wish? To once again have your land stolen and your people enslaved?"

He sighed, stroking her thigh with his thumb. "I wish we could have that child. We deserve that child."

She looked away from him. "As Buddhists, we're supposed to accept suffering. But in this area, I struggle to do so. I'm not strong enough. The pain . . . the want . . . are too great."

"Yet your struggle endears you to me even more."

"Why?"

"Because I know that you suffer not only because we can't produce an heir, but because we can't behold the beauty that we would create together."

She nodded, finally meeting his stare. "It's I who can't create such beauty. I who am deficient. I must have done something vile in a past life. I tainted my karma."

He kissed her hand once again. "You're wrong. Because you do create beauty—in the way that you look at the world, in the way that you look at me."

"But I—"

"Think of the unborn daughters and sons you just saved with your idea about the warning fire. With that thought, you created life; you created beauty. And that's why I shall love you forever. When I see the world, when I see its beauty, I'm reminded of the blessing that is you."

Voisanne secretly followed her younger sister, Chaya, through the sprawling outdoor marketplace, which was filled with hundreds of vendors and shoppers. Most every item for sale—whether onions, mangos, peppers, star fruit, lemons, bowls, fabrics, or knives—was displayed on a bamboo mat laid out on the ground. Chickens clucked in cages, while turtles and eels tried to escape from deep pots. People knelt before the mats, haggling over prices and quantities. The majority of shoppers were Khmers, though a few Chams were also present. One Cham, a high-ranking official by the look of his dress, walked with a leashed peacock in tow.

Located to the west of Angkor Wat in a field that had been cleared of everything except for towering trees, the marketplace smelled of saffron, cooking fires, flowers, and steamed rice. Voisanne had never spent much time there and was surprised to see how adept Chaya was at navigating the crowds and bargaining for various commodities. As she hid behind a tree trunk or a merchant's wares, Voisanne wondered what Chaya was thinking. Her little sister's shoulders seemed to slump, yet her gait was brisk.

Longing to embrace Chaya, but knowing that she must wait until the right moment, Voisanne rubbed her hands together. Her heart thumped with increasing vigor, and perspiration glistened on her skin. She glanced about, looking for suitable places to reveal herself, but seeing only chaotic crowds. To her right, a group of Khmer children kicked a leather bag in the air, keeping it aloft with their feet, knees, and heads. Farther to the west, beyond the market, a few dozen men were gathered around a pen to watch a pair of boars fight. Even from such a distance, Voisanne could hear the men cheering on the creatures and exchanging bets. In this way Khmers and Chams were alike—both groups seemed to enjoy betting on battles between animals of similar size and strength.

Chaya placed a melon inside her bag and headed back toward Angkor Wat, passing a burned-out structure that had been destroyed in the invasion. She followed the footsteps of an old blind woman who used two poles to make her way. Chaya was about to pass the woman when a puppy ran into the market, chasing a squirrel. The puppy darted about, yapping, and disappeared into an alley bordered by the merchants' carts and wagons. Increasing her pace, Chaya followed the puppy, calling out to it. She passed piles of bamboo baskets, a man asleep on a hammock, and a woman combing a girl's hair.

The puppy's yelps continued, and Chaya hurried on, turning to her right and walking into an irrigation ditch that was used to control floodwaters. The ditch, now dry, was almost as deep as Chaya was tall. She followed it until she arrived at a brick tunnel that led under a street. Barking emerged from the tunnel. Chaya stooped low and stepped forward.

At that moment Voisanne said her sister's name.

Chaya paused and turned around slowly, as if expecting to be punished. She looked up and her eyes met Voisanne's. The bag of produce fell to the ground. Chaya started to speak and then stopped, rushing ahead and leaping up even as Voisanne dropped to her knees. They collided, Voisanne falling backward and laughing for the first time since the Chams had attacked, joy overwhelming her.

The sisters embraced. Words tumbled from each, recent histories revealed, questions asked and answered. Chaya seemed older and stronger minded than when Voisanne had last seen her, and yet Voisanne's favorite parts of her personality emerged the longer they spoke—her sass and cheerfulness, her energy and humor. It seemed that despite being a slave to a Cham general, Chaya had endured her fate and captivity better than Voisanne could have dared to hope.

"Are you mistreated?" Voisanne asked while on her knees, stroking the back of Chaya's neck.

"He's not a bad man," Chaya answered. "His wife is as vile as a viper, but I think he pities me."

"He does?"

"Oh, you should see how he looks after me, Voisanne. He makes sure that I have enough to eat, and he even bought me a mosquito net to sleep under."

An image leapt into Voisanne's mind, and her hand stilled against Chaya's skin. "He hasn't . . . touched you, has he?"

"No."

"Are you sure?"

"He's kind, Voisanne. In some ways he reminds me of Father. I told him that a few days ago, and I think it made him happy."

Voisanne hugged Chaya again, squeezing her tight. "How lucky we both are. We were given to good Chams, to men who could have hurt us but chose not to."

"But I went to him. I wasn't given to him."

"What do you mean?"

"I escaped from the Chams who captured us on your wedding day, and I ran straight back home. When the general came I told him that it was my house, that I still wanted to live there even if my family was gone. I told him that I'd wash his clothes and cook his food, that whatever he needed done I would do. As long as I got to stay."

"And he agreed?"

"Of course he did. His wife arrived a week later. She loathes me and makes my life difficult, but I get my revenge on her. Every day I get my revenge."

"How?"

"I put spiders in her bed, a scorpion in with her jewels. She hates it here, and I'm the reason why."

Voisanne smiled. "I'm so glad you seem to be doing well."

"Now I am. At first I cried for many days and nights. Sometimes I still do. But it feels good to get my revenge, to hear her scream. And I think he likes it when I torture her. Sometimes he gives me a little smile, and I know what he's thinking."

Leaning forward, Voisanne kissed Chaya on the cheek. "We're going to escape, you and me. But not today."

"Why not?"

"Because we have nowhere to go. And it sounds like you're safe for now. Better to plan ahead to ensure that we aren't captured. Because if we were, we could end up in worse situations."

Chaya straightened. "Then I'll really get her. Tonight when she's asleep, I'll drop a—"

"I've missed your jokes," Voisanne said, helping Chaya stand up. "How they used to make me laugh."

"You'll hear them again when we're in the jungle. Probably more than you care to."

Voisanne handed Chaya her bag. "I want to stay with you, but I must go. So return home. And each day, after the market, walk through this alley. One day I shall await you, and on that day, we'll leave together."

Chaya nodded, squeezing Voisanne's hand. "Do you think . . . that Mother and Father can see us?" she asked. "Do they know we've found each other?"

"Yes, I believe they do."

"I hope so. That would make them happy. Wherever they are, I want them to be happy."

Indravarman had shut down the road leading to and from the city. Under the shade of the towering trees, he stood alongside his highest-ranking officers. The Chams were gathered in a circle around the spot where Jayavar and Ajadevi had begged and observed. A large and smooth boulder was the center of their attention. Khmers had been touching it all morning, flocking toward it as if one of their Gods were standing upon it and granting wishes. The boulder was nondescript, from a distance no different from any other, but upon closer inspection anyone could see that the words inscribed upon its smooth face could inspire a kingdom:

Angkor shall be ours again.

—*King Jayavar*

Rage flooded through Indravarman as he studied the boulder, believing that it was no hoax, that Jayavar had stood unmolested in this same spot. The Khmer had been here. He had avoided the patrols, slipped past the defensive perimeter, and spoken to his people. He'd inspired them, given them hope. Surely word of his return was already spreading throughout Angkor, arousing a previously vanquished people.

Indravarman glanced up and down the deserted road. In the distance, lines of Cham warriors kept Khmers at bay. Clouds of dust hung about thousands of restless feet. His fury boiling over, Indravarman drew his sword, stepped to the boulder, and swung his blade at Jayavar's words. Steel met stone in a bone-jarring jolt and the sword shattered. Still holding the hilt, which was connected to half of the blade, Indravarman spun away from the boulder. His chest heaving, he eyed his officers one by one.

"I'd have you all on your hands and knees, pushing this abomination into the moat," he said, glaring at them. "But the Khmers would find that amusing. So let a score of those onlookers do it. And when they're finished, kill them and add their bodies to the water!"

No one made a reply. A man standing next to Asal glanced away, as if afraid of Indravarman. What remained of the king's sword plunged forward into the officer's belly. His eyes widened; he clutched at the hilt and then toppled backward and writhed upon the ground.

"I'll have no cowards in my army!" Indravarman shouted. "You hear me? Jayavar is no coward. He came here, past all our eyes, and mocked us! He gave hope to his people when they should have none."

One of Indravarman's longest-serving generals cleared his throat. "Then kill them, Lord King. Kill them all."

"We need the Khmers! How will we feed our army if the Khmers do not harvest their crops? How will we forge new weapons without their blacksmiths? Every day more of our people come, but for now we're like children who haven't been weaned from their mothers' milk."

"Then kill only their young men, Lord King. Anyone who might hold a spear against us."

Indravarman dropped his ruined sword. "Is that the only counsel I am given? Would it not be better to force these men to labor for us? To hold them accountable for the well-being of their families?" He cursed, then wiped the sweat from his eyes. "Am I surrounded by nothing more than a circle of fools?"

"Kill Jayavar, Lord King, and the stone will not matter," Asal said. "Keep it. Mount his head on it, and all opposition to you will vanish."

"How do I kill a man who won't face me?"

"He must have come here, Lord King, to speak to someone, to convey a message. Discover who this someone is, and you shall discover Jayavar's whereabouts. A secret so large surely cannot be kept."

"And then we ride forth and attack him?"

"We do. We will."

Indravarman turned to study the boulder. Part of Jayavar's name was chipped from where the sword had struck it. Perhaps Asal was right. Perhaps it was better to embrace the truth than to deny it. "The stone shall stay," he said. "But make a proclamation that Jayavar's head will someday adorn it and that whoever brings his head to me will be given its weight in gold."

Several of the officers murmured in agreement. Indravarman looked from man to man, aware of their strengths and weaknesses. Most of the officers were loyal, bright, and brave. Despite his words to the contrary, it was a formidable group. Yet not a single man measured up to Asal, neither on a field of battle nor in a debate of strategy.

Indravarman took the nearby general's sword, then nodded to Asal. "Walk with me."

They headed north, proceeding parallel to Angkor's moat. Since the road had been secured, the area was quiet and safe. Sunlight filtered through the thick canopy above, creating glowing rays that illuminated dust particles. A rooster pecked at the earth, digging for an unseen insect. To their left, the towers of Angkor Wat soared like the peaks of a distant mountain range.

"Do you not fear me?" Indravarman asked, wondering if he should draw his blade and kill Asal right now, before the man's power endangered his own.

Asal had never feared death. His mother had said that one day they would be reunited, and since then he had never run from danger. Yet now, as he thought about his life, about how Voisanne was becoming a part of it, he wanted to see where this path might take him. He could imagine happiness, and so, for the first time in many years, he was afraid of what Indravarman could do to him, could take from him. And yet to acknowledge as much would be a mistake.

He shook his head. "If I please you, Lord King, I see no reason to fear you. And I will please you."

"How?"

"By finding Jayavar. Not by searching the jungle, but by searching Angkor. Because there are people here who know where he is."

"Po Rame is already looking for these same people."

Asal nodded. "Then Po Rame and I are bound to meet."

"Your old grudge . . . will it come to light?"

"Yes, Lord King."

"What if I command you to bury it?"

"Then I shall. But he'll never do the same. He'll come for me one day, and once we meet, the world will have one less assassin."

Indravarman nodded. Though he wanted to pit them against each other, to see who would fall, they were both of value to him for the time being. Po Rame was deadlier but also, Indravarman believed, more predictable. He had no decency, no attachments. Asal, alternatively, was perhaps too principled. And that made him dangerous.

"You're to leave him be," Indravarman said.

Asal agreed, his pace faltering only slightly.

"I shall tell him to do the same," Indravarman added, though his words were only half-truths, for once Jayavar was found, Asal would have to die.

"Yes, Lord King."

"We're all Chams, Asal. We must work together to defeat our common foe. Bring me Jayavar's head and you shall save your own."

Later, after the sun had slid below the horizon and the world went dark, Asal and Voisanne sat on a rattan mat, eating dinner. Asal had grown tired of dining as a king would, with golden utensils and much pomp and circumstance. He'd asked that their meal be prepared in the way that his mother would have made it—with a few ingredients and a simple presentation.

Holding special stout leaves to scoop up their food, Asal and Voisanne ate fried catfish covered in a thick sauce made from ginger, sugar, garlic, and water. Both ate using their right hands and often paused to wash their fingers in a bowl of water. Rather than sip through bamboo tubes like most high-ranking members of society, they drank palm wine from wooden cups.

As Asal ate, he glanced occasionally at Voisanne. Since she had learned of her sister's well-being, her features had become even more radiant. Her eyes appeared fuller and her smile was more enchanting. She had resumed using perfume made from jasmine flowers, as well as wearing brightly colored skirt cloths. Khmer jewelry had been made available to certain women, and several gold hoops encircled her ankles. A silver bracelet inset with circular pieces of jade adorned her right wrist.

Asal had asked her to dine with him because he had good news to share. But he wanted her to eat first, as she was thinner than most women her age and he worried that if dysentery was to strike her down, as it did so many Khmers and Chams, she wouldn't have the strength to survive.

While musicians plucked at harps, shook bells, and blew on conchs from somewhere distant, Asal sipped his wine. He watched Voisanne finish her fish and then wash her fingers. She moved with the grace of a court dancer. Everything about her seemed elegant, and he wondered how she must see him—with his bulk and muscles and scars. He must appear as a brute, as out of place beside her as an elephant next to an orchid.

"I've been thinking, my lady, about your sister," he whispered at last, setting down his wine cup.

She looked up.

"I want to see you reunited. You both deserve that. And I think I know how to bring you together."

"How?"

The music stopped. Silence seeped into the room as candles flickered in the corner. Asal shifted on the mat into a kneeling position, drawing closer to her. "At first . . . I thought that I'd steal Chaya away. But I've come to know her master, and he's an honorable man. So there is no need to steal what can be bought."

Voisanne leaned toward Asal. "You could buy her?"

"Why not? I think that honesty would be best in this circumstance. I could tell him that you're my . . . companion and that it would please you to be reunited with your sister. If I ask him for a favor, I think he will grant it."

Reaching forward, Voisanne took his hands in hers. "And she would live with me?"

"No, my lady. Because anyone who lives in that house is too close to Indravarman. We should keep her far from him. As my slave, she'd take care of my horse. She'd live with other slaves. But you could see her often, and I would be good to her. She would be free in all but her title."

"When, Asal? When might you do this?"

He smiled. "What about tomorrow?"

Her hands tightened around his and she embraced him, her breasts pressing against his chest. She looked up, then kissed him, her lips warm and full against his. "You give me . . . life," she whispered, kissing him again. "I thought mine was gone . . . yet you gave it back to me."

"I want . . ."

"Tell me what you want."

"You, my lady. I want you."

"Then you may have me."

"But not like this."

She pulled ever so slightly away from him. "What do you mean?"

He looked down at her, saw the richness of her eyes, smelled a trace of her perfume. "When I'm with you, I feel . . . as I did when I was a child," he replied.

"How so?"

"Because, my lady, the world with you in it . . . seems new. And beautiful." He traced the contours of her upper lip with the tip of his forefinger.

"So why do you hesitate?"

"Because I want you to want me, not to feel indebted to me. Now you're indebted to me because of Chaya. And so you come to me. You offer yourself to me. You offer a gift that I've dreamed of, longed for. Yet I want to receive that gift only when you're a free woman, when you're indebted to no one."

She kissed his fingers. "You're a gift too, Asal. After a long drought I feel that the Gods favor me with blessings of rain. They brought you to me and for that I'm so very grateful."

"Thank you, my lady."

They continued to talk as the candles burned low, sharing their pasts, their hopes for the future. Finally, when the sun's approach had hidden the stars, he helped her to stand. He walked with her through the sleeping palace, through the still city, toward her quarters. Near the end of their journey, as they passed a dark pond full of lotus flowers, he took her hand. Warmth spread between them, causing them to linger near an ancient garden, to smile in the darkness.

They reached her quarters. Though he didn't want to leave her or these new, wondrous feelings she inspired, he said farewell, bowed, and turned.

His pace was slow as he walked away.

He looked for her footprints on the path they had followed.

Part Two

Part Two

Eleven

Rebirth

Kbal Spean, Early Dry Season, 1177

everal days of difficult travel to the north of Angkor Wat, the land gradually began to undulate, like the surface of a sea. Valleys, hills, and outcroppings of rock dominated the area. A series of streams and lakes supported a variety of trees, flowers, animals, and fish. Even in the dry season, the landscape was lush.

Nowhere was this abundance of resources more evident than at Kbal Spean. Set deep in the jungle, Kbal Spean was a religious site created by Hindu priests. A small river ran through the area, and it was there that the priests had left their mark. Hundreds of ancient carvings could be seen in the bedrock beneath and beside the river. In places the clear water ran over images of Shiva, Vishnu, and Brahma; over lotus flowers, cows, crocodiles, and Sanskrit writings. These had been carved decades earlier by priests when the river was almost dry. The boulders that bordered the water were also covered in carvings, as were the walls of small caves and the faces of stone overhangs. The sacred images were still well defined, as if they had been recently created.

Having left Angkor more than a month earlier, Ajadevi and Jayavar sat beneath a waterfall, which must have roared in the wet season but was now just a steady, soothing cascade. The pool beneath the waterfall was the length and width of several spears. Immense trees drowned out most of the sun, though patches of light illuminated the ground like large, glowing leaves. A head-high anthill perched on one side of the pool. Other spaces were filled with flowers, bushes, stalks of bamboo, and thick vines that dropped from the canopy. The air was moist and full of rich scents.

A short walk downriver sprawled the Khmer encampment, which now boasted nearly five thousand inhabitants. Since Ajadevi and Jayavar had returned from Angkor, groups of Khmers had been appearing on a daily basis at Banteay Srei. These groups were carefully screened by Khmer officers and, once approved, led to the secret base at Kbal Spean. Though most of those who undertook the long trip were warriors who had escaped the Cham attack, ordinary citizens—farmers, priests, weavers, cooks, and children—had also made the journey. A contingent of seven hundred Siamese mercenaries was also present, with more expected any day. Though the Khmers and Siamese were old enemies, promises of gold had served to strengthen the unlikely alliance. Jayavar had convinced the Siamese leaders that victory was possible, and with victory would come great riches.

A pink butterfly fluttered above the pool, prompting Ajadevi to rise from a boulder and step forward. The water was cool against her feet. She saw that scores of circular, patterned balls called lingas had been carved into the bedrock of the river and she wondered how the priests had accomplished such an extraordinary feat. The lingas, she knew, were phallic in nature and represented the essence of Shiva. Careful not to step on a linga, she moved into deeper water and sat down, then splashed herself, washing away sweat and grime.

"How long will we wait to attack the Chams?" she asked her husband, not eager for the fight but aware that Jayavar was.

He waded into the water and lowered himself beside her. About to respond, Jayavar paused when a sentry posted in a nearby treetop called out that a contingent of new arrivals was approaching, carrying the right combination of banners. Once this visual code was verified, shouts were exchanged, and the newcomers were given instructions.

"Each day I expect to hear that the Chams have found Banteay Srei and are marching on us," Jayavar replied. "Our strength grows with every sunrise but so does the threat of discovery."

"We've taken precautions. It would be hard for them to surprise us."

"Yes, though they did so once before and it cost us our empire."

She nodded, studying the stone lingas, wondering why the female pedestal, the yoni, wasn't present. "The Siamese elephants have been a blessing. And the horses."

"Indeed. Indravarman will not expect any of us to be mounted."

How long would it take to carve a linga? Ajadevi asked herself, marveling at the patience necessary for such a task. A month? She imagined a priest carving a linga in the middle of the dry season and then watching as the river rose higher, submerging his work speck by speck. Did the rise and fall of the linga symbolize the wheel of rebirth?

Though Ajadevi venerated Buddha and his many teachings, she admired Hindu priests and what they could create. Angkor Wat was the culmination of infinite dreams and aspirations. And so was this small, almost unknown river with its ever-changing images of Shiva and Vishnu.

"We must attack him in a place of our choosing," Jayavar

said, rubbing his foot. "He shall outnumber us, and somehow we must counter that advantage."

"What do your officers say?"

"That we should raid the Cham homeland and draw him out of Angkor."

Ajadevi considered the strategy, still looking at the lingas. "To do that would make us no better than him. And would it not greatly prolong the conflict?"

"It would."

"Better to fight him near Angkor. Fight him there and end this struggle."

He sighed, pausing to stack stones. "If we march toward Angkor, will you do something for me?"

Her gaze swung from the stones to his face, and she eyed him with suspicion. "What?"

"Stay here. Now that Nuon may be with child, she will require your counsel. And if a son is born, he shall one day need guidance."

Ajadevi bit the inside of her lip, wondering how much Nuon pleased him. The woman was young, beautiful, and seemed eager to laugh. In another time and place, Ajadevi would have considered her a rival, and treated her as such. But here in the jungle with the empire at stake, Nuon and her child must be nurtured and cherished.

"I shall train her each and every day," Ajadevi replied. "But then I shall ride with you."

"Why? Why must you ride with me when you know the outcome is likely to go against us?"

"Because I belong with you. And if you're to die, then I wish to die beside you."

He shook his head. "You pretend otherwise, but you're a stubborn woman."

"Perhaps."

"Do your signs tell you as much? That we should be together?"

"My heart tells me. Do I need more than that?"

"If Indravarman captures you, he will—"

"Claim me for himself?"

"Yes."

"Then he would die. One night he'd awaken choking on his own blood. And then wherever you were, into whomever you'd been reborn, I would find you."

"You would find me. I know you would."

She turned to him, touching a scar on his knee. "Our love gives us solace, which gives us strength. And so we must share that same faith with everyone. We must inspire them before they go to war. Better yet, we must bind Khmers and Siamese together."

"I'm trying. I conduct war councils and make efforts to encourage people in camp. I spend time with the Siamese and with our countrymen. But how can I achieve more?"

A monkey screeched from somewhere above. Ajadevi thought about the simple ceremony they had recently conducted to crown Jayavar their king. She had advised staging a more extravagant event, but he'd refused, saying that it would have been wrong to bask in personal glory while so many of their people were suffering.

"I think we should celebrate the Festival of Floats," she finally replied. "Could a more perfect place for it exist?"

Jayavar smiled. The Festival of Floats was held to honor nature, to ask forgiveness for polluting the earth and water. Ever since he was a child, it had been one of his favorite celebrations. "Yes," he replied, smiling. "That will give the children something to do. As we prepare for battle, they can make the floats."

Ajadevi stroked his old scar. "You must make a float too, Jaya-

var. Our kings have always made floats and you must be no different."

"I will. Though sometimes I don't see myself as a king. Perhaps fate does, but why should fate be so omnipotent? Why
should I have this power when others are born as slaves?"

Her fingers paused. "But through rebirths, slaves can become
kings. So you should see yourself as others do. I see a man who
has celebrated all of life's festivals with me, who has celebrated
the festival that is life. And whatever the Chams have taken from
me in the past, whatever they may take in the future, they cannot
steal the imprint of you from me. Just like the river cannot re-
move these carvings from itself, no one can pull you away from
me, or me away from you. That is our destiny. Do not question it,
Jayavar, but embrace it. You are our king. Not because of fate, but
because your past lives and deeds have made you so."

Boran had never been so far north of Angkor. He walked ahead
of Soriya, Prak, and Vibol, leading them through the jungle. Two
days earlier they had left their boat, hiding it amid clumps of
ferns and then setting out on foot, each loaded down with heavy
slings full of supplies. Boran carried the Cham axe, which they
had retrieved after saving Vibol. He eyed it from time to time but
did not want to wield the weapon.

As Boran made his way along a game trail, he thought about
Vibol, wishing that he would laugh as he once had. The Chams
had injured his spirit more than his body; the bruises and cuts
had healed, yet his mind remained in a dark and distant place,
inaccessible to those who loved him. Boran didn't know if his son
was afraid, humiliated, or angry at himself. Perhaps all three
emotions swirled together. Vibol had so desperately wanted to be
a man, but his first foray into manhood had ended in disaster.

Unsure what to say to his son, or how to make him laugh as he once had, Boran felt helpless and frustrated.

For the past several weeks Boran had sold fish to Chams while Soriya, Vibol, and Prak had stayed behind. Boran had studied the Cham camp and gotten to know the officers in charge of gathering supplies. His prices were cheap, and the Chams had come to welcome the arrival of the Khmer, hurrying out onto the long dock to greet him. And while Boran threw fish after fish to his enemies, he had counted the ships, men, horses, and elephants. He had also made note of defensive positions, arriving troops, and the well-being of the men. Each morning Prak asked for more details, and each evening Boran returned with information. While their father traded, Prak and Vibol caught fish and their mother mended nets.

Once Boran and his family had heard about Khmers gathering in the north, they faced a difficult decision. They could stay and further befriend and spy on the Chams, or they could try to rejoin their countrymen. In the end Soriya had come to Boran and whispered that it would be best for Vibol if they left the Great Lake and went far from the place of his capture and beating. Though Boran knew that if they left the lake they could never return as fishermen and could not directly poison the Chams, he agreed with his wife. Near the water, hiding from the men who had nearly killed him, Vibol had become a shadow of his former self. He would not emerge from this shadow until something in his life was different. Soriya believed that the right young woman or the sight of his people might heal him. But something must change.

Boran had spent years in the jungle, but he didn't know these thick woods. Following nothing more than rumors and his instincts, he headed due north, eager to rendezvous with his king's forces. Sometimes the family traveled with other Khmers, but often these groups split apart so as to more easily avoid Cham patrols. The days were long and the nights longer. The farther they got from their home, the more fear gnawed at them, turning their stomachs sour, making them imagine dangers when the jungle was quiet.

Though Boran had usually considered himself to be their family's leader, the deeper they moved into the jungle, the more he turned to his wife and sons. Soriya understood Vibol better than anyone, and Prak was adept at planning. Aware that his family was being tested as it never had been, and that they were all succeeding, Boran's pride in his loved ones swelled to new dimensions.

Now, as he stepped over a fallen log, he let Soriya and Prak pass him. Vibol's eyes were downcast, as usual. Boran reached out and held Vibol's arm just long enough for Soriya and Prak to take several steps ahead. Sighing, Boran rubbed his sore neck, then offered the Cham axe to Vibol. "Would you carry it, my son? My body aches."

Vibol started to shake his head but then stopped himself and reached for the weapon. He set its shaft on his shoulder. "This won't frighten the Chams, you know," he said quietly, walking ahead.

"I know."

"Then why do we carry it?"

"Because it's a good weapon, and you can give it to one of our warriors."

Vibol made no reply, skirting an immense anthill that rose from the middle of the trail.

Boran didn't see any ants and wondered if it was occupied. Sometimes a dormant anthill could survive for many seasons. "If we don't save Angkor," he said, "its buildings will be as quiet as that anthill. Our people will disappear."

"We were never a part of Angkor, Father. Angkor is for the rich."

"But we swam in Angkor's baths; we walked its streets. Of course we were a part of it."

"We were guests. It wasn't our home."

"You always wanted to go there. After every catch, you wanted to visit."

"I was a fool. I am a fool."

Boran reached out to Vibol, who moved away from his outstretched hand. "Why do you say what isn't true?"

Vibol shook his head. "I'm not going to talk about it."

Boran followed his son, hating to see him so beaten down, wishing that his faith could be restored. Somehow, he must be made to realize that everyone made mistakes, that misery was a common experience. "Because I've wanted to protect you," Boran said, keeping his voice low, "I've never spoken of my failures. My biggest failures, that is. But like you, I have them. Everyone does."

"What failures?"

Boran walked onward, his mind drifting back to a distant time and place. "When I was young . . . I had a little brother."

"No, you didn't. Just sisters."

"That's what I told you, but it isn't true. I had a baby brother. One day I was alone with him on the shore of the Great Lake. The wind was strong, and I was making a fishing spear. My thoughts . . . were occupied elsewhere . . . and when I finally looked up . . . he was in the water. He was gone."

"Where did he go?"

Boran breathed deeply, trying to steady his voice. "I was responsible for him. And yet . . . I failed him. He drowned that day. He drowned because of me. And for a long, long time, I didn't want to go back to the water, didn't want to pray to Gods who had abandoned me. But then, when you and Prak were born, it felt right to go back. I felt that my brother had returned within you both, and I wanted to show him the lake, because he'd always enjoyed it."

"You did?"

"And I'm so glad that I returned to the water. When I'm on it, when I see you smiling on it, I know that my brother is also smiling. He's watching us pull in all those beautiful fish and he's grinning from dawn to dusk."

Vibol slowed down. "I can't imagine . . . losing Prak."

"I know. And that's why I tried to hold you back, to protect you. I couldn't endure the thought of letting another loved one die."

Between two tree branches, a large gold and black butterfly struggled to free itself from a spider's web. Vibol brought his gaze back to his father. "Why didn't you tell me earlier about your brother?"

"Because I thought you were too young to hear about his death. Now I know that you're old enough, brave enough. You walked straight into the camp of our enemy, and even though you were caught, you were brave, and I couldn't be more proud of you."

"You are? You truly are?"

"Yes, my son," Boran replied, putting his hand on Vibol's shoulder, squeezing it tightly. "Because it seems to me that bravery doesn't lie in the outcome but in the doing. And your actions . . . they told me . . . they tell me that my boy has become a man."

Vibol tried not to smile, but Boran saw the corners of his lips rise.

*   *   *

At the height of the dry season, when rain and cool breezes were distant memories, crowds of Khmers flocked to Angkor's community bathing areas. The vast moat teemed with tens of thousands of people throughout the day. Children chased frogs in the shallows. Men lounged in the deeper waters. Women beat clothes against rocks, scrubbed themselves, and spoke in small groups. Chams had started to visit the moat as well, and warriors swam from side to side, racing one another as their officers shouted encouragement.

Standing shoulder deep in the water, Thida, Voisanne, and Chaya huddled together toward the middle of the moat. Nearby, a koi, presumably a gift to a Khmer official from a Chinese diplomat or trader, nibbled around the broad leaves of a lotus flower. As long as Thida's arm, the koi was gold and white. The creature moved with the grace and dignity of a more revered species, at ease in the water in the same way that an eagle commands the sky.

Thida watched as Chaya climbed on Voisanne's back, laughing at her older sister. Three weeks earlier, Voisanne had told Thida about Chaya, and Thida had grown used to the sight of the siblings frolicking together. A part of Thida enjoyed watching Voisanne and Chaya playing. Another part of her was jealous of their relationship. It wasn't fair that Voisanne had Chaya and Asal in her life, two people she cared about.

Most of Thida's nights were spent with Indravarman. And though he had never beaten her, she remained terrified of him. His inability to locate Jayavar was a constant source of rage, which could boil to the surface in a heartbeat. Thida tried to keep him happy by misleading him, either through her words or her actions. She applauded his wisdom, whispered endearments, and touched him as if he were the father of her children. Thankfully, she never had become pregnant. At least the Gods had been kind to her in that regard.

Indravarman had called for her earlier that day, which surprised her as he was almost always out in the field. She had gone to him, expecting the worst, and was startled to be greeted by a smile. He told her that his spies had discovered groups of Khmers to the north, near an ancient temple. The Khmers seemed to use the temple as a base. Indravarman's plan was to lead a large contingent of his best warriors into the jungle. The warriors would be accompanied by cooks, blacksmiths, healers, priests, and women. Thida was expected to ride with them. Most Cham officers were taking their wives or concubines. Asal hadn't asked Voisanne to join him, but, desperate to have her friend beside her, Thida had begged her to go. Voisanne was reluctant to leave her sister, though in the end she had agreed. The force would depart at dawn.

Thida hadn't spent much time in the jungle and was worried about insects, snakes, scorpions, and predators. Even though she would be surrounded by warriors, the thought of sleeping in the open left her unsettled. She was also afraid that the Chams would find the Khmers and kill them in the manner that Indravarman had described to her—by sticking prisoners with hot spear points until the air reeked with the scent of burned flesh.

If Thida was forced to leave without Voisanne, she wasn't certain she could face the jungle. But the prospect of having Voisanne beside her slowed the throbbing of her heart, the rasping of her lungs. Voisanne would protect her, would keep her fears at bay.

After Chaya leapt off Voisanne's back and headed toward the koi, Thida reached for her friend's hand. "You're sure that it's all right to leave Chaya behind?"

"She's safe here and can attend to her duties. One of Asal's men will look after her. I've met him twice and trust him."

"How can you trust a Cham?"

Grinning, Voisanne turned away from one of Chaya's splashes. "Because I trust Asal, and if he vouches for someone, then that's good enough for me. Besides, I think it's better to have Chaya here than out in the jungle. The Chams know that she's his slave. None would dare harm her. And she has nothing to fear from Khmers."

Thida nodded, squeezing Voisanne's hand. "Thank you . . . for agreeing to come with me. I've never been deep in the jungle."

"It's beautiful."

"Nothing is beautiful . . . with Indravarman beside me."

"But he won't be beside you, Thida. He'll be out looking for Khmers. I'll be beside you and there's nothing that we need fear."

Thida looked away. "Nothing? You say that because you haven't heard his boasts about the coming battle. You haven't heard him say how he'll capture and torture our people."

Voisanne called out to Chaya, telling her not to swim too far away. She then turned her attention back to Thida. "What does he say?"

"You don't want to know."

"Tell me."

Thida did as Voisanne asked, describing in detail Indravarman's threats and promises. "He'll kill them all," Thida added. "Even the women and children. Because they have all defied him."

Voisanne looked toward a group of children playing in the shallows. Their laughter carried over the water. "Then we'll have to warn our countrymen," she whispered. "I don't know how, but there must be a way."

"If Indravarman learns that we've—"

"Would you have us do nothing, Thida? When we could save them?"

Thida started to speak but stopped, unsure how to answer. She didn't want to see her people tortured, but the thought of trying to outsmart Indravarman terrified her. "He has so many spies," she said. "They tell him everything, and if we make a mistake he'll skin us like animals. I've seen what he does to his enemies, and he'd do even worse to us."

Voisanne nodded. "Somehow I'll warn our countrymen. You needn't worry about it. Pretend that I said nothing."

"Maybe it's better . . . if I don't know. That way Indravarman won't see through me."

"Fine. That's just fine, Thida."

"Thank you. You're such a good friend. I really don't deserve you."

"You deserve to be happy. We all do. And I think that someday . . . we all will be. I don't know much about the world, about war and kings. But I think that we'll be happy again."

Thida squeezed her friend's hand again before releasing it. "Go play with your sister. She's calling for you. I just want to stand here and watch you. Watching you two together makes everything feel normal."

"I'll be back."

Smiling, Thida gazed at Voisanne as she swam into the deeper water. The sisters met, splashed each other, and for a moment Thida forgot about Indravarman.

Then a war elephant trumpeted and Thida's thoughts darkened. What Voisanne didn't understand, what she couldn't fathom, was that no one ever really tricked Indravarman. He let them think that they had. He let Thida think that she had. But in the end, he understood everything. There was a reason why he was the master of two kingdoms, why men feared him and died for him.

Indravarman would find the Khmers. And he would find whoever betrayed him.

*   *   *

Within the Echo Chamber at Angkor Wat, the evening light was subdued, mostly shielded by the room's thick walls. Unlike the vast majority of the temple, the Echo Chamber was unadorned with carvings. Simple sandstone blocks had been fitted together and formed a small, rectangular room with a ceiling twenty feet high. Doorways stood at the east and west sides of the room, providing glimpses of the surrounding temple.

Voisanne remembered when her father had taken her to the Echo Chamber and how he had explained its secrets. She smiled at the vision of him holding her, showing her just what to do. He had been a patient man, and it was no surprise to her that his favorite place in all of Angkor was this one.

Grateful that she could now smile at such memories instead of weep over them, Voisanne took Asal's hand. In the month that had passed since he had freed Chaya, Voisanne had seen him every few days. His duties often carried him outside the city as more and more skirmishes with Khmer forces occurred. Yet when he returned, he always sent for her, and she came quickly to dress his wounds and tell him about her day.

Voisanne and Asal usually met in his room, but on the eve of their departure from Angkor alongside Indravarman's army, she yearned to bring him somewhere special to her, somewhere that had been a part of her former life. She wouldn't have wanted to come to the Echo Chamber alone, but with him at her side, she felt at ease. Of course, she still mourned the loss of her loved ones. Yet that loss no longer overwhelmed her. She had Chaya. She had Asal. And she had hope.

"What do you think?" she whispered, squeezing Asal's hand and looking up to his face.

He studied the chamber. "The rest of Angkor Wat is so beautiful, so extraordinary. What's so special about these unadorned stones?"

"This is the place where wishes come true. Where the Gods can hear you. And I think they should hear us before we leave their city."

"How do wishes come true here?"

"Stand with your back pressed against the stone. Then strike your chest with your fist seven times and make your wish."

Asal stepped back against the sandstone blocks. They were cool against his skin. He looked up at the high walls, which tapered slightly toward the center. His fist struck his chest again and again, producing a sound akin to a large bell ringing in the distance. The sound reverberated, traveling upward, encompassing them with its purity. Entranced by the noise, Asal forgot all about his wish. "It's magic," he whispered when the sound had finally faded.

"My father used to take me here," she replied. "We would listen and wish."

"How does it work?"

She shrugged. "How does the sun work? Or the stars?"

"And other Khmers? They come here to make wishes?"

"Every day. To wish. To pray. It's here where we think the Gods can most easily hear us."

"Then let them hear you, my lady."

She smiled and then settled against the stonework, keeping her spine straight and shoulders back. After closing her eyes, she struck her chest seven times and listened to the sound of faraway bells. The sound traveled within her, lifting her up, carrying her into another time and place. She wished for peace. Not revenge or bloodshed, but simply peace. If the Chams would leave Angkor, life could be beautiful again.

The Echo Chamber quieted.

Asal shook his head in apparent wonder. "What if, my lady, we wish for something together? Will the Gods be even more likely to hear us?"

"Yes. I think so."

"Then let's wish for the joy of our loved ones, that they've been reborn into better lives."

Cham and Khmer beat their chests, listened, wished, and smiled.

"I could stand here all night with you, talking to the Gods," Voisanne said, pleased that Asal was as enchanted as she was.

"You think they listen to us? That they care about us?" he asked.

"Sometimes. But right now . . . I don't draw strength from them . . . but from you."

"You're the strong one, my lady, the noble one."

She squeezed his hand. "When you call me that, I feel warm inside. I smile inside."

"My lady, my lady, my lady."

Laughing, she pulled him toward her. "May I tell you something?"

"Yes."

"When I was engaged . . . I longed for many things. For my lover, of course. But also for a home. And for foolish things like jewels and servants and power."

"Most people covet such things."

"But you don't."

"No."

"And no longer do I." She paused, her pulse quickening as she looked up into his eyes. "Instead . . . instead I long for you. I tell you that now, in this room, because I hope the Gods will grant me this wish."

"They already have, my lady."

She shook her head. "No. They tease me, is all. Because I don't have you. As long as Indravarman is our master, I don't have you."

"But—"

"I want peace, Asal. With peace comes you."

"He isn't a man of peace. I've seen such hearts, but his bleeds with a darker blood."

Leaning closer, she pressed her lips against his ear. "Then we shall have to run. When the time is right, we shall have to go."

"He would hunt us."

"So we'd live in fear?"

"Yes."

She thought about an existence in the jungle far from Angkor. "I would rather," she whispered, "live a short, beautiful life than a long, gray one. And with you, it would be beautiful. Chaya would be with us. We would laugh and touch and be so happy. And even Angkor, with all of its majesty, can't offer me such things."

"I would be a fugitive. We would be destitute."

"It seems to me . . . that wealth doesn't offer the joys that freedom does."

He brought her hand to his lips, kissing it. "Then we shall go, when the time is right. But please keep this between us and the Gods."

Nodding, she started to leave but stopped herself. "Let me make one final wish," she said, leaning against the wall once again. She struck her chest repeatedly, heard the bells, and silently begged her Gods to listen to her, to let her escape with this man she was growing to love.

Twelve

The Call of Battle

The Cham force left Angkor shortly after dawn. Three hundred warriors rode on horseback at both the front and rear of the long column. Between them walked two thousand foot soldiers, as well as contingents of slaves, priests, and supply officers. Due to the narrow trails, war elephants weren't used. Horses pulled carts laden with rice, salted fish, vegetables, weapons, and armor—items needed for the several-days' journey and looming battle. Scores of wives, concubines, and high-ranking officials rode on carts thick with padding and pillows.

The army's presence was keenly felt in the jungle. The clink of shield against spear, the groan of wooden wheels announced the coming of men and mayhem. Deer and leopards hurried ahead of the Chams, and flocks of birds rose from nearby trees. Scents of sweat, dung, oiled leather, and perfume lingered.

Near the head of the column, on a massive white stallion, rode Indravarman. Though wisdom dictated that he would be safer in the center of the force, he had always led his men into battle. Behind him were his most trusted officers, each on horseback and dressed for war. Ahead of him were fifteen Cham warriors who hacked at the undergrowth along the trail with long blades, widening the path. The going was methodical, laborious, and yet progress was made. The army slithered forward, deeper into the jungle, heading north toward the Khmers.

Indravarman had informed his officers of his spies' discovery—that groups of Khmers were gathering in the north near an old temple. These groups were believed to have been joining up for some time, indicating the possibility of a much larger assembly, one likely led by Jayavar. If indeed Jayavar was raising an army near this temple, Indravarman wanted to annihilate him without mercy, and so he marched from Angkor with a formidable force.

The Khmers would likely be slowed by children, as well as by the sick and old. Though the Cham army moved without haste, speed could be employed when necessary. Mounted warriors could charge forward at a moment's notice. Large contingents of Khmers would lack such abilities, and the Chams were confident that heads would be taken. In fact, wagers were being made as to who would kill Jayavar and collect the bounty that Indravarman had placed upon him.

Asal had been on dozens of similar expeditions and was used to the way that men spoke about upcoming battles, with swagger and bravado. It was usually the youngest warriors who did the most bragging. And they would be the first to cringe and weep when blades opened bellies, when horses fell in thrashing, tangled messes of hooves and mud. In any real battle that pitted equal foes against one another, most of the young would die through their own rashness, timidity, or inexperience. A few would survive, and days or weeks or months later, when their next battle approached, most of these men would remain silent in anticipation of the slaughter and suffering to come.

Asal wasn't worried about himself as he followed Indravarman through a bamboo thicket. Instead, he occasionally glanced backward, wondering about Voisanne's location and how he might protect her if they were attacked. Though it was unlikely that Khmers would intentionally harm her, in battle anything was possible. A stray arrow could single her out. A warrior filled with bloodlust could deem her his prize.

Asal's duty was to stand by and protect the king. But if wave after wave of Khmers came, would his feelings for Voisanne overcome his sense of duty? Without question, if he left Indravarman's side, after the battle was over he would be seen as a coward and a deserter. No mercy would be shown to him.

Several days earlier, when Voisanne had beseeched him to allow her to join the expedition, he hadn't been pleased. For the first time since he had known her, he'd been frustrated with her. Yet he had kept his tongue in check, aware that she was trying to placate Thida. Instead of voicing his displeasure, he had counseled her on what to do if they were attacked—how she should hide beneath a shield or a cart, how she should present herself to Khmers or Chams, depending on who won. He might not be able to come for her, and she would have to fend for herself.

Asal wished that they weren't in the midst of an army, but back at the Echo Chamber. In that moment, he had felt fully alone with her, as if Angkor Wat encircled and protected them from all eyes and ears. Even within his room at the Royal Palace, he didn't feel safe with her. At any instant, Indravarman might summon either one of them or split them apart forever. Asal was aware that his king knew that he cared for her, and this knowledge made him leery. It didn't help matters that earlier, as they had left Angkor, he'd seen Po Rame studying

Voisanne. If left to his own devices, Po Rame would hurt her to get to him.

Careful not to be seen doing anything unusual, Asal tilted the inside of his shield toward him. With his free hand he searched for Voisanne's note and unfolded a square piece of deerskin. On its underside she had written: *In the Echo Chamber I prayed for myself. I prayed that I am so blessed as to have you for my own.*

He traced her words with the tip of his forefinger. Then he folded up the hide and tucked it beneath the iron rim of his shield. He still found it hard to believe that she seemed to long for him in the same way that he coveted her. In so many ways they were as different as sky and sea. She was a Khmer; he was not. She came from wealth; he did not. She was beautiful and gracious, while he was known for the strength of his sword arm and little else.

Asal had been loved by his mother and knew what such affection felt like. And while he had expected to find a woman, to give her sons and daughters, he had never anticipated caring for her beyond a sense of duty. He would provide, protect, and perhaps share a smile. But never had he expected to think about a woman's face as a battle drew near, to wish that he could touch that face while candles burned low.

In so many ways, Asal was surrounded by enemies. Indravarman would gut him if the mood struck. Po Rame surely planned his death. Equally dangerous, hundreds of Khmers were within a few days' march.

The only person Asal trusted was Voisanne, yet by merely trusting her, by allowing himself to be consumed by thoughts of her, he was placing his life in greater danger. She represented love and goodness and hope—gifts that he coveted more with each passing day. But such gifts, he knew, would come at a price.

Asal didn't want to fail his countrymen. He was proud of his heritage, of his ancestors. The Khmers had inflicted as many grievances on his people as had been done to them. He was a Cham and would always think of himself as one.

Yet he was falling for a Khmer. And he could not stop falling despite the perils created by their union.

Soriya and Prak sat at the edge of a long and narrow clearing. An immense ficus tree had recently toppled, creating a swath of space in the deep jungle. Standing on the tree trunk were five Khmer warriors whom they had met the previous afternoon. The men had been headed away from Angkor, and Boran and Soriya had decided to travel with them. The Khmers were scarred, kind, and well armed.

Since dawn, the warriors had been awake, practicing their swordplay on the broad trunk of the fallen tree. Boran, Soriya, Vibol, and Prak had watched, fascinated, as the men faced one another, one pair at a time. Maintaining wide stances on the tree trunk, they swung and parried, using heavy bamboo poles instead of steel. The thump of wood against wood rang out, unsettling birds and silencing other creatures. The men fought until one was struck down or forced from the tree.

After they had clashed against one another several times, one of the warriors asked if Boran and Vibol wanted to try. Boran had shaken his head, but after some uncertainty, Vibol had stood up and climbed the tree trunk. He'd listened carefully as the warrior gave him instructions, then picked up a heavy pole. At first his clumsiness with the weapon was apparent to everyone, but Vibol was strong and swift, and he began to swing the pole with ease. To his parents' surprise, he smiled, then asked his father to engage him in a mock battle. Boran agreed, and father and son stood apart. Soon they swung, strained, and sweated, urged on by the warriors.

Vibol had won their fight, and now, as Prak sat on a boulder beside his mother and played his flute, he asked himself if his father had let Vibol win. The other men must know, but Prak could only guess. And he guessed that his father had fallen on purpose.

His mother shifted next to him, her fingers dipping and twisting a needle as she mended a hole in Boran's extra hip cloth. "Do you wish that they'd asked you?" she said quietly, a necklace of jasmine flowers covering much of her chest.

Prak started to shake his head but stopped, not wanting to lie. "I wish," he replied, "that my weaknesses weren't so obvious."

"We all have weaknesses."

"Maybe. But some are hard to see and others are hard to miss."

"Would you join them . . . if you could?"

"If they asked me."

She sighed, setting down her needle to reach for his hand. "I'm no warrior, Prak, but it seems to me that a mind can also be a weapon. Your ideas are worth a hundred swords. The men up there . . . if they saw a weakness, that's because they didn't see the real you. They don't know what you're capable of."

"But you do?"

"Of course I do. And you can do as much as anyone."

He smiled, believing her words though sometimes he worried if a woman would ever commit to becoming his wife, to bearing his children. Then he wondered what his mother might like to hear. She had endured as much as any of them—a witness to the destruction of their home, to her son's capture and beating. "When the war is over, what do you want?" he asked, setting aside his flute, aware of the sunlight on his face.

"Me?"

"Yes, Mother. You."

"I want it . . . to be over. For my loved ones to be safe. Nothing more than that."

"Just dream. For a moment, allow yourself to dream."

A man fell, laughing, from the tree trunk. The others, along with Boran and Vibol, encouraged the vanquished warrior to climb up and renew the fight.

"I want a home," she replied. "Near the water."

"But not the Great Lake?"

"A stream would be nice. A stream near a river. That way your father could still do what he does best."

Prak thought about how water had been as important to his mother as it was to his father. She constantly used it—whether to wash, cook, or bathe. In the past, she'd always walked to a stream and filled her heavy wooden containers. Aware that she had slowed, that she wasn't as strong as she once was, Prak asked himself whether he could ease her future burdens. "Water is heavy, Mother. You're already stooped from carrying it."

She laughed. "Are you going to invent a lighter water?"

"No, but what if . . . what if we built our new home so that a stream flowed beneath it? I could line a small stream with smooth stones, so that it wouldn't get muddy. And this stream could go under a room. When you needed water, you could lower a gourd into the stream, then pull it up with a rope. You'd never have to travel for water. It would be with you always, and you'd even hear its trickles as you went to sleep."

She squeezed his hand. "I . . . I'd love to have such a home, Prak. But could you build it?"

"I see no reason why not. As long as we were careful where we built it, and stayed away from areas that flood. You could have your water . . . and Father could keep his boat nearby."

"How happy that would make us both."

"I want you to be happy, Mother."

"I know. That's why you sit with me, why you play your flute when you could be doing something else."

"I like to play."

"And I like to listen."

Prak smiled, his expression changing as Vibol grunted in pain. "The warriors up there say a battle is looming."

Soriya nodded but made no reply.

"And if a battle is looming . . . maybe we should be going," Prak added.

"We can't."

"Why?"

"Because Vibol can't live with himself, or with us, if he thinks . . . deep down . . . that he's a coward."

"But what if he's hurt? What if Father's hurt?"

She squeezed Prak's hand harder, staring intensely into his eyes. "You can't fight, Prak. But as I've said many times, you can think. So, please, use your mind. It's a gift from the Gods. You've listened to your father talk about the Chams; you understand the strengths and weaknesses of their base. Please think about more ways to defeat them. Your idea about starting a fire is a good one. It's a beginning. But what if the battle is fought in Angkor? What if ten Chams burst into the open right now, their swords held high? You must answer these questions, because I . . . I know what I can do and what I can't do. And try as I might, I can't think of how to defeat the Chams. But you can. And perhaps that's why the Gods stole your sight. Perhaps they stole it to give you another sort of vision, a vision that can save us all."

Prak nodded, his mother's words seeming to echo in his mind. Sensing her needs, her longing for reassurance, he promised her that he would think of a plan to protect his family.

But he had already tried throughout many days and nights to

do just that, and no matter how many times he envisioned the intricacies of the future, he always saw his brother rushing off into battle and enduring a hideous death.

If Vibol died, then the spirit, the life force, of their entire family would die. Prak's parents would walk on dead feet, think with dead minds.

Whatever needed to happen, whatever sacrifices must be made, Prak had to ensure that such a future never came to pass.

Sitting alongside the river that comprised the core of their encampment, Ajadevi gazed at Nuon, the woman who had married Jayavar in a simple ceremony and whom Ajadevi believed carried his child. In many ways, the river and Nuon seemed alike. Both were beautiful and vibrant. At only nineteen years of age, Nuon reminded Ajadevi of her own youth, creating a sense of nostalgia that the older woman rarely experienced. Ajadevi remembered falling in love with Jayavar, all her senses heightened as he sat beside her. How grand their dreams had been.

Fortunately, Ajadevi still saw the world as a collection of miracles. A tree was no more or less than the sum of the thousand trees that had stood in that same spot before it. A child was a cup containing the memories, hopes, and delights of both the present and past consciousnesses.

The miracles that she saw every day sustained Ajadevi, giving her strength in times of darkness, fulfilling her when she was reminded of her empty womb. And Nuon was such a reminder. Without a moment's thought or prayer or yearning, Nuon had done what Ajadevi could not—create the possibility of an heir.

When thinking about Nuon and the gift that she would someday give Jayavar, Ajadevi reminded herself of Buddha's noble eightfold path; of how, through releasing her own attachments and desires, her spirit could finally reach Nirvana. Her supreme goal was to find Nirvana, and she knew that she must force away thoughts of jealousy and self-pity. Yet at times she could not, which disappointed her for many reasons, just one of which was her failure to follow Buddha's path.

For much of the day Ajadevi and Nuon had stayed near the river, talking about Nuon's future duties. The younger woman understood her unique circumstances and was wise enough to listen carefully to Ajadevi's advice. Now, as they sat on a fallen log with their feet in the water, they ignored their surroundings and focused on each other. Women collecting water were hardly seen. An ancient carving of Vishnu was more like a shadow than a work of art. The clang of sword upon sword as warriors trained made no more impression than the wind in the trees, an elephant's trumpets, a child's laughter, or the buzzing of cicadas. Though thousands of Khmers occupied a relatively small area of the jungle, to Ajadevi and Nuon it seemed that only the other was present.

"But are you sure, my lady?" Nuon asked, her palms against her belly as if it were already swollen and needed support. "Maybe I'm not with child. Maybe I'm just sick."

Ajadevi had gone over the signs a dozen times. She was almost certain that Nuon was pregnant. "It's good to feel ill," she replied. "A sour stomach means that your child is strong."

A half smile crept across Nuon's face. "What if . . . the child is a girl?"

"If you have a daughter, you shall do two things."

"What?"

"Love her more than you do yourself. And become pregnant once again. Because while a daughter will give you countless joys and blessings, our empire needs a son. Without a son, without an heir, we are doomed."

Nuon nodded, her round and pleasant face covered in a sheen of perspiration. "But if it's a boy, my lady, I won't know how to train him."

"That's why I am here. To help you."

"But I'm only an untried woman."

"You are whoever you want to be. Why do you worry about your age, when you have already lived so many lives? As a Buddhist, I'm certain that your karma must be good to have brought you here, to have blessed your womb. Surely you've done beautiful and wondrous things. You've already been a mother, a son, a leader. So why not draw upon these lives to do what must be done?"

A horse neighed in the distance. Nuon glanced toward it. "But I . . . can't feel these lives."

"Do you feel your mind?"

"I'm not aware of these lives. I'm aware of my mind."

"Do you dream of things that you've not yet experienced?"

"Yes."

"Where do you think dreams come from, if not from your previous consciousnesses?"

Nuon shook her head, her hands clenching into fists. "But how, my lady, can dreams help me raise a future king?"

Ajadevi stood up. "Let's walk."

The two women stood and started upstream, toward the larger carvings. Ajadevi pointed out images of the Hindu Gods, explained each of the God's attributes and the symbolic elements of each carving.

"Unlike you, I'm not a Hindu," Ajadevi said. "And yet both Hindus and Buddhists believe in rebirth. And you and I both see these carvings and are inspired by them. We both . . . share the same husband. In some ways, we're more akin to sisters than not."

"I'd like to be your sister."

"And as your sister, I shall help you. So don't burden yourself with unnecessary worries. We shall train your son together. He shall be a fine man, an excellent ruler."

They continued to walk, rising higher, flanked by the river on one side and trees on the other. Khmers of all ages dominated the immediate landscape. Women repaired shelters, weaved, cooked, and skinned game. Men spoke about and practiced the art of war. Children were mostly left on their own.

From time to time, Ajadevi glanced at the golden bracelet that graced Nuon's wrist. It was exquisitely made, inset with alternating precious stones—small sapphires and emeralds. The bracelet could have come only from Jayavar, who occasionally accepted gifts from newcomers to their camp. Ajadevi remembered when he had given such treasures to her. She didn't long for them as she once had, but wondered about the manner in which he had presented the bracelet to Nuon. He might have offered it to her from a sense of duty, or a newfound devotion, or a combination of the two. The gold looked lovely against her smooth brown skin, suiting her perfectly. He had chosen it well, which proved to Ajadevi that he thought more about Nuon than he claimed.

The younger woman looked up, and Ajadevi glanced away from her wrist. They continued to walk, skirting a group of archers that was practicing rapidly notching arrows and firing at distant targets. Though most of the arrows struck home, a lone archer was chastised by a commanding officer for his inaccuracy. The man lowered his head in shame.

"May I tell you something?" Nuon asked when they rounded a bend in the river and found themselves alone.

Ajadevi stopped. "Of course."

"King Jayavar . . . when he comes to me," she whispered, "he's kind to me."

"He is a kind man."

"What I mean to say is that he's kind to me . . . but he's not with me. I think . . . I think he is with you."

Ajadevi glanced around, then settled her gaze once again on Nuon's face. "What do you mean?"

"I've never been in love, my lady. I don't know what it means to be in love. But when I mention your name, something changes in his eyes. A light comes into them. And his voice . . . it quickens. He's with me, but he leaves me at those moments, and I think travels to you."

"He cares very much for you, Nuon. I know he does."

"Yes. But he loves you, my lady. Maybe you're right that I should listen to my past lives. Maybe they do tell me things. Because they tell me that he loves you in the most beautiful way, that he's with me only because he has to be. And I'm happy for you. To feel such love, it must carry you to wonderful places."

Ajadevi nodded, trying and failing to suppress a smile. "It makes me . . . feel light on my feet. Like I'm not a woman, but a spirit that rises up into the sky."

"Do you think that's how I'll feel about my child?"

"I do."

"But I worry about the Chams. King Jayavar's child will be a threat to them. And they destroy all threats."

"They try, Nuon, but they fail. King Jayavar lives, does he not? He stands within these woods, creating an army to retake our land. He should be dead and yet you've made a miracle together. That miracle won't perish. I say this not because I'm certain that we shall prevail, but because love has taught me one thing."

"What?"

"That I, that you, shouldn't be afraid to stand in the light. We are deserving of it. And when we're in the light, miracles will come to us. They may come after suffering, after grief. But come they shall. This life, so beautiful, so rife with wonders, is without end, and nothing the Chams can do will ever change that."

In the jungle, day turned to night with surprising swiftness. The soaring trees drowned out the light, prompting a drop in temperature. As the sun fell, countless bats emerged, wheeling about the open spaces in pursuit of insects. While crickets chirped and frogs croaked, the Cham army made preparations for the evening. Underbrush and small trees were cleared to provide suitable grounds for the horses. Warriors were assigned to outposts along the perimeter. Meals were cooked and served.

The Chams were confident of their strength, and officers felt no need for stealth. Campfires sprang up. Men shared gourds of rice wine as musicians beat upon drums and women searched for their lovers or patrons. Though at first glance the Chams might have appeared to be in disarray, nothing was further from the truth. Of the twenty-six hundred warriors, two hundred were stationed outside the fires, hidden in undergrowth, enduring mosquitoes and jealous of their comrades. All of Indravarman's men wore their quilted, short-sleeved armor and kept their weapons nearby. They also wore their lotus-flower headdresses—enlightened and prepared for battle. If the Cham force was attacked, officers and their men would spring to action in a few heartbeats.

In the middle of the encampment, within a large tentlike structure made of bamboo and silk, Indravarman, Po Rame, and Asal sat on a Chinese carpet and peered over an elaborate map. Asal and Indravarman had laid their swords beside them. Po Rame carried no visible weapon, but Asal was certain that tucked within the folds of the assassin's hip cloth was a killing instrument of some sort.

Asal knew that Indravarman was happiest in the field pursuing an enemy, and certainly tonight was no different. The big man had already consumed a vast quantity of food and wine. His voice, always loud, had become even more boisterous. He moved with a newfound energy, pointing from spot to spot on the map, slapping Asal on the back. His confidence was infectious, and Asal felt a growing conviction that Jayavar would soon be caught. The war would be over.

But what that end would bring remained a mystery to Asal. What would become of Voisanne? Her king would be dead and her way of life shattered. Would she continue to care for him when his people had taken so much from hers? Such questions unsettled him, and even though he wanted to go and find her in the darkness, he had to force himself to pay attention to Indravarman and Po Rame as they discussed the assassin's discoveries.

"Why would they gather at this temple of women?" Indravarman asked. "The map shows flat, indefensible terrain. And if the temple is small, it wouldn't be worth fortifying."

Po Rame leaned forward, the huge tiger claw that hung from his neck swinging away from his chest. "The prisoner . . . did not know."

"He did not know or he would not tell?"

"He told me everything, King of Kings," Po Rame answered, smiling. "A red-hot blade makes even the strongest warrior talkative. Isn't that right, Asal?"

Asal stiffened. "I wouldn't know. Nor would I care to."

"But you heard his screams. Do you think that dung eater held anything back from me?"

Willing the memory away, Asal shook his head. "I think a man will tell you whatever he believes you want to hear when he's in pain like that. So I have far less faith in your confessions than you do. And he was no dung eater. He resisted you until the end."

"You speak like a Khmer, a builder of pretty things, not armies. It seems you've been spending too much time with that wisp of a woman."

Asal's eyes narrowed. He raised his right hand and pointed his forefinger at Po Rame. "Stay away from her, assassin. If you value your life, stay far, far away."

"I go where I want, when I want. You should know that by now, Khmer lover."

"Then come to me with a blade in your hand. Come tonight and see what happens."

"Enough!" Indravarman yelled, slapping Asal on the cheek with the back of his hand. "If either of you acts upon your hatred, I'll have you skinned alive! Understood?"

Asal, the side of his face turning red, repressed a nearly overwhelming desire to strike back. "Yes, Lord King."

Po Rame nodded, removing his hand from inside his hip cloth.

"Our common enemy," Indravarman added, "is Jayavar. You say, Po Rame, that he is near this temple. And I believe you. I believe that when someone confesses to you, he's telling the truth."

"Those words were his last, King of Kings. A man's last words are always the truth. Even a Khmer's."

Indravarman contemplated Po Rame's declaration, rubbing the iron that lay beneath the skin of his belly. "Then we shall find him there. You shall find him, Asal. You shall find him in battle and capture him."

"Capture him?" Asal repeated, his hate suddenly forgotten.

"I wanted his head, but that was then and this is now. Now I want him alive. I want to bring him back to Angkor in chains. There his execution will be bloody and public. Once the Khmers see that their savior is dead, their defiance will end. And capture his woman, Asal. The two of them, I hear, are true lovers. They should die in each other's arms."

Asal knew that Jayavar would be protected by his strongest warriors. Trying to capture the Khmer king was likely a sentence of death. "You honor my men and me," Asal replied, bowing slightly. "When the time comes, I'll face him."

"Prove your worth to me, Asal. Prove to me that my faith in you is well placed, that I needn't take away your title, your power, or your woman."

Asal tried to keep his emotions in check. "I shall, Lord King," he replied, wondering why Indravarman found it necessary to keep testing him. He had been nothing but loyal and was weary of such distrust. And he was increasingly worried about Voisanne. Both Indravarman and Po Rame could use her to control him, to hurt him. Without question she was in danger.

Unable to think of any immediate recourse other than to continue to please Indravarman, Asal peered closer at the map. "Do you see the valleys, Lord King, to the north of the temple?" he asked.

"Tell me something that I do not know."

"If I were Jayavar, I would hide in one of those valleys. I'd use the temple as a beacon, but not a base. I'd bring warriors north, to that beacon, and then lead them to my true base."

Indravarman grunted. "Which valley? Which valley would you lead them to?"

Asal leaned forward, studying the map. "This one," he said, pointing to a valley that rose from either side of a river. "An army needs fresh water, Lord King. It needs food. And where better to find both than along this river? In a valley like this one the Khmers could hide. They could build an army. Our scouts cannot see through rock. Five thousand Khmers could hide in that valley, and we'd never know it."

Outside the silk structure, a horse neighed. Indravarman ignored the noise, continuing to study the valley. "I shall name this valley after you," he said, "if Jayavar is there and you bring him to me."

"Yes, Lord King."

"Would you like that? To become immortal?"

"I have known men who thought themselves to be immortal," Asal replied, glancing at Po Rame, "and I've seen such men dead after battle. I've killed such men myself."

"Where is your vanity, Asal?" Indravarman chided. "The boldest of leaders all have vanity."

"Vanity is a shield best carried by others, Lord King. I only wish to serve you."

"Then capture the false king. Bring him to me in chains and you will have served me well."

Nodding, Asal stood up and left the structure. Outside, the air was heavy with the scent of cooking fires and horse dung. Asal glanced from fire to fire, wondering where Voisanne might be. He was weary of threats and hatred and war. He longed to go to her and to hold her. For so much of his life he had been alone, enduring uncertainties with no one beside him. Somehow he'd always remained strong.

But on this night, he did not feel strong. He felt alone. And yet he could not risk going to her, because by doing so he would draw eyes in her direction. He would invite the stares of killers.

Asal walked toward the camp's perimeter, passing into darkness. He sat against the trunk of a dying tree. How can I be with her? he wondered. How can I be with her when they've trapped me? When I'm who they need me to be and not who I want to be?

He looked up, searching for stars. The sky was obscured by trees, and he felt as if he had been locked within a windowless room. He yearned to feel the presence of the Gods, or of Voisanne. But such lights did not enter his world. All he could sense were his own fear and an impending doom.

At some point, Voisanne would need his protection. Where would he be when that moment came? And if the king wanted her dead, how could he be confronted and brought down?

How could Asal betray his people and not die of shame?

Thirteen

Flight Through the Jungle

Two days after practicing swordplay on the fallen tree, Boran led his family through a seemingly endless thicket of bamboo. He followed in the footsteps of the Khmer warriors, moving as they did with caution and stealth. The way that the warriors traveled often unsettled him. Sometimes they laughed and were careless. At other times they seemed to float between the trees, making less noise than a stream flowing over stones. Boran could never predict how the men would react to the flight of distant birds, a scent of smoke, or a freshly broken branch. He felt increasingly out of his element and yearned for open waters. This far north, the jungle was too thick and ominous, too full of Chams that they both tracked and fled from.

Boran knew that Soriya and Prak were equally disconcerted. They had told him as much, and yet walked without complaint. Only Vibol seemed renewed by the expedition. He bantered more and more with the warriors, studying their movements, learning how to interpret the remnants of a campfire or the sound of an elephant's trumpet. Boran had raised his son to be a fisherman, and while Vibol had excelled at pulling catfish and eels from the waterways, he had no passion for it. His passion, Boran now understood, was for doing what the warriors did—discussing how Angkor could be retaken, practicing swordplay, and moving as if he were a part of the jungle.

Boran was pleased by his son's desire to see justice served. But he also feared losing him and wished that life could return to the way it was before the Chams arrived. If the two armies met, Vibol would fight, and Boran would stand beside him, because he'd never let his son go into battle alone.

A battle could steal so much from Boran. He might be killed and never see his loved ones again. He might watch his son die. Such thoughts weighed upon him just as rain makes a leaf hang limp. He felt defeated, though no battle had been fought. On several occasions he was tempted to ask Vibol to turn around, and yet he never uttered such words. To turn around would be to abandon his people and, more important, his son. So Boran tried to maintain a pretense of high spirits while leading his family onward.

Now, as he thought about Soriya, and how his days with her might be numbered, he twisted in her direction. She smiled at him, and he leaned close to her, whispering that he loved her. It wasn't often that he expressed his affection, and she looked at him questioningly, letting her sons pass by.

"Can't I tell my wife that she pleases me?" Boran asked, his voice low.

Soriya began to walk again. "But why now?"

"Because I haven't said those words in a long time. Too long."

She nodded, stepping around a waist-high anthill that rose from the middle of the trail. Leaning toward him, she whispered, "Are we making a mistake?"

"I . . . I don't know."

"If we continue ahead . . . we may lose our son. But if we turn around, he'll travel without us."

"Which do you fear more?"

Sighing, she shook her head. "I can't let him go on alone."

"Nor I."

"But how can you keep him safe when the Chams come?"

"These men . . . they're training him."

"They don't care about him. They're using him. And a boy can't fight a man."

"I know. That's why I'll be beside him."

"But, Boran, you're only a fisherman. Forgive me for saying so, but I've seen you with a sword, and those men toy with you."

Boran looked toward the warriors, knowing she was right and frustrated by his own shortcomings. "What would you have me do? You speak as if I've countless paths to choose from and am going the wrong way. Which way should I go, Soriya? He wants to fight and he's being taught how to do so. Maybe that will save him. Maybe it will save me. I've asked myself, day after day, the very same questions that you're asking me. It's not like I'm on the river, setting nets. I don't know what to do."

"I'm sorry. It's just that—"

An urgent call came from the lead warrior. Boran froze. Suddenly the men doubled back on the trail, moving like the wind through the trees. Vibol was leading Prak, holding his hand, running ahead of their companions. Boran spun Soriya around and followed her as she ran after the warriors, his heart threatening to burst from his chest.

Prak tripped on a root and fell to his knees, prompting Soriya to cry out and reach for him. Vibol helped his brother up, while Boran pulled the Cham war axe from his son's hands. He stood, facing the north, awaiting whoever shared the trail. But then

Soriya tugged on his arm, and once again they were running, dodging and ducking foliage, struggling to stay on their feet.

To Boran's surprise, the warriors led them to a banyan tree and urged them to climb. Boran started to argue but then nodded and helped his loved ones maneuver their way up through a web of intersecting branches. They climbed until the ground was far below and they had a partially clear view of their surroundings.

"Why don't we run?" Boran whispered, his chest heaving.

The leader of the warriors, who had a long scar on his face and a broken nose, leaned closer to Boran. "Because I wish to see."

"To see us die?"

"They aren't Chams, fisherman, but Siamese. So let's watch them come and go."

Boran shook his head, wondering why Siamese wouldn't butcher them just as readily as Chams. He started to ask as much but was silenced by a glare from the warrior. Helpless, he looked from Soriya to Prak to Vibol, nodding to each of them, trying to encourage them when he felt as if he were an eel trapped in his own net.

Several black birds rose in the distance. Boran sought to slow his breathing, his right hand still around the shaft of the axe. He thought he saw the glint of steel. A horse neighed. A foreign scent drifted to him. Peering through the branches and leaves below him, he attempted to make sense of what was happening.

Between gaps in the foliage, the army appeared. Though they were an arrow's flight away, Boran could see immediately why the Khmer warrior had recognized them as Siamese. The newcomers, who walked briskly, wore hip cloths and tunics made of brightly colored fabric. Elaborate patterns graced the garments. Atop the men's heads were pyramid-shaped collections of beads, shells, and feathers. Unlike the Khmers and Chams, who usually carried small circular shields, the Siamese held rectangular shields that protected them from neck to knee. Almost all the warriors wielded steel-tipped spears. White feathers were attached to the middle and top of the spears. Overall, the Siamese warriors formed a tapestry of sorts, an array of colors and patterns the likes of which Boran had never seen. Though the temples of Angkor were unrivaled in size and splendor, most Khmers wore simple clothes and only a few jewels or rings. The Siamese, it seemed, decorated themselves as much as possible.

Boran watched the army pass. He tried counting the warriors but quickly grew overwhelmed by the task. Hundreds and hundreds of Siamese must have been present. The clink of shield against shield, the shuffling of innumerable feet, were plain to hear. Several Siamese appeared to look up at the banyan tree, but no one bothered to come closer. The warriors marched with haste, moving faster than Boran would have thought possible. Their spears and heavy shields didn't seem to slow them down as they moved into and out of sight.

When the army was finally gone, Boran turned to the scar-faced Khmer. "Why are they here?" he asked.

The man smiled. "There is a rumor," he replied. "A rumor that King Jayavar has sent for Siamese mercenaries, that he has asked them to march to the Citadel of Women, as we do. And if that rumor is true . . . maybe the Gods are once again pleased with us. Maybe we can hope."

Boran saw Soriya nod at the warrior's words, as if she also believed that the sight of the Siamese portended a better to-morrow.

But Boran wasn't sure. So many men and weapons could only result in a great many deaths. And how he could protect his family from such destruction remained a riddle.

When the Khmer warrior told everyone to climb down the

tree, Boran was tempted to ask his loved ones to stay. Yet he found himself moving with the others, dropping from limb to limb, approaching a fate he feared.

Asal urged his horse toward the front of the column. Two scouts he had sent ahead of the main force should have returned by now. He'd worked with the men before and always found them reliable. Their tardiness unnerved him.

The jungle was as dense as any Asal had ever experienced. Thickets of bamboo dominated the immediate landscape, though they were dwarfed by much taller teak, ficus, and banyan trees. Even in the dry season, moss grew on seemingly every stone, trunk, or fallen branch. Slanting rays of sunlight penetrated gaps in the dense canopy, illuminating patches of the jungle floor.

Though the men around him marched along the trail without pause or concern, Asal's disquiet increased with each passing moment. Something wasn't right. His horse seemed skittish, the jungle creatures too quiet. Fifty paces ahead of him, fifteen of his countrymen used swords to hack at the undergrowth. Stalks of bamboo shuddered and fell. Ferns were yanked from the ground.

Asal had informed Indravarman of the missing scouts, but the king had not shared Asal's concern. All reports indicated that the Khmers were massing farther to the north, near the old temple. Yet Asal felt as if he was walking into a trap.

Pulling back on his reins, he halted his horse and called for the men to ready themselves for battle. They looked at him in confusion, and he repeated his order, unsheathing his sword. He peered ahead, trying to understand what his senses were telling him.

He had started to turn his horse around to confer with Indravarman when the jungle erupted with war cries. The green foliage parted, revealing screaming men who carried spears and large shields and were dressed in colorful hip cloths and tunics. The Chams had a few heartbeats to draw their weapons and brace themselves. Asal realized that he wasn't about to be attacked by Khmers, but by Siamese.

Whoever commanded the attacking force had planned the ambush site well. In the confines of the narrow trail, the Cham horses panicked. Several bolted into the undergrowth, tossing their riders. Even as he realized that they were outnumbered and doomed, Asal shouted at the men around him to hold their positions.

Then the Siamese struck.

Several hundred paces toward the rear of the column, Voisanne heard the screams and the hiss of arrows, and she remembered Asal's words. Yelling at Thida to follow her lead, she tumbled out of the padded cart and crawled beneath it. The clash of steel against steel rang out, as did the shouts of Chams, Siamese, and Khmers. Hearing the cries of her countrymen, Voisanne was tempted to crawl from beneath the cart and seek help. But as soon as she moved, men began to fall, clutching at mortal wounds, screaming for aid that did not arrive. Thida shrieked beside her, covering her ears, her eyes wild with fright. The roar of the battle increased. Voisanne moved toward the middle of the cart and was able to see only the feet and calves of nearby men.

A warrior dressed in a bright red tunic fell, writhing with a spear in his belly. Seeing his agony, Voisanne thought of Asal. She called out to him, though her voice was overwhelmed by the clamor of battle.

The cart shuddered. A horse toppled, its hooves striking a wooden wheel. Smoke filled the air and soon Voisanne felt the heat of flames. She shouted at Thida that they had to leave. When the other woman only curled into a ball and shut her eyes, Voisanne tried to drag her out from under the cart. But Thida wouldn't move. Voisanne squeezed her friend's hand, then left her, suddenly desperate to run.

Outside the cart, the chaos of battle was overwhelming. She saw packs of Chams fighting against Siamese and a few Khmers. Two of Indravarman's men stood in front of her, and when they fell, Siamese darted forward, eager to plunder and pillage.

Voisanne ran, frantic to escape the blood-splattered warriors who seemed to see her and only her. She rushed away from the trail, crashing through undergrowth. Fallen logs and thorny bushes slowed her progress, but she paid such obstacles no heed, ignoring the slashes on her legs and feet. She ran around two immense anthills, fell, and then dashed into a thicket of bamboo. A dozen paces behind her, a man shouted in a strange tongue, and she didn't need to turn around to know that he was Siamese. Understanding that she was his prey, she ran as never before.

Yet he ran faster, and slammed the butt of his spear into the small of her back. She cried out, falling into a clump of ferns, bracing for his attack even before he was upon her.

When his line of men buckled, then collapsed, Asal fled along with everyone else. Only he didn't dart into the jungle but back toward where he thought Voisanne would be. Aware of how the Siamese would treat her, he ran and fought like a fiend, plowing into and over his enemies, giving little thought to his own well-being. He quickly came to what remained of Indravarman's personal guard, took a sword strike on his shield, killed the Siamese warrior, and then dragged Thida from beneath a burning cart.

"Where is she?" he shouted, his voice nearly lost amid the cries of the fighting and dying.

Thida made no reply but glanced toward a thicket of bamboo. Asal left her, twisting away from a thrown spear. A woman's shriek rang out. Asal jumped over a crippled horse and ran toward the thicket, battering saplings aside with his shield as he held his sword high.

A Siamese was tugging at Voisanne's skirt cloth when Asal burst into the thicket. The warrior looked up, then grunted as Asal's foot struck him hard in the side. He rolled off Voisanne, reached for his discarded spear, and stared in disbelief when Asal's weapon cut through his arm, severing it from the spear. The Siamese shrieked. He gazed at his bloody stump, then died when Asal reversed his sword strike, bringing the blade up from the dirt and blood, cutting deeply into his enemy's neck.

Hearing cries from other Siamese, Asal dropped his shield. Voisanne was trying to stand but trembled uncontrollably. "Can you run?" he asked.

She threw her arms around him, and for a moment he wanted to stay there, holding her, comforting her. But the Siamese were shouting triumphantly, so he pulled away from her, cut slits down the front and back of her skirt cloth, took her hand, and led her deeper into the thicket. At first she stumbled and wept, but as they ran together, knocking aside everything in their path, he felt strength flow back into her. She moved with purpose, letting him lead her but not slowing his progress. Pride for her swelled within him, and he increased their speed, knowing that she could keep up.

At the scene of the attack, the rear guard of the Cham force had regrouped and driven the Siamese back, away from the burning carts and the dead. Indravarman, flanked by his personal guards, fought like a wild beast, his great strength making his sword fast and deadly. Veteran Siamese warriors seemed to offer him no more resistance than children. Enraged by their ambush, he cut them down one by one, pressing into the jungle. Though his officers tried to halt his counterattack out of concern for his safety, he led his men forward, coated in his enemies' blood. He knew that even with the success of his strike, his army had been crippled. Hundreds of his men were dead or injured, and he would have to withdraw back to Angkor and regroup. Jayavar would live to see another day.

After he beheaded a Siamese with a sweeping sword stroke, Indravarman realized that Asal had been right. The disappearance of the scouts should have prompted caution. His enemies were running away, and the king turned, looking for Asal, knowing he had been at the front of the column where the worst fighting had taken place.

Are you dead? Indravarman wondered. Did the Siamese take your life before I could?

The Chams who still stood shouted in triumph, though Indravarman realized that in most ways he had been beaten. Cursing the dead Siamese, stepping on their bodies, he made his way back to the burning carts. He saw Thida sobbing against the base of a tree. Po Rame was already interrogating a wounded enemy warrior. Most of Indravarman's other officers were present. But where was Asal? If he had died, where did his body lie? If he lived, where had he gone?

Within their encampment to the north, Jayavar and Ajadevi sat atop a hill that overlooked their valley. Though the dense foliage obscured much, occasional breaks within the trees allowed glimpses into the base camp. Horses ate from thatch baskets, children played, warriors trained, supplies were unpacked by weary porters, and the river glistened. From so far above, the Khmers were almost unheard, though the clang of metal on metal occasionally rang out, as did trumpeting from their few war elephants.

Jayavar's gaze swung around the encampment's perimeter as he studied the outposts of their sentries. It would be impossible for a Cham army to approach undetected. The Khmer warriors would be forewarned of any attack, and would have ample time to prepare their defenses. Women, children, and the elderly would be sent to caves alongside the river while the men formed lines on top of nearby hills. The Chams would have to fight while climbing up the hills or wading in the river—difficult tasks considering that Khmer archers would fill the sky with arrows.

Still, despite the advantages of the terrain, Jayavar had no wish to engage the enemy here; instead he would take the battle to his foe. The Chams must be driven from Angkor, crushed so completely that they would never return. Repelling an attack in the valley would not accomplish that. Only by retaking Angkor, by celebrating victory within its confines, would they reclaim their kingdom.

The problem was that Jayavar wasn't sure how best to retake Angkor. He would be outnumbered on all fronts—in men, horses, elephants, and resources. His only solace was that several large contingents of Siamese mercenaries had already joined his force, with more to follow. And while payments to the Siamese would nearly bankrupt his treasury, Angkor could not be retaken without their aid.

As usual, Jayavar's thoughts stalled when it came to planning his attack. A bird took flight from the jungle far below, drawing his gaze. For the second time in as many days, he sensed someone watching him from the distance. He started to reach for the hilt of his sword, but stopped, trusting his intuition but also aware of the perils of paranoia. His grandfather had constantly obsessed over real and imagined threats, a distraction that had weakened his rule.

Willing himself to relax, Jayavar studied his wife, noting that spending so many weeks outside had darkened her complexion. Her golden bracelets and necklaces were gone, as were all other material indications that she was an exiled queen. Only her upright posture and the sharpness of her stare hinted that she was someone who commanded attention.

Though Jayavar spent much of his time surrounded by his officers, who were bright and brave, he knew that each of them was replaceable. Ajadevi was not. Her counsel was wise, her actions selfless. She made no effort to flatter him when it came to strategy, or to stroke his ego at the expense of making sound suggestions—something that his officers were prone to do. Nor did she claim expertise where she had none. Certainly when it came to planning for the battle, she trusted his judgment more than her own, although she was always ready to debate various tactics.

Since their escape from Angkor, Jayavar had realized that without Ajadevi he would have been lost. The deaths of his children would have overwhelmed him. And while he still mourned their absence in his world, he felt compelled by the needs of his people. Khmers of all walks of life depended on him. Ajadevi illuminated this need, day after day, and gave him the strength to do what must be done.

"If I were a temple," he said quietly, balancing an oblong stone atop a round one, "you would be the walls that allowed me to reach great heights. Without you I'd crumble."

She smiled. "One day, when we drive the Chams from our land, you shall be a hero to our people. Your face should grace the sides of a temple, a face for our people to celebrate and remember."

"It is a plain face. I am a plain man."

"But you'll be a hero. And heroes need to be celebrated, immortalized. Without heroes a culture will never aspire to greatness."

He shook his head. "Then it should be your face. Anything we build to celebrate victory should honor you."

Far above, a hawk screeched, circling on the still air. "I dreamed last night," she said, studying the hawk.

"Of what?"

"I saw fire. I saw pain. But from that pain came something beautiful."

"Tell me more."

"Most beautiful things—life or wisdom or contentment—are born from pain. And our victory shall be born from pain. We haven't felt it yet. We haven't suffered enough yet. But in the end, we shall win. And when we do, Angkor will rise to even greater heights. Our kingdom will be unequalled. Not because of its riches or strength, but because of its people. You will treat them well. You will empower them. And for that you shall be forever cherished."

He shifted on the boulder. "I cherish you."

She turned her body toward his. "But, Jayavar, I shall not live forever. This war may claim me. And if it does, you must go on. You must find fulfillment through your people. You must lead them to the destiny that was meant to be theirs."

"You cannot leave me, my love," he replied, still trying to balance the stone, using it to distract him from the horror of her words. He knew too well that he'd be unable to endure the loss of her so soon after his children had departed. He would try to lead his people, try to empower them as she wanted, but would fail.

"Tell me about Nuon," Ajadevi said quietly. "I see that she

wears a bracelet of gold and precious jewels. Such a treasure could only have come from you."

"Yes, I gave it to her—because she shall need status if she has a son. The bracelet gives them both power."

"Yet I have seen you smile together. Surely the bracelet means more than just status. Tell me, what is it like . . . to be with someone so young? Does she make your heart race?"

The stone fell from his fingers as he looked up. "She has a curious and engaging mind, which can be pleasing for a time," he replied. "But that time is fleeting. It begins; it ends. With you, there is an appreciation of the moment, but never a yearning for what will come next. The present is not fleeting. It does not end. With you, I know a contentment that I don't experience with Nuon."

The hawk screeched again. Ajadevi studied the creature, nodding to herself. "You see how it circles us?"

"Yes."

"If this war claims me, if I fall, that's how I would circle you, even in death. I shall be reborn, and you shall see me in many places."

"Tell me . . . where I would see you . . . so that I'd know where to look."

"You shall see me . . . where there is life. When dawn comes, I'll be beside you. When you feel water against you, know that I'm there. And when the time is right . . . when I've been reborn into another, I will return to you, and you'll feel my touch and hear my voice."

"Do you believe in such things . . . because of what Buddha said? Because you trust him? Or do you sense truth in his words and follow your own instincts?"

"I believe in what he said. But also because I believe in love. I believe that love binds us together like nothing else."

He finally succeeded in balancing the oblong stone atop the other. Then he placed his hands on her knees, squeezing them tight. "All of that may be true. I will wish it to be true. But still, please don't leave me. I must see your face in my world."

The hawk screeched again, and she knew at that moment that she would die first, that he would have to endure her passing. To flourish as he must, he would need beauty in his life; he would need the promise of hope and love. With her remaining days, whether they were five or five thousand, she needed to bring more light into his life. Because without light he could never be the king that she felt he might be. And her people needed such a king. They yearned for him.

"I love you," she said, then kissed him. "And you should know that . . . you heal my wounds as I heal yours. I feel the loss of my loved ones less keenly in your presence. My own shortcomings seem less abundant. And these are precious gifts that you give to me. Nothing can take them away."

He kissed her.

She thought of the approaching war, of the death and destruction that were sure to come, and closed her eyes.

Fourteen

Found

Jayavar yawned, raised his head, and looked at his sleeping wife. He gently pulled a silk blanket over her bare shoulder, reached for his sword, and then moved to his knees. As he stood up, he studied the light of dawn, wondering what kind of day it would be. Outside their quarters, the temporary shelters protecting his people glowed faintly alongside the rest of their surroundings. By his order, all of the shelters were made of bamboo and thatch, configured without patterns or straight lines to camouflage the encampment.

The first contingent of Siamese mercenaries had brought bolts of silk and coarser cloth, as well as weapons, tools, food, and medicine. New arrivals from Angkor also carried essential supplies, and as the days had passed, items that had been scarce became abundant. Only warriors were lacking. As far as Jayavar was concerned, he could never have enough men. Even with the Siamese mercenaries, he expected the Chams to outnumber them two to one. And while the advantage of surprise would likely be his, the challenge of overcoming such a numerical imbalance stole his sleep and solace.

Careful not to wake the hundreds of sleeping men, women, and children around him, Jayavar made his way around trees, shelters, and fire pits. The river seemed even lower than the previous day, exposing more of the carvings. Glistening images of Shiva and Vishnu dominated the sides of rock faces and captured Jayavar's stare. He nodded to several guards, then began to follow a trail that led to the top of a nearby hill.

As he climbed higher, the smells and sounds of the encampment were replaced by those of nature. The scent of orchids lingered. Birds scratched at the dirt, trying to uncover worms and grubs. Snails created holes in broad leaves, and millipedes as long as his hand crossed the trail. Somewhere a woodpecker hammered away at a hollow tree trunk or limb.

Jayavar climbed quickly, trying to strengthen his muscles as he would soon need all of his vigor. He was unaware of the soft footsteps behind him, of an elaborately carved spear held by a small hand. As he often did, he thought about how best to attack the Chams, whether he should fight them in Angkor or try to draw them outside the city. If he attacked them in Angkor it was possible that enslaved Khmers would join in the fight. But such a battle might damage the city, and Jayavar loathed the thought of such defilement.

Indravarman would likely expect Jayavar to try to capture the war elephants. With such powerful beasts, Jayavar could negate the sheer numbers of the Chams. Every warrior knew that a hundred war elephants were worth a thousand men. Yet Jayavar hesitated in pursuing the elephants because it was such an obvious tactic. It would be better, he thought, to fight where the elephants would benefit neither side, perhaps in a dense part of the jungle, or the swampy borders of the Great Lake. But how to draw Indravarman away from his resources was a riddle that Jayavar could not solve.

He reached the top of the hill, which was heavily forested. Though he couldn't see them, Jayavar knew that sentries were stationed along the spine of the hill, sitting in the tallest trees. These men had the best eyes and ears of all his troops. If the Chams came, an alarm would be sounded. Battle lines would be formed, loved ones protected.

The thought of fighting the Chams in the valley made sweat break out on Jayavar's back. His breathing quickened. He glanced below, then to the sky. To fight here would be to die, because Indravarman would surround them, and the sheer numbers of his men would wear them down. No, the battle had to be fought to the south, within sight of Angkor Wat. At least then, when Khmers fell, they could look up and see the temple, see the place of their Gods.

Jayavar knelt on one knee. He closed his eyes and began to pray, wishing for the safety of his people, for an end to the Cham occupation, and for the well-being of his loved ones—both the born and unborn. With such focus and longing did he pray that he didn't hear approaching footsteps. They went from soft to loud, from tentative to rushed. A sword was lifted. Jayavar opened his eyes, recognizing the Khmer warrior, seeing his own death but unable to do anything about it. The sword was raised higher. Then a spear flew from amid the undergrowth. The throw was weak and the spear wobbled. Yet it struck the dirt in front of the attacker, causing him to stumble, his sword to waver.

Jayavar spun to his right, lifting his own blade and deflecting the blow that was meant to take his head. He leapt up, his years of training and experience overcoming his fear. His sword became an extension of his arm, of his will to live, rising and falling, filling the dawn with the sound of its strikes. Screaming a battle cry, his assailant attacked with renewed vigor, but Jayavar met each sweep and thrust with his own blade. Emotions entered his consciousness. He thought of Ajadevi, and how this man wanted to take him from her. The knowledge enraged him, and his heavy sword suddenly felt like nothing more than a sun-bleached stick. The sword began to dance, to twist and leap and soar.

The assassin was struck in two places before he even hit the ground. By then he was dying. Remembering the spear, Jayavar whirled around, saw a boy, and stepped in his direction. The boy lifted his hands, screaming. Only then did Jayavar halt his blade's descent.

For a moment, man and boy stood staring at each other, chests heaving, thoughts chaotic. Then the boy fell to his knees, bowing low. Jayavar glanced around and saw that the assassin was dead, but still he did not sheath his sword. "The spear . . . it is yours?" he asked, his voice unsteady.

The boy nodded.

"And this man, do you know him?"

The small head twisted from side to side.

"Speak," Jayavar commanded. "Tell me what I need to hear."

The boy looked up, but said nothing.

"Tell me!"

A tear ran down the child's face. "You rescued me . . . Lord King."

"What?"

"That day . . . in the jungle . . . when the Chams were chasing us. You carried me."

Jayavar remembered the slave boy he had picked up as they had fled the Cham invasion. "But why are you here?"

"I made . . . that spear for you . . . Lord King. I wanted to give it to you."

"So you followed me? And when the assassin was going to strike, you threw your spear?"

"Yes. But it was . . . a weak throw. I'm so sorry. Please forgive me."

Jayavar could once again hear the sounds of the jungle. The woodpecker continued its assault. Crickets chirped and cicadas screeched. Jayavar relished the sounds. Grateful to be alive, he bent down and took the boy's hand, helping him to his feet. "What is your name, child?"

"Bona, Lord King."

Jayavar studied the jungle, making certain that it was free of additional threats. "Thank you, Bona. I owe you my life. But, please, call me 'my lord.'"

The boy lowered his gaze. "But I missed him . . . my lord."

"You caused him to stumble. You gave me time when I had none."

"He was going to kill you, my lord."

Jayavar nodded, walking to the dead man. He examined his attacker, searching his hip cloth for hidden weapons or orders. Something hard had been sewn into the material, which Jayavar ripped open. Several gold coins tumbled to the ground.

Cham coins, Jayavar said to himself. A paid assassin. A man who would kill his king for the promise of riches. He will not be the last to come for me. But the question remains, who paid him? Someone in our camp or back in Angkor?

Jayavar mused over the matter while turning the coins in his fingers. Unable to determine an answer, he picked up the fallen spear. He inspected the weapon, tracing his forefinger along the elaborate carvings. "Did you make this, Bona?"

"Yes, my lord. For you."

"Have you tracked me before? Weeks ago, when we first hid in the jungle? And then again yesterday?"

"Yes. I'm sorry."

"Do not be sorry."

"I only wanted to see you . . . and to give you the spear."

"It is a fine weapon. As fine as any I've seen."

"Thank you, my lord."

Jayavar remembered how he had saved the boy and how the child's mother had come running for him. "Are you a slave, Bona?"

"Yes, my lord. So is my mother."

"And your father?"

"He's dead."

Nodding, Jayavar thought about how best to reward the child. He studied the spear, continuing to trace the intricate engravings. "Bona, would you like to be our swordsmith's apprentice? I know him well. The fires make him irritable, but he's a good man. He could teach you much."

Bona looked up. "But . . . my lord . . . I'm to—"

"You're to do whatever we agree upon this day. And if we agree that you're to be the swordsmith's apprentice, then that you shall be."

The boy smiled, rising on his tiptoes. "Thank you, my lord. My mother will be pleased."

"Go then. Go and tell her what you did today. I shall talk with the swordsmith. Find him tomorrow. His place is by a crook in the river, downstream from our position."

"Yes, my lord."

When Bona started to turn, Jayavar reached out to him, holding him by the shoulder. He studied the child's face. And though it was a face that bore no resemblance to his own, he wondered if Bona had been summoned to this hill, if one of his sons or daughters had shown him the way. "Why did you come here?" Jayavar asked, his voice soft.

"I had to come," Bona answered. "When I saw you leave the camp . . . I just knew I had to come."

A half day's march to the south of the ambush site, Voisanne followed Asal down a game trail. For most of the morning they had been quiet, and he had held his sword before him. He'd prayed for the men that he'd left behind, wondered how he would explain his flight to his king, and studied the jungle for further dangers.

Having not seen or heard any Siamese since the ambush, he'd recently sheathed his sword and begun to whisper questions to Voisanne. He asked about her family, her dreams, and her beliefs. Unlike most of the men she had known, he didn't redirect her answers toward himself, so that he could speak about his own experiences. Rather, her answers led him to more intricate and discerning questions. He wondered what she had wondered, what she'd asked herself in the dead of night.

Between the pauses in his queries, Voisanne thought about how he had come back to her, abandoning his position and his men so that he could save her. Without him, her fate would have been cruel, and in all probability the Siamese warrior would have killed her. She had sensed her looming death, and now that she was alive, she realized how very much she wanted to live. Though she believed in rebirth, she longed to experience the joys of existence as she was right now—a young woman who had already seen the worst that life could offer.

"Why did you return for me?" she asked, her voice low.

"I missed your insults. It had been too long since you called me a dog or a cowardly Cham."

"No, really. Tell me why."

He pushed a half-fallen stalk of bamboo aside, sweat dripping from his brow. "Because, my lady, when I was fighting all I could think of was you."

A smile graced her face. "Why me?"

"Because I couldn't bear the thought of you being hurt."

"I've been hurt before."

"But not with me nearby."

She nodded, noting animal footprints in the dried mud. Though she was no hunter, she thought the deep tracks were likely those of a tiger. "Back in Angkor," she said, "I was making you a gift."

"You were?"

"Yes. A necklace. I was fashioning it with a piece of jade. To show you, my lord, how I feel about you."

"My lord?"

"If I'm your lady, then you are my lord."

He smiled, turned, and gestured toward the jungle around them. "So we rule over this kingdom? Over plants and trees?"

"Yes, my lord. It's our domain. Our subjects scurry about us."

His laughter surprised her. It was deep and robust, and she had never heard it before. "And our thrones?" he asked.

"Come," she said, taking his hand. "I will show you."

"Please do."

She smiled, leading him forward, feeling light on her feet. At first she walked, but then, weary of caution, she increased her speed, keeping her hand around his fingers, running along the trail. He laughed again, and she ran faster, heedless of the branches that slapped at her arms, of the monkeys that screeched overhead. She ran as she had as a child, not quickly to get from one place to another, but to feel the joy of movement, the air against her face. Bushes blurred, roots flashed beneath her feet, and still she ran, wanting him to see her strength, to realize that she was not afraid of the unknown. She ran and ran, splashing across streams, continuing to lead him ahead. A sense of euphoria filled her, though she wasn't certain if it came from being alive or from being alone with him. While they had known privacy in his chambers, the solitude of the jungle was liberating and cathartic. No one was watching over them, listening to them. They were truly king and queen of this unrivaled domain.

Her chest heaving, Voisanne slowed her steps, sweat glistening on her shoulders. She followed a stream that led to a deep pool beneath a banyan tree. Finally releasing Asal's hand, she waded into the pool and dived beneath its surface. The cool water was invigorating. She called out to Asal and laughed as he hurried to join her, remembered his sword, and returned to the shore to lean it against a boulder. Soon he was beside her. She splashed him, tried to escape his retaliation, and was suddenly in his arms.

What happened next surprised her, for without thought she leaned forward, wiped the beads of water from his face, and kissed him. His lips were soft, but she didn't notice that softness, didn't feel the water rising to her chest or the ray of sunlight that struck her shoulder. She sensed nothing but her yearning for him, and she pulled him toward her. He lifted her up—their hands clasped behind each other's backs, her breasts pressed against his chest. Her feet rose from the sandy bottom. She was weightless and in wonder. Leaning forward, she kissed him as she had run, with a flurry of movement, with elation born from hope. He was all that mattered, for in him she had found a sense of oneness that some people called love.

Her hunger for him overwhelmed her and she continued to kiss and clutch at him. She groaned and wrapped her legs around him, pressing herself against him. Their movements became more frenzied. He stumbled, then righted himself and carried her to shore, where he tried to lay her down. But she rose to her knees, still kissing him. He leaned down and his mouth moved to her neck and then to her breasts. She arched her back, crying out as he kissed and caressed her, clutching his bound hair.

They rolled to their right and she found herself atop him. His hands eased under the backside of her skirt cloth, squeezing the firm rises of her buttocks. She moaned, then kissed his lips and neck. Her mouth opened wider, and she bit his shoulder, as if intent on consuming him. Clasping her harder, he whispered of his desire, of how he'd longed to touch her for many days and nights.

His words prompted her to move faster—her thoughts fleeing as her instincts exploded into action. Again they twisted, and suddenly he was on top of her. He broke the string of her skirt cloth and pulled it aside. Her fingers ensured that soon he was also naked.

Voisanne had always thought that rebirth would come to her after death, but as she rejoiced in his warmth, she felt as if she had already traveled from one life into the next.

Farther to the north, still a day's journey from the temple of Banteay Srei, or the Citadel of Women as it was more commonly known, Vibol, Prak, Soriya, and Boran sat beside one another. While the Khmer warriors were scouting ahead, the family stared into the jungle toward a dead horse. The mount had been wounded by two arrows but must have thrown its rider and made its way from the site of the battle, because there were no other signs of fighting. It had died amid a group of thick ferns, either killed or discovered later by predators, for not much of the horse remained. The arrows were gnawed and bloody. The carcass was already covered with insects and soon would be no more than a scattered collection of bones.

As his mother applied a healing ointment to a cut on his forearm, Vibol thought about the horse, which had cast a pall over his family. Even so deep in the jungle, so far from the Chams, it seemed as if war followed them, creeping after them like the mist of a cool morning. And while Vibol was gladdened by the knowledge of their proximity to the Khmer stronghold, his mother in particular appeared to grow more tentative with each new step. She had told him that morning that they seemed to be marching toward death, that they should reconsider their path. When she looked at him for a reply, he nodded but said that he would go on alone.

Vibol believed that his future lay in being a warrior, not a fisherman. He had tried his hand at his father's trade and excelled at it. But when the Chams came, a hook and net had saved no one. The Chams had killed with their strength, they had beaten him with their strength, and they must be driven from Angkor by strength.

At first a need for retribution had motivated Vibol. He'd wanted to avenge his people and himself. But now he fought for the future, because he believed that unless the Chams were forced from Angkor, his loved ones would always fear what lay ahead. They could never rest in peace if Chams were nearby. He certainly couldn't. Not when he'd seen what they had done, the horrors that they so readily inflicted. Having the Chams as overlords was like fishing from a boat filled with snakes. Sooner or later, one would bite.

Though he was convinced of the necessity of his choice, Vibol regretted the hurt he was causing his loved ones. Prak brooded and played melancholy songs on his flute. Their mother clung to them both in ways that she hadn't since they were children. And their father tried to learn as Vibol did, to fight with a sword and defend with a shield. But his father was no warrior. He had lived a life that depended on patience—sitting on his boat, searching the surface of the water for fish and eels. From what Vibol had seen of warfare, battle was for the quick of mind and body. His father was neither.

"I should go on alone," Vibol said, as he had several times before.

His mother stopped tending to the wound on his arm. "Why do you say that?"

"Because all of you should stay together. It's my place to leave and yours to stay."

Prak closed his eyes. "You think the blood of brothers is so different from the water of rivers?"

"I—"

"The water is connected. We're connected."

"But I don't want to take you where you don't want to go."

"Don't tell me what I want," Prak replied, shaking his head. "Do you think that just because I can't see, I can't help? That I should just run away into the jungle? Am I a burden to you, Vibol? Now that you've found your warrior heroes, am I slowing you down?"

Their father cleared his throat. "They say that we're only a day away from the temple, from our people. You haven't slowed us down, Prak. You never have, and no one has ever thought that."

"But everyone expects me to run away."

Vibol reached out to his brother, wishing that he could see, but burying that wish deep down where Prak would never sense it. "I want you to come with me. I've always wanted that."

"Maybe my eyes don't work, but my ears do. And I don't believe what you say."

"Then you're not listening to me."

"I'm not?"

Vibol swatted away a mosquito. "No. Because—"

"Leave me be."

"Because when we're together, it's your mind and my eyes that make us work. That's always how it's been, how we've caught the biggest fish, bartered for the best price, found the courage to talk with girls who live in palaces. We did all those things together, and you were just as much a part of them as I was."

Prak turned away from the scent of the dead horse. "What do you want me to do?"

I want you to survive, Vibol thought. I want you to keep Mother strong in case something should happen to me. With you and Father beside her, her grief would pass. Maybe not in a month or a year, but someday it would. "I want you to do," he finally replied, "whatever you want to do."

"I want to go on. I've been thinking of plans, ways to attack the Chams. I want to destroy them just as much as you do."

Vibol saw his mother flinch. "We'll be careful," he said, staring at her. "I promise."

She looked away.

From ahead on the trail, voices came to them. The warriors were returning. Boran took his loved ones' hands and pulled them closer together. "I've always tried," he said quietly, "to keep you boys far from war. Because strong, poor boys often go to war. In war, such boys can make names for themselves, find wealth for themselves. But war is vile, like a carcass in the water. It corrupts the pure. It maims the innocent. You may look up to these warriors, and you may be right to do so. They seem to be decent men. But remember that their backgrounds are humble, like yours. And when the fighting starts, when the poor drench the earth with their blood, the rich will stand ready to seize whatever hasn't been destroyed. That's the nature of war. You'll fight and suffer and bleed. And those who haven't fought will claim the spoils of the day."

"But, Father," Vibol said, "some wars must be fought."

Boran nodded. "Wait, my son. Just wait. I've been thinking

long about these things, as long as it takes to set dozens of nets, and I'd like to share my thoughts. Because I agree with you. Some wars—a few among many—must be fought. It seems to me that kingdoms on the whole are good, but they sometimes are led by men with malice in their hearts. And when that happens, when a kingdom attacks its neighbor, that neighbor must defend itself. Otherwise a people, a way of life, may cease to exist. And that's where we find ourselves now, as the Chams have taken away what we hold most precious. Our homes are gone, our people dead or enslaved. And though I wanted to run from this war, to take all of you in my arms and flee somewhere distant and beautiful, I can't go to this place. I can't go because our way of life is more important than my life. And if I must die so that your daughters and sons will live as free people, under our laws and banners, then so be it."

As his mother stood up and walked away, Vibol stared at his father, finally understanding his actions. For so long, in his most secret heart, Vibol had feared that his father was a coward. This fear had turned him away from the man he had always loved, but he realized now that his father was as brave as the returning warriors, as anyone. His father didn't want to fight but would fight, not for himself but for his children and their children.

Vibol felt ashamed that he had doubted his father, the man who had taught him to fish, to read the wind and water. They had laughed together, cried together, and his father was no coward. "I'm sorry," he whispered, reaching out and clasping the thick, scarred hands that he knew so well. "I'm sorry for being such a fool."

His father squeezed his hands. "Just stay with me, my son. When the fighting starts, stay close and in that way we can safeguard each other."

*   *   *

Sitting atop his wounded horse, Indravarman rubbed the dried blood of his foes from his face, still enraged that his force had been ambushed and decimated. Though he had thousands of warriors at his disposal back at Angkor, he'd expected to return with Jayavar in chains, not with his honor and reputation in tatters. Surely the knowledge of his humiliation at the hands of the Siamese would embolden the Khmers.

Indravarman eyed the jungle, hating it. He was tired of insects and bats and thorns. Though desperate to fight his foe, he longed to do so on an open field of battle, where he could see his enemy, where strength could meet strength. Fighting in the jungle was for cowards, allowing them to hide and then kill.

Once Indravarman had gathered his men and charged the Siamese, they had scattered like minnows before a heron. Yet the damage had been done. The front of the column, which should have been as sharp as a spear point, had been shattered. Asal and other officers of high rank had been at this point, and they had failed him, allowing the enemy to achieve a complete and overwhelming surprise. Four hundred Chams were either dead or badly wounded. Worst of all, Jayavar was still free.

His rage boiling over, Indravarman struck the rump of his horse with an open hand. The mount, already wounded from a sword stroke, flared its nostrils but only briefly increased its pace. Indravarman called Po Rame forward, remembering how the assassin had disabled a Siamese officer with a simple flick of a spear. The Siamese had broken later under Po Rame's instruments, begging for his life and revealing the details of Jayavar's offer. The man had been bought by gold, and when Po Rame was finally done with him, Indravarman had stuffed a coin down his throat and watched him choke to death.

The trail was wide enough so that Po Rame could guide his horse forward until it walked beside Indravarman's. "Yes, Lord King?"

"Why am I surrounded by weaklings?"

"I don't—"

"Jayavar makes promises with gold he doesn't have, drawing Siamese into his ranks like flies to a corpse. And my men run like children at the first sight of the enemy!"

Po Rame smiled inwardly. He made no reply.

"Where is Asal?" Indravarman demanded, again hitting his horse, wanting to put distance between himself and his other men. "Why did his position crumble?"

"His woman is gone, King of Kings. They say he came for her even before the fighting started."

Indravarman swore, remembering how Asal had worried about the missing scouts. "If he deserted his post, if what you hear is confirmed, he shall die by fire. Cowards are always best killed by fire."

"And his whore?"

"She'll die beside him."

"A . . . fitting fate."

"You'd rather have them for yourself, to do with as you wish?"

Po Rame nodded. "I'd rather, Lord King, look into their eyes when they die. Fire would keep me too far away."

"Why? Why do the dying concern you so much?"

"Because it's in death that a man gives you his soul."

"You're a taker of souls, Po Rame? You consider yourself a God?"

"I—"

"You think you could take my soul?"

"Your soul shall live forever, King of Kings."

Indravarman spat dust from his mouth. "I despise the jungle, Po Rame. You seem to take pleasure in its shadows, but I detest them. Give me an open field of battle and let me see my foes."

"The jungle is for peasants, Lord King. As for your foes, let me dispatch them for you before they desert you once again."

"You speak of Asal?"

A shaft of sunlight penetrated the canopy to fall on Po Rame. He raised his hand, shielding his face. "The Khmer lover fled when you needed him, when your life was in danger. I'm told his sword was still sheathed."

"But up until now his counsel has been valuable, Po Rame. It was he who advised me to approach Angkor using barges, he who has led some of my best men to victory after victory."

"And yet now, Lord King, where is he?"

"With his Khmer," Indravarman replied. "And she shall die. But he may live a short time longer. I have need of him yet. I want Jayavar alive, and Asal might be the man to bring him to me."

"I will—"

"We lost four hundred warriors, Po Rame. Tomorrow, when we return to Angkor, pick four hundred of the fittest Khmers you can find. Round them up. Stand them in a courtyard. Then have our men practice on them with their spears and arrows. You may take as many souls as you like."

Po Rame clucked his tongue. "And then should I search for the coward?"

"No. Because like a loyal dog, he will return. If he can explain his absence, he'll live. Not because I feel merciful, but because his mind is sharp as his sword. And for the time being I need a few sharp minds."

"But once the false king is—"

"As I told you before, once Jayavar is mine, Asal can be yours."

"Thank you, Lord King."

"So pray to your Gods, pray to yourself, Po Rame, that the end is upon us. For my patience is waning. It's left me before, and when that happens my mind goes blank, my generosity becomes a thing of the past. And the people around me start to die."

*   *   *

The campfire was small and fickle, swaying in the slightest draft, illuminating only a few paces of ground. Asal had built it not for warmth, of which they had plenty, but to keep the evening's mosquitoes at bay. He and Voisanne rested beneath an outcropping of limestone near a stream. The half cave was deep enough to allow them to lie under it with only their feet exposed. On the other side of the fire, he had erected a bamboo fence that would hide the flames. Someone would have to be quite close to see the fire, and since Asal and Voisanne had left the game trail and found this secret place, he wasn't overly worried about discovery. Of course, he kept his sword and shield next to him.

Asal had cut thick ferns and laid them on the floor of the shelter, creating a bed of sorts. They had eaten wild fruits and nuts, bathed in the stream, and placed short, sharpened stakes around the perimeter of their encampment in case some person or beast approached in the dark. As the sun had set, they prayed together, calling upon their Gods to grant favors both small and large. In addition to asking the Gods to protect Voisanne, Asal had prayed for his men. He had always fought with their best interests at heart, but for the first time in his life, he felt as if he'd failed them. He should have sensed the ambush a moment earlier, should have pulled his men back into a more defensible position. Worse, he'd been forced to leave them to their own fates in order to protect Voisanne. His emotions had overruled his sense of duty, and while he felt blessed to have rescued Voisanne, he wished that he could have also saved more of his men, some of whom he'd seen fall beneath Siamese blades.

Now, as Asal and Voisanne sat cross-legged near their fire, he studied their environs, making sure that he had properly prepared for the night. Several spear lengths away, a thicket of bamboo ran alongside and into the stream. Taller trees rose to obscure the darkening sky. Frogs croaked, crickets chirped, and bats darted this away and that, avoiding branches as they chased insects. The stream gurgled, its waters illuminated faintly by the fire.

Asal closed his eyes, again musing over the ambush. He knew that many of his countrymen had died in the attack and wondered if Indravarman or Po Rame had been killed or wounded. The king would have been protected at all costs. And yet it was possible that an arrow or a spear had taken his life. In that case, many of Asal's problems would be solved. He could kill Po Rame before the assassin came for him. He could escape with Voisanne and her sister. Freedom might be his.

Careful not to create delusions, Asal reminded himself that Indravarman was highly skilled at war. He had most likely survived the ambush and would demand to know why Asal had fled. To protect himself, Asal had better concoct a convincing excuse during their journey back to Angkor.

"What are you thinking?" Voisanne asked, turning to him.

He saw how the firelight danced on her face, glowing on her smooth skin, on her lips. He had felt those lips and remembered their softness, wanting to touch them again. "Perhaps, my lady, you should escape tomorrow. I'd ensure that your sister followed in your footsteps. I could bring her to you."

"No. I have to escape with her."

"But Indravarman knows about you. And this knowledge places you in danger. He doesn't trust me, and to get to me he might use you."

"How can a king not trust his officers?"

"Because treachery was his path to power. Because his father, who led many, was betrayed and killed by a fellow officer. Indravarman fears what was done to his father; he fears that what he's done to others may be done to him. Moreover, he's never sired a son or a daughter. His blood does not flow in another, and because of that failing he trusts no one. He clings to power by removing those who might oppose him."

Voisanne shifted her position, resting her head against his shoulder. "Will you come with Chaya and me when we flee?"

"Where will you go?"

"I must go to my people. Not for myself, but for Chaya. She needs friends. Someday she will need suitors. And she can have neither while hiding in the jungle with me."

Asal nodded, putting his arm around her. Though he feared for the future, and remained torn about the prospect of betraying his countrymen, his spirits were buoyed by the sensation of her skin against his. He finally replied, "Your people might not welcome me."

"But Jayavar is forgiving. I've met him twice, and he will remember me. And when I vouch that you're to be trusted, I think that he'll believe me."

The fire was faltering, and Asal added two branches to it, then studied the darkness, ensuring that they were safe. "There was a time when I would have gladly died for my homeland. Now I contemplate running from it."

"Please don't run for me."

"If I run, my lady, it will be for us both."

"But maybe . . . you would risk too much. Maybe you should stay."

She looked away as she said these words, and he did not believe she meant them. "For most of my life," he replied, again stoking the fire, "I've felt as if the Gods have abandoned me."

"Why?"

"I've felt cheated in that everyone I loved was taken from me. My mother, my father, my siblings all died. My memories of them are faint, too faint. And worse, the memories that could have been never were." He paused, turning to her, surprised at himself for revealing his secrets, but needing to speak of them. "I've tried to convince myself that I wasn't cheated, that the best parts of my loved ones exist in me."

"They are in you."

"Perhaps. I do enjoy the sea, as my mother did. And my father taught me about hawks, which I still seek in the sky."

"I've seen you looking up . . . from time to time."

He smiled. "I look for him. I swim for her."

"You see, such things can't be stolen."

"I've tried to tell myself that. But after a battle, when I've endured loneliness and regret, I've still felt wronged—slighted by the Gods."

She moved against him. "I don't always understand the Gods," she said, running her hand along his thigh, "but I think that they can be fickle, granting favors one moment and ignoring our pleas the next."

The fire crackled, sending sparks toward the black sky.

"You speak the truth," he said. "Because now I no longer feel cheated, but blessed. The Gods brought me to Angkor; then they brought me to you. Some of the wrongs in my life have been righted. And that's why, my lady, I'll go with you. I'm not so foolish as to turn from such a blessing."

"You truly see me . . . in this way?"

"I see you . . . as something that fills the emptiness inside me, that warms the cold, that brightens the night."

She smiled, still stroking his thigh. "A warrior-poet. I've found myself a warrior-poet."

"I'm less the poet, my lady, and more the warrior."

"Then I'd hate to be your enemy."

It was his turn to grin. "When we return to Angkor, I'll find a way for us to escape. But it may take time. You must be patient and tell no one our plans. Not even your sister. When the time is right we'll simply come for her."

"And then we shall run? To my people?"

"Yes. We'll run for days and nights, and I don't know where the paths will take us."

An owl hooted in the darkness, prompting Voisanne to toss another branch on the fire. "I think you should trick Indravarman," she said. "If he's as mistrustful as you say, you should convince him that someone else is about to betray him. We could persuade Thida to whisper into his ear that you believe a traitor exists, and that you plan to track him to the north as he heads for a rendezvous."

"Yes . . . a version of that might work. But be careful, my lady. Be very careful. Treachery is Indravarman's weapon of choice, and if we fight him with that blade, he could turn it against us."

"Then maybe we should just sneak away in the night and run."

"Patience, my lady. You must have patience. Even though it suits you poorly."

She threw another stick in the fire and sparks flew. "What I must do is escape with you, because the Gods have also cheated and blessed me, and we can't waste this unexpected gift. It might not come again."

"You're the gift," he replied, kissing her lips. "A gift that I see, that I hear, and that best of all . . . I feel."

She leaned back so that she was lying on the ferns and looking up at him. He bent down to kiss her again, moving unhurriedly, like the dancing flames. He tried to further slow himself, for they had last come together in frantic need, and this time he wanted to savor their union. The Gods had blessed him, and he longed to honor them, as well as Voisanne. She was to be cherished, celebrated, and he could do neither if his desire overrode his control.

His lips and hands moved upon her, professing his feelings to her. He spoke not with words but in the way he held her. Though so much of him rejoiced at the sight of her, a part of him also feared that she would be pulled from him, that two people could not stand in the path of war and emerge unscathed.

Soon they would be back in Angkor, where he would be unable to protect her, to share his feelings as he was now.

Asal's lips parted from hers. His pulse raced, and he wanted to slow it, to make everything remain forever as it was now. But the fire burned, the trees swayed, and he bent down to kiss her again, his hands moving with more speed, his mind, body, and soul restless to consume all that she had to offer.

Fifteen

The Pain of Paths

he temple of Banteay Srei was as Ajadevi remembered it. The only major temple in the Angkor region not created by a king, Banteay Srei wasn't much larger than a cluster of ten homes. Built by a wealthy patron of the Hindu Gods, the site was made of light red sandstone and was much more detailed than the massive temples to the south. Surrounded by a head-high wall made of large, laterite blocks, the temple consisted of a platform that supported three towers.

Ajadevi and Jayavar had followed a long raised walkway to the main entrance, which brought them to a second walkway. This structure was roofed and graced by smooth pillars. At its end were several courtyards and a pair of ponds. The platform supporting the three towers was covered in intricate carvings that depicted demons, Gods, dancing women, snakes, and lotus flowers. Large swaths of sandstone had been carved to re-create heroic scenes from the Hindu epic *The Ramayana*. And though the temple was devoted to Shiva and Vishnu, inscriptions also championed the poor, the blind, the weak, and the ill.

The carvings were so intricate, it was said that only women could have made them. And, in fact, many of the carvings were of female dancers and guardians. Smiling feminine faces were everywhere, adding serenity and beauty to walls, columns, and towers. The Citadel of Women, as it was known by many, could not have been a more apt name. Whoever had designed the temple surely meant to celebrate women as well as the Gods.

Standing on the platform between two of the towers, Ajadevi stared to the south. Though the temple grounds boasted open courtyards and lotus-filled ponds, towering fruit-bearing trees rose from just within the surrounding wall. The bare-trunked trees were more than two hundred feet tall and featured leafy canopies. Khmer warriors had secured ladders to the trunks and nailed wooden platforms near the trees' summits. The views must have been unparalleled, and Ajadevi wondered whether the sentries could see all the way to Angkor.

"You were wise to inspect our position here," she said, turning to Jayavar.

"This place," he replied, "is the eye of the needle. It is the key to our future."

"If the Chams come, our troops will be well positioned to see them."

He nodded, his face glistening. "Yes, and our men on the ground will have time to flee. But our men in the trees will likely be sacrificed."

Ajadevi looked up, suddenly aware of how long it would take to climb down from such a vast height. Not long after the warnings had been given, the sentries would be surrounded by Chams and killed. "But how can we help them?" she asked.

"Nothing can be done. They might have enough time to climb down; then again, they might not. But they are volunteers. Most were wounded in the attack on Angkor. Some have arrows and will fight. When the time comes, the others will leap from the trees."

Though accustomed to the casualties of war, Ajadevi shuddered at the thought of men jumping willingly to their deaths. "Then we must attack the Chams before they discover us here."

"And we shall. But we need more time."

"Tell me why."

Jayavar wiped the perspiration from his forehead. "Because many of the Siamese mercenaries haven't yet arrived. Nor have most of our spies returned from Angkor. I'm somewhat blind to the Chams' numbers, to their defenses, and still lack a complete battle plan."

"How long will you need?"

"At least half a moon. We shall celebrate the Festival of Floats and then attack."

Ajadevi sighed, then turned around slowly, studying the thousands of carvings that graced walls and towers. She felt empowered within the Citadel of Women, as if the strength of each female face had somehow infused her with wisdom. The faces were telling her something, she was certain. But what they were saying she could not surmise.

"What?" Jayavar asked, turning so that he could better see her.

She walked over to a tower and touched one of the dancing women. "Banteay Srei doesn't soar, but of all the temples, it may be my favorite." Her fingertips traced the contours of the carving's face, lingering on its eyes. "And yet this temple was not built by a king, but by a commoner."

"What of this commoner?"

"Perhaps you place too much emphasis on your own designs for battle. Perhaps there's someone among us, a commoner, who has seen the Cham defenses and can give you the ideas you seek."

"But I've made inquiries. No one has come forward."

"Ask again," she replied, then studied the small groups of Khmer warriors clustered around the temple. The men seemed grim, she thought, aware that the usual banter among warriors was lacking.

"You must inspire them," she said. "You must inspire your people."

"I have ideas on how to do so, but might you have another?"

"You should make a float for the festival. And when we celebrate, you should set your float among the others. Speak to our people then, as you would to me. Not as their king, but as someone who cares for them, who loves them. Let them know that we shall win this battle and that it's one worth fighting for; that after we've won, our empire will be greater, and more noble, than it's ever been."

A dog barked, its cries echoing off the nearby walls.

"Look around you, Jayavar," she continued. "See how the temple inspires? How the dreams of its makers can still be felt on this day? You must inspire our people just as our temples do, by convincing them that they're part of something far more beautiful and glorious than themselves. That's what Khmers have always believed and what we must continue to believe."

His hand went from the hilt of his sheathed sword to the stone face that she had just touched. "Your father told me once, when I was courting you, that his pride in you was unequalled."

"He did?"

"He said that I'd come to cherish you above all else, and he was right. While there was a time when I coveted power and possessions, those desires have faded with the passing years. Now I simply long for this war to end so that we may spend the rest of our days together in peace, as I believe we were meant to."

"But we shall not spend them idly, my love, for we'll have so much to do."

"I agree. And those accomplishments will mark the summit of our lives."

She smiled, envisioning such a future when she need not worry about death and despair but simply how to share their blessings with those less fortunate. "When this war is over," she said, "we shall build hospitals and roads and courtyards. But we shall also build a temple to honor you, a temple with your face on it."

He shook his head while scratching a smudge of green lichen from the carving. "You make me into more than I am."

"Perhaps."

"And when this war is through, what shall I do to honor you?"

"Live, Jayavar. That is how you will honor me. Because the enemy will come for you and I so very much need you to live."

He had opened his mouth to speak when the sound of a horn pierced the air. The horn blew twice, indicating that a group of supporters, likely Khmers, was approaching. Four blows would have indicated the presence of Cham warriors. Jayavar's hand once again went to his sword hilt. "Come, my queen," he said. "Let's see who has arrived."

She watched him walk away, so familiar with the cadence of his movements. After a few paces, he turned around, seemingly surprised that she wasn't beside him. And so she went, as she always had and always would. She took his outstretched hand and squeezed it, and something within her trembled at the permanent yet untested nature of their connection.

Within one of the courtyards of Angkor Wat, Thida watched Indravarman practice his warfare. He wielded a bamboo pole, as did his two opponents. Though smaller men, they were skilled with their weapons and took turns assaulting him. Thida had seen Indravarman fight on several occasions but couldn't remember witnessing the fury that seemed to explode now with each of his attacks. A blurred shape, his pole swept and darted, humming as it sliced through the air. Each of his adversaries had been struck, and large bruises had already formed on their battered flesh. Yet Indravarman showed them no mercy, attacking as they retreated, using his pole, his fists, and even his knees. Drops of sweat and blood darkened the gray sandstone beneath their bare feet.

When Indravarman had his back to her, Thida glanced up at the magnificent towers of Angkor Wat, hoping that the majestic sight would overwhelm her memories of the previous day. She had stood beside the king as four hundred Khmer men had been rounded up, speared, and left in a pile for everyone to see. Wives and children had clung together, shrieking, and the cries still reverberated in Thida's mind. She had never seen such horror, and the very thought of it made her legs tremble. At one point she had started to ask Indravarman to stop the killings, but the intensity of his gaze had silenced her.

The fight continued, and when someone grunted, Thida turned back to the melee in time to see a man roll away from the king, clutching his side. Indravarman kicked him, then spun to face the other Cham. Thida wished that the smaller man's weapon would strike home. She feared Indravarman to a degree that she would not have believed possible. He'd brought so much suffering to her people. With each passing day she saw, heard, and felt their anguish.

The king shattered the second warrior's pole, then reversed his strike, bringing his weapon up and into the man's chin. Flesh split and blood flew. The Cham crumpled, and as he lay writhing, Thida couldn't help but pity him. Not one of the many observers came to his aid until Indravarman dropped his pole and walked away. He strode toward Thida, his body glistening with sweat. Despite spending so many nights with him, she was still surprised by his size. He was an immense man who moved with the speed and dexterity of someone much smaller.

"Walk with me," he said.

"Yes, Lord King."

He led her away from the courtyard and into a hallway. A golden bas-relief graced the near wall, and Thida studied the carvings of various Gods and demons. Cicadas buzzed. The scent of burning wood lingered. Indravarman turned to his right, proceeded up a long flight of stone stairs, and came to the second level of Angkor Wat. He then entered another courtyard and climbed a long, steep stairway that led to the top of the temple. For a moment Thida wondered what would happen if she pulled him backward. The fall would be terrible, perhaps even fatal. With one tug on his shoulder she could send him toppling and take control of her own fate. Yet she did nothing, merely following in his footsteps, soon panting with effort.

They reached the summit of Angkor Wat, stepped through massive, elaborately painted doors, and walked to an opening in the western wall that provided an unparalleled view of Angkor. Thida leaned against the parapet, her fists clenching at the sight of her country. Gardens, canals, and rolling green hills attracted her gaze, drawing her in and not letting her go. The bronze and gold towers of several temples sparkled in the mid-morning light. Birds wheeled beneath her, riding thermal breezes.

"A beautiful land," Indravarman commented absently.

"Yes, Lord King."

"Do you understand why we came here?"

She glanced up at his broad face, wondering how she should answer. "Isn't your land as beautiful?" she asked.

"Perhaps. But when you can have two sapphires why would you make do with one?"

"I don't know."

He grunted, then wiped sweat from his eyes. "Do you think me harsh? For how those men were killed?"

"What . . . what did they do, Lord King?"

"They did nothing. But their allies hid, plotted, and attacked. If such crimes went unpunished we would live in a lawless land. And I need law. I need order. Without them we'd be no better than the savages who live in the mountains, who make good slaves but are useful for nothing else."

"Yes, Lord King."

"I don't savor cruelty. Truly I don't. But it's a weapon and I will use it as needed."

"I hope that . . . you're not attacked again. Then, Lord King, there will be no reason for more cruelty."

Indravarman laughed. "How my timid Thida speaks up. You must be quivering inside."

She nodded, leaning slightly away from him. "I only want peace."

"Then tell me, are you willing to help achieve it?"

"What do you mean?"

"What has your friend Voisanne told you of my man Asal? I know him to be strong and able—the best of my officers. He is a crutch that I have leaned on from time to time. But his absence troubles me. Why have they still not returned?"

She shrank away from the fierceness of his stare. "I told you, Lord King. She ran away, and a Siamese warrior hurried after her. I heard her scream. Then Asal grabbed me . . . and he ran after them. I called for them but . . . but neither answered."

"Do you think they died?"

"I don't know."

"If they died, why were their bodies not found?"

"Lord King, I know only what I've told you," Thida replied, understanding that Voisanne needed her protection and trying to honor that need. "She doesn't care for him. Nor he for her. She pretends to, but that's all."

"Perhaps they deceive you."

"Perhaps."

Indravarman peered toward a distant temple. "Do you know why I worry over their fate?"

"No."

"I worry because I value him. I need a few good men and he's such a man. But every man has a weakness. Some covet gold. Others seek fame and glory. Maybe Asal has found salvation in that woman. If he has, that makes him harder for me to control. And a king needs to control his subjects."

Thida nodded, wondering what he wanted from her. "I don't know him, Lord King."

"But you know her. And you shall tell me what she says of him."

"But, Lord King, he isn't here. Nor is she."

Indravarman clenched his jaw, his facial muscles tightening. "I am both an easy and a hard man, Thida. Give me what I want, and I shall be easy. Deny me those wants, and I shall be hard. So when they return, as I believe they will, ask her about him. Women are cunning creatures, and I expect to learn much about those two from you."

She glanced up at him and then lowered her eyes. "I will try, Lord King."

"The dead have tried, Thida. They tried and died. The living . . . they have done more than try. That is how they live. Do you understand me?"

"I—"

"If you want to live, if you wish to avoid an unnecessary and unpleasant fate, you shall do as I say."

"Yes . . . I will."

"Good. Then come to me tonight, when the moon has risen. I shall reward your loyalty."

"Thank you, Lord King."

He turned away so suddenly that she was startled. Striding down the hallway, he ran his fingers along the carvings of dancing women, then turned a corner and was gone.

Thida tried to steady herself, to slow her breath. She thought about Voisanne and tears formed in the corners of her eyes. She trembled. Though she would never seek to betray her friend, Thida was terrified that Indravarman might see into her as easily as he did into others. She'd witnessed how his paranoia had led to the execution of both his friends and his foes. If he was worried about Asal, then he would look to her for answers. But what answers could she give? How could she possibly protect herself and Voisanne? To do both required skills that she did not possess. Until that very moment, deceit had never been a part of her life. She had always been taught the virtues of honesty, of truth.

To protect her friend, she would have to lie—an art for which she had no skill.

Thinking about the unfairness of life, of how others laughed and smiled while she suffered, Thida closed her eyes, prompting a tear to fall. She shuddered, filled with a sense that the world was too cruel for her. She had not been raised for such a world. Her mother had been too kind.

Boran waited patiently on his knees with his head bowed low. He had never been in the presence of a king, and despite the sweat that rolled down his back, his mouth felt dry. After glancing to his right to ensure that Prak was also prostrate, Boran rehearsed what he would say if questioned. The Khmer warriors who had accompanied Boran's family were in the midst of explaining to Jayavar and several of his officers what they knew about the Cham positions. When they finished, it might be Boran's turn.

Jayavar stood in front of a lotus-filled pond and the Citadel of Women. He was a broader man than Boran had expected, thick with aged muscles. His face was pleasant, however, and his voice and mannerisms encouraged conversation. Unlike the kings of stories and legend, Jayavar wore no jewels. He was dressed as a common warrior, carrying a round shield with a sheathed sword at his side.

Somewhere unseen near the temple were Soriya and Vibol, awaiting the conclusion of this meeting. Boran wished that they were with him. They would have enjoyed listening to the king.

The warriors finished their report, answered a few more questions from Jayavar, and left the courtyard. One of the king's men called Boran and Prak forward, and the fisherman's heart surged at the request. He rose to his feet, walked toward Jayavar, and again got down on his knees, lowering his head.

"Please stand," Jayavar said softly, motioning upward with his hands. "There is no need for formality here."

Boran nodded, though he kept his gaze downcast as he stood up. "Thank you, Lord King."

" 'My lord' will suffice."

"Yes . . . my lord."

"I am told that you've seen the Cham encampment at the Great Lake and that you possess an idea of how to defeat them there."

Boran started to speak and then stopped, his carefully rehearsed speech failing him. He was the son of a boat maker, a man who had no right to stand before a king. "My lord, we are . . . simple fishermen."

"Yet without fish we all would surely starve."

"Yes, my lord."

"Kindly tell me what you saw at the Great Lake. Tell me everything."

Boran glanced at Jayavar's face, then lowered his gaze. "They have many men there, my lord. At first it was . . . maybe two thousand. Then some went away—maybe half."

"And the number of war elephants and horses?"

"I counted forty elephants, my lord, but could hear more. The horses . . . maybe two hundred."

"And the boats. Please tell me about the boats."

Boran smiled for the first time since meeting the king. He understood boats. His confidence growing, he looked up. "I believe, my lord, that the boats are important to them."

"Why?"

"Because they're large, well manned, and come and go at all hours of the day. The Chams use them to bring supplies from their homeland. They're always carefully guarded, my lord. Smaller vessels, full of warriors, protect the bigger ones. And sometimes . . . sometimes, my lord, I think the Chams pile our treasure into these boats. I see the glitter of gold, and then the boats wallow deeper in the water."

Jayavar's fists tightened. "And what is your idea for how to defeat our enemy?"

"If it . . . pleases you, my lord, my son should speak," Boran replied. "For it's his idea. That's why I asked that he accompany me here."

The king nodded, and Prak straightened. To Boran's surprise, his son didn't keep his head low, but stood proud and ready. "Before I say anything, my lord, I should tell you that I'm nearly blind. My ideas come from my thoughts, rather than my eyes."

"As they should."

Prak smiled. "Thank you. Thank you very much."

"What do your thoughts tell you?"

"They tell me that the Chams could be trapped at the water's edge. I heard their laughter many times. They don't seem worried about an attack. They feast and laugh and sleep."

"And how would you attack them?"

Prak's hands came together. He remembered what his mother had said about needing to protect his brother, to save him with a plan that would ensure their victory. "The Chams are wound up like a ball of fishing line," he replied, his voice quickening. "They were cutting down trees to make room for their men, though for a while now I haven't heard their axes. And the stink of their encampment makes me think that they're packed tightly together."

Jayavar shook his head. "Armies always stink."

"Did you know that we sold them fish? We tricked them. And when we were tricking them an idea came to me."

"Tell me."

"The land where they've camped is so dry. During the wet season, the lake was higher, and all sorts of plants and trees grew in that wetness. But we're now in the dry season. The Great Lake is low, and all of that land, where the water previously was, is filled with dried-out bushes and trees. This time of year the wind often blows to the south, from Angkor toward the Great Lake. If we came from the north, if we waited for such a wind, we could light a fire that would race toward the Great Lake. That fire could trap the Chams, forcing them into the water, away from their elephants and horses. We could follow the flames, attacking from the land, or we could fight them from boats. Either way, we'd be in a far better position than they are."

To Prak's surprise, Jayavar laughed. "You say that you cannot see, but you've seen everything."

"I think fire would panic them, and when we came rushing in, they wouldn't know what to do. We would crush them, and maybe we could capture some of their elephants and horses. I've heard that no one can ride an elephant like a Khmer. Why don't we capture some for our warriors?"

Jayavar smiled again. "Retaking Angkor will require many steps. But yours could be the first. Indravarman wouldn't expect an attack at the Great Lake."

"And there are other Khmer fishermen selling their catch to the Chams. What if that catch was poisoned, or old enough to make some of the Chams sick? We could sell the old fish, then attack the next day."

The king turned to Boran. "Your son is wise beyond his years. Where did such wisdom come from?"

"I don't know, my lord. Certainly not from me. My life and thoughts are simple."

"My wife shall want to meet you both," Jayavar replied. "And to meet the rest of your family. She told me this morning that you'd be coming. She told me to listen to you, and I'm glad I did."

Prak didn't notice his father bowing. "But how did she know?" he asked without thinking. "How did she know we were coming?"

"Because, like you, she has the gift of vision. She sees signs. And the signs said that you would come."

"I wonder if—"

"We should leave, my son," Boran interrupted. "The king is a busy man." He turned to Jayavar. "When you're ready for us, my lord, when the queen is ready, we'll be yours."

Jayavar nodded, moving his hand to his sword hilt. "There is a secret place, my new friends, not far from here. It's full of water and fish, and I think you will like it very much. I will soon travel there. And I'd be honored if you would accompany me."

"We'll gladly go with you, my lord," Boran replied, lowering his head once again.

The king bid them farewell and turned to one of his officers.

Boran took his son's hand and led him away from Jayavar, squeezing Prak's palm firmly. When they were beyond earshot of their fellow Khmers, Boran told his son of his pride in him, because he'd advised a king and that king had listened. He added, "I think I just watched my son become a man. And the best sort of man."

"What kind of man is the best?" Prak asked, the temple a blurry red mountain before him.

"The kind who doesn't think of himself, but of others. And that's you, my son. The Gods may have taken your sight, but they replaced it with a strong and noble spirit."

"Thank you, Father."

Boran pulled his son into an embrace. "If something . . . should happen to me in the days ahead, remember what I just told you, that you're the best kind of man and that my pride in you is as deep as the waters of the Great Lake."

"But nothing is going to happen to you."

"True enough, my son," Boran replied, though a chill seemed to rush through him despite the heat of the midday sun. "Come," he said, "let's go find your mother and brother. They won't believe that they're about to meet the king and queen."

Voisanne and Asal sat in a long and narrow boat that had been painted red, equipped with a silk canopy, and featured a prow carved to resemble a dragon's head. The creature's face was green, its gaping jaws crimson, and its teeth and eyes white. The boat had most likely once belonged to a high-ranking Khmer official. At some point during the Cham occupation, the invaders had seized it. When Asal and Voisanne had come across the craft, he'd commandeered it from a trio of Cham warriors who seemed eager to give up the tedious task of guarding it.

The boat, a pleasure craft, was designed for the canals and moats of Angkor. Asal stood near the stern and used a long bamboo pole to propel the vessel forward. Voisanne sat near him on a wooden bench that spanned one side of the craft. She often glanced up at him, as well as looked ahead. From time to time the towers of Angkor Wat emerged from behind the trees. Taking on a golden sheen from the late-afternoon sun, the towers appeared as magical incarnations, too perfect to have risen from the minds of mortals. Voisanne both cherished and shrank from the sight, rejoicing in the beauty of her people's accomplishment but also fearful of once again being under control of the Chams. The past two days had been among the happiest in her life. She had laughed, run, swum, and been loved. Returning to Angkor, something she had always looked forward to, now seemed like the end of a beautiful dream, one from which she did not want to awaken. When she awoke, Asal would no longer be at her side. His shoulder wouldn't be there for her to rest on. His voice wouldn't be the last thing she heard before sleep swept her up. And instead of kissing him whenever an urge possessed her, she'd have to wait until he was with her and they were shielded from prying eyes.

"May I tell you something?" he asked.

"Of course."

"You might not like what I have to say."

"Then be careful, my big Cham, how you say it."

He lifted the pole from the water, thrust it forward, and dropped it again below the surface. Up ahead, a duck arose from the canal, its wing tips making circular ripples. Asal's smile faded as the ripples spread out and the duck climbed into the sky. "When we first sailed down from my homeland," he said, "I thought all Khmers were . . . beneath us."

"Why? Why would you think that?"

"Because that's what we were taught. Our minds were filled, cup by cup, with falsehoods. And I drank up all such tonics."

Near where the duck took flight, a snake swam across the surface of the canal, gliding with grace and speed. "I never felt that way about Chams," she replied.

He nodded, lifting the pole again. "But when I first glimpsed the towers of Angkor Wat, I wondered if what I'd been taught was wrong. Because I failed to see how something so extraordinarily beautiful could have been built by a people who were anything but extraordinary."

The distant towers drew her stare, rising like sculpted mountains, shimmering as the sun drifted toward the horizon. "My whole life," she replied, "has been spent in the shadow of Angkor Wat. And there's no place I'd rather have been."

"Beauty abounds in your land, my lady. I see it everywhere. In your temples, in your jungles, and . . . and in your face."

Her smile was fleeting. "But if you thought Angkor Wat was so extraordinary, why did you attack? Why did you seek to destroy such beauty?"

"Because a warrior does as he's told. Because sometimes fear is more inspiring than beauty. And I feared your people . . . and my king."

"And now?"

"Now only my king concerns me."

She lowered her hand into the water, watching miniature waves spread out from her fingers toward the shoreline, which was a tangle of plants, shrubs, vines, and trees. "I think fear comes from the unknown," she replied, watching the landscape. "Maybe if Chams lived in Khmer cities and Khmers lived in Cham cities we wouldn't be afraid of each other. We would still be different from each other, of course, but maybe it would be easier to see the beauty of both places."

"There is, my lady, beauty in both places."

"Tell me about the beauty of your homeland."

He lifted the pole, swung it forward, and dropped it again. "Our land is not unlike yours. We have valleys, rivers, lakes, end-less fields of rice. But while you climb hills, we climb mountains—steep and uninhabitable places where the Gods have left their marks."

Voisanne asked him more about where he was born, but her mind was suddenly elsewhere. Angkor Wat seemed closer, and she didn't want to go home, not yet. "If not for my sister, I'd run away with you," she said, interrupting him. "We could take this boat and head in the opposite direction, toward a place where we'd know peace."

"And I'd go with you, my lady."

"May we stay here just one more night?"

The pole slid down his hands until his fingers tightened. "I . . . I don't . . ."

"I understand that you must get back to your king. That he awaits your return. But will one more night make a difference?"

"He is . . . a demanding man. I have thought long about a story to tell him, a story that will calm his anger. I have a plan. But still . . . he will be hard to placate."

She nodded, trying to hide her disappointment. "Of course. Then we must go to him. Please forgive me for asking."

"There's nothing to forgive." He lifted the pole. The boat crept forward. Then he stopped once again. "But I also need no for-giveness, whether from the Gods or from Indravarman. And surely he can wait until tomorrow to see me."

"But you said—"

"I was once inspired by ambition, my lady, but now I draw inspiration from something else. And why should I return from this place one day earlier than necessary? Indravarman needs me. He relies on me. He won't harm me because he believes I can help him."

"Are you sure?"

"Yes. At least for now. At least until he feels safe within your borders. So let us enjoy our remaining time together. I shall re-turn to him tomorrow."

She smiled and rose, standing beside him. The thought of spending the rest of the day and night with him flooded her with anticipation. The sights and colors around her appeared so much more vibrant than they had only a moment before. Burdens seemed to ease from her shoulders. And unburdened, she felt younger, full of the same joy and playfulness that she had pos-sessed as a child.

"What was that?" she asked, pretending to search the nearby shoreline.

Asal leaned away from the boat, following her gaze, crying out as she pushed him from behind. He fell forward, landing in the water with a mighty splash and disappearing for a moment. He surfaced, spat out water, and laughed.

And then she was laughing with him. He grabbed the side of the boat and heaved downward, and she let herself fall toward him, striking the water, aware of his arms coming around her. She kissed him, no longer focused on the towers of Angkor Wat but on him. When their lips parted, she admired the strength of his features, taking delight in his delight.

They kicked for the shoreline, dragging the boat behind them. A patch of pink lotus flowers graced the water's surface, and they took care not to disturb them. Soon their feet struck the mud. They emerged from the water, passing a rotting log that was covered in flat white mushrooms.

The sun was dropping below the horizon, painting the landscape in hues of orange and amber. Asal started to kiss her again, but Voisanne stopped him, wanting to watch the wonders around her unfold. He was a part of those wonders, and she held his hand, pointing from sight to sight, in awe of the magnificence of the moment. The still water reflected the colors, creating a never-ending tapestry of reproductions.

The light faded slowly. Still holding Asal's hand, Voisanne stood up, looking toward Angkor Wat, proud of the towers, proud of Asal for appreciating their beauty. Her father had always told her that perfection was a word invented by poets and didn't exist in the world. And until that moment, she had believed him. But now perfection was tangible, as real as the air that she drew into her lungs. The world's ailments fell away. Instead, the triumphs of the Gods flooded into her, lifting her up toward a brightness that she had never before seen or felt.

Only when her feet were truly off the ground did Voisanne realize that she was in Asal's arms. Only then did she kiss him again.

Sixteen

The Scent of War

aving never seen so many people outside Angkor, Soriya eyed the vast encampment with awe. Temporary shelters made out of bamboo frames and covered with thatch seemed countless in number, though they were naturally camouflaged within the jungle. Cooking fires had been built in special stone ovens that hid the light and smoldered in front of many of the shelters. Women cooked rice and baked fish. Children played in the narrow river, for the most part unchecked, though mothers occasionally told them to avoid the intricate carvings.

Soriya wanted to enjoy the waterfalls, pools, and trees, as well as study the images of her Gods. Yet her gaze drifted repeatedly back to the warriors who so dominated the landscape. Both Khmer and Siamese fighters sharpened weapons, repaired shields, practiced swordplay, or slept after a long night on duty as sentries. Most of the men were serious, ignoring laughing children or beseeching wives. The Khmers were dressed in simple hip cloths while the Siamese preferred colorful tunics. Though the two groups had fought many battles against each other over the years, they existed peacefully now within the valley, bonded by a shared purpose—to drive out the Chams. The Khmers wanted their city back. The Siamese mercenaries coveted the gold that a victory would bring.

Since her family had arrived at the Khmer base the previous evening, Soriya had hardly seen her loved ones, who had been welcomed into the Khmer army. Prak wouldn't fight but had been on hand as his father and brother were given a shield, sword, and spear. In the few moments that Soriya had spent with Prak since his encounter with the king, he appeared to have swollen with pride. In fact, both of her boys, and even Boran to a certain degree, seemed filled with energy and eagerness as they mingled with scores of Khmer warriors and officers. Boran had told her that while he feared and despised war, it felt agreeable to be a part of something larger than himself, of a noble effort to return their land to their people. And Soriya, for all her misgivings about their course of action, was pleased that Prak had advised the king and that Vibol seemed to have been reborn.

Now, as she walked down a path near the river, she looked for her loved ones. The trail dropped, circumventing tree trunks, boulders, and immense anthills. Soriya said hello to strangers, smiled at some children who were making floats for the festival, and said a quick prayer while standing before a carving of Vishnu. She had asked Vibol to meet her near one of the waterfalls after he had finished some training, and hoped that he would be there.

Away from the river, on a slope leading up to a high ridge, Soriya saw that a group of officers had gathered around the king. He was standing on a boulder and talking quietly with them. Twenty paces beyond the officers, a ring of warriors ensured that no one else approached. As the king spoke, he pointed up the slope with a bamboo pole, thrusting the pole in various directions.

Some of the officers appeared to nod. As they moved, rays of sun-light reflected off their weapons and shields. Soriya wondered if Jayavar was discussing the recent Siamese attack on Indra-varman's force. He had been delighted to receive the news of the confrontation, which had been successful enough to at least stall Indravarman's thrust into the jungle.

Soriya turned from the gathering when she heard the distant waterfall. She increased her pace. Somewhere a horse neighed. Alongside the river, a swordsmith and a boy affixed steel spear-heads to long poles as thick as Soriya's wrists. She imagined one of her loved ones being impaled by such a weapon and her gait faltered. You aren't warriors, she thought. Please don't think you are.

A hundred more steps brought her to the waterfall. To her surprise and relief, Vibol stood on a flat boulder, apparently studying a carving near his feet. He carried a shield and spear. A sheathed sword hung from his side. The war gear made him look older, and even somewhat unknown. She called out his name and he turned to her, then motioned that she should follow him.

They entered the jungle and walked along another trail as it climbed a nearby hill. After passing a group of Siamese warriors and some Khmer children who laughed and waved at the foreign-ers, Soriya and Vibol made their way to the summit. The crest sprouted thick hardwoods, and shade was abundant.

Vibol leaned his spear against a tree. "Why did you want to see me?"

She realized that his right arm was bleeding from a long, nar-row wound. "Did a sword strike you?" she asked, reaching to touch him.

"It's nothing, Mother."

Nodding, she looked around for plants with healing proper-ties but saw none. "I'll fix that. I'll find some—"

"Don't. We're training and everyone has them."

"It doesn't look like nothing. Such wounds often fester."

He reached for his spear. "Why are we here? Why did you want to see me?"

"Why wouldn't I want to see you?" she replied, biting her bottom lip. "You're about to rush off to war and of course I want to see you."

"No one is rushing off anywhere. We'll be ready."

She glanced again for the right kind of plant, worrying about the wound. "I need to tell you something," she said.

"What?" he answered as nuts fell from a nearby tree, prompting him to look up and see a monkey.

"Please, Vibol. Please listen to me."

"I'm listening."

"Please do. I don't know how many more chances we'll have to talk, and I want to ask you something. It's important. And it will take a moment."

"So ask me."

She touched the edge of his shield, wishing that he didn't carry it. "Are you here . . . Did you come all this way because of that girl, that girl you kissed and the Chams killed?"

"What?"

"Prak told me about her, how you favored her and maybe even dreamed about her."

Vibol's jaws clenched. He started to speak and then stopped. "She used to smile at me," he replied quietly. "She smiled at me a lot."

"Why do you think she smiled so much?"

"I don't know."

"You made her smile, Vibol. And I'm sure she made you smile too. Didn't that feel good?"

He nodded absently, wiping away blood that oozed from his

wound. "Why are you talking to me about this? What does it have to do with coming so far?"

"Because I want you to know two things. First, that I support what you're doing here. I understand it. And second, I want you to make someone special smile again. I want her to make you smile." Soriya paused, waiting to continue until his gaze drifted up to hers. "Because when I look back at those days, they were when you were the happiest. You didn't talk about revenge or swords or anger. You just laughed and made excuses about needing to go into Angkor. And I want to see you like that again. So you must promise me one thing, Vibol. One promise and then I'll never ask you for another."

"What?"

"If the fighting goes bad, you must swear that you'll take your father's hand and run. Run like you've never run before."

He slowly shook his head. "Warriors don't—"

"You must run. Otherwise you'll never know that feeling again, that taste of love. Don't you want to experience it again? Don't you miss it? Please, my son, fight if you must. Take the fight to your enemies. But if the day is theirs, then you must flee. You must survive."

Vibol started to protest but stopped, finally nodding. "I don't think we'll lose. But if . . . if we're routed, I'll do as you say."

"Thank you."

"But we'll win."

"I know. I believe that. But if you don't, then you run. And bring your father. Prak and I will be waiting for you. We'll need your swords, Vibol, because the Chams will hunt us. You can still run and be a man. You can protect us from them. And later, when all the fighting is over, you can find a girl who makes you smile. You can make each other happy."

He wiped his wound again. "Don't worry, Mother. I've always been fast. So is Father. And if we lose, I'll do as you say. I'll run."

Once more she thought about the long spears, wishing she could protect him from their wicked points, terrified by the thought of steel within his body. She leaned forward, hugging him, squeezing him with all of her strength. He stiffened at first, but then she felt his muscles relax. He held her, promising that all would be well, that he was as fast as any animal in the jungle.

She made him repeat his promises, squeezed him again, and with great reluctance finally let him go. "I love you," she whispered, taking her necklace of fresh jasmine flowers and placing it around his head.

He smiled at her, nodded, and then, to show her his speed, hurried down the trail toward the warriors below.

Asal strode forward with grace and determination, trying to push thoughts of Voisanne out of his mind, worried about how the king would react to his delayed return. Though he had spoken confidently to her about Indravarman's reliance on him, he'd said such words while looking at her face, while being captivated by the possibility of spending another night with her. Now, so far from her, he regretted his choice. He should have returned earlier. While it was true that Indravarman relied on him, the king could still put him to death. Other minions would step forward to take his place.

In the distance Asal saw Indravarman and Po Rame, who stood atop a platform that was as high off the ground as a man could reach. Within a stone's toss of the platform, numerous war elephants were chained to various trees. Some used their nimble trunks to pull tender leaves from nearby branches. Others flapped their ears, shuffled their feet, and trumpeted. Cham warriors practiced mounting several of the elephants by stepping onto the beasts' raised left knees, then grabbing their left ears, and hoisting themselves atop the creatures' necks. The Chams were practicing while dressed in full war gear, and spears fell, curses rose, and men lowered their heads in shame.

Maintaining perfect posture, Asal announced himself to the king's guards, walked past them, and climbed up a ladder leading to the platform, which was about five paces long by three across. A flicker of a smile flashed on Po Rame's face. Indravarman didn't bother to turn around.

"Lord King," Asal said, dropping to one knee and bowing his head. "It pleases me to see you."

Indravarman grunted and continued to study the elephants. Slaves tended to many of the creatures, bringing them baskets of bananas and grass, applying poultices to wounds, and checking that the chains were properly fastened. Though the area had once been fertile, the elephants had trampled the undergrowth, and dust rose whenever they moved. Flies buzzed on their dung and sores.

"Explain yourself," Indravarman finally said. "Explain why it took you four days to return to Angkor when it took me two."

Asal readied an answer that he'd prepared the previous night, when Voisanne had been asleep in his arms. "Toward the end of the battle, Lord King, after I had killed many Siamese and my position had crumbled, I realized our women were in danger," he replied, creating a version of the truth. "My first duty, of course, was to you. And so I ran for you, but was cut off by countless Siamese. I slew several, but would have fallen if I had fought on. Instead, seeing that our women were unprotected and hearing their screams, I pursued their attacker, killed him, and again tried to return to you. But the Siamese were thick between us, and I was forced to go deeper into the jungle."

"But your position was at the head of our column! You left it for a woman?"

"My position was lost, Lord King. Please forgive—"

Indravarman spun around, kicking Asal hard in the jaw and knocking him from his half-kneeling position. "You pursued your woman and not your king? What if the Siamese had surrounded me?"

Asal had expected the blow. He returned to one knee, his jaw throbbing. Though he kept his gaze downcast, he watched his king's hands, fearing that they might dart to the hilt of his sword. "My men . . . will vouch for me, Lord King," he replied. "I alone warned them of the attack. I alone readied them. I fought with them until we were overwhelmed. My hands were wet with Siamese blood, and I—"

"Your men did vouch for you, which is why you still live. They said you fought like a lion. But lions are proud creatures, Asal. Perhaps too proud to return to their masters. Cut a lion loose, and who knows where it will go."

"Yet I am here now, Lord King. To serve you faithfully, as always. And I bring news."

"Then stand, fool, and share it."

Asal rose to his feet. "I interrogated a Siamese," he said, beginning the lie that he had so carefully prepared, a lie that was based on his suspicions. Though a part of him felt as if he was about to betray Voisanne, he knew that he must give Indravarman something. "The Siamese was a high-ranking officer, privy to information. He told me that he was supposed to lead his men to the Citadel of Women, and that—"

"But we know this!"

"But we didn't know, Lord King, that the Khmers would then take the Siamese to a nearby valley, where the true Khmer army awaits. And where Jayavar is planning his retribution."

Indravarman rubbed the iron in his belly. "We suspected as much."

"Yes, Lord King. We did. But my prisoner confirmed our suspicions. And looking at him, it occurred to me that some of our men speak both Siamese and Khmer. We could dress such men as Siamese, and they could travel to the Citadel of Women. After they were brought to the secret base, one of them could slip away and return to us. He could then lead our army directly to the Khmers. Surprise would be our ally. Victory would be the outcome."

Po Rame chuckled. "It took you four days to conjure such a plan? A plan that any child could devise?"

"Simple plans are the best," Asal answered. "Any warlord can tell you that."

"Warlords don't flee from battles. Cowards do."

Asal's hand dropped to his sword hilt. "With your permission, Lord King, I'll rid the world of this—"

"Yet you did run, Asal," Indravarman replied. "And you took four days while we took two. It seems to me that you felt a greater duty to your woman than to your king."

"You will always come—"

"And now is not the time for the petty differences between you two to be settled. Now is the time to serve me."

Asal's hand dropped from his sword. "My plan, Lord King, will work. We can end this war."

Indravarman nodded, then spat dust from his mouth. "A week ago, I would have let you seek out this valley, while other men were sent to the temple, as you suggest. But now . . . now my faith in you has wavered. I see a warrior. I see a keen mind. But I also see a man divided. A Cham, yes. A man who has served me well. But also a man who has let the spells of a woman affect him. The next time you're faced with such choices, return to me in one day instead of four; kill ten Siamese instead of three. Do these things and your woman shall live. Fail me again and I shall gut her like a wild boar."

Asal tried to speak but could not. He nodded, his gaze lowered.

"I let you live only because I admire your plans," Indravarman added. "And we shall proceed against the Khmers as you advise. Three thousand more warriors will arrive from our homeland in ten days, landing at our base on the Great Lake. Once they do, we'll march on our foe, intending to attack them in this valley. So you shall continue to carry a sword, to lead men, to act as my council. But for the rest of this day you'll set your weapons down and become a slave."

"What . . . would you have me do, Lord King?"

Indravarman gestured toward the elephants. "The foulness of this place offends my senses. Clean it up. Rid these fields of dung."

"Yes, Lord King."

"Only do not use a shovel, but your hands. And be thankful that I've let you keep them."

Po Rame laughed, using his index finger to point from elephant to elephant, pretending to count them. "Better wash, slave, before you seek your woman again. Wash and pray that she doesn't find me more appealing."

Though he wanted to warn the assassin to stay away from Voisanne, Asal knew that by drawing more attention to her, he'd only place her in greater danger. Ignoring Po Rame, he unbuckled his sword belt and set his weapon on the platform. "My plan will work, Lord King. If it doesn't . . . you may have my hands."

Indravarman pursed his lips. "There is another reason you still live, Asal. I'm in a benevolent mood, for soon we'll find the Khmers, and after every last drop of their blood has been spilled,

I'll ponder which of our warriors deserve fame and wealth. Some will receive these spoils. Others will collect elephant dung for the rest of their lives. And you, Asal, you must decide which of those men you will be."

Asal nodded, then climbed down the ladder and approached a massive bull elephant not more than twenty paces away. Without hesitation, he bent down and used his hands to scoop up a pile of dung. The dark matter was warm in his hands. Flies buzzed against his face. And Po Rame's laughter echoed in his ears.

Yet Asal almost smiled. His plan had worked. He was still alive. Best of all, after the day had passed, he would wash himself in the river, tend to those of his men who had been wounded in the ambush, decide how and when Po Rame would die, and then return to Voisanne.

He imagined her face, recalled the fullness of her lips, the heat of her body. For her he'd gladly clean up after a thousand elephants. He'd scoop up dung as if he had been born to do it. The only way that Indravarman could truly punish him would be to take her from him, and to avoid that awful fate, he simply needed to outsmart the king.

He needed to run.

Because their Cham guard would not likely follow them into the moat, Voisanne removed her skirt cloth, covered her privates with a cupped hand, and stepped into the dark water, following Thida. Holding her skirt cloth with her other hand, Voisanne waded out, the water rising from her ankles to her knees to her belly. Since the day was overcast and cool, the moat was not as crowded as usual during the hot season. Still, children chased water bugs, warriors cleaned wounds, and women washed their bodies, their hair, and the clothes of their loved ones.

Across the waterway, a group of Khmer men was gathered around what Voisanne assumed was a pair of fighting roosters or boars. Behind the men and across a road sprawled the marketplace, which was dominated by scores of stalls and many hundreds of shoppers. Occasionally, the shoppers were obscured as elephants moved along the road, either pulling wagons or carrying several Cham warriors. Dust rose from beneath the beasts' feet, hanging like a cloud over everything and everyone. It seemed to Voisanne that more elephants were on the move than usual, and she wondered why.

On the other side of the moat sprawled Angkor Wat. As she stepped backward into an empty stretch of water, Voisanne eyed the temple, which dominated the entire western horizon. The perfect symmetry of the soaring central towers held her gaze, and she wondered who had dreamed up the site. She couldn't imagine where such inspiration came from and was glad that Angkor Wat not only moved her, but had also made Asal question the necessity of the Cham invasion. Perhaps there were other Chams who felt as he did—that the builders of such a wonder ought to be celebrated instead of subjugated.

Though not even a full morning had passed since she had said good-bye to Asal, Voisanne felt as if she hadn't seen him in days. She missed him more than she had ever expected to, feeling vacant in his absence, as if he'd once dwelled within her but had gone away. The memories of their laughter and conversations and lovemaking weren't enough. She needed his immediate presence in her world, and her thoughts focused on how and when they might be brought together.

When Thida finally reached an area of water that was unoccupied by either Khmer or Cham, she turned to Voisanne and hugged her. Voisanne held her friend tight, stroking the back of her head, the water up to their shoulders. "I'm sorry I left you when the Chams attacked," she said quietly. "But I couldn't stay there. I had to go."

"Don't be sorry. You did what I should have done."

"But friends don't leave friends. I thought of myself when I should have thought of you."

Thida shook her head, eased away from their embrace, and began to wash her skirt cloth. "Indravarman found me and . . . laughed at me."

"Why?"

"Because I screamed when I saw him. He was covered in blood. His face was . . . crazed. And I just screamed."

"And he thought that was funny?"

Thida nodded. "He laughs at me because I'm weak. Because I cry. I think he enjoys seeing me distraught."

Guilt flooded into Voisanne as she remembered leaving Thida beneath the burning cart. "Just because he's as big as a mountain doesn't mean that he's strong."

"He is strong."

"If he were strong, Thida, I don't think he'd laugh at you. He wouldn't revel in your fear. That's what the weak do. They lift themselves up by beating others down."

Thida wrung her skirt cloth. "I don't know. Everyone fears him. And why would everyone fear him if he were weak?"

"Asal doesn't. At least, not much."

"Well, he should."

An elephant trumpeted. Voisanne remembered how Asal had told her to keep silent about their plans for escape. She wanted to honor his wishes but was conflicted because of the guilt she felt over leaving Thida. "You're not weak," she reiterated, squeezing Thida's hands. "And you can prove it."

"How?"

"You can escape with us. Asal is making arrangements. In a

few days, he and I shall leave along with my sister. You should come with us, Thida. And when you do, you'll prove to Indravarman that he misjudged you, that there's more strength in you than he ever knew."

"He'll kill us."

"Only if he catches us. And he won't."

Thida backed away, shaking her head. "No. It's too dangerous. He watches you, Voisanne. And if you leave the city, he'll hunt you down."

Stepping forward, Voisanne gently pushed aside a pink lotus flower floating on the water's surface. "We know that he watches us. But we can still escape. Just because a snake watches a frog doesn't mean that the frog will be eaten."

"You don't understand him! He has spies everywhere. He—"

"Shh," Voisanne interrupted, putting her finger to Thida's lips.

"Maybe . . . maybe I am weak," Thida said, "but I've heard how his executioners peel the skin from men, gouge out their eyes, cut off their manhood. That's how Indravarman treats those who cross him. And you will be crossing him, Voisanne. You'll cross him in the worst possible way."

Voisanne glanced around, suddenly afraid. Fortunately, neither Cham nor Khmer was nearby. "But I think . . . that is how he rules. He creates fear. He depends on it. He believes that your fear has made you a beaten woman, Thida. But you don't have to be beaten. You don't have to spend every day in fear. Asal is smart and strong. His plan will be good. And when we're free, you can go back to being whoever you were before Indravarman swept into your life. Don't you want to be that person again?"

Thida nodded, though she looked away.

"Then come with us. When the time is right, I'll get you. Just be ready to go."

"And you'll . . . stay with me?"

"I promise," Voisanne replied, taking her friend's hands. "I won't leave you again. When I did that, I was afraid, just like you were. And I'm not going to be afraid anymore. Because fear is what Indravarman is counting on. The only way to beat him is to take that away from him."

A koi broke the water's surface—a flash of orange and white that disturbed the reflection of the sky.

"I'll . . . be ready," Thida said quietly.

"And tell no one."

"I won't."

Voisanne squeezed Thida's fingers. "It's all going to be fine. Have faith in the future, Thida. Have faith that goodness will overcome wickedness, that your strength will overcome your fear."

Later that day, as the sun had started its descent, Po Rame followed Thida while she walked along Angkor's streets. One of the assassin's informants, whom he'd assigned to report on Voisanne, had told him of their emotional meeting earlier that afternoon. Though the informant hadn't heard what was discussed, he had seen their hugs and tears, and after the meeting he had followed Voisanne back to Angkor Wat, where she had prayed. Oddly, she had then purchased a small cooking pot, spices, and a bag of dry rice. Only when Voisanne had returned to her quarters did the informant seek out Po Rame and tell him about Thida.

As Po Rame followed Thida down an alley, he wondered why she had been so distraught during her rendezvous with Voisanne. Certainly the woman could have been airing her grievances against Indravarman, or perhaps she was simply lonely. But Po Rame believed that the cooking pot and the rendezvous were connected. Normally household slaves bought such goods and prepared the meals. A woman of Voisanne's position had no use for the cooking pot and wouldn't be expected to buy one.

Thida left the most populated part of the city and headed north, following a tree-lined road. Po Rame trailed her at a distance, dressed as a common Cham warrior, hating the attire but believing it was necessary. He studied Thida's movements, unaware of a pair of blue butterflies circling each other to his right. Nor did he hear the cry of cicadas or the banter of passing priests. His senses were completely homed in on Thida. She was more a part of his world than the dirt beneath his feet or the trees that filtered out the weakening sunlight. He was convinced that she was still distraught. Her uncertain gait told him as much, as did the way she clenched and unclenched her fists. Something was troubling her, something perhaps that she had learned from her rendezvous with Voisanne.

Though a part of him wondered if he should expend so much time on a pair of women, Po Rame knew that his old adversary, Asal, was on dangerous ground. His tardiness had almost cost him his life. Encouraged by Po Rame's allegations, Indravarman had been close to gutting him. And yet in the end Indravarman had let Asal live, mainly because the king counted on him more than he would care to admit. He respected him as well, treated him as more of an equal than any other man, including Po Rame. During the past several months, Po Rame had felt particularly slighted by Indravarman's favoritism toward Asal. While it was true that Asal had planned much of the invasion of Angkor, Po Rame had also experienced more than his share of successes.

Despite Indravarman's reliance on Asal, Po Rame knew that the king would not stand for another failure or betrayal, and Po Rame believed that Asal and Voisanne's relationship could be exploited. Something between them wasn't right. He needed only to determine what that something was and then bring it to Indra-

varman's attention. At that point the king would allow Po Rame
to do what he had longed to do for several years—slit Asal's
throat and watch as his life force emerged and offered itself for
the taking.

The farther Thida walked from Angkor Wat, the fewer people shared the street. She had nearly reached the northern gate to
the city, which overlooked a portion of the moat. Of course, the
gate was mostly for decorative purposes, as the only way to cross
the moat on foot was via the causeway on its western side. Po
Rame allowed the distance between himself and Thida to increase. She seemed unaware of him.

Thida stepped into a drainage ditch that bordered the street.
In the wet season the ditch would be full of water that would run
into the moat. But now the ditch was dusty and brimming with
weeds. She continued walking until she arrived at a smaller street
that ran perpendicular to the one she had been following. At this
intersection the ditch entered a brick tunnel that ran beneath the
secondary street. She paused at the entrance to the tunnel, bent
over, and called out.

Po Rame watched as Thida removed something from within
the folds of her skirt cloth. She whistled softly, holding out her
right hand. Po Rame was reminded of her beauty as she leaned
over, her high, full breasts swaying. Thida's long, thin legs seemed
to glow in the dying light. Suddenly Po Rame felt an urge to ex-
tinguish such beauty from the world, to look into her eyes as he
choked the life out of her. His victims had been old and young,
men and women, healthy and sick. But never had he stolen life
from someone as beautiful as Thida. In a world where objects
were usually more striking than the people who made them, she
was a notable exception. Her face and body were so perfect in
their dimensions and contours that surely the Gods must have
spent much time creating her.

Understanding why his king desired Thida, and craving her for himself, Po Rame crept closer. He heard a kitten's cry come from the tunnel, which prompted Thida to shake her hand and whistle louder. After a Cham warrior leading a horse had passed by, Thida tossed something into the tunnel. She waited patiently, then called again.

Only when the street was almost empty did the kitten emerge. It had a gray back and a white belly. At first it sniffed at Thida's outstretched hand, then rubbed the side of its head across her fingers. It nuzzled against her, arching its back. Thida took the kitten in her hands and stood up. She cradled it, kissing its forehead.

Po Rame moved closer. He was now only about twenty steps from her. He sat down in the shade, set the old spear he carried on the ground, and pretended that he had a splinter in his foot. He plucked at the imaginary splinter, all the time looking at her, listening to her. As long as no one else was present on the street, her words carried to him. At first she told the kitten how good it was to see it. She asked if it was hungry, fed it something, and then stroked its back. The kitten meowed, prompting her to kiss it again.

An elephant and its Cham rider approached and Po Rame cursed his luck. He wished he could kill with a stare, then imagined the warrior toppling off the elephant and the beast turning away. Neither event happened, however, and Thida turned to her left, placing herself between the beast and the kitten. An instant before her gaze fell on him, Po Rame focused on the imaginary sliver, swearing as he pretended to pick at his heel.

The elephant disappeared through the northern gate. Po Rame continued to pick away, nodding to himself when she refocused her attention on the kitten. She held it against her chest, saying that she was sorry for not bringing more food, but that the kitten would have to learn to survive by itself because she would soon be leaving.

Po Rame's fingers stilled at her words. As far as he knew, Indravarman had no intention of taking Thida outside the city again. And if that was true, why would she speak of leaving? Did she plan to flee without his consent? Is that why she had been so emotional with Voisanne in the moat?

For a moment Po Rame considered interrogating her then and there. But Indravarman had not ordered him to shadow her, and if she was innocent of any wrongdoing, the king would be furious with his unwelcome intervention. No, it would be better to continue to watch her. If she fled, he could capture her and return her to Indravarman. At that point, if betrayal had been on Thida's mind, Po Rame was certain that Indravarman would give her to him.

His pulse quickening at the thought of possessing her, Po Rame pretended to pluck the sliver from his heel. He stood up and walked toward the northern gate, staying in the shadows, avoiding even the dying light of the sun. Her voice changed to a whisper and she held the kitten close, against her chest and under her chin. What she said to it he did not know. But when she looked up at him, he smiled. If she left Angkor, if she took a step in the wrong direction, he would be there.

Are you afraid to leave? Po Rame said to himself. Is that why you argued and wept in the moat?

Still deep in thought, he stepped through the northern entrance to Angkor. Before that day he'd always believed that Thida was too weak to run. But perhaps Asal's woman was fueling a mysterious fire within her. Perhaps they would run together. If they did, Asal could be blamed, regardless of whether he had anything to do with their flight.

Eager for the coming days, to see how the plans of his quarry would play out, Po Rame dropped the old spear, his pace increasing. If Thida did run, she would start a chain of events that would be very much to his liking. Three lives might be given to him, to do with as he pleased. Which soul, he wondered, would add the most strength to his own? With Thida came beauty. With Asal came power.

Voisanne was more of an enigma, but whatever wisdom, knowledge, and strength she had gathered throughout her many lives would become a part of him. And when the light of her passed into him, when he trapped her soul within his own, he would be closer to becoming a God.

In time people would fall on their knees before him. In time even Indravarman would beg for his favor.

But first he had to catch those who would run. He had to lay a trap.

Jayavar thought the cicadas seemed louder that night, even though a nearby fire crackled and popped, hidden within a tall circle of cut timber. The blending of the insects' buzzes created a constant hum that was strangely comforting. He was certain that his ancestors had gone to sleep listening to the same noise. Did the Hindu Gods hear it? he wondered, thinking about the nearby carvings of Vishnu and Shiva. Or had they created cicadas to lull mortals to sleep?

In some ways, Jayavar thought, his army was like the cicadas, for though the insects made so much noise, he rarely saw them. Despite their multitudes, they remained all but invisible. His warriors were much the same, a powerful force that blended into the landscape when needed, that would soon fill the air with battle cries.

Jayavar glanced behind him into the bamboo and thatch shelter where Ajadevi slept. Her belly had ached for much of the afternoon and she had become uncharacteristically downcast, saying that she missed the companionship of her sisters. Her words and pains had caused him to worry. Too many of his acquaintances had developed an ache in the belly, breast, or head and died a few months later.

As he had several times already, Jayavar prayed for her health and well-being. Her stamina wasn't what it used to be, and he wished she wouldn't demand so much of herself. He had asked her to slow down, but it was obvious that she would continue to push herself, and push him, until the Chams were defeated.

Standing up, Jayavar surveyed the landscape. Though great effort had been taken to cloak the cooking fires, he could still see faint orbs of light that dotted the deep valley, a sight that made him uncomfortable. If a Cham scout happened into the immediate area, surely he would realize that the Khmers had taken refuge here. Prudence demanded the fires be put out, yet Jayavar made no such order. The fires kept mosquitoes, snakes, scorpions, and tigers at bay. Back in Angkor his people lived in stilted homes and slept under fine nets. But in the jungle they had no such luxuries. So the fires were a gift, albeit a dangerous one.

A man coughed. Jayavar turned toward the sound, worried that disease would find its way into their camp. Dysentery was a curse that had plagued his people since the dawn of time, and on any occasion when Khmers were crammed tightly together, this curse might rise up and claim many lives. Jayavar had no idea how to combat the disease. Healers had told him that fast, fresh water was helpful and he felt blessed by the presence of the nearby river. So far his people had been mostly spared, though a few had succumbed to the fevers of malaria.

We need to be back in our homes, he thought. We've lingered here long enough.

He crept toward his shelter, smiling at how Ajadevi slept, with her knees drawn toward her chest as if she were still a child. Certain that she was in a deep slumber, he moved behind his shelter where he had hidden some discoveries he'd made earlier that day. A white, crescent-shaped boulder, polished by the passage of the river, first caught his stare. He picked it up, trying not to grunt, and carried it into the shelter. With care he set it beside Ajadevi, then positioned it so that its profile faced in her direction. He walked outside again and gathered five peacock feathers that he'd found on a game trail not far from the river. The feathers, dominated by green threads and blue orbs at their ends, were among nature's most wondrous creations, he thought. He placed them against the boulder, arrayed to resemble a fan. Last of all, Jayavar collected a pomegranate, star fruit, and mango, which he set beside the boulder.

Ajadevi liked to awaken to beautiful sights, and Jayavar hoped his arrangement would please her. He had put thought into choosing each object, for she would look from the stone to the feathers to the fruits, seeing purity and purpose in each. She would tell him what she saw, then ask why he had chosen the white rock instead of a red one, or the feathers instead of flowers. They would talk, smile, and the pain in her belly might be forgotten.

After studying his wife's face, Jayavar left the shelter. He thought of his unborn child, wondering if the world would be graced by a girl or a boy. A boy would be better for the empire, but Jayavar had always delighted in his daughters and would be happy to have another girl enter his life.

Whether I have a son or a daughter, I must bring peace back to my people, he thought. Because all sons and daughters deserve peace.

The nearby fire popped, casting a spark into the sky. Jayavar thought about the coming days. First they would celebrate the

Festival of Floats. Then he would address his warriors. And finally his army would march to the south. A battle would be
fought, the biggest battle of his life. He'd have to lead his men,
and there was a strong chance his life would end and that his succession of rebirths would continue.

Jayavar wasn't afraid of death because he believed that Buddha was right—that karma was crucial to the evolution of the
soul, and Jayavar had always tried to be kind and just toward others. His soul would most likely ascend. And yet, when the eyes of
this body ceased to see, Ajadevi would be taken from him. The
greatest gift he had ever known would cease to be the most important part of his life. Ajadevi would be with him in spirit, and
she'd come back to him, but the face he so cherished would no
longer be the first sight he saw in the morning or the last of the
evening.

The fear of such separation causing his breath to quicken,
Jayavar crept back into the shelter. He shifted one of the feathers
to the right. He twisted the pomegranate so that a small bruise
wouldn't show. And then he lay down beside her, drawing her
close.

Seventeen

Tributes

wo days later, not long after the city's roosters announced the coming of dawn, Voisanne made her way to the Royal Palace. She had wanted to see Asal the previous day, but he'd been outside Angkor's gates at an unknown location. No word had come from him until this morning, when a slave knocked softly on her door and handed her a sealed message. The writing was in Asal's hand, asking her to come to his quarters. She'd left immediately, moving through the darkness like a living shadow.

The Royal Palace—with its towering ceilings, tiled floors, and columned rooms—was illuminated by flickering candles. Slaves used thatch brooms to sweep the hallways. Cats prowled around open spaces in search of mice. And a trapped swallow fluttered this way and that, seeking an escape from the imposing walls. Most Cham officials and warriors, as well as their servants, slaves, and courtesans, were still asleep.

Voisanne walked to Asal's room and pressed her hands against its door, thumping her thumb on the wood. She sensed movement within the room and then the door swung slowly open. Asal reached for her hand and led her inside. She saw immediately that his eyes were bloodshot and his face haggard.

"When did you last sleep?" she whispered, squeezing his fingers.

He leaned down and kissed her. Then he touched her face, traced the contours of her jaw, and once again pressed his lips against hers. "I have much to tell you," he said quietly. Before she could answer, he shut and barred the door behind them. They moved to his bedding on the floor and knelt on his silk blanket, facing each other, their knees touching.

She saw the concern on his face and leaned forward. "Why did you send for me?"

"Because the end draws near," he whispered.

"Tell me."

He nodded, but instead of speaking, he kissed her again. "I've missed you, my lady. Only a short time has passed since I saw you, but it felt like an eternity."

"I know," she replied, nodding. "For me as well."

"Things that I once cared for have become meaningless."

"Such as?"

"Ensuring that my sword didn't have a fleck of rust." He glanced at his weapon, which was propped up in the near corner. "I used to scrub that blade until it shimmered like the sun. Now all I care about is that it's sharp."

She liked the sensation of his knees touching hers. She wished that she could feel more of him. "And now . . . since your sword no longer needs to shimmer . . . what catches your gaze?"

"You, my lady. You're all I need."

"I'm only a woman."

"And the sun is only a light in the sky."

She brought his hand to her lips and kissed a scarred knuckle.

"I made you something," she said, and reached into her skirt cloth and removed a necklace. A thumbnail-size piece of unfinished jade had been crisscrossed with a silver wire and hung from a thin strip of leather. "I found this stone at the edge of the river when I was with you. I thought it seemed strong and wise, just as you are."

He smiled, examined the stone, and then placed her gift around his neck. "Thank you, my lady."

"You're welcome, my big Cham."

"I shall always wear it."

"The stone suits you."

"You suit me."

The morning light filtered into the room. Voisanne knew that soon people would be waking. "Why did you send for me?" she asked.

He beckoned her closer. "I've found a guide," he answered, his words barely audible. "A Khmer guide. We shall leave tonight when the moon rises over the horizon."

Her pulse quickened. "Leave for where?"

"That's up to you."

"Why?"

"Because we have two choices. We can run from war. We can find a secret place where we'll remain unseen. Or we can run to your people. But the second course will be a perilous one. Indravarman's spies are on their trail. They near them. Soon a fresh horde of my countrymen will sail into the Great Lake. Indravarman will assemble every man he has, march north, and attack and overwhelm your people."

Voisanne stiffened, shaking her head. "Then we must warn them. Please, please tell me that we can warn—"

"I knew your answer would be so," he replied. "And, yes, tonight we'll strike out to warn them. Tell your sister to be ready.

We'll meet on the north side of Angkor. Across the moat there is a teak tree that's recently fallen. Meet at this tree."

"And Thida. I have to bring Thida."

"Why?"

"Because I left her when the Siamese attacked in the jungle. And I can't leave her again."

"Then bring her. But tell no one else. Travel with enough provisions to last for three days but no more than that. Once Indravarman learns that I've fled, he'll send men after us. They won't know which path we've taken, but they'll be fast. We will need to move even faster."

"What about a horse? Could we leave on a horse?"

"Horses neigh. Their tracks are easy to follow. Once we get beyond Angkor, a horse would be a blessing. But near the city a mount would be a curse."

She nodded, pleased that she'd had the foresight to purchase items for their journey, but also fearful of Indravarman's wrath. "And you'll go with me to my people? You'll help us?"

"I'll help you. And if that means helping your people, then that's what I'll do."

"But you risk so much."

"I risk losing you, my lady, if I don't help you, and that's a risk I shall never take."

She moved forward, spreading her knees apart so that she straddled him. Her lips pressed against his, and she pulled him against her. "Will we be fast enough?" she asked, then kissed him again, fueled by desire and fear. "Will they catch us?"

"They will try, my lady. But we'll have a good start on them, and I think that shall be enough. I know where your countrymen gather—at least where some of them do. We can find them, and you can warn them."

"And what will you do?"

He glanced at the door. "There is a man . . . an assassin . . . who will come for me. I'll have to kill him. Then my fate will be in the hands of your people. I hope they're as worthy as they seem."

She squeezed his shoulders. "I'll protect you. But I don't think I shall need to. You'll have told them about the approaching army. They'll trust you."

"If they trust me . . . they may expect me to fight for them."

"No. You can't fight against your own people."

"I'd rather not," he admitted. "Most of my people are good. It's Indravarman who leads them astray."

"And if he falls?"

"Then my people will return to their homes. Your people will be free."

Someone coughed in the hallway outside. "My people must kill him," she replied, still whispering.

"Yes, but he's a very difficult man to kill. Many have tried."

"Maybe—"

"I must go, my lady," he interrupted, then kissed her brow. "Preparations for war are under way, and if I'm not a part of them, Indravarman will suspect me of treachery. So slowly walk back to your sister, then to Thida, and tell them of our plan. And meet me tonight, when the moon has first risen, by the old teak tree across the moat."

"I shall be there."

He started to get up, but she held him still. "What?" he asked.

"I need to tell you something—that I love you. Because to-night we'll run and I have no idea when I'll have another moment of peace with you. So when you're running, when you're leading us through the jungle, remember that I love you and that when all of this is over I shall be yours and yours alone."

*   *   *

Later that day, when the sun reached its zenith and she felt as if she were a coal in a roaring fire, Voisanne walked toward Angkor Wat. For once her eyes didn't stray to the majestic towers. Instead she gazed at the ground, her feet falling rhythmically on hot sandstone. She had just come from a clandestine meeting with her younger sister and smiled as she thought about Chaya's exuberance. Her sister's emotions had always been close to the surface, her laughter easily provoked, her wit incessant. When Voisanne had told her about their coming escape, Chaya had barely managed to stifle a shriek before leaping into Voisanne's arms. After curbing her sister's enthusiasm, Voisanne had told her where and when to meet, stressing the importance of stealth. She had left her in the stables where she was tending Asal's horse.

Voisanne had also met with Thida and whispered about the coming night. Thida's reaction was the opposite of Chaya's. The very thought of sneaking away under a full moon had made her visibly nervous. She'd wrung her hands, glanced about in all directions, and often stopped in midsentence to compose herself. Voisanne tried to convince her that an attempted escape, even with its inherent dangers, was safer than remaining with Indravarman. In the end, Thida had promised to meet Voisanne by the old tree, and Voisanne swore that they would flee together, hand in hand if need be.

Now, as Voisanne made her way through the long corridors of Angkor Wat, she considered the coming night, deciding how to best leave her quarters, which route to take, and if she should somehow darken her skin so as to blend into the night. Her emotions lay somewhere between Chaya's and Thida's. She was eager to escape her Cham masters, to be with Asal, and felt enormous pressure to warn her people of Indravarman's imminent attack. But she was also fearful of what the night would bring. Perhaps a guard would see them escape. Perhaps the assassin who was Asal's enemy would track them down. Too many variables existed to ensure the future she longed for, a future defined by the peace of kingdoms and the companionship of the man she loved. Life seemed so tenuous, and her growing fear prompted her to seek out the Echo Chamber. She needed to pray.

The chamber was cool, quiet, and empty. Voisanne moved to an unadorned wall, pressing her shoulder blades and spine against the stonework. She closed her eyes, struck her fist on her chest seven times, heard the sound of bells ringing in the distance, and began to pray. At first she prayed for her ancestors, feeling guilty that she had not thought of them for several days. Then she begged for safe passage that night. She beseeched the Gods to watch over the small band of friends and loved ones who would flee in the darkness. This band would be noble and good, she promised. They would each contribute to the world in meaningful ways.

Please, please help us, she thought, then struck her chest another seven times. My father said that in this place, more than in any other, you listen. So please listen to me. I know that I'm nothing to you but a speck of dust, but just as you did, in the coming days I shall face demons and I need your help. I can't fight them alone. So will you help me? Will you help a woman who doesn't have the strength to lift a sword but who isn't a coward, who will do what I can to save my people? We built this place for your pleasure, and we deserve to live and to build again. Grant us this victory, Gods of all Gods, and I know that we shall build for you again.

Voisanne turned around so that she faced the wall. She kissed the stonework, something that she'd never done. The bodies of her loved ones had touched this same spot, she knew, as had those of her countrymen. Though stone could not speak, though walls

could not whisper, the chamber was a place of life, of magic.
How else could a beating fist be turned into ringing bells? And
since the chamber was endowed with life and magic, surely the
Gods could hear her pleas. Although she was a speck of dust, did
not countless specks of dust comprise the universe?

A Khmer girl entered the chamber. Voisanne smiled at her
but the gesture was unreturned. The girl's eyes were bloodshot
and an acute sadness seemed to grip her. Voisanne had an urge to
hold her, to tell her that everything would be as it was, that her
prayers would be answered. Sniffing, the girl placed her back
against a wall but paused before striking her chest.

"Would you like me to pray with you?" Voisanne asked softly.
"To pray for you?"

The girl nodded, a tear dropping to her cheek.

Voisanne moved next to the child. She felt the wall against
her back, her fist strike her chest. Once again the bells sounded.
Only this time Voisanne did not pray for her own needs, but for
this stranger, this girl who was not so different from herself.

To everyone who was eager to celebrate the Festival of Floats,
darkness couldn't fall swiftly enough. For generations the festival
had been one of the most popular events in Khmer society, an
event during which participants asked forgiveness of the earth for
having polluted it during the past year.

More than five thousand Khmer men and women lined the
banks of the river, while their children gathered upstream near a
special bamboo platform that had been built across the water.
The children held plate-size floats that had been carved from the
wood of fallen trees. Surrounding a single beeswax candle that
rose from the middle of each float were orchids, chrysanthe-
mums, and lotus flowers. The candles hadn't yet been lit.

On the far end of the platform, away from the children, stood Ajadevi and Jayavar. She smiled at the sight of the laughing youngsters. Several weeks earlier, when she had first thought of holding the festival, she'd sent a courier to Siam asking for a delivery of candles as well as essential items such as medicine and weapons. The candles had arrived a few days earlier—each tall and thin, carefully wrapped in silk.

Everyone was waiting for complete darkness. The night was already almost black, and most kings would have signaled for the celebration to begin. But Jayavar was a patient man and he was waiting until the best possible moment to launch the candles. Somewhere downstream drums beat rhythmically. Voices brought to life a song sung by their ancestors: a song asking forgiveness from the land and water.

Jayavar held a float that he had made with Bona, the former slave boy whom he had saved and who had saved him. On several recent occasions, after meeting with his officers and discussing strategy, Jayavar had sought out Bona. The two unlikely companions had sat near a crook in the river and created their float together. While doing so they had spoken of topics that Bona understood and embraced—the jungle, its creatures, and the beauties abounding in Kbal Spean. In some ways, Bona reminded Jayavar of his children, and he felt at peace when he was with the boy. They smiled and occasionally even shared a laugh. Jayavar had begun to care for Bona and to devise plans that would ensure his survival and ultimate happiness.

"It is time," Jayavar said finally, prompting a group of men and women who held larger candles to move from child to child, lighting their floats. Of all the children, Bona was nearest to Jayavar. He smiled though his hands were empty.

Jayavar walked to the center of the platform, his pulse quickening, his convictions gathering and strengthening like storm clouds. He had rehearsed his speech alone in the jungle, speaking out loud, wanting to get the words just right. For once he hadn't shared his thoughts with Ajadevi. He hoped to surprise her, and to please both Khmers and Siamese.

He bowed to the people downstream, held his float high above him, and nodded. When he spoke next, he did so deeply, projecting his voice far into the night. "If, my friends, I told you that somewhere in the universe there lies a world where colors dazzle the eye, where the air is sweet and fragrant, what would you say?"

Murmurs rose along the river's edge. People were not used to being asked questions by their king and they were unsure how to reply. Seeing the uncertainty on the faces downstream from her, Ajadevi smiled, encouraging more responses.

"If," Jayavar continued, "I told you that somewhere in the universe this world exists, and has magical creatures that fly beneath a golden sun and is filled with endless water and valleys and mountains, what would you say?"

The replies were louder this time—responses offered by men and a few women.

Jayavar smiled. "And what if I told you that this world is pure and beautiful and perfect? That stars sparkle like diamonds in the night? That life rises and falls and yet rises again? Would you think that this world is too good to be true? Would you believe that this world is nothing more than a dream? Or would you pray to be delivered into it?"

A young girl called out, "I want to run across this world!" Her words prompted many smiles. "Can I?" she asked her king.

"But, my child," Jayavar replied, "you already run across this world, because the place I speak of is here. We stand within it now. We savor its beauties each day. We smell flowers, walk beneath trees, drink water that flows down from mountains. This world, which is unique in all the universe, lies directly beneath our feet. It is our home."

People laughed and clapped their hands.

Jayavar gestured for Bona to approach. Together they held their float still as a woman lighted it. "Because we are tenants of this world, we must protect it," Jayavar continued. "And for the trees we have felled, for the water we have dirtied, for the plants and creatures we have eaten, for the air we have sullied, we must ask forgiveness. So this is what we do tonight. We place our floats in this river and ask that the earth forgive us for our defilement."

Dropping slowly to their knees, Jayavar and Bona lowered their lighted float into the water. They released it gently. The current gathered up the offering, spinning it, then pulling it downstream. People cheered. Jayavar straightened, thanked Bona, and gestured for the other children to come to the platform and release their floats. He stepped aside to allow them room. Bona bowed, grinned, and headed downstream. Ten children hurried forward, set their lighted floats into the river, and then crossed the platform so that another ten children could do the same. This process went on as floats drifted down the river, each resembling a shimmering star in the blackness, a star that moved and twisted. Along both sides of the shoreline Khmers and even some Siamese applauded the floats, which varied in size and ornamentation according to each child's tastes.

When the last float was placed in the river, the celebration began in earnest. People cheered, clapped, and sang. Children splashed in the shallows while adults sipped rice wine from bamboo containers. The floats continued to flicker and shimmer, partly illuminating the figures of Vishnu and Shiva carved on nearby boulders.

Ajadevi moved closer to Jayavar, taking his arm in hers, smiling as the last of the floats rounded a corner of the river and children began to run along the shoreline, chasing them. "You're right about this world," she said. "In all the universe there may be only one such place, and we should not take it for granted."

"I could say the same about you," he replied, turning to her. "Except that I would say it with certainty."

She smiled. "Remember our first Festival of Floats? Yours tipped and foundered."

"While yours sailed past?"

"I think you were trying to impress me with the sight of so many flowers placed upon it."

"When have I ever not tried to impress you?"

Cheers arose from around the bend. Jayavar's smile faded, and Ajadevi wondered if he was thinking about his children. They had always delighted in this night, just as he had been forever beside them, helping to create and launch their floats. "Do you hear them?" she asked.

"The children?"

"Your children."

He glanced upward toward a slice of starlit sky. "Every so often in my dreams they speak to me. And from these dreams I never want to awaken. Yet Bona did find me. Sometimes I think that they sent him to me, that they dwell in him. I see glimpses of them in his smile, in the way he moves his small hands as he speaks, like Chivy did when she was trying to make a point."

Ajadevi smiled and kissed him again, then guided him to a sitting position at the edge of the platform, so that their feet dangled into the water. "Tonight's festival is more important than ever."

"Why?"

"Because soon we'll wage war on our enemies, and nothing pollutes the earth like war. Soon we shall have much to ask forgiveness for."

He nodded. "In a few days all the Siamese mercenaries will be here, and then we must march."

"When you march, Jayavar, when you lead, you must do so as a king."

"What do you mean?"

"You've shown your people the nature of yourself, how you're gentle and noble, good and pure. But now you must show your ferocity. To lead lions you must be a lion."

"You needn't worry about how I shall lead my men, nor about the strength of my sword, Ajadevi. Just because I've buried my thirst for revenge doesn't mean that it's been quenched. Just because I've grieved doesn't mean that I've forgotten my duty."

"Your destiny, Jayavar. Your destiny."

"Angkor's destiny. That is what I will fight for, what I will kill for."

She turned to him. "Good."

He stepped into the water, which rose to his knees. Extending his hand to her, he helped her off the platform. "Let's celebrate this night with our people. Let's celebrate as one. Because war approaches and we shall not hear laughter, as we do now, until many long days have passed."

Much later that same night, Thida and Indravarman lay in his oversize bed, which, in the fashion of the Chinese, was raised off the floor and layered with soft fabrics. A silk sheet had been cast aside and half of it had fallen to the floor. Surrounded by an almost transparent mosquito net, Thida was naked and on her side, facing Indravarman. For some time she had been pretending to sleep, hoping that he would also close his eyes, but he remained propped up on an elbow, drinking rice wine. For the most part he was still and silent, but every so often he would grunt or mutter to himself.

Normally Indravarman fell asleep soon after their sexual encounters, or sent Thida on her way, but he seemed preoccupied tonight. She knew that he had a bevy of Cham women also at his disposal and wished that he would call one of them, as he sometimes did. Soon the moon would rise, and she was increasingly worried about being late for the secret rendezvous with Voisanne. Thida's breathing started to speed up. Sweat glistened on her back. She imagined Voisanne waiting for her in the darkness and began to panic, terrified of being left alone.

Thida opened her eyes and then slowly sat up. She wiped her brow, staring at Indravarman's flat face rather than his naked body. "I can't sleep, Lord King," she said quietly. "The heat is too much."

He sipped his wine. "What would you have me do?"

"I . . . I'd like to return to my quarters. The breezes there are much stronger than—"

"No wind exists tonight. The Gods make no mischief."

She looked down, rubbing the back of her hand. "Still, Lord King, I'd like . . . I'd like to go if I may."

"I'm waiting for someone. When she arrives, you may leave."

"And is she—"

"Silence, woman! Must you fill my head with your senseless questions and laments? When she is here you will go. No sooner or later."

Thida shrank away from him, fearing his temper. She knew what he was capable of and suspected that only her beauty had protected her from his fists. Indravarman safeguarded beautiful objects, and to him she was an object, little different from a golden statue.

Through a window at the far end of the room, Thida could see the faintest light outside and worried that the moon had already risen. They might be waiting for her, wondering where she was and preparing to flee. "No," she whispered unconsciously, wringing her hands.

Indravarman's brow furrowed. "What?"

"Nothing . . . Lord King. But may I have some wine?"

"Why? You've never drunk my wine before."

"Because I think . . . it will help me sleep."

Indravarman handed her his bamboo cup. She drank deeply, resisting the growing urge to leap out of bed and hurry toward the rendezvous point. Almost never did she stay so late in his room, and she couldn't believe her ill luck. If she had known that he would keep her so late she would have thought of a better excuse to return to her quarters. She silently cursed her stupidity. When would the woman arrive? Why was she so tardy?

Thida handed the cup back to him and glanced at the window again. The light outside seemed to be getting stronger. She felt trapped. The room appeared to become unsteady, as if she stood on the deck of a small boat instead of resting on a bed. Walls tilted, her thoughts became muddled, and her skin itched. Again she imagined Voisanne waiting for her, growing restless and impatient. Soon they'd leave, and when that happened Thida would have no one.

She lay back on the bed, praying for the other woman's arrival, squeezing the sheet with her right hand. Without question the moon was already out. Her coconspirators would be under the tree, looking to the south, across the empty moat. She wanted to be swimming in that water, to be calling out to them. Instead she was an arm's length from Indravarman. She felt bound and gagged and immobile—as helpless as an infant left alone in the jungle. Though she tried to hide her emotions, she was restless and agitated.

A knock sounded on the distant door. A woman's voice called out. Profound relief surged into Thida and she sat up quickly, bumping into Indravarman's arm. He started to respond to the woman, then turned to Thida. His eyes narrowed. She shrank from him, but suddenly his hands were around her throat. He pressed his thumbs against her windpipe and she couldn't breathe.

"Why do you wish to run?" he demanded.

She struggled against him, clutching at his thumbs, her chest heaving.

He released her, then slapped her across the face. She cried out, trying to roll from the bed. The mosquito net became entangled in her arms and was ripped from the ceiling. He struck her again, producing whimpers and tears. "Where do you seek to go with such haste?" he roared.

She shook her head. She tried to flee him. Then she saw the rage in his face, she saw his open hand rise once more, and words tumbled from her. She sought to stop herself, but the words kept coming. She wept, told him everything, and finally pleaded that he be merciful.

Indravarman picked her up and threw her against the nearby wall. He began to shout, calling for his men. Thida screamed. She screamed to her friend that they were coming for her, that she should run and never stop running.

The king's fist flew through the air, striking Thida on the side of the head, turning light to dark, horror to nothingness.

Beyond the moat on the northern side of Angkor Wat, Asal, Voisanne, Chaya, and the Khmer guide hid within the branches of the fallen teak tree. They had been waiting for so long that their skin had dried after swimming across the moat. The moon had risen and drifted partway across the sky. Though it was still

the dead of night, time seemed fleeting, and everyone was restless.

His hand on the hilt of his sheathed sword, Asal closed his
eyes and prayed. He didn't want to leave Thida behind, but they
had already waited too long and taken too great a risk. They
should have been far into the jungle by now, having put a substantial distance between them and their soon-to-be pursuers.
Asal knew that Indravarman would send men after him, likely Po
Rame and some other trackers. These men wouldn't know the
exact route that he'd take but would assume that he was fleeing
to the north.

Asal finished his prayer, peered through the branches surrounding him to study the moat, and leaned close to Voisanne.
"We have to leave," he whispered. "We've lingered too long already."

She squeezed his free hand. "Why is she late? She promised
me that she'd come. Something must have happened."

"All the more reason to leave now."

"But I swore an oath to her. I left her once, and I promised
that I'd never fail her again."

The Khmer guide, a weathered man who had already seen five
decades come and go, urged haste. Chaya tugged on her older
sister's skirt cloth. It was obvious to Asal that Voisanne was torn.
Yet at this point, fear needed to be the stronger motivator. And to
drive that point home, Asal put his lips against her ear. "If we're
caught," he whispered, his words audible to no one but her, "your
sister will suffer grievously."

She looked at him, nodding. "We should go."

"You go. I'll stay a short time longer, because of your oath,
and then follow."

"No. We have to stay together. I won't leave you behind. Not
when—"

His finger touched her lips. "I can move faster than you on the trail. I can wait. And I'll catch up."

"But—"

"Your oath to her is important. You've told me as much. You shouldn't have to break it because I lost my courage."

"Asal, please come with us. Please. You've nothing to prove to me. Nothing at all."

"If we flee, and she's caught, Indravarman will skin her alive. Let me stay for a short time, and then, with or without her, I'll find you."

She shook her head but was pulled away from him by her sister and the guide. Breaking from their grasp, she embraced him, kissing his lips, his cheek, drawing him as close as possible. She told him of her love for him and he smiled at her words, echoing them with his own. The guide once again explained his intended route, saying that he would leave twice-torn leaves as signs. Asal thanked him, promised that he would soon catch up to them, and kissed the back of Voisanne's hand. "Now run, my lady. Run as I know you can."

She started to reply but was pulled from him. Her face was wet with tears and he longed to kiss that wetness. Instead he smiled, waved farewell, and watched them depart, vanishing into the darkness of the jungle.

As soon as they were gone he unsheathed his sword and peered over the moat. He would stay until the moon reached its summit. Then he would run. He would run and never look back. But until that moment he'd linger, because he knew that the oath was important to her, and he longed to see it fulfilled. Also, if Thida came to this place and they were gone, if she were caught, her screams would be heard across all of Angkor. Those screams would be on his conscience, on Voisanne's conscience, and would be a heavy burden to carry.

Without Voisanne's presence, Asal became more aware of the night. A breeze rustled the dried-out leaves of the dying tree. The soil was damp beneath his feet. The moon, already too high in the sky, seemed to shimmer. As he had many times before, Asal wondered about its features, which were plainly visible on this night. The moon seemed young, yet old; strong, yet feeble.

Reaching upward, Asal touched the necklace that Voisanne had given him. He kissed the jade, imagining how she must have wrapped the silver wire around it. Not since his parents died had someone thought about him in such a way, and he suddenly wished that he was beside her. In a life full of uncertainties, he felt sure of only one thing—that he should stand next to her, beholding the beauty of her face and her spirit.

A shadow appeared across the moat. Asal squinted, wondering if his imagination was toying with him. Or perhaps Thida had finally arrived. Perhaps she would come to him and they could flee together.

The moon dimmed as a cloud drifted in front of it. Asal peered into the moat. He thought he heard a splash. Though he wanted to call out to Thida, he dared not use his voice. Instead he crouched within the branches, his knuckles whitening on his sword hilt. Somewhere a dog barked.

The edge of the moat was about fifty paces away and Asal saw a figure materialize. Only this figure was not thin and narrow, as Thida would be, but broad and seemed to carry a spear. Another shadow appeared and then another. At that moment Asal knew that he'd been betrayed. He turned to flee but realized that he would only lead his pursuers to the woman he loved. He could run in the opposite direction, but then the approaching men might simply choose to head to the north, as they had likely been told to do. They might find Voisanne. And Asal could never flee when that possibility remained. He had to kill these men.

The shadows emerged. There were eight of them, and they moved like warriors, bent and ready for action. Each held a shield and a spear. Spreading out, they crept straight toward the tree, and Asal wondered how many he could surprise before they were upon him. He kissed his necklace again, then beseeched the Gods to give him strength, to make his sword dreadful that night. He needed to be dreadful; otherwise he would never see Voisanne again. The thought of such separation made his chest heave, and so he tried to focus his energy on the approaching men, looking for the stoutest, the man who would be most difficult to bring down and so should be slain without warning.

Asal spied such a man—a huge and muscled brute who carried a thick spear. The warrior neared Asal's hiding spot, and without a word Asal swung his blade through a small branch, grunting as the weapon struck his countryman's side, where it bit deeply and became lodged against bone. Asal let go of the hilt and grabbed the dying man's spear. He thrust it into another warrior's chest, deflected a blow with his shield, and whirled, swinging his spear like an axe, trying to keep his attackers at bay. One man shouted a war cry and rushed forward. Asal bent low and pushed up with his shield, throwing the warrior upward. The man landed on a broken branch, screaming as it pierced his leg, but Asal wasn't aware of the warrior's misfortune. He was already rushing forward, trying to take two Chams by surprise. Perhaps the Gods had been listening, for they did grant him strength, and while thrusting with his spear he lifted the edge of his shield up hard under a man's face, breaking his nose, sending him reeling backward. Asal spun around, aware that four more adversaries remained. Something struck him on the side of the head. His knees buckled, but he did not fall. Blood obscured his vision, and he stabbed wildly with his spear, attacking his foes, taking the fight to them rather than being surrounded and overwhelmed.

Just as he slew another warrior, many more Chams emerged from the water, emerged like shadows in some dark underworld. He didn't see them come, yet he felt the shafts of their spears as they beat him down, pulverizing him as the world spun around him and he stumbled to his knees. Finally dropping his weapon, he tried to protect himself with his shield, but feet, fists, and elbows slammed into him, battering him as the monsoon rains might assault a leaf, relentless and unforgiving.

He thought of Voisanne. Run, my lady. Run.

And then darkness swept into him.

Eighteen

Apologize

They had hurried all night through the jungle, moving beneath the light of the full moon and then, when it fell below the horizon, using torches to illuminate the trail. The Khmer guide kept a manageable but constant pace, pausing every few hundred steps to make two rips in a prominent leaf. At each fork in the trail he left a sign, which hopefully would bring Asal to them. Though Voisanne had asked him several times if they might wait, the guide had resisted, instead reassuring her that all would be well. Asal would catch up with them.

Yet it was now morning and he still hadn't arrived. Voisanne tried to stay strong for the sake of her sister, but the task was becoming increasingly difficult. She felt as if she had abandoned him, and feelings of guilt, worry, and frustration flooded her. As she placed one dusty and scratched foot in front of the other, she wished they could go back in time. They should have all left together or stayed together. Were it not for Chaya, Voisanne would have remained, but her little sister had to come first.

Though dawn wasn't long gone, the day was already becoming hot. Sweat ran down Voisanne's spine and into her skirt cloth. Fortunately, they passed many streams and stopped often to cool themselves. While Voisanne and Chaya drank and bathed hurriedly, their guide would climb a tree and look to the south. So far, he'd seen nothing that gave him any concern. But neither had he spied Asal, and each time he descended with no news, Voisanne lowered her gaze and grew quiet.

Now, as they entered a vast section of the jungle that had been scorched by fire, the guide paused to study their surroundings. He had already lived longer than most Khmers would and seemed to consider each choice with equal parts patience and caution. Though most of the giant trees were unscathed, the undergrowth had been burned away, leaving charred embers, ash, and a barren landscape the likes of which Voisanne had rarely seen. The normal sounds of the jungle were missing.

"What happened?" Voisanne asked, standing atop a blackened boulder.

The furrows on their guide's brow deepened. "Lightning."

"What should we do?"

He glanced in all directions, seeming not to hear her. To head across the charred land would leave prominent tracks. But to circle the area would add time to their journey. "Can you go faster?" he finally asked, looking from Voisanne to Chaya.

Voisanne nodded.

"Then let's make haste," he replied, heading straight into the wasteland.

Chaya skipped after him. For a moment, Voisanne was jealous of her sister's childhood innocence. Despite the horrors that had befallen their family, Chaya remained upbeat. She believed that their loved ones had already been reborn into better lives, and she didn't dwell on uncertainties.

The sisters could now jog beside each other, and though their pace was swift, Voisanne suddenly needed to talk about Asal. "Tell me how he treated you at the stables," she said. "What was he like?"

Chaya smiled. "But you know him better than I. You asking me that is like a fish asking a rabbit how to swim."

"True, but still, what did you think of him?"

As she leapt over a charred log, Chaya beckoned Voisanne onward. "He came to the stables only once. He showed me how to care for his horse, how to avoid its kicks. Later, he said I looked like you. And then, after I'd finished cleaning and we were talking, he must have been thinking about you, because he wasn't really listening to me, and he called me 'my lady.'"

"He did?"

"He didn't even notice he did it. He just smiled when I told him. And when he was about to leave, I asked him why he called you that, and he said it was because you deserved it. Because you were noble and good. Of course, I said he was crazy. But he just kept smiling."

The breeze lifted a swirling cloud of ash into the air. Voisanne held her breath and hurried forward, sweat beading on her face. "I think . . . he sees me as his queen."

"Then he must be blind."

Voisanne grinned. "Someday, Chaya, someday you shall be someone's queen."

"And why would I want that?"

"Why not want it?"

"Because the lives of queens are boring. Why would I want to sit on a throne and do nothing but look pretty? I might as well be a fern."

Voisanne remembered running through the jungle with Asal,

then making love with him on the riverside. Nothing she'd done with him had been boring. "I wish he would catch up with us. It's been too long."

"He's probably out gathering flowers for you, or doing something else gallant."

"I hope so."

"Last night, when we were waiting by the water, I saw how he touched the necklace you made him. You cast a spell on him, that's for sure. You charmed a Cham."

"He's a man, Chaya. Just a man."

"A man who calls you 'my lady.' And if he does that, he must be your king. He's hardly just a man."

Voisanne saw the scorched shell of a dead turtle and wondered how many creatures the fire had killed. Winded, she slowed their pace, letting their guide pull ahead of them. "Do you know who I want him to be, Chaya?"

"No."

"The father of my children."

Chaya stopped, dust settling around her feet. "Then we shouldn't have gone. We shouldn't have left him all alone."

I know, Voisanne thought. I left him because of you, but I should have sent you ahead. I should have stayed.

"What?" Chaya asked.

"Nothing."

"Tell me."

"It's just . . . each step I take, I feel as if I'm drawing farther away from him. I rush to the north, but what I want to do is run to the south."

"Then let's run to the south."

Voisanne shook her head. "If I could, I'd pick up a sword. I'd fight my way to him. I'm not afraid. But . . . but since I can't do

that, what I can do is what he asked me to do. I can pray, I can go
north, and when I finally see him, I can use my strength and love
to fill him with whatever he needs."

Chaya pointed toward the guide, who was now far ahead.
"He wants us to hurry."

"You go. I shall be right behind."

"But why?"

"Because I want to leave him a message. Here in this blackened dirt."

Chaya nodded, then scampered ahead. Voisanne dropped to
her knees. She placed her forefinger on the ground. Pushing
down, creating a trail within the soot, she wrote: *I have only one
request of you, my love. Wherever I have gone, you must go. May the
Gods give you wings. May they fill my eyes with the sight of you.*

Voisanne's tears left dimples in the ash. She stood up. Though
her body trembled, her mind propelled her forward, ahead into
the bleakness where she must travel.

Statues loomed over him—Gods who had been created from
stone and covered in gold. They seemed to whisper in the darkness in a language too divine for him to understand. The Gods
leaned toward him. Though their faces showed pity, they made
no move to release him. His bonds weren't severed. His pain lingered. He remained tied to a wooden column with his hands behind his back, upright only because of the ropes that encircled his
legs, midsection, arms, and chest.

With one of his eyes swollen shut and a hundred aches assailing him, Asal wished the Gods would set him free, from his
bonds or from his pain—preferably both, though even one would
be glorious. He silently begged the grinning figures to do as
much, but they made no such effort. Closing his good eye, he

tried to fall back into the darkness. Voices rang out from somewhere. Footsteps echoed in his mind.

"Voisanne?" he asked, or at least he thought he asked.

Water splashed against his face. He gagged on it, turning away. A hand slapped his cheek. As more water poured over him a voice emerged—the voice of his king. He tried to turn from the voice, to pretend he didn't hear it, but the water pulled him into the present. The Gods seemed to drift away from him. He saw them more clearly now—statues that had been stolen from temples and brought here, statues that were too beautiful and precious to be gathering dust in a dimly lit room.

Through Asal's good eye Indravarman also materialized. The king seemed larger than usual, even as he stood next to one of the Gods. Behind him were Po Rame and two guards dressed in war gear. Po Rame was smiling.

Asal tugged at his bonds but could barely stir. The movement produced waves of pain that swept through his head, shoulders, belly, and groin. Only his hands and feet seemed uninjured, though they tingled from the constriction of the ropes that held him.

"You must be wondering why we are here," Indravarman said, stepping forward, his face impassive.

Again Asal struggled to free himself, straining until the room began to spin around him.

"We are here because many of my men admire you. And I don't want them to hear your screams. Down here, in the bowels of the Royal Palace, you'll be mute, as you should be. No one knows that you're imprisoned, so no one will think to save you—not your men, not the Gods, and certainly not me. If you wish, you may pray. But the Gods shall not listen. They do not listen to insects at their feet, and you're nothing but an insect."

"My men—"

"Be silent!" Indravarman roared, his open hand slamming

into Asal's cheek. "I'll tell you when to speak! You who tried to steal my woman from me, who tried to dupe me. She told me all about your plans, told me as she begged and wept. I gave you everything a man could want and in return you betrayed me!" Again the king slapped Asal, this time on both sides of his face. "Now I command you to speak. Why did you seek to flee in the night? Why did you try to take what was not yours?"

Asal spat blood. "Lord King . . . I—"

"I'm no king of yours! I'm a conqueror, a leader of armies! I don't reign over insects. I step on them."

Though Asal tried to focus his good eye, the room continued to spin. His right ear rang from Indravarman's last blow. "I always . . . fought well for you," he managed to say.

"Yes, you did fight well. Why then did you betray me? Why did you try to flee?"

"Because . . ."

"Tell me!"

"Because you . . . threatened Voisanne. When you did that . . . you lost me."

Indravarman started to swing his hand again but stopped, a smile eclipsing his scowl. "A whore caused you to break your vows to me?"

"She's no whore."

"But she soon will be, Asal. Because right now my best men are tracking her. She left a half day ahead of them, but how far do you think she will get? And when they catch her she'll become my whore. You'll watch as I ravish her, again and again. I wonder what will happen then. Will you still care for her? Because how will you be able to tolerate, much less care for, one of my whores?"

"Leave her be!" Asal shouted, thrashing against his bonds.

Indravarman laughed, then motioned the guards and Po Rame forward. He said something to them, but Asal could not hear him. He was gripped by such despair that only one desire seemed to make sense—his frantic need to protect Voisanne.

The guards moved behind him. Smiling, Po Rame reached into his hip cloth and produced a sliver of bamboo the size and length of a feather's shaft. "I'd take your eyes, Khmer lover," he said, "but the king of kings wants you to see. And so I'll be pleased in other ways."

Reaching out, Indravarman placed his hand on the side of Asal's sweaty face. "Po Rame believes he can break you in a very short time. I told him that you'd be stronger. So humor me, Asal. Last longer than he expects."

A thin hand held the sliver of bamboo in front of Asal's good eye. "It doesn't look like much, does it?" Po Rame asked. "But how it can hurt." He stepped behind Asal, out of his sight.

When Asal felt the guards grip his left arm and thumb, he struggled against them. He twisted and cursed and heaved against the ropes, but he was held immobile. Po Rame laughed as he took the piece of bamboo and placed it behind Asal's thumbnail, thrusting it deeper and deeper into his flesh until it moved past the bottom of the nail and lodged against the knuckle. Pain was instantaneous, horrific, and all-consuming. Asal surged against the ropes, fighting as he never had, thrashing and biting and producing more than one cry of hurt from his oppressors.

His forefinger was gripped. Again the pain came, enveloping him in an overwhelmingly acute sensation of agony that exploded within him. He screamed. He fought. He raged.

In the end, he tried to think of Voisanne, to imagine her running into his open arms with joy and love etched on her face. He called to her, pleaded with her. And she appeared for a glorious instant, filling him with light.

Then she was gone.

He screamed until the pain simply became too much, shutting down his mind and his body, plunging him into a place where not even dreams existed.

"It's not much of a fever," Soriya said quietly, placing a piece of honeycomb between her son's lips, "but I want you to rest all the same."

Vibol looked up at her, thankful for the sweetness of the honey. He lay within their sleeping quarters, a three-sided bamboo and thatch structure. The four of them had built it not long after arriving at the Khmer base and finding an open space near the narrow river. They felt relieved to be near water once again, and faced with the decision of where to build, the choice had been easy. The interior of the structure was nondescript save for a small bouquet of flowers that Soriya had set in each corner.

"Tell me what you've been doing," she added. "How in the world did you get so many bruises?"

"We practice with wooden swords."

Soriya shook her head, all too aware that real blades would do more than darken flesh. "But there are so many. Why are there so—"

"I left more on others than I received. A lot more."

"But these on your belly. Why aren't you protecting your belly?"

He glanced away and then returned her stare. "Those are from wooden spears. It's hard to block them with a shield."

She started to speak but instead rubbed a paste with healing properties on his injured flesh. "When the fight comes . . . please stay away from the spearmen."

"I'll fight whomever I have to, Mother."

"Then get a bigger shield. Do something."

"Fine."

Nodding, she continued to apply the paste. "I'm glad that this fever is a gentle one, and yet it's slowed you down."

"Only for a day. Then I must return."

"A day for me to heal you. I can do that."

A group of Siamese warriors passed in front of their shelter, each as colorfully dressed as the next. They laughed, arms around one another, and walked along the river.

"They're strange soldiers," Vibol said as he lay with his head supported on a rolled-up deerskin.

"How so?"

"Sometimes they sing when they fight. And their singing makes them strong."

"Maybe you should sing."

"Khmers are already strong. We don't need to sing."

She saw that his elbow had been bloodied at some point and began to coat it in her paste. "Tell me about last night. You were all gone for so long."

"Father didn't tell you?"

"He did, but maybe he forgot to mention something."

Vibol wiped sweat from his brow. "We had a war council. The king and queen were there. So were a score of Khmer and Siamese officers."

"And you?"

"And us. Thanks to Prak's plan. At the beginning of the council, the king asked Prak to explain his plan about the fire and then for us to describe the area. And the queen, she asked nearly as many questions."

Soriya smiled at the thought of her loved ones talking with such people. "What is she like?"

"Smart . . . no . . . more like wise. She seems very wise."

"Why do you say that?"

Vibol scratched at a scab on his shin. "She has a way of speaking that . . . that makes you think she's as old as the mountains."

"And the king?"

"I've seen him practice with his sword. He's fast . . . though he seems to tire."

Soriya nodded, then stood up and stepped outside their shelter to where a small pot was perched above a fire. She removed the pot, poured some steaming liquid into a bamboo cup, and returned inside. "What about his mind?" she asked, then blew into the cup.

"He understands war. He took Prak's plan, which was simple, and talked about ways to make it better."

"And they treated you well?"

"Yes, Mother. They treated us well. Very well."

She smiled again and handed him the cup. "Sip on this. It will help with the fever."

He did as she asked, then grimaced. "It tastes like dirt."

"I know. But it will help. My mother gave me the same drink when I was young and ill."

After finishing the tea made from roots and leaves, he handed her the cup and closed his eyes. "Maybe I'll sleep."

"Let me put out the fire. It's too hot."

"No, it feels good. I'm cold."

She leaned forward and rubbed his brow. "I know, Vibol, that you're a man. But for today I can treat you like a boy. And that makes me happy."

He started to protest but relaxed as she gave him another piece of honeycomb and then massaged his pains away. "Tell me a story . . . of when I was a boy."

Continuing to rub his forehead, she thought back through the years. A long and thick millipede crawled across the floor of their shelter, and, knowing it was poisonous, she used a stick to flick it into the fire. "Do you remember Prak's pet turtle?" she asked.

"A little."

"When he was eight, your father brought him a turtle. We made a pen for it at the edge of the river. You and Prak would go down every day and play with that turtle. And though you liked it, Prak loved it. He talked with that turtle. He fed it. He even slept with it once." Soriya paused, then used a damp cloth to wipe sweat from Vibol's face. "But one night, something got into that pen. An old tiger, maybe. For it was a big, hungry beast, and it gnawed at the turtle until only its scarred shell was left."

"I remember."

"Prak wouldn't stop crying. Father and I were comforting him and you just slipped away. One moment you were there and the next you weren't. Father went looking for you while I stayed with Prak. It wasn't long before you came back. You'd caught another turtle, and when you gave it to your brother I don't think I'd ever seen you smile so wide."

The corners of Vibol's lips rose. "I used one of Father's nets to make a trap. There were some turtles sunning themselves and I chased them right into it."

"Well, whatever you did worked, because Prak was so happy. And he had that turtle for a long, long time. As you can imagine, he built a perfect, safe pen for him."

Vibol nodded and opened his eyes. Soriya continued to wipe his face, still smiling at the story. "I'll stay away from the spearmen," he said, reaching for her hand. "I promise, Mother."

She nodded, bending down to hug him.

He reached for her, and suddenly it was as if the years had gone backward. He was simply a boy who needed the comfort of his mother, of the person who had brought him into the world and who understood the beauty of turtles and memories and to-getherness.

Trembling, Thida shuffled through a dimly lit corridor of the Royal Palace. She carried a tray that held the simplest of meals—a bowl of rice and a cup of water. Walking was difficult, and she had to pause often, leaning against a wall as she tried to gather her strength. Something inside her was broken, she knew, shattered that morning when, in a fit of rage, Indravarman had beaten her unconscious. Ever since she'd awoken from that horror, breathing had been a tortured affair. Blood had seeped upward, into her mouth, nauseating her.

She came to a stairway, almost fell, but collected herself and proceeded down the wooden steps. It was even darker below-ground. Through her swollen nose she detected the presence of dampness and decay. She coughed, producing a searing pain in her lungs. Gritting her teeth, she tried not to cry. But tears came anyway, spurred by the thought of the previous night, of how she had failed Voisanne. Now that same friend was being tracked and would soon be captured. Equally horrible, the man who had tried to free them both, a good man by all accounts, had been tortured in the chamber below. Indravarman had told her as much just before he beat her. He had called her unspeakable names, enraged by her betrayal. In the end, she had simply col-lapsed.

The lower level of the Royal Palace was used for storage. The corridor through which Thida passed was lined with rooms con-taining weapons, foodstuffs, fabrics, carts, timber, rugs, deer-skins, cooking supplies, and bound scrolls. Thida hadn't been here before but knew that Asal was locked in the very last room, protected by a single guard. Indravarman had said so and more.

He had bragged about Asal's screams, about how remarkable it was that a bamboo splinter could produce such pain.

Thida set her tray down on a small table, then wiped her face free of tears. Raising her hand to her face made her wince in pain. She coughed again, spat blood, and closed her eyes. Still shaking, she picked up the tray and shuffled forward, worried that she might fall at any moment. She wanted to fall, to let darkness come to her, but she wouldn't allow herself such a release—not yet. First she had to undo the misery she had caused, if such a thing was possible.

Thida felt that she'd failed so many times in her life. She still lived only because of her beauty, because of what her mother once said was a gift but Thida saw as a curse. Without her beauty, she might have been killed when the Chams first arrived. If so, by now she'd have been reborn, hopefully full of strength instead of beauty, with hope instead of fear.

Because her whole life had been defined by weakness, Thida was determined to die doing something noble; at the very last moment, she would redeem her many years of feebleness. She prayed for fortitude as she approached the room that held Asal. She prayed that the knife she held beneath the tray was as deadly as she believed.

Thida knocked on a thick, wooden door and said that she was commanded to bring food for the prisoner. A rough voice answered, and she was tempted to turn away. Then the door swung open. Ten paces in front of her sagged Asal, tied to a column. He was bloody and beaten, and she almost called out to him. Instead she muttered hello to the guard and stepped inside. He shut the door behind her, and as soon as he had locked it, she turned to him. She was trembling, and he asked her what was wrong. The tray tilted in her hands, falling to the floor, the bowl of rice shattering. The guard looked down, and with all the strength that she could summon, Thida lunged upward with the knife, plunging it beneath his chin and into his throat. Blood spurted from the wound, and she shrieked as he fell backward, clutching at the knife. He toppled to the floor, pulled the blade from his throat, and thrashed about, his feet striking the wall. Gasping, he clutched at the wound, but soon his eyes glazed over and he was gone.

The sight of the dead man caused Thida to reel. She spat out her own blood and tried to steady herself. Each breath she drew seemed to bring more acute pain. Tremors ran up and down her body, causing her to breathe too fast and deep. She bent down, picked up the knife, and struggled toward Asal. His eyes were open. He said something, but she didn't comprehend his words. With trembling hands she cut the ropes that bound him. After pulling them off, he held her up, and it seemed as if suddenly he were rescuing her instead of the other way around. She wept against his shoulder, and he stroked her back with his uninjured hand, trying to soothe her.

Though she still found it hard to breathe, though blood continued to gather in the back of her mouth, she nodded to him. "Thank you," she said.

"What has he done to you?"

"He . . . he broke something in me. I bleed inside."

"We must find you help."

She shook her head. "No one . . . knows you're imprisoned. Just walk out of this place."

"I'm taking you with me."

"No. Go alone."

He picked her up, cradling her in both arms. She cried out at the pain the movement brought and told him to stop, but he paid her no heed. Instead he struggled over to the guard, awkwardly pulled the dead man's sword from its sheath, and then unlocked and opened the door. She continued to cry, and to her surprise, he kissed the top of her head. "It will be all right," he said. "Everything will be all right."

She felt his feet moving beneath her as he limped forward, and the corridor began to drift by. "Tell Voisanne . . . that I'm sorry," she whispered.

"There's no need for that. And whatever you wish to tell her, you can do so yourself."

Unable to help herself, she spit out more blood. She didn't want to think of herself as dying, and so she tried to believe him. She watched where he went, noting that he must have known the Royal Palace well as he shuffled this way and that, staying belowground until the last moment, at which point he managed to climb a teak ladder and exited the building through a narrow doorway.

Outside, the sun seemed brighter than ever. Giant trees stretched upward, as if trying to touch the Gods. Many people were about, but strange sights were not unusual, and no one seemed to take notice of them. He was simply a wounded Cham warrior who was carrying his Khmer plaything. Indravarman had been so pleased, she remembered, to tell her how Asal's imprisonment and torture were a secret, how his men would not be given the opportunity to choose between their king and their friend. Perhaps it was because no one knew that Asal had been confined that no one bothered to question him. He went wherever he wanted to, all the time whispering to her that she would be fine, that he was going to get a horse and take her to a healer.

In time he did find a mount, and with her positioned in front of him, they headed into the jungle. He did not ride to the north, as she asked him to, but to the west. Nearby, he promised, was someone who could help her. He thought her rib was broken and that it was cutting into her lungs, but he swore that such wounds could be healed. She wanted to believe him, tried to believe him, yet she knew she was dying. Breathing became arduous, then nearly impossible. Suddenly she didn't want to be on the horse, but on the ground, in a beautiful place. She begged him to grant her request, and finally, after much debate and pleading, he did as she asked, stopping atop a hill that provided a view of Angkor Wat in the distance.

Asal lifted her from the horse, then sat on a boulder, holding her so that she could see the temple. In the afternoon sun it seemed to shimmer with fire, its towers like blazing mountaintops. She didn't think the temple had ever looked so beautiful, not even under a full moon or bathed in the colors of dusk.

"I am . . . unafraid," she whispered, then smiled as he kissed her brow again. His eyes glistened, and she understood, for the first time, why Voisanne cared so much for him. "Go to her," she added. "Love her."

"Save your strength, lady," he replied, stroking her forehead with his good hand.

"I have . . . no such thing."

"Your strength, not mine, brought us here."

A breath seemed to catch in her throat. She struggled, winced at the pain, and finally drew in air. "Where should I look," she asked, "for my loved ones?"

"They will come to you, lady. You needn't look."

"But how . . . how will they find me?"

He started to speak and then stopped, brushing his eye. "If you wish, I shall bring them to you."

"How?"

"I shall . . . send them a signal. And they will come. I promise you that they will come."

"You'll . . . burn me?"

"Yes, lady. If that is what you wish."

"It is."

He kissed her forehead again, and she smiled at his touch. Even now, in the midst of her pain, it felt good to be cared for. It had been so long since someone had touched her with tenderness.

The colors of day seemed to fade. The distant temple beckoned to her. It ebbed and flowed. Her ancestors were coming, he promised. They were moving faster than the light of dawn. Their voices were songs, their faces golden. Soon she would be with them again, and with that union would come the joys of youth, the beauties of a world seen through new eyes.

She believed in his words. And as they began to transform from words into truths, she squeezed his hand, wanting him to know that he was right, that she would never be alone again.

Nineteen

First Sight

After he had built a funeral pyre, laid Thida's body on it, prayed for her, and lit the dry wood, Asal climbed onto his horse and rode hard to the north. Behind him smoke billowed upward, and he hoped that his promise was being granted, that her loved ones were following his beacon. He would have liked to have stayed beside her longer, until the flames had finally died away, but with Voisanne in danger he had to ride forth.

He found her trail not far beyond Angkor Wat and followed it northward. With a horse he had the advantage of speed and yet was far enough above the ground that he often had to drop down to inspect the dried earth. To his dismay, he realized that a group of five or six men was also tracking her. They made no effort to conceal their tracks and clearly were not concerned about being followed. He couldn't tell how far behind they were from Voisanne and her sister but guessed they would catch them soon.

Because of his relentless haste, on several occasions Asal lost the trail and was forced to backtrack. These instances were maddening as he could ill afford such delays. Part of the problem was that his left eye was still swollen partially shut. His ears also rang. His body ached, though his surging emotions masked some of his pain. On his left hand, his thumb and first two fingers were bloodied, throbbing, and useless. Yet his smallest fingers were undamaged and so he could grip light objects when necessary.

As dusk arrived, Asal slid off his horse and, leading it forward, followed the trail on foot. He walked with only a few breaks to quench his thirst, using a series of makeshift torches and the light of the moon to make his way. In the middle of the night he came to a burned area of jungle and found remnants of a message that Voisanne had left for him. He was able to read only a few words, for many feet had trampled the area, but he recognized her writing. And with that recognition came both joy and dread. She had been alive a short time ago, but her pursuers were surely getting closer.

Asal lingered at the site for only a moment and then pressed forward with renewed vigor. In the barren wasteland the tracks were easy to follow, and he rode his horse as fast as he dared, covering a large distance before dawn. His torn fingers started to bleed, but he didn't pause to bandage them. Instead he continued onward, thankful for the wasteland because the men he followed were on foot, and with each passing moment he must be gaining on them. If he reached them before they caught up to Voisanne, he would simply ride around them and go to her. But if he was too late, then he would have to somehow best five or six men with only one working hand.

As dawn finally arrived, Asal sensed that he was nearing his foes. The wasteland ended, and, fearful that he would lose the trail in the dense underbrush, he slid off his horse and pulled it behind him, his gaze rarely leaving the ground, his feet soon gouged and bloodied. He made no attempt to move with stealth, for that would slow him down. Birds squawked and took flight, announcing his approach. He did not eat, and rarely drank, running as he never had, pushing himself through his exhaustion. Only when his knees buckled and he suddenly collapsed did he rest, his lungs heaving, his legs trembling. He soon climbed back on his mount and rode on, leaning down so that his good eye always remained as close as possible to the trail.

For the most part, Asal focused on following footsteps. But when they were obvious and required no thought, he prayed, beseeching the Gods to grant him speed and strength. He begged them to protect Voisanne and her sister, saying that they were innocent and should be spared. His prayers included Thida, as he hoped that she was already reborn and in the company of her loved ones.

The farther Asal rode, the more something unfamiliar and sinister grew within him. He had always fought for his people and his future. His sword had never been bloodied because of hate or revenge. But now, as he prepared for possible battle, rage filled him—fueled by the unjustness of Thida's death, the prospect of Voisanne's demise, and memories of the bamboo being forced beneath his fingernails. So much unnecessary suffering was mostly the work of one man—Indravarman. To conquer an enemy was the right and expectation of any warrior, and Asal found no fault with the invasion of Angkor. It was the occupation that enraged him, because despite all of Indravarman's musings and philosophies, ultimately he was nothing more than a greedy, unjust ruler. His greed demanded that Thida be at his side, and that same greed had ruined her. His unjustness ensured that he sent men to bring Voisanne back to him, when he could have easily let her go. What purpose would her capture and suffering achieve other than to punish him, Asal, who had served Indravarman faithfully for many long years?

The memory of the king's boasts about what he would do to Voisanne fueled Asal like nothing else. Only now, as he rushed forward, did he realize what a powerful weapon hate was, because it allowed him to push himself harder than he ever had. He loved Voisanne and he wanted to fight for love, and yet it was hate that drove him. The men he tracked had been sent to hurt and humiliate her. Though they wouldn't ravish her, as Indravarman surely demanded such spoils for himself, Chaya's immediate fate would be something else altogether.

Remembering how Thida had suffered in his arms, how she had wept, and how, despite his desperate longing to help, he had been unable to stop the life from flowing out of her, Asal rode faster. Though his fingers still bled, he did not feel them. Though his eye was still swollen, he could see. The footprints below him seemed fresh. Propelled by the belief that he was nearing the men who would dare to take his loved one away, he smashed his good hand against his horse's flank, urging it ahead. Branches tore at his shoulders. Animals fled before him. And onward he went, dominated by thoughts of vengeance and welcoming the powers brought by his rage.

Of the six Chams, five were warriors and the other excelled at tracking. Though the tracker's quarry took precautions so as not to be followed, the two women left many signs of their passage for him to follow. He saw where their feet had turned over rocks on a stream's bottom, where they had bent branches away from their faces. Their footprints were smaller than those of the man who guided them, and the Cham saw many more of these lesser indentations. It seemed that the group traveled with speed rather than with stealth. They wanted to reach the Khmer base as soon as possible, for there lay safety.

The Cham tracker hadn't slept for a full day and night but wasn't overly tired. He had been promised gold if he returned the women to Indravarman, and now, as he drew closer to them, new strength surged through him. He whispered to his comrades that soon they would see their prey. They were to kill the Khmer guide and return the women to Angkor without pause. The women were to be frightened and humiliated, but left physically un-harmed.

The breeze shifted, blowing from the north, and the tracker paused. He could detect the faint presence of perfume in the air, and this new sign prompted him to smile. The women were close. They still tried to maintain speed but must be winded and ex-hausted. Someone not used to such a journey would be near the breaking point by now.

To his surprise, the breeze caught and carried a sound—a woman's cough, perhaps. Suddenly fearful that his prize would be saved at the last moment by a group of fellow Khmer travelers, the tracker turned to the men behind him, whispered that he would run and they were to follow him. He told them to ready their spears.

The cough came again, and the tracker stepped forward, walking, then running, his arms swinging back and forth. He avoided dead branches and fallen twigs, his bare feet striking the dry ground. The men behind him ran with much less stealth, but for once, he didn't mind. The women had impressed him in many ways, covering much more ground than he would have thought possible. But they hadn't been fast enough. In the end, they had faltered.

Thinking of the gold that would soon weigh down his hands, the tracker increased his pace, no longer even trying to be quiet. The best part of a hunt was the final, desperate moment when his quarry realized it had been caught. And that moment was about to unfold.

Holding her little sister's hand, Voisanne wearily led Chaya forward, wishing that her cough would stop. They'd been eating dried fish while walking, and in her exhaustion and haste Chaya had choked. She had gagged and retched, heaving as she tried to draw in air. The piece of fish had finally fallen free, but Chaya couldn't seem to clear her throat. In the dense, quiet jungle her coughs seemed unnaturally loud.

"We must hurry," Voisanne whispered, then helped Chaya over a fallen log.

"No."

"But, Chaya . . . we're almost there. Another half day's walk is all."

Their guide hissed at them to stop speaking. He stepped to his left, off the trail, and proceeded down a slight hill to where a stream gurgled. As they had many times before, they began to struggle up the stream, water splashing against their shins. Voisanne patted Chaya's back, trying to reassure her that everything would be fine when, in truth, Voisanne felt as if her world were crumbling. She was increasingly convinced that somehow Asal had been caught. Perhaps he'd waited too long for Thida, or maybe they had departed together but were overtaken by Indravarman's men. The thought of Asal in chains seemed to steal the breath from her lungs. They should have left as one or stayed as one. Something as precious as love could not split in half and be expected to survive.

Her foot slipped on a mossy rock and she fell to her hands and knees. She tried to stand, but her limbs seemed to be made of lead instead of flesh and bone. A profound weariness gripped her. The water was cool, and she wanted to lie down and let it carry her where it liked. Why was she going north, she asked herself, when Asal was to the south?

Their guide hurried back downstream and lifted her out of the water. She started to protest and he cursed, pulling up on her limp arm.

The jungle changed then, from a place of quiet subtleties to one of movement and noise. Men ran shrieking from the undergrowth. The Khmer guide thrust his spear toward the first attacker, but his weapon was deflected by a shield. He whirled, swinging his spear over the water, trying to keep a pack of Chams at bay. But they encircled him, drawing closer, taunting him as they poked and prodded with their own spears. His fate was obvious to everyone, especially to him, because he suddenly screamed and charged at one man, flicking his weapon forward. The spear point struck the Cham's shoulder and he staggered, but the other warriors howled in rage and plunged their weapons into the Khmer. He fell, dying, and they stomped on him, forcing his head underwater until his lungs drew no more air.

A rock held in her right hand, Voisanne stood in front of Chaya, shielding her. The men laughed as she pivoted, looking for some sort of escape. She thought of how she had been taken on her wedding day and that memory provoked an overriding sense of panic. Grunting, she threw the rock with all her might. One Cham ducked, and it struck another in the thigh. But then the men dropped their spears and closed in on her. Chaya shrieked. Voisanne beat their hands away. When their fingers seized hers she clawed, scratched, kicked, and bit. She was knocked into the stream, and for an instant water filled her lungs before she was dragged upward. Someone struck her in the belly. She couldn't breathe. Her sister was being held by two men, one who gripped her feet and another who had seized her arms. Voisanne gasped, trying to get up. But the men clutched her tightly, their fingernails digging into her skin. A rope was produced, her hands bound. When her breath finally returned, she screamed for help, but one Cham, older than the others, slapped her hard. She screamed again, and his second slap was even more vicious.

Silence fell. Chaya was also tied up. Both women were then thrown into the water. Voisanne crawled over the smooth rocks to her sister, putting her bound hands over Chaya's shoulders. They wept together, shuddering in the shallows as the Chams treated their wounded comrade and plundered the dead Khmer. The Chams started to laugh, gesturing toward Chaya, their crude movements making her cry. One warrior dropped the dead Khmer, then stepped toward Chaya, reaching out to squeeze her earlobe and lift her up.

"Leave her be!" Voisanne screamed. "Leave her—"

The older Cham shouted, and the younger warrior grimaced, then pushed Chaya backward, on top of Voisanne. The men laughed as Chaya began to sob, calling out to a father who wasn't there.

Voisanne had lived through the death of her loved ones. She had endured. But as she held her weeping sister she knew that she lacked the strength to survive a second capture and imprisonment. Death would be a far better alternative, for both of them. To die together, to be reborn together, held much more promise than a life of suffering, a life without Asal.

The killing end of a broken spear glittered in the water. Voisanne stared at it, and Chaya must have seen and interpreted that stare, for she nodded.

Still trembling, Voisanne lifted her bound hands back above her sister's shoulders and face. She reached underwater for the spear. When her hands touched the thick shaft, she dragged the weapon closer, shaking her head while she moved, denying what the moment meant, the action needed to do what must be done. She glanced at her sister and saw the beauty within her. Suddenly she couldn't imagine slashing the steel across Chaya's throat.

"No," Voisanne whispered. But instead of dropping the weapon, she began to rub the spear point against her bonds. She did so underwater, wincing as she accidentally cut the side of her right wrist. A trail of blood uncurled within the clear water. Still she worked, sawing back and forth, desperate for freedom.

The rope parted. Though her hands were no longer bound, she kept them together, turning toward Chaya, pretending to console her while she dragged the arm-length broken spear underwater.

As the Chams continued to deal with the injured shoulder of their companion, Voisanne cut at Chaya's bonds. She didn't know what she would do if and when Chaya was freed, but it felt good to be doing something. Hope surged within her.

But then she moved too quickly, and the steel sliced into Chaya's thumb. Her sister cried out.

One of the Chams stood up on the far bank. His brow furrowed. He stepped toward them, into the clear water.

Asal knelt closer to the ground, trying to determine where the footprints had gone. He had been following them along the hardened trail, but they seemed to have abruptly disappeared. Usually he could discover a twice-torn leaf or a snapped twig that indicated the direction that had been taken, but no such markers existed. He cursed, hitting the ground with the palm of his uninjured hand. Without question he was close to Voisanne and Chaya, but so, he believed, were their pursuers.

Now that he was forced to move with patience, his aches and weariness were more pronounced. His three battered fingers throbbed. His body was sore and unresponsive. Only his eye seemed to have improved, the swelling no longer much of a problem. Yet because of his weariness, focusing on the trail was difficult, and he wondered if he was missing an obvious sign.

His horse neighed softly, as if letting him know that it was also exhausted. Asal stood up, patted its neck, and then looked back in the direction he had come, thinking that he should backtrack.

The scream startled him.

He gazed about the jungle. Again the cry came, and he recognized Voisanne's voice. Without thought, he leapt onto his mount, and while turning it to the right, unsheathed his sword. When his horse balked at moving into some thick underbrush, he brought the hilt of his weapon down hard on its flank, prompting it to charge ahead. Branches tore at his shoulders and thighs, but he demanded more speed.

The slope of a hill fell away from the trail, and they plunged downward. A stream shimmered below. At first Asal saw only water and boulders, but then he noticed struggling figures a few hundred paces upstream. Distracted as he was, a limb almost knocked him from his mount. He recovered, kicked his horse with all his strength and held on to its mane as they dropped like a tumbling stone.

It would have been wiser for Asal to attack with surprise, but he saw that Voisanne was fighting with a man in the water and shouted her name. The Chams nearest to him turned in his direction. They stepped back, reaching for their spears even as he sent his horse careening into them. Two enemy warriors went down beneath its hooves, but then his mount stumbled and Asal was thrown over its head. He landed in the water, somehow managing to hold on to his sword, instinctively knowing that if he dropped it he would die.

Though the breath had been hammered from his lungs by the force of the fall, he stood up. Three Chams remained uninjured, and they all had found their spears and shields. They encircled him like predators surrounding a wounded but dangerous prey. The spears were longer than Asal's sword, and as the Chams began to thrust their weapons at him, he could only beat their attacks aside. Yet Asal had seen blood flowing from a wound on Voisanne's hand, and the sight had filled him with rage, empowering him and his blade.

"Leave and you live," he said in his native tongue. "Stay and you die."

His countrymen pressed closer, stabbing and retreating, moving around him so that he was forced to defend himself from all directions. One of the men slipped on a rock, and Asal leapt toward him, his sword humming in the air, cutting through the warrior's spear and slicing deeply into his side. The man fell, screaming. The two other Chams rushed forward as Asal pulled his blade free. One spear tip missed his neck by a handsbreadth. The other grazed the side of his hip. Asal shouted in fury, knocking down the spear shaft with his left forearm and slashing sideways with his sword. Again his blade struck home and a Cham cried out, blood spurting from a wound in his thigh.

The warrior who had barely missed skewering him in the neck had pulled back his spear and thrust it forward again. Asal twisted so that the weapon slid past him, as did the man. But suddenly Asal's right foot became lodged between several rocks. He tried to jerk it free, yet it was held fast. The warrior regained his balance and slammed the butt of his spear into Asal's belly. As Asal doubled over, the Cham dropped his spear and in one fluid motion pulled a hunting knife from a leather sheath and swept it toward Asal's face. Asal leaned away from the strike and the blade missed him, but his foot was still trapped and he fell backward. Sensing victory, the Cham stepped forward, his weapon held high.

When the warrior abruptly shuddered, Asal kicked at him, unsure what had happened. The man fell, clutching at his back. He toppled into the water, a broken spear shaft protruding between his shoulder blades. Voisanne stood behind him, her feet spread wide. The wound she'd given him was painful but not fatal, and Asal kicked his foot free and hacked down with his sword, killing the warrior. The remaining Chams, all wounded, pleaded for mercy, but he cut them down without hesitation, only dropping his blade when the stream had reddened with their blood.

Voisanne stood shaking in the center of the water. Chaya was holding her sister's elbow and sobbing. After running to them, Asal gathered them both in his arms. He held them tight, promising that they were safe, that no one would ever hurt them again. When he saw that their wounds were superficial, a profound relief flooded through him. His legs trembled. His breaths came in quick gasps. He kissed the tops of their heads, thanking the Gods for granting him speed and strength. And he thanked Thida.

Asal held them until the water finally ran clear once again. "We should go," he whispered, then kissed Voisanne's hand. "Come, my lady. Let us go."

"But your fingers. What happened to your fingers? And your face?"

A bird squawked from far above, and he glanced up. "Indravarman . . . captured me."

"And you escaped?"

"I was freed. Thida freed me."

"Where is she?"

Asal told Voisanne the full story, recalling their final words and the fire he had built around her body. "She died . . . with a smile," he said. "She wanted to be reunited with her loved ones, and I think she saw them coming for her."

Weeping, Voisanne bent her head down and leaned against him. "Do you believe that she is with them?"

"Yes. Because I was there. I saw how she smiled."

Chaya, who had so far remained silent, eased away from them. "What were they going to do with us? Why were they—"

"It's all right," Voisanne replied, reaching out to her.

"But those men . . . They wanted to hurt us. They were going to hurt us and I don't—"

"They can no longer hurt you," Asal said. "So you needn't worry about them."

She shook her head. "We have to leave here. Right now. I can't stay here. Not in this place."

Asal picked up his sword. "We shall leave in a moment. But first, if it's agreeable to you, I'd like a word with your sister." Chaya's eyes squeezed shut and she seemed to gather herself. She nodded. Asal thanked her and led Voisanne to the muddied shore.

"What?" Voisanne whispered, wiping tears from her eyes.

At first he didn't speak but simply smiled at her. Though his fingers still ached and his hip bled from where the spear point had grazed him, he was filled with joy. "When Indravarman had me," he said, his voice softer than the gurgle of the stream, "all I thought of was you. In the end, when the pain was the worst, I saw you, I heard you, and I felt you."

"I'm so sorry. I wanted to go back for you. I almost—"

"Shh," he said, touching his good forefinger against her lips. "There's no need for that, my lady. No need at all. I asked you to go ahead. You did what we all knew must be done. And a part of you was with me. A part of you lingered."

"I won't leave you again. Not in this life or the next."

His smile returned. "I never thought I'd love a woman . . . as I love you."

"Why not?"

"Because I didn't think life could be so beautiful."

She kissed him, and would have kissed him again, but he collected himself enough to break slightly away from her, to whisper that Indravarman must have sent men after him and that they should flee. She asked about Thida again, nodding at his words, praying while he spoke. When she continued to pray, he turned from her, walked back into the water, and carried Chaya to the horse. He lifted her upon it, then helped Voisanne climb up behind her.

Using a short lead rope, Asal guided the horse to the north, following the stream. A snake glided across its glistening waters. He looked upward, glimpsed the sky, and thought of Thida, hoping that whatever world she now inhabited was as beautiful as this one. Bowing, he thanked her again.

Behind him the siblings began to talk, and he smiled when he heard vigor flow back into Chaya's voice. Knowing that they might be pursued, he was tempted to ask them to whisper but, for the moment, he remained silent.

Near the southern end of the Khmer encampment, Jayavar led Ajadevi along the river's edge, greeting his people when they bowed or knelt as he passed, raising their spirits with words of encouragement. Now that battle was imminent, and because there was a strong chance of a Cham spy or assassin hidden within their midst, two trusted bodyguards walked about five paces behind the king and queen. These men carried swords and unusually large shields. The bodyguards were present at Ajadevi's insistence. Jayavar felt that they made him look vulnerable to his people and that it would be difficult for them to draw inspiration from someone who appeared fearful. But Ajadevi had managed to convince him that the threat of assassination was too great to ignore. Without Jayavar, the Khmer cause would be lost.

The floor of the valley slanted to the south and the river rushed forward, cascading over boulders. Mist glistened in the air, giving sustenance to moss that grew along the shoreline, most notably on tree trunks and fallen branches. A space had been cleared near the water where crates of provisions had been stacked. Older Khmer men inspected wares, took notes, and tried to salvage a damaged cart. Farther away from the river, several war elephants were tied to trees.

The trail, which Hindu priests had created generations before, began to narrow. Jayavar pressed ahead. He stepped around chest-high ferns, his left hand leading Ajadevi forward, his right on his sword hilt. A smooth boulder bisected the trail and he paused, motioning for his bodyguards to remain still. They nodded, spread apart, and studied their surroundings.

Jayavar guided Ajadevi to the other side of the boulder. They took a few more paces, then moved toward the river, stepping from the trail onto a patch of sand that dropped into the water. Minnows darted about mossy rocks. A blue-winged butterfly fluttered above its reflection. In the distance, the beat of the swordsmith's hammer rang out against an unseen anvil. Jayavar thought of Bona, and decided to seek him out later in the day, to resume teaching him how to use a bow and arrow. Through his smiles and eagerness, the boy brought a welcome sense of peace into Jayavar, a feeling that the world still held promise.

"There's something I wish to tell you," Jayavar said, turning toward Ajadevi.

She looked up at him, a ray of sunlight dropping from her

forehead to her chin. "Then share your preoccupation, Jayavar. I've sensed it easily enough."

He smiled. "I would like to thank you."

"For what?"

"I saw you yesterday with Nuon. You were bathing together, and her entire world was you. I don't know what you were telling her, but whatever it was, she was consumed by your words."

Ajadevi shifted away from the ray of light, which had fallen into her eyes. "I wanted her to understand that her role will not be to merely stand and look lovely by your side. If she has a son, she must protect him. Just as she must protect you. She doesn't think that she's old or wise enough for such responsibilities, but I told her that age is irrelevant. What has yet to be learned in this life has already been learned in others."

Water bugs darted atop the nearby water, fleeing the attack of a finger-size fish. "I know that at times it must be difficult for you to counsel her," he said. "And to see me with her. I would not be strong enough to share you with another man."

She looked away.

"And that, Ajadevi, is what I wish to thank you for today," he continued. "To acknowledge your selflessness, your strength. You give more to Nuon than you do to yourself, and I shall always be grateful."

"I merely . . . fulfill my duty."

He squeezed her hand. "Come, my love. Follow me. There is something I wish to show you. A gift from me to you."

Once again they followed the narrow trail, stepping over roots, avoiding the glistening strands of broken spiderwebs. A bamboo thicket rose directly before them. The stalks, as thick as an arm and twenty feet tall, rubbed against one another, creating a series of groans and creaks. Jayavar paused at one of the stalks, holding it. He turned to Ajadevi. "You were right to bring us to this valley," he said. "This place has been good for our people. It has been good for me. It's brought healing to us all."

She nodded. "We needed to heal."

"Like you, I've been a Buddhist for many years. But I still cherish the Hindu Gods. This place, with its carvings of Vishnu and Shiva, fills me with peace. And before war, I need peace. I need to know what life will be like after all of the misery."

A monkey screeched.

"Why did you bring me here?" Ajadevi asked. "You could have told me these things anywhere."

"Because I've seen how many of our people pray near this water. How they touch the carvings and bow their heads. They draw great strength from this setting."

"They do."

"But a few of our people, like us, are Buddhist, and we also need a place to pray and draw strength."

She smiled, reaching for his hand. "Show me."

He led her around the bamboo thicket. It was larger than most and appeared very old. Moving with patience and care, he sensed her eagerness, which filled him with joy. Everything she did, it seemed, she did with him in mind. She was the most self-less person he knew, and it felt good to be doing something for her.

At the far end of the thicket, the river broadened and swung to the west, creating a deep pool of slow-moving water. Facing the water at the edge of this pool was a slightly larger-than-life-size statue of Buddha, who sat with crossed legs and rested his upturned palms on his lap. An orange sash covered the left shoulder of the Buddha and was wrapped around his midsection. Scattered about the Buddha, candles burned within golden bowls. Sticks of incense that had been stuck in the damp ground smoldered and filled the air with the scent of sandalwood.

Without a word, Ajadevi stepped forward, entranced. She studied the Buddha's face, which was dominated by a wide and gentle smile. The statue had been carved from the same dark stone that lined the river and had been used to immortalize the Hindu creations.

Ajadevi placed her hands together and bowed. She closed her eyes, praying as the bamboo swayed behind her. Jayavar watched her with pride and contentment, believing that he had helped to create a deeply spiritual place, one that would be used by his people for centuries to come.

He added his prayers to hers, asking for victory in the coming battle. The victory he sought was not for greed or power, but for liberty. His people needed to be free to live and pray and die as they saw fit. As their king, he knew liberty was the greatest gift that he could offer, and yet as of this day, he'd failed to give it. His people had been conquered and subjugated, and this failing would define his very existence until the Chams were driven from his land.

"How did you manage this?" she asked, finally opening her eyes.

"Our first day here, I walked this river's banks. I saw the Hindu carvings and was moved by them. I saw people praying to them. And I asked a stonesmith if a statue of Buddha could be created. Five masters were soon working on it. They labored day and night so that it could be finished in time. I asked that this place be built for those of our people who are Buddhists . . . and for you. Because it's you who gave me the gift of first sight."

"What do you mean?"

"You showed me how to see, Ajadevi. Some beauty . . . like that of Angkor Wat or of a child, is obvious. But other beauty is harder to discern. How can beauty be seen in hardship, in a fallen tree as well as in a soaring tree? How does beauty survive, and how does it blossom, at a time when so much of it has been stolen from the world? After the Cham invasion I was lost. And though I still grieve for my loved ones, though I still aggravate you with my laments, I believe that my children are with me, that their beauty has become a part of me. I want to live because of them, because through my deeds I honor their dreams. You and you alone gave me this faith, this ability to see, to look past the ugliness of life and glimpse its radiance. And for that gift I shall be forever grateful."

She turned to him, embracing him. "Thank you. Thank you for seeing."

"You have given my life renewed meaning. I'm a king without a throne, but if we win this fight, then I shall try to cast as much beauty into the world as possible. With you beside me we shall feed the hungry, cure the sick, give hope to the downcast. Our empire will rise to new heights, and a thousand years from now, people will walk the streets we paved, marvel at the sights we built, and be reminded that their part in this world is not a small one, that every man and woman can aspire to greatness."

"That's why we cannot lose this fight," she replied. "That's why I shall come here every day and pray for victory. Because victory shall give you the chance to build such a world. And I know you can build it."

He shook his head. "We can build it. Together."

"The Chams will come for us, Jayavar. I see their looming presence like smoke on a windless day. They'll come for us and we must attack."

"And we will. Soon. I need only a few more days to prepare."

She leaned toward him, taking both of his hands in hers. "You should go. You should ready your men. I shall stay here and pray."

Nodding, he started to turn away.

But she held on to his hands. "Thank you for . . . believing in me."

He smiled. "How could I not believe in you? In the one who shall stand beside me in life and death, throughout this life and every one thereafter?"

Twenty

Final Preparations

ndravarman stood beside what had once been a large funeral pyre. The charred ends of logs and branches dominated the outside of a scorched circle of earth almost as large as an elephant. In the center of the ashes lay the charred and broken remains of a human skeleton. Jewelry had been found amid the remains, and Indravarman held blackened rings and a misshapen necklace. He remembered giving the items to Thida. She had pretended to be pleased with the gifts and had worn them without exception, but he had suspected that she'd displayed them solely out of fear.

In the two days since Asal and Thida's escape, Indravarman's trackers had combed the jungle near Angkor, looking for clues. Finally a farmer had said that a Cham warrior had brought a woman to this place, held her, burned her body, and left with great haste. As soon as Indravarman had heard the information, he'd rushed to the spot, unsure why he felt compelled to act quickly. It was his beating, he was certain, that had killed Thida. And though he didn't regret beating her, he wished that she still lived. Her presence had brought a comfort to him, a sense of contentment that he rarely knew.

In the end, he had misjudged her. He had thought her beauty was her strength. But after he had struck her, after he had taken her beauty away, that was when she had found her courage. She had killed a guard, freed Asal, and escaped into the jungle. She had become more potent, and therefore more desirable, than ever before.

Indravarman hated his foes; he hated weakness. But he did not hate Thida and was sorry that she was dead. There would be other women, of course, but none would rival her beauty, and he doubted that any would dare to stand against him as she had. She was more like himself than he had ever believed, and he was glad that she had died with honor.

Asal was another matter. His betrayal was like a deep wound in Indravarman's side. He had spurned his king for nothing more than love. Indravarman felt that he had given Asal the opportunity to claim fame and fortune, and in return he had received from Asal only treachery. The knowledge that Asal might have already joined the Khmers profoundly rankled Indravarman. Asal knew too much, having attended recent war councils and spoken with Indravarman on several occasions about how to best use the approaching Cham reinforcements. These three thousand warriors would arrive in five days after traveling across the Great Lake. Shortly thereafter, Indravarman would lead his forces north to the Khmer stronghold. But many things could happen during that time, especially if Asal were to seek out the Khmers and gain the trust of Jayavar. As a military strategist, Asal was unpredictable, a trait that Indravarman had always welcomed. Patience was needed in war, but so were guile and audacity.

Indravarman dropped the rings and necklace, then rubbed

the iron in his belly. That iron had been placed beneath his skin by his father, who proclaimed that all his sons were to be warriors. They would live and die by the sword, and how better to know steel than to make it a part of you?

"We'll never catch him," Indravarman said, eyeing the trail to the north.

Po Rame, who had been inspecting Thida's remains, turned and approached his king. Several Cham warriors near the charred wood stepped aside for the assassin, giving him a wide berth. "But neither will we see him again, Lord King," he replied, stopping next to Indravarman.

"You think him a coward?"

"Yes."

"Then you're a fool, Po Rame. I've seen him in a dozen fights, and he's downed killers when the rest of his men were dead or wounded."

"But why, Lord King, would that seeker of whores risk a fight against us? He's gone. He's free. And he won't—"

"He loves a woman! A Khmer woman! Her people fight against us and so he may take up their cause. When we last saw him your bamboo was in his fingers, and you think he has no reason to hate us?" Indravarman kicked the rings at his feet. "You excel at killing, Po Rame. You're a master of death and treachery. But you misjudge Asal. He'll go to Jayavar and share our secrets."

"Then we should attack, Lord King. March north tomorrow. Now that one of my men has discovered the false king's true base in the valley, we should destroy him there."

"I have three thousand of my best warriors arriving in five days! You would have me split my force? By splitting my men I invite disaster. The Khmers could defeat us to the north, then come south and destroy the new arrivals. If I wait a week to march, I'll vastly outnumber them and will rid the world of them once and for all."

Po Rame nodded, then turned his body away from the midmorning sun. "We have able spies, King of Kings, within the Khmer encampments. These spies have tried to reach the false king at the river and at the temple, but he's closely guarded. Surely the Khmer lover, if he indeed goes to those dung-eating peasants, would be treated with suspicion. No one would protect him. He could be killed with ease."

Indravarman considered the notion. He could send word via carrier pigeon to his spies in the north. Asal could be targeted. But messages were sometimes intercepted, and if he alerted the Khmers to Asal's importance, then surely his council would be sought out and heeded. "Send messages," he finally replied. "But cloak your words in codes. Let your spies know that the traitor is to be killed."

"Yes, Lord King."

"But if they fail, Po Rame, then your task will be to discover his whereabouts. If he hides in the jungle, I want him skinned alive and staked to the earth. If he meets us on the battlefield, I want your spear in his back. I want him to suffer, then die."

"I'll do all—"

"Because treason is contagious. It festers like a disease, moving from one body into the next, infecting the weak and endangering the strong."

"I'll finish, Lord King, what I began with his fingers. And then I'll steal his soul."

Indravarman smiled for the first time since seeing Thida's skeleton. "You'd like that, would you not?"

"Yes."

"Once again, because it amuses me, tell me why."

"A man, Lord King, is a collection of lives, of memories, of knowledge. And when I steal a soul all of these powers find their way into me."

"And that's the source of your strength?"

"One source, King of Kings. One source among many."

A Cham warrior began to urinate on the ashes, and Indravarman shouted at him to stop. The warrior bowed low, holding his stance until his king dismissed him. "He dares to piss on the remains of my woman?" Indravarman said to Po Rame, an edge to his voice.

"A careless weakling, Lord King. A man beneath us."

Indravarman thought of Thida, wishing that she were beside him, disbelieving that one of his men would so carelessly defile her. "Let me see how you'll cripple Asal when you meet him on the field of battle. Let me see how you'll strike him in the spine."

"On that fool?"

The king nodded, then watched as Po Rame walked toward the warriors, moving with ease and grace, as if his mind were on nothing more than where to place his feet. The men parted again to let him pass, only this time he dropped his hand behind him, into his hip cloth. Steel flashed in the sun. The offending warrior screamed and fell. Other Chams drew their weapons but Indravarman shouted at them to make no move.

The injured Cham tried to defend himself, but his legs were unresponsive. He cried out, asking for help that did not come. Using his elbows, he began to crawl away from his assailant.

Po Rame glanced at Indravarman, who nodded, then stepped closer to see how a soul was stolen.

The knife, now red, descended again, this time with leisure rather than haste. Screams seemed to echo within the clearing. Po Rame bent low, pressing his forehead against his victim's, holding him tight.

Ashes stirred in the wind.

Whether a soul had escaped or been captured, Indravarman wasn't certain.

He turned and left.

The Citadel of Women was just the reprieve that Ajadevi needed. She was tired of the endless preparations for battle, and though she often attended war councils and was usually pleased to offer her husband advice, she had needed to escape the beautiful yet shadowy confines of the valley. Convincing Jayavar that she would be safe at the temple wasn't easy, but in the end he had encouraged her to leave—accompanied by ten of his best warriors.

Banteay Srei was located on the plains to the south of the valley. The fertile land was home to many varieties of towering trees—behemoth creations that would have rendered most structures inconsequential but seemed to draw Ajadevi's gaze to Banteay Srei.

She remembered seeing the temple as a little girl and feeling empowered by it. While countless statues and bas-reliefs of female dancers and guardians graced Angkor Wat, these works of art were a part of Angkor Wat's landscape. Banteay Srei, conversely, appeared to have been built in honor of women. Of course, carvings of the Hindu Gods were present, but even these seemed of secondary importance to the feminine faces and figures that adorned so many of Banteay Srei's walls.

Ajadevi stood at the base of the tallest tower. Wanting a clearer view of the grounds, she left the interior of Banteay Srei and headed toward its outer courtyards. She passed through these and came to the southernmost part of the wall that surrounded the complex. The stone blocks that comprised the wall were no longer perfectly joined, allowing her hand- and toeholds that she used to climb to the top. She sat down, nodding to the warriors who followed her at a distance, thankful for their loyalty and vigilance. Though she tried to stop her mind from going to such a place, she couldn't help but wonder which of them would die in the coming battle. Surely these warriors would be in the thick of the mayhem, eager to avenge their families and country.

After saying a prayer for the men below, as well as for their wives and children, Ajadevi stared to the south. Soon the Chams would come. Keeping the presence of nearly eight thousand Khmers and Siamese a secret was an impossible task. A spy would arrive, assess the military strength of the force, and then depart for Angkor. Perhaps Indravarman already knew of their location and was merely making his preparations. Armies, Ajadevi was well aware, were not made for speed. They were assembled, instructed, and then laboriously moved from one place to the next.

Still, the Chams would come. Jayavar preferred to fight them in a place of his own choosing and would soon lead his forces to the south. They were waiting for a final contingent of Siamese mercenaries. When these men arrived, Jayavar would have more than seven thousand warriors under his command—a respectable force for certain, though he would still be outnumbered by the Chams. One of the reasons he wanted to fight close to Angkor was that he hoped once the battle began, Khmers from the nearby city would join the fray. If enough ordinary Khmers joined the fight, the balance of battle could be tipped in their favor.

The loud flapping of wings caused Ajadevi to look up. She was surprised to see an osprey flying past. The bird with its white chest and black wings was large and swift. Within its talons it carried a piece of fluttering red silk larger than one of its wings. Ajadevi had seen the nests of such raptors, which were often composed of bits of cloth as well as sticks and branches. The osprey must have found the red silk from the Siamese part of the nearby encampment.

The bird flew south, disappearing behind the canopy of a broad tree. Ajadevi thought about its arrival, intrigued that she had seen such a beautiful bird and that it had carried a piece of red silk. Surely the bird was a sign, though one she could not yet interpret.

A fly buzzed about her head, but she paid it no heed. She envisioned the osprey, wondering where it had gone and why it had sought out the red silk. Did it warn her of coming blood? Of betrayal? Or was Jayavar in imminent danger?

Frustrated by the lack of answers, Ajadevi closed her eyes, certain that she was meant to see the silk. She had been sent a sign, yet it was up to her to properly read it. Standing up, she began to walk along the wall. The stone blocks were warm against her feet. She passed from sun to shadow, constantly thinking about the bird and the silk. When she reached the eastern edge of the wall she turned around and headed back, unaware of the lizards that scurried away from her approaching feet or the warriors who followed her every movement.

When the answer finally came to her, she stopped. The bird had carried a banner. Her people had always fought under banners, yet those had been the standards of kings. Perhaps it was time to create a new banner, one that celebrated people rather than a man. They needed a symbol to fight under, something to inspire them, to show everyone that what they bled and died for was noble and grand.

"Angkor Wat," she whispered. "It has to be Angkor Wat."

She imagined how the flag might look. The strip of red silk in the osprey's talons should be a part of the image, as should the central towers of Angkor Wat. Her people would die for those towers, she knew. Under a banner of Angkor Wat, they would bring the fight to their foe.

Pleased with herself, Ajadevi was about to step down from the wall when, to her surprise, the osprey returned, this time without the fabric in its talons. It flew from the south, high above the treetops, toward their distant encampment. She watched it for a moment, clucking her tongue as it disappeared from view.

What are you trying to tell me? she asked. Why have you come again?

At first, the sky was devoid of answers. But the more she contemplated, the more apparent it was that the flight of the bird, the direction in which it had traveled, hinted to her that someone was approaching. This person would be a stranger to them but should be heeded. He or she would come with open arms, seemingly weak but in truth far from it.

Ajadevi had always believed in signs. She had seen her first one as a young girl. She could still remember the sight of the staggering ox that was a prelude to her father's illness. The ox had died before her eyes, and shortly thereafter, her father had died with her beside him. Life was a series of echoes, she believed— moments in time that came and went, different with each cycle and yet connected.

The osprey had once carried a banner. It had returned, flying in the direction of her husband. Someone was coming to him, someone who had no banner but who could be trusted in the dark days ahead.

She climbed down the wall and asked the ten warriors to accompany her back to their king. Certain she had been drawn to the temple to see the bird, Ajadevi asked the men to move with haste. Soon events would unfold of which she could foresee only part, events that were infinitely larger than she was. If she did not act with care, she and, more important, Jayavar would be overwhelmed, as powerless as ospreys in the midst of a storm.

Back at the Khmer encampment, Soriya and Boran knelt inside their shelter, oblivious to the activity around them. Boran's fingers were blistered from training with a spear and shield, and Soriya was in the midst of wrapping them in thin strips of fabric that she had soaked in a healing paste. Though his hands were hardened from many years of fishing, it seemed that the hilt of his sword and the handle of his shield rubbed against him in all the wrong places. Soriya could have wrapped his fingers faster, but she wanted to talk with him and meant to delay his departure. She knew he wouldn't like what she had to say and needed more time to steel her resolve.

"I should return," he said, clenching and unclenching his right fist. "Vibol and Prak are with some officers describing how the Chams are positioned on the Great Lake. I should be with them."

"But our boys are so eager to be men. Maybe they should be left alone to speak as men."

"Yes, but I've spent more time at the Cham base. I might remember something that they've forgotten."

"Then go. But if you would . . . please wait a moment. There's something I need to tell you."

"What?"

Her pulse quickened, and she shifted on the thatch mat that covered the ground beneath their shelter. "I've been talking with other women," she said quietly. "Many intend to travel with their men when the army marches south."

"So?"

"So . . . I'd like to travel with you. As would Prak."

"But you agreed to stay here together."

"That was before I heard from the other women. They said I should come."

Boran shook his head. "If the battle is lost, the Chams will find our women. They'll hurt them."

"If you lose, the Chams will also come here. Our fate would be no different."

"That's not true. You'd know of our loss. You and Prak could hide. We hid once before and were never found. Why not hide again?"

"Because I don't want to leave you and neither does Prak," she replied, taking his bandaged hands in hers. "Please, Boran."

He swore, something she rarely heard him do. "You'd put yourself at too much risk," he replied. "Put Prak at too much risk. If we lose the battle, Khmer riders will be sent here. Whoever stays will be warned."

"And the Chams will hunt them down like animals. Better to die there, with you, than to hide here for a few days in terror. That's what many of the women think. And I agree with them."

His hands tightened upon hers. "But you might escape. It's possible."

"The king's wife is going. She'll be there with him. Why shouldn't I be there with you? Why should we be different?"

"He can find another wife! He can find ten more!"

"No. Everyone knows he loves her. He'd wither away without her. And she without him. That's why she's going. Because she refuses to hide in the jungle here. She'd rather live or die by his side."

"But Prak. You must think of Prak. The Chams would take him as a slave. He'd spend the rest of his life enduring beatings and taunts. Is that how you'd have him live?"

Soriya started to reply, but the image created by Boran's words made her eyes well with tears. "That . . . that wouldn't happen."

"Why not?"

"Because those of us who go . . . we go with poison. If the battle is lost . . . the poison is used."

"No!"

"It's what Prak wants. He agrees."

"You speak of horrors."

"But the queen will do the same. It was her idea. She's bringing enough for everyone, but even so I collected some red-capped mushrooms. They—"

"And so our people would die. Rather than flee, rather than survive to fight another day, our people would die."

"As one. We'll live or die as one."

"Then the queen isn't as just as I thought. Nor as wise."

It was Soriya's turn to shake her head. "That's not true, Boran. To live or die as one is wise. And it will be life, she thinks. She believes that you'll win."

"We'll be outnumbered! Even with the Siamese."

"I know you always think of me, and of our sons," Soriya replied. "So please think of this—what if the king follows Prak's plan? How can he not be there to see his own plan unfold? If you lose, he can't run away in fear, in shame. And if you win, then let him share in the glory. Let that one moment carry him forward for the rest of his days. Because he'll need something to lean on when we're gone."

Boran let go of her hands. He reached up to rub his aching neck. "They say that we'll leave in two or three days," he said, looking down. "Are you telling me that in such a short time all of my loved ones may be dead?"

"I'm telling you only what I must."

"Right now . . . the world seems to be a bitter place."

She leaned forward, putting her arms around him, holding him tight. "Yes, but if we win, then it will be such a beautiful place. So win, Boran. Keep Vibol safe and win."

He rested his head against her shoulder. "Our sons need to see our strength. But right now, I don't feel strong. I feel lost. And I miss our old life. I want to be on the water with them, with you."

"I know. So do I. But you're strong, Boran. That's why I've looked for you to lead us. Because you've always been strong."

"As have you."

"No. Not at the beginning. Not when the Chams first came. I was weak. Very weak. But lately I've tried in my own way to help. I'm sorry that I haven't done more for you. I haven't been strong for you."

"Why do you say that? You sit here and tell me that you're willing to take poison, that you'd rather face our foe than flee. You mend my old nets without complaint, cure my aches when you have so many of your own. You couldn't do what you've always done without being strong."

She closed her eyes, disbelieving his words but glad to hear them. "If I may ask . . . what is your decision?"

"About coming with me? You ask as if I control you. You're like a deep river, Soriya, smooth on the surface but swirling underneath. I'd rather you stay, but if you must go, if Prak must go, then I won't stop you."

"Thank you."

He shook his head, his gaze drifting to a bouquet of irises that she had fashioned in the corner. "The Gods . . . seem so cruel. Because we've built so much, you and I. And in a matter of days . . . it could all be lost."

"I know. But if our sons are to live as men, we have to stay. Isn't that what we both believe?"

He nodded.

She brought his bandaged forefinger to her lips and kissed it—something she hadn't done for many years. Suddenly their youth seemed so very distant. Her memories were still crisp and plentiful, but at that moment they weren't enough. She yearned for the freedom to claim the future. She needed the promise of blissful sights and sounds that she had yet to discover.

If she must, she would take the poison. She would give it to Prak. But she would have to die first. Because regardless of what Boran had said, she wasn't strong enough to watch her son perish. Her child, who had brought her so much joy, whom she loved far more than herself, would have to die alone.

As they neared the Citadel of Women, Voisanne grew increasingly nervous. She was excited at the prospect of seeing her people once again, but she was worried about how Asal would be treated. She trusted him with her life and she had grown to love him, and yet her countrymen would see only a Cham warrior who must be vanquished. Surely they were eager for vengeance, and Asal might prove to be an irresistible target.

Sitting behind her sister on the horse, Voisanne let her gaze follow the trail ahead and then drifted back to Asal's broad shoulders. Sweat glistened on his skin, and once again, she asked to exchange positions. He politely declined, saying that the jungle was unsafe and that he should remain on the ground.

I'll protect him, she thought, as Chaya jested about a butterfly that seemed to follow them. He's always protected me, and soon it will be my turn to stand in front of him.

The trunks of immense trees came and went, different in hues and textures. Despite the great canopies, the trail seemed to brighten, perhaps due to the absence of smaller trees and shrubs. Voisanne thought she smelled smoke. An elephant's trumpet seemed to reverberate around her.

The jungle vegetation continued to thin out as they proceeded. Asal unsheathed his sword, using his injured hand to pull

their horse's lead rope. Gaps in the foliage appeared ahead of
them. Light streamed in their direction.

Banteay Srei first appeared as if it were a miniature Angkor
Wat, its sculpted towers rising skyward in the clearing. Shouts
erupted, and Asal dropped his sword, then knelt on the ground.
As Khmer warriors rushed forward, Voisanne leapt from the
horse, calling out that they came as friends. She was ignored, and
the warriors confronted Asal, demanding to know his intentions.
He bowed, but stayed silent, as his accent would betray his origins. Sensing danger, the Khmers fanned out around him, their
weapons held ready. Voisanne stepped in front of Asal, shielding
him from their spears and swords with her own body. The weapons flicked at her, but she did not retreat.

"I know the king!" she shouted, stepping ahead toward the
glistening blades. "And I demand to see him!"

Though she exaggerated, the warriors became uncertain, their
weapons wavering. "Why bring a Cham into our midst?" asked a
thin man who held a heavy silver horn that he looked ready to
blow.

"He comes as our ally," Voisanne replied, still holding her
hands up. "And he has information for our king."

The Khmer frowned but seemed to relax. "Bind him," he said.

Voisanne started to protest, but Asal told her that they had a
right to bind him, that he would do the same if their positions
were reversed. Men came forward with ropes and tied his hands
behind his back. He winced when they jostled his injured fingers,
and Voisanne pleaded with them to be careful. She thought that
they would listen to her, but then their leader lifted his silver horn
and slammed it down hard on Asal's head. She screamed as he
crumpled, screamed as the men wrapped rope around her hands
and also reached for Chaya.

One of her countrymen cuffed her, yet the blow didn't silence her protests. She struggled and fought, terrified by what they might do to Asal, clawing and biting and kicking even as hands encircled her neck.

Fingers pressed against her throat and still she raged. But then she could no longer breathe.

Darkness approached, lingered, and then, after what seemed an eternity of suffering, was replaced by light.

Someone picked her up. She tried to call out to Asal, to Chaya, but her voice seemed to be trapped within her. She made no sound as she was carried away.

Through the haze of Asal's pain and disorientation, the world came slowly into focus. He was outside in a courtyard, which seemed to be raised off the ground. Immediately before him a tower stretched upward, graced by carvings of dancing women. To his left a sandstone walkway, the same height as the courtyard, was supported by pillars and led to the tower. The ground below was dominated by a garden and a pond covered in lotus flowers.

He lay with his hands tied in front of him inside a circle of seated Khmer warriors. A woman was talking—Voisanne. To his surprise and gratitude she no longer shouted but spoke firmly and with confidence to the obvious leader of the group. Asal had never seen the Khmer king but the man must be Jayavar. She bowed her head when answering him, and though he wore no jewels, the men near him were deferential toward him.

Remembering his own necklace, Asal was relieved to see that Voisanne's gift still lay against his chest. He sat up slowly, clenching his jaws at the pain that movement brought. As he stirred, Voisanne started to rise and call out to him, but the king placed a hand on her shoulder and she grew still.

At first no one spoke. Asal gazed at Voisanne, saw how she nodded to him, and he relaxed against his bonds. Outside the circle of Khmers, fires burned, cloaked within structures of wood and stone. Though the canopies of nearby trees were dark, their trunks were partly illuminated by the flames. Bats wheeled about in the underbelly of the sky, chasing unseen insects.

Asal counted eight Khmers plus Voisanne and Chaya. Neither sister was bound. The moon was out, prompting Asal to wonder how long he'd been unconscious. A fair amount of time must have passed, he realized, because the wound on his head had been bandaged and blood had dried against his skin. He was also hungry.

"I am Jayavar," the king said, nodding. "Tonight I've been told an unlikely story by the woman beside me. I would like you to repeat that story. Repeat it and we shall talk. Tell me a different tale and I shall consider you a spy."

Asal understood that he was being tested. He bowed his head, introduced himself, explained his position in the Cham army and his relationship with Indravarman. Then he told the story of how he had come to know Voisanne. He did not mention his feelings for her, but he spoke at length of how he had tried to help her flee and how Indravarman had captured him. His explanation of his escape provoked a series of questions from the king, who seemed to deem this part of his story improbable.

"I've seen your fingers," Jayavar replied after silence fell. "But one could inflict such damage on one's own flesh. And one could ride here pretending to be Indravarman's foe when actually acting as his instrument."

Asal nodded. "Yes, Lord King. I could be that instrument."

"But you could also be his foe. To that end, why would you betray your people?"

"I would not—I do not betray my people," Asal replied. "I betray Indravarman, Lord King. I betray him and him only."

"Tell me why. Because my spies say that he's not someone who should be betrayed lightly."

"Your spies speak the truth."

"Then why would you cross him?"

A nearby fire crackled. Cicadas chirped. Asal thought about his response, wanting to honor Voisanne. "I met a lady, Lord King. And this lady needed to be freed. She was in danger."

"You betrayed your king for love?"

"For a lady, Lord King."

"And you commanded men?"

"Many."

"These men you left behind—you deserted them?"

Asal stiffened at the king's choice of words. "I led my men to many victories. I cared for them. But, yes, I left them. Indravarman forced me to choose between duty and . . . and this lady. I chose her. And if any man thinks me a coward for making that choice, he does so at his own risk."

"I would think that at my own risk?"

"Yes, Lord King. I'm afraid so."

Though the Khmers around him muttered and reached for the hilts of their swords, a smile spread across Jayavar's face. "Your honesty impresses me. Tell me, what will Indravarman do?"

Asal had suspected that he would be asked such a question and he had his answer ready. "He's cautious, Lord King. He won't commit his men to battle unless he's sure of victory. And so he'll wait for reinforcements."

"When will they arrive? And how many?"

"Three thousand men will land in five days. They'll come across the Great Lake, arriving at our base on its shore."

"And how many warriors will he then have?"

"Nearly seventeen thousand, Lord King."

Jayavar offered no response. Cicadas' cries and the swooshing of bat wings dominated the night.

Asal knew that to ensure his future with Voisanne he needed to help the Khmer king. A gift must be offered and delivered. He bowed once again. "Indravarman is strong, Lord King. Do not underestimate him. He's strong and his men are well trained. But he has killed his rivals, and if he were to fall, the Cham army would be leaderless. His anointed successor is feeble and back in our homeland."

"So if he fell, your army—at least your army here—would be a snake with no head?"

"Kill Indravarman, Lord King, and his men will have no heart. The day will be yours."

Jayavar nodded, then glanced at Voisanne. He appeared to study her before whispering into her ear. She bowed, nodding repeatedly. Asal had a sudden urge to reach out to her, but he forced himself to remain still.

"I would like to share an idea with you," Jayavar said, "and to hear you assess it. But if I do so, you shall remain bound and guarded until the fight is over. Is this agreeable?"

"I offer my services, Lord King, because if Indravarman wins, I lose."

"Please call me 'my lord.' Formality isn't needed so deep in the jungle."

"Yes . . . my lord."

"Soon I shall attack his base on the Great Lake, destroy his force there, and then, with my men dressed as Chams, will sail to meet the approaching ships. I have been warned of these reinforcements by my spies, who echo your words. The three thousand warriors the ships carry will think we are their comrades, and we shall surprise them, rout them, and return to shore. When we finally march to Angkor, Indravarman's force will have been greatly weakened. We will approach Angkor, seize the elephants kept near the city, and crush the remaining Chams."

Asal closed his eyes, imagining the confrontations. "You'll fight three small battles instead of one."

"Yes."

"And by doing so, you'll overcome the advantage of his numbers."

"If all goes according to plan."

Opening his eyes, Asal considered the risks. "You'll be most vulnerable, my lord, in the boats."

"Why do you say so?"

"Because if something goes wrong, your entire force will be trapped and annihilated."

"And if you were my man, Asal, what would you have me do?"

Asal recognized the fierceness of Jayavar's stare. He acknowledged it, nodding. "I'd use fire arrows, my lord," he answered, a part of him still reluctant to participate in the death of his countrymen. "Your enemy's boats will be filled with warriors, but also with supplies—horses and hay and weapons. Light the boats on fire and panic will ensue."

Jayavar smiled again. "I had this same thought, Asal. I'm glad that it also came to you. Know that if we win, and if your words prove to be truthful, you shall be freed. You may return north to your people, or stay with ours."

"Thank you, my lord."

"And know that I don't think you a coward for what you have done. I've also been blessed to know the embrace of love, and know that its power is unrivaled." Jayavar stood up, then stepped outside the circle.

The fire crackled. A Khmer warrior approached Asal. But

Voisanne asked if she could speak to him alone, just for a moment. After a pause, the man nodded, and as he stepped away, she came forward, embracing Asal. Her body pressed against his, she whispered that everything would be fine, promising that she would care for him, as he had for her, saying that they would always be together.

Though Asal knew that in war promises could fall as readily as men, he kissed her forehead, letting her fill him with dreams, daring to believe that they would come true.

Long after the Khmers had left the courtyard at the Citadel of Women, and as dawn was about to reveal its colors, a small man untied himself from beneath the raised walkway that led to the temple's main tower. The spy had been hiding, strapped under the platform, throughout the entire night. He had positioned himself in such a way for several days, hoping that a group of Khmer officers would elect to discuss strategy in the nearby courtyard. Last night the spy's efforts had been rewarded.

He shook his hands, which tingled and ached from inaction. Grimacing, he finished untying himself and slowly dropped to the ground, still under the platform. His knees buckled and he collapsed, lying in weeds between two rows of stone columns that supported the walkway.

Gradually sensation flowed back into his limbs. He clenched his fists, wiggled his toes, and flexed his thighs. The sky seemed to be lightening, and he wanted to head south as soon as possible. A horse and supplies would be waiting for him not far from the temple.

Though the spy hadn't heard everything that had been said between the king and the traitor, he had comprehended enough to know where the Khmers would attack and where they would be vulnerable.

The spy slowly stood up, moving like a shadow. A few fires encircled the temple, and distant conversations drifted toward him. Avoiding the flames and the voices, he shuffled under the walkway, heading toward the entrance to the complex.

Over the past several years, the spy had uncovered secrets that Khmers would have died to protect. Yet this discovery could eclipse all others.

Remembering what Po Rame had taught him, the spy resisted the urge to flee into the darkness, continuing to move slowly, blending in with the landscape.

Only when the temple was far behind him did he start to run, eager to share his secret, to rejoice in the spoils of victory.

Part Three

Part Three

Twenty-one

Horizons

North of the Great Lake, Mid–Dry Season, 1178

ollowing markers left by trusted scouts, the Khmer army moved like a giant centipede through the jungle, twisting around trees, splashing across streams, navigating the contours of the land. At the front of the force marched men who held long swords and slashed at the undergrowth, widening the passageway. The work was exhausting, and the men had to be replaced often, rotating to the rear of their brethren. Behind these trailblazers were some of Jayavar's best warriors, who rode horses and carried shields and spears. If the Chams attacked, these mounted men were to charge their foe, allowing the Khmers time to organize defensive positions.

Farther down the line marched twenty-five hundred foot soldiers, simultaneously watching the jungle and avoiding the steaming piles of dung left by the horses. The middle of the Khmer column was dominated by scores of wooden carts pulled by oxen. The carts were piled high with provisions and each was guarded by a pair of archers. More than fourteen hundred women and children had elected to travel with the force and walked behind the supply carts. Though normally Jayavar would have insisted that the women and children stay behind, he had expressed a simple concern to his men: If he took all the warriors to battle, who would remain to protect their loved ones?

The very old and very young had been left behind, along with a token force of three dozen spearmen who would keep bandits at bay. Everyone else had marched to the southwest, following a course that would take the army to the Great Lake in a semicircular manner, so as to avoid discovery.

Behind the women and children came another substantial group of Khmer warriors, followed by seventeen hundred Siamese. The foreigners wore their brightly colored tunics and hummed songs as they marched. Secretly worried about treachery, Jayavar had placed two thousand of his best fighters behind the Siamese. At the rear of the column rode five scores of Khmers mounted on horses.

In all, Jayavar commanded about seventy-two hundred men. A sizable force to be certain, but far less than what Indravarman could bring into battle. Jayavar's plan depended on catching the Chams by surprise both at the lakeside and on the water. When the Chams finally realized what was happening, Jayavar hoped to be headed back toward Angkor. He would then throw all his men into an assault meant to recapture his war elephants. Once he had the elephants, he hoped that Khmer citizens would join the fight. With luck, Indravarman would be trapped between the Khmer army and its citizens, a position that would all but ensure his destruction.

While Jayavar and Ajadevi rode gray stallions near the front of the column, Asal and Voisanne walked among the women. His hands were still tied in front of him, and an experienced Khmer spearman had been assigned to watch his every move. Asal had asked Voisanne to study the jungle, and she did, following his gaze with her own, becoming increasingly nervous as they drew closer to their enemy.

Soriya also walked with the women. Behind her, separated by a hundred Khmer warriors, strode Boran, Vibol, and Prak. Since most of the men marched beside a companion, Vibol and Prak spoke quietly, while slightly ahead of them Boran asked an older warrior about the coming battle. Prak was interested in what the army looked like, and Vibol described for him the scene of so many warriors and weapons.

"It's quite a sight," he added, using the shaft of his spear as a walking stick. "The sunlight falls through the trees, and the spear points and sword hilts glitter like thousands of stars."

"What else?"

"The Siamese wear so many different colors. I can't help but watch them."

"As much as you did the pretty girls in Angkor?"

Vibol smiled. "Maybe not that much. But still, they're interesting to look at." Noticing that a web of exposed tree roots lay ahead, Vibol reached for Prak's elbow. "But what I like most are the battle standards."

"Tell me about them."

"They're tied to the ends of spears. The banners are red silk, but in the middle is a white silhouette of Angkor Wat."

"Do the men carry them with pride?"

"Yes," Vibol answered, and then thought about how his brother must feel. "Do you want to carry one? I'm certain I could find you one, and if anyone should carry one, it should be you. The fire and poisoned fish were your ideas."

Prak nodded. "Yes, though King Jayavar may have other battle plans in mind."

"Why would he waste time doing that? Your plan is perfect."

The men in front of them slowed; a cart had broken down.

The split wheel was removed. Then the sound of a hammer thudding into thick wood echoed off the trees. Men grumbled about the delay, but more quickly than anyone expected, the column began to move forward again.

As the warriors spread out, Vibol glimpsed a jagged scar on one man's back. The scar was as long as Vibol's hand, and he wondered if the man had been wounded in battle. Thinking about how easily a blade could cut through flesh, Vibol looked up at his spear tip. He'd practiced thrusting it into bundles of thatch and shook his head at the memory, knowing that it would be far different to pierce an enemy's flesh. The bundles of thatch merely toppled. A man would thrash and bleed and scream.

As he had many times before, Vibol wondered what it would feel like to have steel slice into his flesh. Would the pain make him weep? Would he shame himself? What would happen if his father was maimed? Did his father fear dying or failing his king and countrymen?

The march continued. The odor of the column wafted backward—an unpleasant combination of dung, urine, and sweat, with only a trace of the flowers that the Siamese wore.

The army was as loud as it was pungent. Horses neighed, warriors cursed, carts creaked, and weapons clinked. People were under orders to keep their voices low, but the collected whispers of nearly nine thousand tongues ensured a constant buzz.

As Vibol walked in silence, he continued to think about the coming battle. "If you . . . if you could see, would you fight?" he asked his brother.

Prak took a few steps before answering. "It's all right to be afraid, Vibol. We're all afraid."

Ahead, a man coughed, then hacked.

"Remember," Vibol said, "when we talked about finding a pair of pretty sisters in Angkor and marrying them?"

"How can I forget? And it was you who talked about it mostly. You're the reason we took so many trips to Angkor, why we bathed until our skin was as wrinkled as dates."

"You enjoyed it too. I looked, but you listened. You listened to their laughter, and I told you when they glanced in our direction."

Prak smiled. "They usually didn't."

"True, but sometimes they did."

"When they were bored, or maybe when they pitied us."

Vibol shifted his grip on his spear, lifting it upward. "I want to live," he said. "I want to laugh with you again, to watch the pretty girls with you and wonder if they'll come our way."

"They will, Vibol. I know they will."

Vibol smiled at the thought. "I hope so. But they must be sisters. Because if they're sisters, we can always be together."

At the periphery of an immense field within the city of Angkor, Po Rame watched Indravarman inspect his troops, who stood in tight formations, their shields glistening in the midafternoon sun. The men were lined up in long columns with their officers at the front. Indravarman was dressed for battle, a shield strapped to his left forearm, his left hand gripping a stout bar inside the shield. Short-sleeved, quilted armor covered his torso. Though he usually carried a sword, on this day Indravarman wielded a huge war axe that was sometimes favored by Chams. The axe was a heavy, unwieldy weapon compared to a sword or spear, but when used by a man of great strength it could be devastating, shattering shields and maiming flesh.

Po Rame was a hundred paces from Indravarman, but his eyesight was excellent and he saw how carefully the king inspected the men he passed. Occasionally Indravarman would ask an officer something, but for the most part he walked in silence. Sometimes he pressed his shield against a man's chest and thrust forward, expecting the warrior to hold his ground. When the man stood firm, Indravarman nodded. When he stepped backward, the king struck him with the edge of his shield or the thick shaft of his axe.

The mood in the field was grim. The warriors in their lotus-flower headdresses seemed eager for battle and looked as if they had prepared for it. Heavy shields were held high and didn't quiver. Muscled arms and legs remained firm when Indravarman tested them. Though the king was larger than almost every man in the entire field, his warriors stood tall. Po Rame wondered if a fiercer fighting force existed anywhere. When they possessed their war elephants, the Khmers were also deadly, but almost all of the beasts were under Cham control in Angkor.

Po Rame was used to waiting for Indravarman, and he remained patient even as the king went from row to row and scattered clouds drifted across the sky. The assassin stood in the shade of a tree, pleased that he wasn't baking in the sun like a commoner. Finally Indravarman shouted to the entire contingent of men, who roared a reply and thumped their spear shafts against their shields. The thunderous, rhythmic beat was comforting to Po Rame as he'd heard it before great victories. To an opposing army, the sound would inspire dread.

The clamor continued as Indravarman thrust his fist into the air, climbed on his horse, and headed in Po Rame's direction. Po Rame untied his own mount from the nearby tree, straddled it, and then rode out to meet the king. Indravarman uttered not a word but motioned for Po Rame to follow him.

The two men galloped across the field, soon heading down a wide road. Chams and Khmers scattered to let them pass, bowing low when they were no longer in danger of being trampled.

Dust rose from the hooves of Indravarman's mount, and Po Rame squinted, wondering why the king seemed to be in such a hurry.

Wheeling to his right, Indravarman guided his mount onto a wide trail that led into the jungle. Many Khmer homes built of bamboo and thatch dotted the area, all supported by stilts. Very few kings, Po Rame realized, would dare to ride without an escort into the land of their enemy, but Indravarman seemed not to give his vulnerability a second thought.

They followed the trail as it climbed toward the top of a ridge. Once at the summit, Po Rame looked to the east and saw that one of the Khmers' vast canals ran parallel to the rise of earth. Indravarman slowed his mount, leapt off, and tied it to a shrub. He had secured his battle-axe and shield to the stallion and now removed both weapons. Po Rame did the same, glad that he didn't sweat nearly as much as the king, who shone with perspiration.

Indravarman eyed the canal, which was so wide that the strongest archer would not be able to shoot an arrow across it. "Why can we not build structures such as this?" Indravarman asked, his open hand gesturing toward the length of the waterway. "The Khmers bring water from the Great Lake to feed their crops, to clean their people. They subjugate nature to their needs while creating monuments for the Gods. We fish and make war and try to appease the same Gods, but our efforts are feeble compared to those of our enemies."

"Yet we defeated the dung eaters, Lord King," Po Rame offered. "What was theirs is now ours."

"Is knowledge a possession, Po Rame? Because they have done what we have not. And I don't think that by conquering them we gain control of their wisdom."

"I think—"

"When Jayavar is dead and his bones are scattered, I shall have a tower built on this spot to commemorate our conquest. This tower shall have the grace, strength, and permanence of their temples. Yet Chams will make it. And in a thousand years, our people will come to this place and remember the sweetness of victory."

Po Rame bowed slightly, thinking about the coming battle, hoping that Asal would fight for the Khmers. If he did, he could be found. And Po Rame would cripple him in the exact manner that his king had ordered.

The prospect of downing his old adversary prompted Po Rame to cluck his tongue in anticipation. Asal would beg for a quick death, a warrior's death, but he'd receive no mercy. On the contrary, Indravarman would demand that Asal's suffering be increased and prolonged.

"Tell me of your man's report," Indravarman said, turning to Po Rame.

"The Khmers march to attack our base at the Great Lake. The rats intend to overwhelm our men and then capture the boats that we have stationed there. The traitor told them about the reinforcements who have sailed from our homeland. The Khmers plan to take the boats that they have captured from us, put on the armor of our dead men, sail out under a false banner, and pretending to be Chams, they will surprise our new arrivals." Po Rame paused, wishing that his spy had overheard the entire conversation instead of select snippets. Unforgivable, he thought, to place yourself too far away to hear everything.

"And that's it?" Indravarman asked, his face tightening. "He knows nothing more? How will Jayavar destroy our forces out on the lake, even with the element of surprise? His men will be weakened from their battle on the shore."

"I don't know, Lord King. The traitor suggested something,

and the false king seemed interested, but my man couldn't hear
what was said."

"A fool."

"Yes, Lord King. I should have——"

"Still, his information is useful. If Jayavar puts all of his men
into our boats and sails into deep waters, he'll be vulnerable."
Indravarman smiled, unconsciously lifting his war axe. "We'll
simply let him sail to us. But we'll have warned our approaching
countrymen and will be waiting with our entire fleet. And we
shall surround and annihilate him."

"And our force on the shore?"

Indravarman chopped the air with his axe. "Will be sacrificed. We won't warn them, won't bolster their ranks. If Jayavar
senses that we know of his plan, he'll change tactics. And I need
him in those boats, Po Rame. In those boats he will be weakest.
Men can run from a battle on land. They can hide and regroup.
But on that endless expanse of water, there will be no place to
hide. Once and for all, I shall destroy every Khmer who dares to
stand against me."

Nodding, Po Rame envisioned how the battle would unfold.
Indravarman would have his best men waiting for Jayavar. Every
resource at the king's disposal would be thrown into the fray.
Victory would be theirs, and the lake would turn red with Khmer
blood. Po Rame's only concern was that the fight would be over
too quickly. Destruction, he thought, should be savored, not hurried.

"The Khmer lover," he said, "marches with his new countrymen."

"How do you know this?"

"My man heard——"

"How does this man of yours hear one thing and not another?
How can he please me one moment and infuriate me the next?"

"I'm sorry, King of Kings, for his failings. He has already been punished. But he promised me that the traitor will march."

Indravarman cursed, chopping the air once again with his axe. It was a weapon that most men would struggle to lift, but he treated it as if it were made of thatch. "Asal is a threat," he said.

"Do you still want my blade in the traitor's back?"

"Of course."

"And if my wound downs him, King of Kings, may I take his life after you're finished with him?"

Indravarman's jaw clenched, but he made no immediate reply. "Cripple him, Po Rame, and find his woman for me. Do those things, and you can take his life."

Po Rame bowed low. "Consider them—"

"Now leave me."

The assassin nodded, then climbed back on his horse. As he rode back to Angkor, he thought about what might go through Asal's mind as he died. As broken as he would be, relief might flow within him when the end came. But Po Rame wanted him to fear the end, to weep in terror and sorrow as darkness closed in on him.

His woman is the key, Po Rame thought. Let him know of her fate and he'll die a thousand deaths. And each time he dies, I'll be there to steal another part of his soul. I'll plunder his strength, his boldness, and even his love. For a God must understand love. I don't understand it, but love makes men behave like fools, makes them risk everything for a woman. So love must be powerful. And whatever is powerful must be mine.

The Khmer army marched all day without rest, finally stopping at a wide and lazy river that fed into the Great Lake. After an elaborate perimeter of lookouts had been established, the majority of warriors, women, and children waded into the river, washing sweat and grime from their weary bodies. Farther downstream, horses were led into the water, where they drank and cooled off.

Near the contingent of Siamese, Voisanne, Chaya, and Asal stood waist deep in a bend of the slow-moving river. Asal's guard watched from the shoreline. Though his wrists were still bound, Asal had otherwise been treated well during the march and didn't seem to mind how his skin was chafing against the ropes. Voisanne had tended to his injured fingers on several occasions after asking an older woman how to treat them.

Voisanne felt conflicted as she washed herself. She was thrilled to have escaped Angkor with the two people she cared about most in the world, yet was saddened by the death of Thida and worried about the future. If the Khmers lost the coming battle, anything could happen to them. Voisanne had been tempted to stay behind with Asal and Chaya, back at the Khmer encampment, but King Jayavar had asked Asal to march with them, thinking that his knowledge of Cham tactics might prove useful.

For most of her life, Voisanne had looked to her father for advice, but now that he was gone, she needed to move forward on her own. Of course, she sought out Asal's opinions, but she didn't want to besiege him with questions and needs, so she often turned inward, relying on her own past experiences. Foremost on her mind was Chaya. Was it right to bring her little sister along with the army, or should she have stayed behind? It was well known that poison was available if the Chams were victorious, but Voisanne couldn't imagine encouraging her little sister to end her own life. If the Chams won, she thought, she'd cut Asal's bonds, and the three of them would try to escape into the jungle. Yet they would be hunted and likely captured, and the notion of what Chaya might endure made Voisanne beseech the Gods for mercy. She prayed so much that day that prayer had become almost involuntary, as natural as breathing.

Chaya laughed at something Asal said, and Voisanne shifted her gaze to him. She remembered how they had first made love near the stream, how he'd moved with boundless urgency and desire. It was as if he had wanted her for a hundred lifetimes and yet had been chained down, unable to touch her, to show her how he felt. When finally given the freedom to act, he'd been overwhelmed. He had consumed her, and for a time she'd been carried to such a place that the world below faded away into nothingness.

As Voisanne watched him laugh with Chaya, her desire to touch him again grew. She wanted to be alone with him, for her passion to become his. Yet now it was she who felt chained down, because privacy was impossible, and soon they might all be dead. Her breathing quickened as she wondered how she could ensure their safety. When the fighting started, she would have to free him and find him a weapon. If King Jayavar punished her, so be it, because she had seen Asal fight and knew that they would be infinitely better protected if he was armed.

I must find a knife, she thought. A small knife with which to cut him free.

Chaya led Asal to shore, then picked up a smooth stone and tried to skip it. Her stone plunged into the water and Asal laughed, causing Chaya to curse and Voisanne to smile. Chaya tried again but fared no better.

"Let me show you," he said, leaning down to pick up a stone. Since his hands were still bound in front of him, his throw was awkward, but his stone still skipped three times across the flat water.

Chaya frowned. "But that's just how I did it."

"You have to flick your wrist."

"I know how to do it. My stones aren't as good as yours. Why don't you find me a good stone instead of telling me about flicking wrists?"

"Am I to be your servant?"

"Yes, so move quickly, you lumbering elephant," she teased, "or I shall give you a whipping you'll never forget."

Voisanne smiled again, surprised at how quickly Asal and Chaya seemed to have forged a bond. He was acting like an elder brother to her, and clearly she wanted such an influence, because as he searched for a stone, she chided him about moving too slowly. He increased the speed of his search, handing her stones that she tossed away with exaggerated disdain.

Smiling, Voisanne watched their antics, then found a flat, round stone as long as her thumb. She whistled, saw Asal and Chaya turn to her, and then lowered her body and flicked her wrist as Asal had done. Her stone skipped six or seven times before settling into the water.

"That's not fair!" Chaya said, laughing. "You cheated."

"I did no such thing."

"You two have been working on this. That's what you did all those days back in Angkor before you found me. You studied skipping! And now you conspire to make me feel like a fool."

"But that needs no conspiracy," Voisanne replied, happy to see her sister laugh. "It's easy enough to do alone."

Chaya tried to suppress a giggle, failed, and then rushed straight at Voisanne, grabbing her hands. The sisters struggled for a moment before Voisanne slipped on a rock and tumbled into the river with a splash. Chaya clapped triumphantly. Asal told her how Voisanne had pushed him into the moat when they were on the boat together, and how he was pleased to be avenged.

Voisanne sat in the water and watched them laugh, aware that her little sister and a Cham warrior now made up her entire family. "I love you both," she said, still watching them. "For a long time, I felt as if the Gods had abandoned me, that they didn't care about me. But I was wrong. They do care. So pray to them, both of you. Pray that this fight goes our way."

€arly that evening, after the Khmer army had marched farther to the southwest, Jayavar and Ajadevi sat atop a ridge that provided mostly unobstructed views in all directions. The army was camped along the ridge with sentries posted at every fifty paces. Because of their proximity to Angkor, Jayavar had forbidden any fires. This order created taxing conditions within the camp, for no one could cook and, worse, there was no smoke to keep the mosquitoes away.

As Ajadevi chewed a piece of dried fish, she rubbed oil from a neem tree on Jayavar's skin. The oil repelled the flying pests, though its effects didn't last long. On top of the ridge, curses and claps rang out as people tried to deal with the insects.

Ajadevi and Jayavar possessed a silk mosquito net but had opted not to use it since so many of their countrymen suffered. Even her renowned patience was tested by the constant buzzing and biting. Trying to relax, to focus on what lay to the south, she breathed deeply.

"What do you see?" Jayavar asked, then bit into a strip of dried fish.

She shrugged. "A million little devils. They're all I can sense."

"They know good blood when they find it. And surely yours must be as sweet as any."

"My blood is old. Old and tainted."

"Nonsense."

She swatted at a persistent mosquito and shifted on the boulder they shared. Frustrated that she couldn't interpret the signs around her, she shook her head, wishing that fires could be lit.

"In a few days it shall all be over," Jayavar said, stacking three stones. "For worse or better, it shall end."

She thought about the permanence and impermanence of life, wondering how they could coexist. "What do you see, Jayavar? You always ask me, but on this night I see nothing."

"I believe victory is possible . . . but I fear betrayal."

"Who would betray us?"

"Many. And if even just one does, we are lost. Because the only way we shall win is through surprise. Indravarman has too many men. If we fail to surprise him, we'll be annihilated."

"Don't let our people see your fear."

"I won't."

"You must speak to them before battle. Tell them what we fight for."

"What do we fight for?"

"The right to live as we want."

He nodded, adding a fourth stone to his pile. "War should be fought for nothing less."

The sun had dropped below the horizon, and waves of amber spread slowly across the sky.

"It looks like an artist spilled orange paint on a blue background," she said.

He agreed but then turned from the sky to her. "In two days, when we strike, I shall have to lead the charge. And the Chams will seek to destroy me."

Nodding, she made no reply.

"If victory is theirs," he asked, "will you take the poison?"

"Yes."

He reached for her hand, his fingers rubbing against her skin. "If we should die, how shall we find each other amid so much space, so much blackness?"

She kissed the back of his hand. She wasn't certain how to

answer and thought about how she would look for him if the poison claimed her. "Remember," she said, "that night so long since past, when you sent up a lantern into the sky?"

"I do."

"You took silk and wrapped it around a rectangular box that you'd made from the thinnest of bamboo strips. The silk was yellow, the box as long as my arm. Positioned near its bottom was a candle."

"A three-wicked candle."

"Yes. And we stood atop Angkor Wat and beheld its beauty, the night full upon us. For the first time you told me that you loved me and that you wanted to honor me by adding my star to the sky."

"And I did."

She smiled as the memory unfurled. "You lit the candle and held your lantern aloft, waiting for the air within it to warm. When it finally did, we released the lantern. It drifted sideways for a moment and we feared it was lost, but then it seemed to surge upward, glowing and strong. It sailed high and far, at one point mingling with the stars."

"It became a star. It's still there, if you look closely enough."

Her smile returned. She leaned over to kiss him on the lips. "If you should fall in battle, hold our star within yourself as you pass from world to world. I shall do the same, and if we both keep our star, our light, within us, surely we shall be brought together again in the next life."

Jayavar nodded, putting his arm around her, drawing her close. "I was right, so long ago, to think of you as that star. Because you've brought such a brightness into my life. You're the one person in the world who sees me as I am."

A mosquito landed on his forearm and she crushed it before it could trouble him. "If I hear you're dead, I shall take the poison. I shall hold our star within me and come looking for you."

"Just be certain, Ajadevi. There are many untruths in war, and rumors are born as quickly as the pests around us."

"If we win," she replied, "we should light another lantern. We should add one more star to the sky."

"Yes."

"Win so that you can give us a second star."

Sighing, he kissed her shoulder, his lips lingering on her skin. "Rest here with me, my love. Rest with me and see what the night will bring."

Twenty-two

Fight on the Shore

wo days later, shortly before dawn, Jayavar stood in the center of a circle of twenty-four officers who were illuminated by a small fire. One of the men was Phirun, to whom Jayavar had revealed himself on the dusty road outside of Angkor. True to his word, Phirun had sent groups of fighters north, and later made the trip himself, commanding a large contingent of able men and women.

Each of the twenty-four officers would soon lead three hundred warriors into battle. Each had been assigned specific goals for the coming fight. Some were told to follow Jayavar's lead and drive straight into the Cham camp. Others were commanded to flank the melee and capture the Cham boats before the enemy had a chance to flee.

Jayavar had spent the previous night thinking about how the battle might unfold, mulling over every possibility. In the end, he decided to use a version of the boy's plan to employ fire. Jayavar was afraid that massive flames might simply cause the Chams to rush to their boats. Certainly some of the enemy would be overrun and downed, but others might escape and warn their approaching countrymen. The success of Jayavar's overall strategy was to surprise the new arrivals, and to do that he needed to ensure that no Cham escaped the morning's attack.

Ultimately, Jayavar opted to start a small, diversionary fire to the west. The smoke would distract the Cham sentries, and perhaps a contingent of the enemy would be sent to inspect the cause. In the meantime, Jayavar would lead his army straight at the Cham base, rushing forward to surprise many of his foes before they had time to arm themselves and form fighting groups. As the Chams had used terror against his people, he would use it against them, scattering their warriors, killing them without mercy.

Jayavar had decided to follow the boy's plans exactly when it came to the poisoned fish, and two days earlier he had sent scouts ahead to tell Khmer fishermen to let their catch spoil before they sold it the following day. The king had no idea how many Chams would be sickened, but he was certain that at least some would not be at their fighting peak. This fact alone might shift the outcome of the battle in his favor.

Since Indravarman commanded far more men, Jayavar was convinced that waging three smaller attacks instead of one large one was the only way that he might drive the Chams from their land. In the first two battles—the fight on the lakeshore and the waterborne attack on the approaching Cham fleet—his force would be larger than that of the enemy, and if his strategies were superior, he might win the day.

As he stood among his men and repeated his earlier instructions, Jayavar wondered which of them would live to see the sunset. They were all strong, brave, and loyal. They had been beaten by the Chams, sent fleeing into the jungle, and craved revenge. Jayavar feared that they might be too aggressive and counseled them to fight with their minds as well as their hearts.

"I cannot afford to lose any of you," he added. "So attack with passion, not recklessness. Think of those you've lost, but don't seek to join them. Instead, honor them with victory."

Several officers expressed their agreement. Jayavar gazed from man to man, each of whom was heavily armed. Of the twenty-four officers, six Siamese were present, including a scarred and toothless man who had planned the successful Siamese ambush against Indravarman's column of warriors. Considering the needs of the foreigners, Jayavar kept his eyes on them. "You were drawn here by gold, and gold you shall have. But know also that we have a common enemy. If the Chams destroy my people, they'll come for yours. So fight with us today not just for gold, but also for your future."

The Siamese beat their shields against their chests. As usual, their movements were synchronized, and Jayavar was glad not to be fighting such men. Again his gaze drifted from face to face. "On the trail," he said, "I asked my wife why we should fight this war. She replied that we should fight to 'live as we want.' And she was right—no desire has ever been more noble. So as you prepare for battle, tell your men of this need, of what was once a certainty but now is a longing. For I, like you, covet freedom. And today I shall have it, either through victory or in death."

Jayavar nodded, hoping to inspire his men, his hand tightening on his sword hilt. He needed to fill them with hope and courage because they would soon be called upon to throw themselves against hardened fighters.

"My days of hiding are over," he added, looking at his men, his voice growing louder. "I was forced to hide, as were you, but thoughts of vengeance have simmered within me since that first night in the jungle. The Chams killed my children. They stole that which was most precious to me. And now, as they defile our temples and our homes, as they mock our history, they think us cowards. They cast their dung upon us because they believe that we're incapable of rising up against them. But they are wrong, my friends. Because on this day we, so small in number, shall redden the ground, the water, the very air we breathe with their blood. And when my sword sings, it will do so through the voices of my children. Your swords will sing as well, and together we shall show the Chams that anyone who threatens our land does so at a terrible risk. We do not seek war. We do not welcome it. But when it comes to us, we shall battle as if the existence of our very souls is at stake!"

Both Khmers and Siamese shouted in agreement, beating their shields and weapons together.

"Good!" Jayavar yelled, the prospect of victory filling him with strength. "Today we shall fight under a new banner. A banner not for a king, but for a people. Draw resolve from it! Carry it forward! And fight to live as you would want, not as the Chams would make you." He unsheathed his sword and thrust it into the air. "As you would want!"

The officers cheered, hoisting their weapons.

Jayavar stepped forward to embrace each man, calling him by name and wishing him victory. He would die for his people and they would die for him. And though he wanted to live, if he had to choose between victory and death or defeat and life, he would choose the former. More important than his fate, or even Ajadevi's, was returning freedom to his people.

At all costs, Jayavar had to win.

Several hours later, after the diversionary fire had been lit to the west, Boran stood next to Vibol and listened to his commander give additional orders. Though what the officer said was important, Boran kept glancing at his son, whose chest rose and fell with increasing vigor. Sweat beaded on Vibol's forehead. His fingers were tight around the shaft of his spear, which trembled slightly, like a sapling in a breeze. Boran had a sudden urge to take Vibol's hand and pull him away from the approaching madness, but he knew that his son would never forgive him. So Boran prayed to the Gods to shelter his family. He beseeched them for protection.

The commander unsheathed his sword. The Cham encampment was near, and all along the jungle, large groups of Khmers and Siamese waited to attack. Men shifted uneasily, ensured that their shields were held fast, and whispered to one another as brothers might—swearing their loyalty and protection. With a possible end so near, emotions were unchecked. Hardened warriors spoke of love and devotion. Officers looked at their men with affection and grace.

A bird's call sounded to Boran's left. He recognized it to be false, and the men around him readied themselves. The call came again and his commander urged them to run. Boran turned to Vibol and kissed his forehead. "I love you."

Vibol nodded, started to reply, but suddenly the men behind him were pushing forward.

Boran followed the leaders ahead of his son, promising himself to always remain between Vibol and the enemy. The jungle rushed past. He leapt over a fallen log, ducked under a branch, careened past a waist-high anthill, and kept running, aware of Vibol's grunts behind him. Men stumbled and fell but rose again, rushing through the undergrowth like a river bursting through a dam. Though shields beat against branches and bodies, the footfalls of the warriors were remarkably quiet.

A Cham shouted. The men around Boran quickened their pace. The jungle thinned, sunlight streaming down. Abruptly the Cham base revealed itself. Boran saw men struggling ahead. The aim of his group was to capture and secure the enemy boats, and his commander warded off a blow but did not engage his attacker, instead circling toward the docked vessels. The clash of sword against shield rang out, as did shouts, screams, and the trumpeting of several war elephants that were still tied to trees.

Boran turned to make sure Vibol was right behind him and then stumbled. A Cham axe whipped toward him, and he barely had time to raise his shield and duck. The weapon hit his shield at an angle, sliding harmlessly away. Even as he regained his balance, Boran thrust his spear forward. Its tip plunged into the Cham's thigh and the man screamed, dropping his axe.

The enemy seemed to be everywhere, and Boran shouted at Vibol to run toward the boats. Several arrows hissed from Cham archers in front of him, thudding into a large Khmer who was covered in the blood of his foes. Knowing that the archers were a mortal threat to his son, Boran charged ahead, holding his shield in front of his torso, feeling an arrow strike the thick timber. Two archers scattered as he approached—dropping their bows and running for the water. Though Boran had always considered himself to be strong, he had never felt such strength as he did now. The thought of Vibol's possible death filled him with fury, and he screamed at the remaining Chams in front of him, drawing their attention away from his son. A naked Cham picked up a comrade's fallen sword and barred Boran's path. The man was well muscled, yet Boran felt no fear, only an overwhelming need to protect his child. He blocked the Cham's thrust with his shield, felt the other's weapon become lodged in the wood, and used the shaft of his spear to beat the man down.

The boats weren't far away, and Boran once again shouted at Vibol to hurry. Fifty paces ahead, a dock teemed with struggling Chams and Khmers. Boran joined the fray, using his shield to knock Chams from the dock and into the water. The hilt of a sword struck him hard in the right shoulder and his arm went numb. He thought he would be overrun, but instead the Khmers around him rallied, forcing the Chams away. Suddenly the dock was theirs.

Boran dragged Vibol to the nearest boat, jumped over its gunwale, and landed awkwardly. Pain shot up his leg, but he turned, protecting Vibol with his shield as a Cham spear flew in their direction. A band of experienced Khmer fighters killed the few Chams on board. Boran's chest heaved and he found it hard to breathe, his right arm still nearly useless. Yet he used the edge of his shield to pull Vibol closer to him. To his surprise, he realized that the tip of Vibol's spear was slick with blood.

Risking a glance toward the shore, he saw that the banners of Angkor Wat were moving forward and that the enemy was being cut down. The Chams had been surprised, and though many fought with courage and determination, they were surrounded and overwhelmed. Some fled for the lake or jungle but were intercepted and struck from behind. Others dropped their weapons and pleaded for mercy but were quickly dispatched. The wounded and the ill wept and wailed but were unheeded. They died in vast numbers.

Suddenly Vibol leaned over the side of the boat and retched. Boran put his good arm around his son, holding him tight, inspecting him for injuries. Seeing none, he silently offered his gratitude to the Gods. He continued to pray as Vibol heaved and sagged, dropping his spear.

Khmers and Siamese began to shout in triumph. Thousands of voices blended into a single torrent of howling sound. This cry, Boran thought, might have been heard by the Gods, because it seemed to echo off the jungle, the water, and even his very flesh. Men around him raised their weapons, and the world seemed to split asunder from the strength of their voices.

Boran kissed the back of Vibol's damp head, still holding him. He looked to the north, wondering where Soriya and Prak were. The vanguard of the army was supposed to arrive after the fighting had quieted, but he didn't see a single woman or child.

"Where are they?" he whispered.

Near the shoreline, the few remaining wounded Chams were speared with appalling efficiency. Boran turned Vibol from the spectacle, directing his gaze toward the open water. Aware that fighting still lay ahead, Boran tried to focus on the undulating surface, tried to imagine what fish might be swimming within sight. Such questions had occupied his mind for all his life, yet now seemed pathetically insignificant.

One son was alive. But his other loved ones were beyond the reach of his senses, and this separation tore at him with as much wickedness as any blade. He didn't want to be here, on a Cham boat holding up one dazed child while the rest of his family wondered if they were alive or dead.

Khmer and Siamese officers started to organize the army, putting groups of men onto the Cham boats while assigning others to guard the perimeter of the camp. Several dozen Khmer *mahouts* scrambled atop captured war elephants and rode them into the jungle. Boran didn't know what would happen next but felt that his day was just beginning.

Vibol finally looked up, his eyes bloodshot, his face covered in dust and streaked with tears. Still trembling, he started to speak but then noticed the red welt on his father's shoulder. "Are you hurt?" he asked, his voice barely audible.

"A branch slapped me on our run."

Vibol's eyes filled with tears. "I wish it were over. I wish all the fighting were finished."

"As do I."

"How much more will there be?"

"Plenty," Boran replied, wanting to be truthful. "Angkor is still full of Chams. The Great Lake is full of them. All we've done is stir up a hornet's nest."

"Oh."

An officer on the shore gestured for the father and son to come to him. Vibol closed his eyes, then picked up his spear and started to step over the gunwale. Boran reached for his elbow. "Wait."

"What?"

"You came here . . . longing to be a man. But I want to tell you that killing a man won't make you one. What will make you a man is taking the more difficult path. And that's the path we've chosen. That path led us to this moment."

"I already . . . killed a man. And I don't feel any stronger."

"You're not. So don't kill to prove yourself. Kill to stay alive, if you must. But not to prove your worth."

"I won't."

"You proved yourself years ago to me on the water. Each and every day you proved yourself. How I enjoyed having you beside me. How I loved those days."

"So did I," Vibol replied, tears once again dropping to his cheeks.

Boran embraced his son, holding him tight. He then watched Vibol climb onto the dock. He followed in his footsteps, moving gingerly because of the pain in his ankle and shoulder. Now that the rush of battle had ended, he felt so very tired and old.

A half morning's row into the Great Lake, Indravarman and Po Rame stood near the end of a long Cham boat. The vessel was far different from the barges that had carried the Cham army into Angkor. This craft, with an upturned bow and a single mainsail, was thirty paces long and six paces wide. Its two sides were lined with oarsmen, while its interior bristled with thirty of Indravarman's best warriors. At the rear of the craft, the captain guided a steering pole that was connected to the rudder. Standing next to him, an older man chanted rhythmically, the oars moving to the sound of his voice.

Many of the men stood and sweated beneath the sun, but Indravarman was seated on a dais padded with silk cushions. Po Rame knelt next to him. Both men were shaded by an elaborate canopy supported by bamboo poles. The edges of the canopy rippled as the boat surged forward, powered by the wind and the oars. The bow of the vessel was carved into a rooster's head, complete with a thick beak and tufts of feathers.

In all, Indravarman's boat carried more than seventy men. About a hundred and fifty vessels of various sizes sailed with him, moving a force of eleven thousand warriors. He had left two thousand fighters back in Angkor to keep the Khmers in line, but the bulk of his army accompanied him. Another three thousand Chams were approaching his position from the south, having sailed an indirect route from their homeland.

Po Rame's spies had predicted that Jayavar would march with about seven thousand men, meaning that once Indravarman met his reinforcements, he would have a two-to-one advantage in numbers. The prospect of such a confrontation caused the Cham king's breathing to quicken. He gazed to the south, searching for his countrymen. Though the sky was free of clouds, a slight haze hung over the water, making it difficult to see for long distances. He knew that the approaching force was near, as swift scout boats had rushed ahead and brought word of the main group's progress.

Indravarman wasn't certain if Jayavar had already attacked the base at the lake, but he suspected that he had. It was wise of the Khmer to try to stage a series of smaller battles rather than one large one. If Po Rame's spy was correct, Jayavar would have assaulted and certainly defeated the Chams by the lake. He should be on the water by now, rowing hard to meet his enemy. Pretending to be Chams, Jayavar's men might surprise and overwhelm the approaching group of warriors. But if Indravarman warned his countrymen about the treachery, they could simply let Jayavar near them, then combine their forces to surround and annihilate him. The war would be over.

Turning to Po Rame, Indravarman unconsciously rubbed the iron under his skin. "When Jayavar realizes that he's trapped, he shall come straight for me," he said. "Slaying me is the only way he can win the day."

"Let the dung eater come, Lord King. Our men will swarm over him like flies on a corpse."

Indravarman grunted. "Both he and I know that if one of us were to fall, the other would win. If he manages to fight his way to me, he shall die on my sword. But if you wish, you may stalk him from the rear. Wound him for me and I shall reward you with his soul."

"Thank you, Lord King. A king's soul . . . even a false king's soul . . . would be a priceless gift."

"And what of my soul, Po Rame? Shall you take it someday?"

"Forgive—"

"If I fall, you'll be nothing. Remember that." Indravarman nodded to himself, thinking that after this battle he would kill Po Rame and feed him to the fish. Perhaps he would look into the assassin's eyes as he died and try to take the power that purportedly had already been stolen.

"You're my master, King of Kings. You'll see that today, when I cripple your enemies."

Indravarman twisted around, peering to the south. "Will Asal come?"

"Most likely."

"He shall come because he's a fighter. He now fights for love, as that passion deceives him. But in his heart of hearts he's a warrior. He knows that he'll never be safe while we live, and so he shall face us."

"Then my blade will find his back."

"Be careful, Po Rame. I've known men who have fought for love, and they're a difficult breed to kill. Such passion may cloud their minds, but it gives them great strength. Cripple him swiftly or you shall die on his blade."

Po Rame nodded, then moved away from the sun and deeper into the shade.

"When this day is over," Indravarman continued, "the Khmer Empire will be finished. We shall return to Angkor, gather more of our forces, slay the city's leaders for their part in this uprising, and populate the land with our people. The Khmers' history, their achievements, their glories, all shall become ours."

"They will—"

"So sharpen your blade, assassin. Put Jayavar down on this deck, and you shall be immortal. Put Asal down as well, and you'll steal the passion of which I speak."

"Yes, King of Kings."

"Now go. Leave me to my thoughts."

Po Rame turned away, but Indravarman barely noticed his departure.

The Cham king stood up. His hand on the shaft of his battle-axe, he soon paced the deck, impatient for the killing to begin.

Back at the former Cham stronghold, Jayavar stood on the shoreline, facing Bona. The boy carried a small shield and a dagger that he had sheathed like a sword. His face bore a pained expression that prompted Jayavar to crouch down so that they were eye to eye.

"My lord, I want to fight," Bona said, his right hand on the hilt of his dagger.

Jayavar smiled. "I know. And fight you would. I've seen your strength, how you can pull back the heavy cord of a bow."

"I can."

"The next time you lift that bow, we'll be hunting together. We'll head deep into the jungle and disappear until the stars are out."

"When can we do that?"

"Soon, my child. But for now I need you to do something else for me. Your mother? Is she near?"

"Yes, my lord."

"Please go to her. She will need you."

"But, my lord, you'll need me more. I want to serve you."

Jayavar put his right hand on Bona's shoulder. "Your father is dead, Bona. My children are dead. That makes us more than a servant and a lord. We are to be companions, you and I. After the Chams are defeated, I would like you and your mother to move into the Royal Palace. You may continue your work as the swordsmith's apprentice, or as whatever else suits you. Your mother may work as she wishes. And when my duties tire me, I shall seek you out. Then we shall hunt, stack stones in a quiet place, or discuss the day."

Bona scratched a burn near his wrist, shifting from side to side. "My lord, the Chams will try to kill you."

Nodding, Jayavar removed a golden ring from his finger and handed it to Bona. "If the Chams are victorious, flee into the jungle with your mother. Return to your homeland. The gold you now carry will offer you a start."

"Thank you, my lord. But please . . . please, don't lose. I'd rather stay with you."

"I know. And though I would like to stay here and continue our talk, I must go. Time grows precious." Jayavar rose to his full height, then squeezed both of Bona's shoulders. "I shall see you soon. Until then, stay safe, my young companion."

"You too, my lord."

Jayavar turned away from the boy. Ajadevi stood in the distance. Now he needed to be with her.

Ajadevi watched him approach, noting how he walked, how his posture was even more upright than normal. She also stood near the shoreline. Around her, scores of enemy boats, docked and anchored, were now manned by Khmers and Siamese. Yet many of these warriors held enemy shields and axes; they wore the short-sleeved, quilted armor favored by Chams, as well as some of their lotus-flower headdresses. From a distance, the Khmers looked like Chams. Hidden throughout the vessels were archers, the tips of their arrows wrapped in cloth and dipped in pitch. When the time was right, the sky would rain down burning bolts, setting Indravarman's fleet ablaze.

As final preparations were being made to get under way, Ajadevi glanced from her husband to the Khmers behind her. Hundreds of women and children, guarded by dozens of warriors, were gathered in a circle. Ajadevi recognized the nearly blind boy and his mother. Without question the boy's idea concerning the poisoned fish had worked, for Khmer officers had reported that many of the Chams had been enfeebled by illness, which all but ensured their slaughter.

Not far from the boy stood the Cham officer Asal and his lover. Asal's hands were still bound, though Ajadevi believed he was no threat. Jayavar, however, was less trusting in the matter.

Once the warriors sailed for battle, the women and children

would take the remaining boats and pull away from shore. Positioned in such a way, they would be protected from Indravarman in the likely event that upon learning of the Khmer attack, the Cham king led an army to the lake. Far from shore, and with every boat gone, the women and children would be safe. After Jayavar defeated the approaching Chams, he would turn his fleet around and return to protect whoever had been left behind.

Ajadevi believed that Jayavar's plan was sound, but she didn't like the thought of being separated from him. Her place had always been by his side, and now, in his moment of greatest need, she would be beyond his reach.

"I should accompany you," she said as he came close enough that his shadow fell on hers.

He shook his head. "This conversation has already occurred."

"But you may need me."

"Yes, I may. But whoever is left behind shall also need you. I'd rather have you in charge than anyone else."

"There are other—"

"No one is as quick as you, my queen. You must stay for the sake of our people."

For the first time in her life, Ajadevi wished that he didn't trust her judgment. He wasn't just saying that she would be the best person to lead the collection of women, children, and warriors—he believed it. "My place is with you," she finally replied, knowing that he wouldn't relent but unable to stop herself from speaking.

A faint smile graced his face. "Whatever I am, it is because of you. You gave me strength when I had none, faith when my doubts were many."

She saw that the boats were full and ready. His officers were waiting for him, standing on the decks, their weapons glistening.

Because many eyes were on her, and she wanted to do him honor and thereby inspire the men he commanded, she knelt on one knee and kissed his hand. "If you should fall, look for our light," she said. "But do not fall, Jayavar. There's still so much for us to do in this life, precious moments still to unfold."

He helped her rise. "You are most precious. I could journey throughout our land, searching year after year, and find nothing and no one as lovely."

Wanting to stay strong in front of the men, she held back her tears. "Return to me. Let me journey with you." She kissed him once on the lips, then stepped backward, knowing that he should go.

"I shall always love you," he said, bowing to her.

"And I you."

He turned away.

She resisted a nearly overwhelming urge to reach for him, to pull him back to her. Willing herself to remain still, she watched him go, tears finally falling to her cheeks. She bit her bottom lip, holding back a shudder, terrified that she would never see him again. Suddenly there were so many things that she wanted to tell him, so many thoughts left unsaid. But she stayed still, watching him move along the dock and step into a boat. He waved to her, then to his people.

The fleet set sail. She watched it fade away, allowing herself a brief moment to lament his departure. Then, thinking of her countrymen, she steeled herself and turned around, ready to organize those who remained. Her first order of business was to ensure that Nuon was in a large boat surrounded by able fighters. The two women exchanged farewells. Then Ajadevi hurried from vessel to vessel, anointing leaders and telling them what she expected.

She wanted to be off this bloody and vulnerable stretch of

land as soon as possible, wanted to be on the water, where at least she could touch its wetness and wonder whether Jayavar touched the same thing.

It didn't take long to board the women, children, and remaining warriors onto the boats. For a reason unknown to Asal, the Khmer queen asked that he, Voisanne, and Chaya travel with her. Their boat was crammed with crying children, worried mothers, and some fighters well past their prime. Despite the many distractions, the queen organized everyone, and soon they set sail. Though his hands were still bound, Asal volunteered to help row and, sitting on a bench, he dipped a long oar into the water and pulled with the Khmers.

They drew away from shore. Other boats followed their lead, and soon their force was safely in deep water, far enough from land that no arrow could reach them. The queen ordered that the sail be dropped, the oars left still, and the anchor lowered. Their craft swayed idly. Mothers fed children. Warriors scanned the horizon. The queen conferred with a wrinkled man who held a spear.

Asal glanced at Voisanne, who was talking with Chaya. Voisanne saw his gaze and smiled at him. She looked at ease on the rocking boat, and he felt a surge of pride. Now that she was reunited with her people, she seemed more confident and mature. Her beauty had blossomed as well. She stood with her back straighter, her head held high. He had fallen in love with her when she was beaten down, and now that she had risen, his attraction to her was even stronger.

Though Asal wanted to leave his post and go to her side, he resisted the urge. Instead he studied the shoreline, certain that Indravarman would lead his army to the lake. It would take some time to organize thousands of warriors and march them here, but before long they would come. Scouts should have arrived already, and seeing none, Asal asked himself about their absence. Aside from birds that circled and pecked at the dead, the shoreline was bereft of movement.

Sweat rolled down Asal's back. The sun beat upon him. He glanced at the queen and saw that she was still speaking with the old spearman. Did they also wonder about the silence? Why no one had appeared?

Asal imagined what Indravarman would do upon hearing that his base had been attacked. The king, who commanded so many more men than the Khmers did, would surely seize the opportunity to crush his foe. As with any looming engagement, scouts would be sent ahead.

Thinking that perhaps the scouts would come by water, Asal scanned the horizon. Yet he saw no one. The Khmer fleet had recently disappeared into a distant haze. The Great Lake was an endless shimmering mirror.

Uneasiness began to seep into Asal. Something was wrong. He knew Indravarman too well to believe that the king would ignore an invading army. Indravarman's plan was unfolding, but what it was, Asal could not guess.

Cursing softly in his native tongue, Asal continued to scan the shoreline and the lake. Though he had felt fear many times in his life, this helplessness was worse. The woman he loved was standing nearby. He could hear her voice and see her face. Yet he felt incapable of protecting her because whatever was happening, he was blind to its intricacies, naked to its dangers.

Indravarman was out there somewhere, and whatever trap he was planning was about to be sprung.

*   *   *

Due south, in the deep waters of the Great Lake, Indravarman waited. He had found the approaching Cham force, and after having alerted its officers to the Khmer plan, there was nothing he could do but sit idle. His boat was at the rear of his fleet, opposite where the Khmers would appear. He wanted to remain unseen until his trap was set in motion and the enemy was completely surrounded.

Restless, Indravarman shifted on his dais. He had told his officers to have their men appear at ease. Music and singing emanated from several boats, and the scent of roasting fish hung heavily in the air. Men rowed, but with no sense of purpose. A few warriors, all fit and young, swam alongside their boats, racing one another. Bets were cast and men shouted encouragement.

Indravarman had spread the word that at most seven thousand Khmers and Siamese would oppose them, and his men were confident of victory. He shared their outlook and was increasingly impatient for the killing to begin. Gazing at his army, he tried to count all the boats but lost track, bored by the tedious exercise. On the flat waters of the Great Lake, his men seemed infinite in number. These were hardened fighters, and with two of his men for every Khmer and Siamese, his force would give him a resounding triumph.

The dream that Indravarman had conjured up so long ago was finally about to come true. He would shatter one empire while expanding his own. After the Khmers had fallen, he would consolidate his forces, demand reinforcements, and then march on the Siamese. Their land was rich in resources, harbors, and history; and he longed to beat down the men who had joined forces with the Khmers to oppose him.

To the north, the lake seemed to shimmer under a thin haze. Indravarman wished that a breeze would arrive, but the Gods ignored his request. Spurning them as they had him, he thought about Asal, believing that he would appear, hoping he would. Asal was now an enemy, and one to be reckoned with. The only death that Indravarman coveted more than Asal's was Jayavar's. Both men posed threats. Both were strong, in part because of their women. Indravarman had heard of Ajadevi's exploits and wanted to take her alive, though he doubted he could do so. She was too wise to let him capture her. Yet Voisanne was another story. She was still young, and even if Asal died, she would want to live. She would attempt to flee and would be tracked down.

Indravarman tried to picture her, thinking that though she wasn't as striking as Thida, her face had held his gaze. He'd given her as a reward to Asal, and she had corrupted him. So she must be much more resilient than he had suspected. She must be a prize.

An oar stroke splashed him, and Indravarman glared at the crewman. He wondered how he might keep Asal alive long enough for him to understand that his woman had been captured and was now the property of a king. Or perhaps he should simply entomb them forever, wall them up in a room of thick stone and let them die in each other's arms.

You should have stayed away from me, he thought, but I know that you didn't. You hate me, and so you shall come. Yet you come only to the end, Asal, like a moth to a flame. Do you not know that your death is imminent, that you rush toward it with open arms?

I was wrong to think so highly of you, as only a fool would return to me. And if you've brought your woman, then you're twice the fool. Because whatever pain I give you, she shall receive tenfold. She stole you from me; she twisted you, and in doing so, she mocked me.

Perhaps you need time to think, Asal. Perhaps being entombed will suit you. You'll want to end her life, her misery, but shall be powerless to do so. Yet you shall see her tears, hear her suffering. Countless deaths she shall die before you watch the light finally fade from her eyes.

Still far away and approaching from the north, Jayavar's fleet moved steadily toward its foe. Wanting his men to see that he did not place himself above them, he held an oar and moved it to the cadence of the captain's voice. Sweat glistened on his face, back, and chest. Though he was pleased with how his plan was unfolding so far, he felt ill at ease. The fight on the shoreline had gone well, but a Cham spear had almost impaled him. It would have but for a man to his left who had lifted his shield at the last moment and saved his king's life.

Jayavar had fought in many battles and had always believed in his blade. But on the shoreline his foes had seemed to be younger, stronger, and quicker than he remembered. His own weapon was slow, barely parrying thrusts, downing only two of his enemies. For the first time in his life, his age had begun to betray him. He had never seen the spear flying toward him, or recognized a warning shout. Equally distressing, while his men, almost all of whom were half his age, charged forward and fought with fury, the surge of bloodlust that always accompanied battle had carried him only so far. In the end, he'd had to rely on his wisdom and experience rather than on the strength of his sword arm. And he knew too well what happened to warriors in hand-to-hand combat when their arms tired and their reflexes slowed.

Battle was a place for the young. Yet he had to lead his men, had to be in the heart of the fight. Somehow he would have to find the vigor to bring down quicker and stronger warriors. Recalling how he'd once seen an old tiger fight off a much younger adversary, Jayavar reminded himself that the old could dominate the young—at least for a moment. His challenge would be how to string together a succession of such moments.

If Ajadevi had sensed his apprehension, which was likely, she had chosen not to speak of it. Nor had he mentioned his shortcomings to her. Their mutual fear held the subject at bay, it seemed, as if by speaking of weaknesses they would become real.

Jayavar eased back on his oar, rowing with less vigor. Sweat continued to roll down his skin, and men on nearby boats applauded his efforts. No one appeared to notice that he was conserving what remained of his strength. He knew that only two great battles remained. If he could survive those, if he could lead his people to victory, he would never need to lift a sword again. He'd rule with peace in mind, and if someday another war became inescapable, he would command from the rear ranks.

For the first time in many years, Jayavar felt completely alone. The weight of an empire pressed down on his shoulders. Based on his actions, his people would rejoice or lament the day's conclusion. In so many ways, he should have felt empowered and encouraged.

Yet, drawing closer to his enemy, he continued to worry, wondering if he had the strength to do what must be done.

As the mothers around her managed their children and the handful of warriors assigned to her boat scanned the horizon, Ajadevi stood at the stern and resisted the urge to pace the deck. With every passing heartbeat she felt Jayavar pulling farther away from her, and the separation left her increasingly troubled.

Though she tried to pray and to look for signs, her thoughts moved with too much speed to allow such focus. She closed her eyes, opened them, wiped her brow, and stared to the south, toward where she had last seen Jayavar. He'd waved and then disappeared, taking the best parts of her along with him.

Ajadevi had usually been content to be a woman, but she wished that today she could transform into a man, grab a sword, and fight beside her king. She would take the battle to the Chams, driving them backward, turning the water red with their blood. She would risk the standing of her karma to liberate her people. Yet she was not empowered to join the fight and could do little but worry, wishing the time would flash by, that Jayavar would return before an approaching cloud hid the sun.

A few of the nearby women spoke about the discomfort of being on the boat, and Ajadevi glared at them, wondering how they could be so oblivious to what was transpiring. Their men would live or die, their culture would thrive or perish, depending on what happened to the south. Every eye, she felt, should be straining in that direction, peering through the haze. And every mind should be praying for victory.

Ajadevi studied the faces around her. She saw foolishness and ignorance, but also wisdom and strength. Her gaze settled on the Cham officer who held the end of an oar despite his bound hands. He was shaking his head and staring to the north, toward Angkor. To her surprise, he muttered something to himself, then shifted on the bench. He seemed restless and ill at ease, the one person in the boat, she thought, whose anxiety seemed to mirror her own.

Without a second thought, Ajadevi moved toward him, unaware of the women who shifted to let her pass. When she made a move to sit on the bench directly in front of the Cham, a Khmer warrior stood up, allowing her access to the space.

"Will you talk with me?" she asked the Cham, then noticed

that the young woman who accompanied him was walking toward them.

He squinted against the glare of the sun that beat upon her back. "Yes, lady."

"Why do you worry? Do you dread the death of your king?"

"Hardly. He's undeserving of the title he carries."

Ajadevi started to speak, pausing a moment as the woman sat beside him. "But clearly you're concerned. Why? We're safe here. Arrows cannot reach us. And we've taken your king's boats. We have nothing to fear."

"Do you see the shore, lady?" he asked.

"Yes."

"Indravarman's scouts should be there by now. Surely some of his men escaped your attack and have reported back to him. Why don't we see his scouts? Why hasn't his army arrived? It should have. If I were he, I'd have sent every man to destroy you at the water's edge."

Ajadevi felt her heart flutter. She glanced at the distant and empty shoreline. "But . . . but why? Why is there no one?"

"No one can be sent if they've been positioned elsewhere." The Cham leaned toward her, his brow furrowing, his words coming fast now. "I think, lady, that your husband is sailing into a trap. I think that Indravarman awaits him out there. Otherwise, why wouldn't Indravarman have arrived at the shoreline by now? Hearing of the defeat of his men, he would have marched forth with great speed, bent on revenge—unless he knew of your attack and let his men be sacrificed so that he could trap your entire force on the lake. Nothing else makes sense, lady. If Indravarman is out there with his army, he will surround your husband. He will slay every Khmer and never have to—"

"Stop!" Ajadevi held up her hand, suddenly knowing that

what the Cham said was true. The signs had told her as much, though only now did she recognize why the wind came and went, why a haze existed to the south. The world seemed to spin around her, but she steadied herself. "We must go to him," she said, raising her voice. "Release the anchor! We must go! And cut away this man's bonds. Right now. Cut them away."

The warrior next to Ajadevi frowned. "But, my queen, he—"

"Cut them!"

The Khmer quickly freed the prisoner.

Panicking, Ajadevi glanced around and saw that there were twenty oars, ten on each side of the boat. But only seven were manned. She ordered her people to start rowing. As the captain unfurled the sail, she grabbed the oar next to her and lifted it over the water, then dipped it below the surface and pulled with all of her might.

Women began to fill the empty benches, the oars awkward in their hands at first, but then moving in unison with the others. The boat seemed to surge forward, casting the water aside, a breeze suddenly buffeting them.

Ajadevi was now positioned so that she faced the Cham's broad back. She saw the muscles around his shoulder blades tighten as he pulled hard on his oar. The young woman whom he seemed to love sat in front of him, rowing as well, her back to him.

"Will we catch him in time?" Ajadevi asked the Cham.

He strained against his oar. "Maybe, lady. But the Gods will need to smile upon us."

The Cham looked to his left. "We must lighten this vessel, lady. All but the most crucial of provisions should be thrown overboard."

Ajadevi commanded that the supplies be cast away. People did as she asked, even children helping to toss a large sack of rice over the gunwale. Heaving against her oar, Ajadevi bit her bottom lip, trying to hold back her tears. She felt foolish for not anticipating the trap, and berated herself for the oversight.

Time and time again, she imagined Jayavar rowing as she was, heading directly into the hands of the waiting Chams. She envisioned the look of horror on his face, and then one of resignation. He would try to protect her and his kingdom; he would fight to the last man. But he would be overwhelmed.

By now familiar with her oar, she thrust it forward and backward, grunting with effort. The oar became her enemy. She heaved upon it as if it were a giant snake that had wrapped itself around her loved ones. The skin of her fingers blistered and split, yet she pulled still harder, the pain making her think of what Jayavar would soon endure.

"Faster!" she shouted. "We must go faster!"

The shoreline receded into nothingness. In the open water, the size of the waves increased, slapping the bow of their surging boat, casting spray into the air. Suddenly the Cham's oar split in half, and he fell backward toward her, smashing into her knees. She helped him up, and he moved to where his lover sat, taking her oar from her. The woman knelt beside him, and he leaned over to kiss the top of her head. Then he was rowing once again. To Ajadevi's amazement, she felt the strength of his strokes propel their boat forward.

Thinking of how he had kissed his loved one, Ajadevi began to cry. She wanted to do the same to Jayavar. Perhaps he was already surrounded by the enemy, fighting for his life.

Her hands bleeding on the smooth wood, Ajadevi gritted her teeth against the pain, pulling harder. Everywhere she looked, she saw signs of death—the upturned belly of a bloated fish, the broken oar handle at her feet, the way the sun hid behind a cloud. She saw so much death, but could not see what she yearned for most—Jayavar.

Remembering what she had told him, she tried to picture

their paper lantern, the star that they had sent so high into the sky. But her overwhelming fear allowed her no solace.

Death awaited him—a lonely death on a beautiful, warm day. And all she could do was row.

Not far from Ajadevi's boat, in a larger vessel closer to shore, people around Prak and Soriya began to talk excitedly. Prak had always excelled at listening to the conversations of others and realized what was happening before his mother did.

"The queen is leaving," he said, sitting on a bench near the gunwale. "And doing so in a hurry."

Soriya shared the bench with him and put a hand on his forearm. "Why?"

"Is she headed out into deep water?"

"It seems so."

"No one knows why," he said. "But the warriors near the front of the boat believe something has gone wrong."

"But she said that she'd stay."

Prak looked around. He was used to the dim light of the jungle, and the relentless strength of the sun made it even harder for him to see. Everything was blurry and white, enveloped in a halo of light that made all features indistinguishable. "The warriors want to follow her," he said, still eavesdropping. "They're arguing, but I think . . . I think we're going to follow."

"She told us to stay."

"Yes, but she needs protection. She must not be out there all alone."

Someone pulled up the anchor. The sail was unlashed and unfurled. Along the boat, warriors headed for their oars and began to row.

"Will you hand me the oar, Mother?" Prak asked. "I'd like to help."

She did as he asked. "What do they say? Are your father and brother in danger?"

"They're unsure," he answered, rowing with strength and ease, aware of the clumsiness of the nearby men. From the sound of the splashes around him, the warriors seemed to attack the water with their oars, beating at it with neither rhythm nor precision. "They don't know how to row," he said softly. "We'll never catch the queen."

"So . . . so tell them. Tell them how to make good speed."

He licked his cracked lips. "Me?"

"They'll listen to you, Prak. People have always listened to you."

The oar moved with speed in his grasp, an extension of his arms. He wanted to believe in himself and yet he had been disappointed when the king had used only a part of his battle plan. He might have been a hero if the fire had swept the Chams off the land. Instead he was only the boy who could neither see nor fight.

"Please tell them, Prak," his mother repeated, squeezing his arm. "For Father's sake. And for Vibol's. We need to hurry."

"I don't—"

"They may be in trouble!"

Prak nodded and closed his eyes, feeling the wood in his hands and the water beneath them, aware of the sudden desperation in his mother's voice. "We must stroke as one!" he shouted, trying to mimic how King Jayavar led. "Not as twenty minds and bodies, but as one! Dig your oars deep into the water, make no splash, and pull with me! Dig . . . pull! Dig . . . pull! That's it! As one! Dig . . . pull! Dig . . . pull!"

He felt their boat surge ahead, and men around him began to

whoop excitedly. A wind born of their strength and unity caressed his face. For a moment, pride washed over him, but then he remembered his father and brother, and was frightened for them.

"We're going to fight, Mother," he said, then felt her squeeze his arm once again. "So when we do, hand me a spear and tell me what to do with it. Be my eyes."

"Are you sure?"

He nodded, certain of the path ahead of him. Some of the nearby warriors began to falter with their strokes, and once again he called out to them, chanting rhythmically. The boat picked up speed, rushing toward an enemy that he could not see but knew was there.

Though even his calloused hands had blistered and cracked, Asal continued to row with strength and determination. Soon they would catch up with the Khmer king. Soon a fight would be joined or started. Indravarman's force would be much larger and better prepared. The Khmers' only advantage would be the fire arrows, which would cause their foes fear and pain. Yet the arrows wouldn't last, nor would they inflict enough damage. Indravarman would simply have too many men.

For this reason Asal knew that Indravarman would need to die. If he fell, his army would stumble. Leaderless, fighting so far from their homes and loved ones, the invaders would lose heart. But killing Indravarman would be nearly impossible. He would position himself deep within his fleet, surround himself with his best warriors, and wait, well rested, as weary men approached.

Asal closed his eyes, knowing that he'd try to get to Indravarman but would likely be killed in the process. His dreams would go unfulfilled. His sons and daughters would be forever unborn. And worst, the woman he loved would be ripped away from him.

He continued to row toward his doom, aware that his final moments were passing but unable to stop what had been started. A profound sadness consumed him, and his senses suddenly seemed more acute than ever before. He heard the cries of distant birds, smelled the water, and felt the warmth of the sun on his skin. Most striking of all was the presence of Voisanne's hand on his knee. She still knelt beside him, trying simultaneously to comfort her nearby sister and encourage him.

Her hand provoked a longing within him. He had wanted to feel her touch for the rest of his days, but soon her hand would leave him. He would be alone. He would die alone.

Afraid that she might have the same thoughts, he leaned over and kissed the top of her head. "The Gods have such beautiful plans in store for us," he said softly, his eyes on hers.

Her lips appeared to tremble. "Tell me . . . of their plans."

"They shall bring us children. And laughter. So much laughter."

"Where? Where will it all happen?"

"In Angkor. In a tidy home not far from the Chamber of Echoes. That way we can often thank the Gods for their gifts."

She bowed her head, then nodded. "I'll thank them every day."

"As will I, my lady. As will I."

"And our children . . . will be happy and healthy?"

"Yes. And we'll grow old together. Like a pair of saplings planted next to each other we shall rise . . . with grace and dignity, our roots and branches intertwined."

"Promise? Please promise me that, Asal."

"I do, my lady. I promise."

She straightened up, kissing his lips, her eyes glistening. "I love you."

"And I you."

"I want more time," she whispered, her hands on his, slowing down the movement of his oar. "I need more time."

An ache rose within him, stealing his breath, clouding his mind. "I know."

"Please give me more time, Asal."

The ache expanded within him, threatening to steal his memories, his very soul. Somehow he forced it away, rowing harder now, trying to focus. "We shall have a girl first," he said. "A beautiful girl who will remind me of her mother."

Voisanne nodded, tears dropping. "What . . . what should we name her?"

He tried to smile. "You think of that, my lady. Think of her name while I row."

A wind had risen, marring the surface of the lake so that it looked like scuffed leather. Ripples turned into small waves, the crests of which occasionally tumbled in rolling bursts of white spray. As the wind strengthened, so did the waves, swells lifting the boats from bow to stern. Masts pitched forward and backward while warriors clung at gunwales, their weapons sheathed, their stomachs uneasy.

Standing in front of his dais with his feet spread far apart, Indravarman stared to the north, searching for his foe. He didn't mind the sudden change in the weather, taking it as a sign that the Gods were interested in the outcome of the looming battle. Their attention had brought the wind and the waves. Their eyes were on him, and he was eager to impress them.

Raising his voice, he shared his thoughts with his men, encouraging them to honor the Gods with a resounding victory, to make them remember their own epic battles against the demons that sought and failed to destroy them. The men cheered at his words, and he asked them to row, to pretend that they were eager to reach the distant shoreline.

"Welcome the Khmers as your brothers!" he shouted, thrusting his fist into the air. "Lure them into our trap, let them believe that they've deceived you, and then fall on them like hounds on a hare! Redden this water with their blood, and let the Gods celebrate your deeds!"

Again the men cheered him, and, fearing that their voices would carry with the wind, he gestured for silence. Gazing from side to side, he studied his surroundings, pleased that the sky was still fairly clear. Though the wind and waves continued to strengthen, a storm wasn't imminent. They would fight in the sunlight, and those who fell on Khmer blades would be reborn into that same light, which surely would be preferable to death beneath a cold, dark sky.

Increasingly impatient, Indravarman ordered his men to row harder. As they put their backs into the task, he felt the vessel heave ahead, bringing him closer to his enemy and his fate. His enemy was about to be vanquished. His fate was to carve his name into the pillars of history, to rule near and distant lands, and to shape the world into a realm of his own making. Once the Khmers fell, the Siamese would follow.

It required only the death of Jayavar to begin this march to ultimate triumph.

"Slay the false king," Indravarman said to the warriors around him. "Slay him and whatever you want shall be yours."

Jayavar thrust his oar into the water and pulled back, still working at less than his full strength. He studied the waves as he rowed, watching them roll forward, aware that they would make it harder for Khmer and Cham boats to come together, for warriors to board one craft from another.

"After we draw the Chams close, we shall use the fire arrows," he said to the men he commanded, raising his voice so that those on nearby boats could also hear. "But at some point the fight will be hand-to-hand. And when that happens, when our boats strike those of the enemy, wait to leap aboard their vessels until a wave lifts us higher than our foes. Jump down on them with your shields and weapons pointing low. Land on a Cham and he shall be easy to kill. Let him land on you and you shall die. Now raise your voices and spread the word to the boats near you. The waves are a gift from the Gods. We must use them to soar above our foe."

A wave slapped against the side of his boat, sending spray into his face. He licked his lips. He took a deep breath, and then another, steadying himself. Soon the Cham fleet would appear. One way or the other, soon it would be over.

Her hands bleeding and afire with pain, Ajadevi rowed onward. She grunted with each stroke, willing herself to push through her misery, to lessen the space between her and her loved one.

Distance is only a state of mind, she told herself. Be with him now. Let him feel you.

Waves battered against the bow. Ajadevi turned to see the Cham officer sweeping his oar forward, the Khmer woman kneeling beside him, her hands on his knee. Their love was as tangible as the wind, and Ajadevi prayed that it would endure the coming fight.

Too much water was crashing over the sides, and aware that it was sloshing around her feet, she asked a nearby boy to start bailing. He bowed to her and hurried away, presumably to look for a container.

Their sail flapped in the wind, a tear emerging in it near where it was secured to the mast. Ajadevi recognized the tear for exactly what it was—a greater power overcoming a lesser one. And yet the fabric stopped separating. For the moment it held fast. She saw the sail as symbolizing the union between her and Jayavar, one more sign among many that this union was about to be torn in two.

"Mend the sail!" she shouted to some idle women, hoping that one might have handy a needle and thread. "Stitch another piece of fabric over the tear! Take the pressure off it!"

The women searched for the necessary instruments, then bent low in apology after realizing that they couldn't fix the rip.

A gust of wind pummeled them, shredding the sail.

"Jayavar!" Ajadevi screamed, knowing he was falling into the trap at that very moment, that despite her bloody hands she had not been fast enough.

Twenty-three

When Banners Fall

o Rame located them first, which pleased him greatly.

"There," he said, pointing to the north.

Warriors asked what he saw, but he paid them no heed. Standing at the stern of Indravarman's boat, he held a trident and an oversize shield that bore a golden image of a seven-headed snake. When Indravarman demanded to know what he had pointed at, Po Rame lifted his long, three-pronged weapon and aimed it toward a speck on the horizon. "The rats draw near," he said.

"I see nothing."

"Yet they come, King of Kings. Soon you'll have your battle."

As Indravarman gave instructions to his men, Po Rame imagined how the fight would unfold, determining where to stand to avoid a possible rush of Khmers, and how best to wait for the right moment. He cared only about wounding Jayavar or Asal. The war against the Khmers did not matter to him. The struggles of men were trivial and fleeting, beneath him in every regard. But to bring Jayavar or Asal to his king might allow Po Rame to end their lives, to become the keeper of their souls. And what better souls could be kept?

The Khmers drew closer, prompting the men around Po Rame to ready themselves for battle though they still pulled on their oars and pretended to be unaware of danger. Soon Po Rame could discern the outline of the enemy fleet, its size paling in comparison to that of the Cham force. The Khmers neared, doubtless expecting victory.

Encouraged by Indravarman, Chams began to cheer on the approaching force, as if they were delighted to have found their countrymen. The fleets neared each other. Po Rame saw Khmer figures, and then faces. He smiled.

Indravarman has won, Po Rame thought. The dung eaters are doing exactly what he wants, and before the sun falls they'll all be dead. Even better, I'll have wetted my steel in the back of a king or a traitor—perhaps both. And if I'm not a God at this moment, I will be one by the end of this day.

In the distance a Khmer waved. His hand tightening on the shaft of his trident, Po Rame bowed, his heart rate finally increasing, his eyes searching among the nearing faces for Jayavar or Asal.

Jayavar stood at the bow, holding a Cham shield and sword, squinting as he peered to the south. The enemy fleet had just sailed into view, and though most of his men still rowed, the five archers aboard were gathered in the stern and laying arrows at their feet as well as testing the tautness of their bowstrings. Pitch had been applied to the tip of each arrow and a small fire burned in an iron cauldron. When the time was right the archers would dip their arrows into the fire, light the pitch, and aim for their enemies' mainsails. Jayavar had told the archers to conceal themselves until the last moment, and so the men were crouched low, mostly hidden behind the gunwale.

To Jayavar's delight, he realized that several Chams were waving. He ordered his men to return the greeting. The enemy boats were under full sail, heading his way. Though they were packed tightly together, he counted sixty-nine of them, which represented a slightly larger number than he had expected, but not big enough to cause him excessive concern. Armed with the element of surprise and the fire arrows, he should be able to overwhelm the Chams.

Waves slapped against the bow of his vessel, the spray cooling Jayavar's skin. Sunlight glistened off enemy shields and weapons. Some of the Chams were singing, for the wind carried their voices to him. He told his archers to be ready and asked his captain to steer toward the largest of the enemy boats.

The distance between the two fleets shrank. Jayavar prayed for victory, envisioned Ajadevi's smiling face, and tightened his grip on his shield and sword. He was about to ask for an increase in speed when the Cham boats started to separate. The boats fanned out to the east and west, revealing a multitude of smaller vessels that had been hidden behind them. These were crammed with warriors and headed straight at the Khmer fleet.

Jayavar felt as if he had been thrown from the top of one of Angkor Wat's great towers. He recognized the trap before any of the men around him did and ordered them to pull back on their oars, to reverse their forward momentum. Their boat slowed, but the enemy came at them with too much speed, spreading out around his much smaller fleet. Fast Cham vessels began to encircle his force. He considered asking his men to turn their boats around, but such a maneuver would take too much time. His warriors would exhaust themselves in a fruitless effort and be weakened before the battle even began.

Twisting around, Jayavar looked desperately for a means of escape, a break in the Cham line ahead of him through which he could save his army. But the Cham boats were two or three deep. To smash into one link of the chain of enemy ships would only bring the others crashing down on him from all sides. A few of his lead ships would likely escape, but the rest would be left behind and overwhelmed.

"Ready your arrows!" he shouted, deciding that their best chance at victory lay in attack. He pointed toward one of the smaller Cham boats that was overcrowded with warriors. "She's your first target! Strike her, then whatever other vessels hold the most men!"

The Cham fleet drew closer. The enemy warriors started to shout, thrusting their weapons into the air. Filled with a sudden rage, Jayavar spun toward his men. "Here come those who stole our land and slaughtered our loved ones! They shout to put fear into our hearts, but do we fear them?"

"No!" came a chorus of replies.

"So silence them forever! Draw your arrows and ready your spears!"

The five archers lit their arrows, notched them on taut bowstrings, and sent the flaming bolts toward the enemy ship. Several arrows struck the sail, and Chams shouted as the fabric caught fire. Aboard other Khmer boats, officers followed Jayavar's lead, and scores of flaming bolts arched over the water, slamming into sails, hulls, and men. The wind fueled the flames, causing them to race across sails, to spread upon sun-bleached beams. Cham archers shot back in return, but their arrows carried no fire and did little damage. Meanwhile, enemy warriors beat at the flames with their shields. Some were successful at putting out the fires, but others were scorched and leapt into the lake.

Jayavar saw that the flames were causing havoc among his

foes, but most of the enemy vessels were untouched and came straight at his fleet, propelled by Chams bent on revenge. Spinning around, he searched for Indravarman's boat, believing that it would be the biggest. But smoke and sails obscured much of his view.

A Cham vessel, the bow covered in flames, came straight at him. "Stand firm!" he shouted, holding his sword aloft, preparing for a jolt as the two boats met.

The burning craft struck his own. He staggered from the impact. "For Angkor!" he cried, stepping forward, aware of arrows whistling past his head, of friend and foe already dying around him.

"Bring me to them!" Indravarman roared at his oarsmen, who had stopped making any effort to row once the fire arrows had begun to rain from the sky. "Bring me to them or by the Gods I'll have all your heads!"

Oars rose and fell. The boat heaved forward. Indravarman continued to shout at his men, furious to behold the damage that the fire arrows were causing. He had planned to wait at the edge of the battle and to enter it only when the Khmers were about to be beaten, but the destruction wrought by the arrows was simply too much for him to witness. Almost half of his fleet was on fire, and though his men had finally brought their boats crashing against those of their enemy, the Khmers were fighting only a fraction of his force. Smoke billowed from burning infernos that had once been sails. Six Cham boats had foundered as their occupants rushed to one side to avoid the flames. Everywhere Indravarman looked, men were in the water, thrashing about as they swam through the carnage toward friendly vessels.

"There!" Indravarman screamed, pointing to a large Khmer

boat that seemed to be inflicting the most damage on his fleet. "Get me to her! Now, curse your souls!"

A smaller enemy vessel full of Siamese warriors was directly in their path, its broadside open and inviting. "Faster!" Indravarman commanded. He moved toward the bow, thumping the butt of his spear into the deck. "Smash through her sides! Bring her down! Now, now, now!"

Whoever commanded the Siamese vessel tried to turn away, but Indravarman's captain steered his craft with cunning, and its reinforced bow slammed into the middle of the enemy ship. Timbers splintered and crashed. Men screamed. The smaller vessel shuddered, then split in two. Siamese were crushed or thrown into the water. Indravarman saw that one swimming man was trying to organize the survivors. The Cham king shifted his balance, threw his spear, and howled with glee when it pierced the Siamese's shoulder.

A burning arrow thudded into the deck near Indravarman. He bent down, smashing it with his shield, smothering the fire. The large Khmer vessel was slightly off their port bow, and he commanded his captain to take him there. Whoever commanded the enemy ship was skilled, for its men had already destroyed several Cham boats.

"Jayavar!" Indravarman screamed in Khmer. "Are you there? Come to me! Come to me, you coward!"

The distance between the two ships shrank. Indravarman reached for another spear, suddenly desperate to fight in hand-to-hand combat, to see terror on the faces of his enemies. The first moment of battle had belonged to them, and the urge for revenge almost overwhelmed him. Why hadn't one of his officers thought of the fire arrows? They had been used before on the open sea. Why had no one foreseen that they'd work in a battle such as this?

"Pull harder!" he shouted again. The Khmer boat was inundated with fighting men, with scores of Chams and Khmers struggling against one another. "Jayavar is on that boat and I want his head!"

The Khmer boat neared. Indravarman threw his spear, saw it down a Khmer, and then reached for his massive, double-sided axe. "The Gods watch us all!" he said, aware of his men behind him, against him. "So don't disappoint them! Or me!"

Bow met bow. Indravarman leapt, sailed through the air, and landed on enemy ground. He lifted his axe and the killing began, joyful and wondrous, filling him with an incomparable power. He pressed forward, his bloody weapon carving a path before him, his rage engulfing his thoughts, giving life to a primeval instinct that drove him on and on, closer to where he believed Jayavar was fighting.

The smoke was merely a black stain on the horizon, but it left no doubt that the battle had begun. While Asal labored at his oar, Voisanne studied the sight, wishing it didn't exist, for surely men were fighting and dying amid the flames. If her countrymen were trapped as the queen feared, then all might be lost.

With each passing oar stroke, the smoke grew thicker and more ominous. If she squinted she could see the faint outlines of boats and the occasional billow of flames. She shifted her gaze to Asal, wishing that they were somewhere else, that Chaya was safe, and that they had all forgotten what it was like to fear, to hate. The war had swept them up, but it was not a war of their making. Why should they forever be forced to walk within its shadow?

She watched the necklace she had made bounce against Asal's chest. Despite his size and strength, he suddenly looked vulnerable, and she cringed at the thought of steel piercing his flesh.

"You needn't fight," she said quietly, her hands on his knee.

"I must, my lady."

"Why?"

"Because if I'm to be with you, in peace, Indravarman must be defeated."

She nodded but made no immediate reply. Waves slapped against the hull of their boat. Distant screams drifted upon the wind. "I'm frightened," she said. "For you. For Chaya. For us all."

"When I join the fight, go to her. Protect her."

"I will."

"And if we lose, if I fall, bloody yourselves and pretend to be dead. My countrymen will only care about the living."

"Yes," she replied, though her answer was a lie, for if the Chams won, she would take Chaya's hand and swim into the deep, into the blackness. They would swim as far as their lungs permitted, and inhale. Rebirth would come swiftly then, and they would seek out their loved ones. A new life would await.

But I want this life, she thought. This is the life I've always wanted.

"I love you, my lady," he said. "I've loved you from first sight. Even when you hated me."

"I was a fool."

The few warriors on the boat had stopped rowing and were readying themselves for battle. The men gathered at the bow while women continued to row. Not much farther than an arrow's flight ahead, scores of Khmer and Cham boats were engaged. Black smoke roiled above some of the ships, many of which were half sunk. Every single undamaged vessel was locked in battle, side to side against an enemy ship. Men fought and died. Cries and screams rose above the clash of sword against shield.

Asal stopped rowing but still lingered by Voisanne's side, his eyes scanning the battle.

"What are you looking for?" she asked as their boat glided forward.

"My king," he answered, then let go of his oar. "I must kill my king."

The fighting was even more intense than Jayavar had expected. Though the fire arrows had damaged the Cham fleet, Indravarman still led more men, and these warriors poured onto Khmer and Siamese vessels, overwhelming their defenders. His own boat was surrounded by several enemy craft, and Chams came at him from all directions, howling and hacking. His best fighters stayed by his side and tried to keep him safe, but his shield was already battered in a dozen places and his sword was nicked and red. He tried to form his men into a battle line not far from the bow, but it was impossible to maintain a position as Chams were constantly leaping over their gunwales from attacking ships.

Jayavar lacked the youth to fight with the savage fury of some of the men around him. Instead he wielded his sword with lethal precision, often blocking a Cham strike and then stepping forward, putting his weight behind each blow. Men fell in front of him and did not rise. The wounded he slew with no mercy, for a downed warrior could inflict grievous damage on an unwary adversary.

The deck near him was cleared of Chams, and there was a momentary lull in the fighting. Jayavar spun around, looking for friend or foe, pausing when he recognized Ajadevi's boat in the distance. It was headed straight for the battle, and he felt a sudden surge of pride and fear. Ajadevi had come to save him. But she was too late. The trap had been sprung.

Distracted by the sight of her boat, he didn't see the Cham

war hammer swinging in his direction until it nearly smote him down. Grunting with effort, he brought his shield up, caught the blow on the hardened wood, and staggered beneath the impact. The warrior dropped his weapon, his hands finding Jayavar's neck and squeezing.

Unable to breathe, Jayavar twisted and punched and fell, but the hands still tightened around his throat.

Several boats away from Jayavar, Boran and Vibol also fought for their lives. Their vessel was being boarded by Chams from both sides. Father and son stood next to each other, using long spears to keep their enemies at bay. As waves lifted and dropped the boats, Chams tried to leap onto the Khmer vessel, which was partially swamped. While some enemy warriors were able to land safely on the deck, others mistimed their jumps and fell into the water or were crushed between the boats.

Boran sought to protect his son from enemy blades but was nearly overwhelmed with threats. Everywhere he looked a Cham axe, spear, or sword seemed to dart forward, seeking to end Vibol's life. Boran screamed at the Chams to come at him, and some did, leaping forward to land near his feet or die on his spear. Those who landed he fought in close quarters, stabbing and slicing with his hunting knife. But he was able to pierce most of the attackers in midair with his spear, as his many years spent hauling in nets and fishing gave his arms the strength to repeatedly thrust his weapon over the water.

Still, even though he had killed and wounded their countrymen, the Chams continued to assault his position, trying to take advantage of Vibol's slight frame and inexperience. Boran shielded Vibol with his own body, though he knew that if he were to fall, his son would follow. During occasional and fleeting lulls in the battle, Boran turned to Vibol and saw the terror in his son's eyes. But before he could offer reassurances, fresh Chams would shout a challenge and try to plunge forward from their boat to his.

Khmers around him called for help that did not come. Their boat, so overloaded with water and warriors, listed to one side, almost flipping over in the swells. Several Khmers and Chams toppled overboard. Boran slipped on the bloody planks, dropped to his knees, and would have died then and there if Vibol hadn't blocked a Cham axe with his shield. With a burst of strength and a savage cry, Vibol threw himself into the Cham, sending him over the gunwale and into the water.

Boran struggled to his feet, his chest heaving, his every thought focused on saving his son. An arrow whipped past his face. The heat from a burning Cham boat was so fierce that he pulled Vibol away from the drifting inferno. The boat neared their own, bumped into it, and then drifted away. Though he wanted to take the opportunity to run to a safer area, Boran had been ordered to hold his position, so he stepped back toward the gunwale, his spear and shield ready.

A different Cham boat, undamaged and full of warriors, came in their direction. "Stay away from my son!" Boran screamed, hurrying forward to face them. "You hear me, cowards? Face me!"

His spear darted out, pierced flesh, and the Chams accepted his challenge, leaping from their boat, trying to engulf him.

It was the queen who saw her husband. He was near the stern of his boat fighting alongside twenty or thirty Khmers. The remainder of the vessel was inundated with Chams, who pressed forward from the bow. The fighting was ferocious. Weapons clashed, men shouted and screamed, and bodies were thrown overboard to make room for new arrivals. Asal watched the queen as she cried out her husband's name, telling him to hold on, that she was coming for him. She screamed when Jayavar fell. He then grappled with a man and managed to struggle to his feet.

Asal was about to head to the bow of their boat and join the Khmer warriors when his gaze stopped on a large Cham who was fighting toward Jayavar. "Indravarman," Asal said, rising to his feet.

Ajadevi overheard him. "Where?"

"Toward the bow," Asal replied, pointing. "He seeks your husband. He believes that if Jayavar dies the war will end."

Ajadevi shouted at their captain to head straight for the Cham king. She then ordered the few archers on board to target him. While she spoke, Asal hurriedly unbuckled his sword belt.

"What are you doing?" Voisanne asked, standing beside him.

He reached behind her back, drawing her close. "In a moment, my lady, it may seem that I run from you. But in truth, I shall run toward you. I shall always run toward you."

"What? Asal, what are you—"

Before she could protest, he put his foot on top of the gunwale and leapt overboard. The water was cool. She started shouting behind him, but for once he paid her no heed. He swam ahead, pausing on occasion to glimpse the fighting before him. Jayavar's ship was getting closer. He heard the thump of swords on shields, the cries of the maimed. Men struggled from bow to stern, often locked in each other's arms. Indravarman cut a Khmer down, pressing toward the stern, toward Jayavar.

Asal hadn't seen Indravarman since his torture and escape. He remembered the king's threats to Voisanne, how he had promised to take her as his own, to rape and ravish her. The thought of Indravarman putting his hands on her flesh, of hurting her with malice and delight, rekindled a profound rage within

Asal. He swam harder, praying to the Gods to give him strength, to make him terrible. He had always been a strong, able fighter, but on this day he would need to be more than that. There were too many of his countrymen on the boat, too many warriors fighting beside Indravarman. And surely Po Rame would be near, waiting in the shadows, ready to strike.

Grant me strength or she'll die, he prayed. Let me fight as a God, as one of you. Just for this day, for this moment. Let me fight as one of you and I shall never ask anything of you again.

A spear splashed into the water near him. He plunged down beneath the surface, kicking harder to avoid other projectiles, drawing closer to the bedlam ahead.

Though the fighting had consumed the Khmer ship, Po Rame had engaged only two foes. He had been forced to kill the young warriors when the Khmers rushed him in a fit of boldness and stupidity. Otherwise, Po Rame had remained near the bow, his gaze often on Jayavar and Indravarman. Too many Khmer warriors still guarded their king, but their ranks were thinning, and soon Po Rame would enter the melee, wading forward through the dead and dying, his trident seeking Jayavar's back.

An unusually large swell rocked the boat, and Po Rame stumbled into a Cham archer. He cursed the man, looked for more waves, and was surprised to see someone swimming in their direction. Whoever it was carried no weapon but swam with great speed, his muscled arms and legs propelling him forward. Po Rame was about to turn away when the swimmer paused to study the nearby boat.

"So you came," Po Rame whispered, instinctively raising his trident.

Asal plunged underwater, disappearing for a moment. He resurfaced closer to the stern, where the Khmers were struggling to stay alive. Po Rame debated asking the archer to shoot Asal but didn't want to announce his presence in case the man missed. Besides, he would rather kill Asal himself.

Po Rame started to edge forward, watching as Indravarman crushed a Khmer with the flat of his axe, beating the man into the deck as if he were a stake. The two kings were separated only by a few men and surely saw each other. Po Rame could tell that Jayavar was a skilled fighter, though he didn't possess the sheer strength of his counterpart.

Worried that he had waited too long, that he would miss out on the killing, Po Rame pressed ahead. A Cham fell in front of him, and a bleeding Khmer thrust a spear in his direction. The thrust had little power behind it, and Po Rame deflected it with his shield, simultaneously jabbing his trident into the man's abdomen. The Khmer fell, screaming.

Battle had never interested Po Rame, but killing had, and now that he had entered the fray, his trident darted about as if it had become the seven-headed snake on his shield. Khmers faced him and died. He fought his way to Indravarman, then circled to the right of his king, hoping to get behind Jayavar. The fighting was fierce, and though he wanted to look for Asal, he dared not take his eyes off his foes. Many were hardened warriors and fought like fiends, determined to save their king. They struggled under a banner depicting Angkor Wat, and whenever its bearer fell, another Khmer would take his place.

Po Rame ignored the screams, sights, and smells of battle. He concentrated only on the men before him, warding off their blows and still moving to his right, flanking the Khmer line. He found himself pressed against the gunwale and, after killing an adversary, he risked a glance over the side, searching for Asal.

Men thrashed about and died in the water, but as far as he could tell, Asal was not among them.

"Where have you gone?" he whispered.

Not ten paces away, Jayavar fell. As his men rushed to protect him, Po Rame slid in from behind them, his trident held low.

To Prak, the battle was not one of flashing swords and shining shields, or of flames and smoke, but of unfamiliar sounds. Men screamed for blood and whispered for mercy. Arrows whistled through the air to splash harmlessly in the water, to thud into wood, or to prompt a shriek. Entire groups of warriors raged, whimpered, and went silent.

Prak's boat had entered the melee not long after the queen's. Immediately they'd been attacked by a Cham vessel, and fierce hand-to-hand combat had ensued. Though the Chams had been driven away, most of the Khmer fighters were killed or wounded. Arrows had also struck down several women, and now nearly everyone on their boat was injured. Four children cowered behind the mast, two men tried to row away from the mayhem, and the remaining women tended to the dying.

Able to discern some of the battle, Prak realized that a vessel was heading in their direction. "Is that boat ours?" he asked his mother, who stood at his side near the stern.

"No . . . I don't think so."

"How many Chams are on it?"

"I'm not sure. The smoke makes it hard to see."

"But are they coming for us? Look closely, Mother. Are they steering in our direction?"

"Yes."

"Then hand me a spear. When the time is right, tell me what to do."

She pressed the thick shaft of a spear into his hands. "I have a shield," she said, her voice quivering. "I'll stand to your left and hold the shield."

Despite his surging fear, the thought of her fighting beside him provoked a sense of pride within him. She might have been quiet. She might have doubted herself. But now, in this decisive moment, she was going to stand beside him and face the Chams.

"How far away are they, Mother?"

"Twenty paces . . . I think. There are six of them."

Prak yelled at the two remaining Khmer fighters to join him in the stern. He wasn't sure if they heeded his request, but he thought he heard oars falling onto the deck. "Tell me where and when to strike, Mother. Straight, left, or right. Just say one of those words and I'll stab away."

Nodding, she shifted closer to him, grunting as she lifted the heavy shield.

The enemy vessel bumped into theirs. Chams leapt from boat to boat. Prak, who stood still, could see only white blurs, but he thought that the two Khmers rushed forward to face them. There was a sudden and violent clash of swords. Someone screamed. Someone else fell into the water. The fighters grunted and swore and died.

Prak sensed the Khmer children gathering behind him. They wept and pleaded. "How many Chams, Mother? How many remain?"

"Two! And they come now! To your right!"

Prak shifted his position, aware of the approaching blurs. Though his vision was weak, his arms were strong, and he held the heavy spear with ease.

"Left!" his mother screamed.

Without thought he thrust the spear ahead to his left, and felt it bite into flesh. The other blur rushed forward. His mother cried out as something smashed into her shield. Even as he yanked his spear backward, Prak realized that she had saved him. "Where?" he shouted. "Where do I strike?"

A searing pain shot through his leg.

"Straight!" she screamed.

Once again he thrust his weapon forward. It struck wood, not flesh, but now he knew where the Cham was and dropped his spear, rushed forward, and slammed into the body of his adversary. They fell together. Prak felt fingers clawing at his face. Somehow he resisted the urge to protect himself, instead finding the man's neck and wrapping his right arm around it, squeezing tightly. He had subdued many large catfish in such a manner, and before long the Cham gasped. The warrior tore at Prak's eyes and mouth, but Prak didn't change his grip. He simply squeezed until his adversary was silenced and went still.

"He's gone, Prak!" his mother shouted. "They're all gone!"

Prak pushed the body from him and tried to rise to his feet. Yet his legs failed him. He knelt on the ground in a state of shock. His mother was speaking to him, but her words no longer made sense. He could barely remain upright, no longer aware of even the sounds of battle or the wound on his calf.

His mother reached for him, and he took solace in her presence, sinking deeper into her embrace, into a place where he knew comfort.

Upon reaching the stern of the Khmer boat, Asal grabbed onto the rudder, the waves lifting and dropping him. Though he wanted to rush into the fray, his lungs heaved, and he forced himself to wait as strength flowed back into him. He looked for Voisanne, but his view was obstructed by the boat's slippery hull.

A woman screamed. Asal didn't know who it was, but the

sound spurred him into motion. He pulled himself up on the rudder, clutched the gunwale, and fell onto a dead Khmer. Without a moment's hesitation, he pulled a sword and a shield from the man's lifeless fingers. Two Khmers saw him and rushed forward, but he called out in their language, saying that he was a friend of Jayavar's. The men hesitated, and Asal saw that the king lay prone on the deck, surrounded by about fifteen of his warriors. A larger number of Chams were attacking them from the bow, pressing forward in a furious onslaught. Jayavar struggled to his feet and raised his sword, the sight of which provoked cheers from his men. They fought on, as did Jayavar, who to Asal's surprise moved to the front of their ranks. Farther down the boat, Indravarman shouted at his men as he swung his battle-axe, splintering shields and cleaving flesh.

Again Asal remembered Indravarman's threats to Voisanne. He imagined the king beating her, and the image filled him with such rage that he ignored the two Khmers' orders to stand back. One of them swung at him with a sword, but Asal cast the strike away with his shield and charged past them, howling at Indravarman to come forward and die. He knocked aside several other Khmers, oblivious to the threat of their weapons. Suddenly he was next to Jayavar. The king was engaged with a Cham officer, and Asal brought the man down with a backhanded stroke of his sword. Jayavar, already wounded in several places, recognized Asal and called out that he was a friend.

Indravarman must have seen Asal at that moment, for he shouted at his men to kill the traitor, pointing in Asal's direction. Chams surged forward. Much of the fighting was too close to use spears, so men on both sides attacked with swords, knives, and axes. Asal stood beside Jayavar, beating away those who sought to kill a king. His sword had never felt so light and free, falling and rising in great arcs, opening the enemy ranks. Men dropped before him, creating a shield of bodies. Still, compelled to attack by Indravarman, Chams came forward, swinging swords and axes, trying to thrust their weapons past Asal's shield. One warrior might have succeeded, but Jayavar caught the descending blade on his own sword hilt. The combatants cursed and struggled, and Asal pulled his sword from a dying Cham and thrust its blade deeply into Jayavar's adversary. A spear darted forward from the second line of Chams, nicking Asal in the shoulder. The blow didn't have much strength behind it, but the blade produced a searing pain, which only increased his rage. He screamed the battle cry of his own countrymen yet attacked them without pause or thought, his sword now a living thing of steel. Men stepped back from him, dominated by fear, and he pressed forward, deeper into the ranks of the enemy. Suddenly he was alone, nearly surrounded, and fighting for survival. He killed two men but would have fallen if Jayavar hadn't pressed ahead to reach his side.

Khmer king and Cham officer fought together against the enemy. They protected each other and slew each other's foes, but Indravarman's men were too many. And the Cham king himself was coming closer, his axe blurring as it swept forward to claim lives.

The shaft of a spear smashed into the side of Asal's head. His vision dimmed, but he still fought on, trying to get to Indravarman. Screaming, he stepped over men downed by his sword and waded deeper among the Chams. He now saw the king as a demon that would rob the world of light and beauty. Asal charged at him like one of the Gods on the walls of Angkor Wat, his sword held high, his face contorted with fury.

Asal met the demon. The blades of their weapons struck, the strength of the blow numbing Asal's arm. Around him, Khmers and Chams struggled and died, and Po Rame crept forward, but to Asal, nothing except the demon existed. He threw himself against it, trying with all his might to bring it down, but it stood tall, resisting his every strike, empowered by its own malice and evil.

Vibol wasn't sure how his father had been knocked down. One moment he was battling a Cham spearman, and the next he lay on the deck, blood oozing from a wound on his forehead. Their boat was swamped, and water sloshed back and forth atop the deck, pushing his father's limp body from one side to the other.

At first Vibol thought his father was dead, and after killing an older Cham, he fell to his knees in despair. But Boran opened his eyes and tried to sit up. The fighting raged around them, and legs knocked into them as men screamed and fought. The deck was covered in bodies.

Vibol had seen too many injured Khmers speared where they lay to leave his father alone. Grunting with effort, he dragged him toward the side of the boat that had sunk nearly to the waterline. Struggling warriors stepped on them and fell in their path, yet Vibol continued to pull his father, weeping at the sight of his wound, which was swelling quickly. The man who had always loved him, who had followed him into this hell, was as helpless as a child.

Someone stepped on Vibol's hand, and he grimaced but didn't draw attention to himself. Smoke wafted over them, perhaps obscuring them for a moment because the fighting seemed to ebb. Vibol reached the edge of the boat and pushed his father overboard. He rolled over the side after him, positioning himself behind his father, holding his head out of the water and supporting his body with his own.

Vibol began to swim, though coordinated movement was

difficult as he shuddered uncontrollably. He didn't know where to go, so he simply headed away from their boat, from a place of death and despair. He continued to weep, thinking that his father would be safe and well if he hadn't forced his family to follow him to war.

"I'm sorry," he whispered. "I'm so sorry."

"No need . . . for that," Boran replied, his voice low and deep, as if he had woken from a long slumber.

"Don't die, Father. Please . . . you can't die."

"I won't."

A spear splashed into the nearby water, prompting Vibol to swim harder. "Leave him be!" he screamed. "Just leave him be!"

Boats loomed in the distance. Some were on fire. Others teemed with warriors. Vibol kicked away from these sights, though at times they seemed to surround him. He wouldn't bring his father to such a place even if he had to swim with him all the way across the Great Lake.

"I want to go far from here," Vibol said, kicking awkwardly, pulling his father away from the madness. "And not ever return."

"Just swim . . . my brave son."

Vibol did as his father asked, heading for a stretch of the horizon that was free of boats and men. He swam into the deep, still supporting his father. The waves had diminished, he realized. The wind had stilled. Yet he felt so overwhelmed. His father's body dragged him down.

Onward he swam. He longed for silence, to listen to the water, to breathe untainted air. Nothing mattered to him now but to be with his father, to hold him as fish passed below, as memories of their companionship unwound behind his closed eyes.

*　　*　　*

Jayavar twisted away from the spear thrust, wincing as the blade impaled the Khmer behind him. Bringing the hilt of his sword down hard on his adversary's head, the king glanced at the nearby boats, praying that help would arrive soon. But everywhere he looked, Khmers and Siamese fighters were being overwhelmed by Chams. The enemy numbers were simply too great.

Believing that they were doomed unless Indravarman fell, Jayavar pressed toward the Cham king, attacking a stout warrior with a sudden burst of fury. The man was quick, however, parrying his thrusts, counterattacking with a series of swift sweeps of his sword. Jayavar was forced backward, nearly slipping once again on the bloody deck. Another Cham joined in the assault and Jayavar desperately protected himself with both his shield and sword. His foes came at him again and again, and it took all of his strength and savvy to stay alive. He knocked aside one sword stroke only to find that the stout man was lunging forward, his blade parallel to the deck. The thrust would have disemboweled him, but Asal disengaged from his fight with Indravarman so that he could parry the blade of Jayavar's attacker, smashing the Cham's sword down with his own. Jayavar stumbled. Two of his men stepped in front of him, and as he got to his feet, he couldn't help but watch Asal fight against the stout Cham.

Though Jayavar had prayed for strength, it seemed that if divine intervention had taken place then surely the power had been given to Asal, for he fought with extraordinary fury and skill. He screamed a battle cry, his sword a blur, his shield battering men aside. The stout Cham was struck twice before his face even registered shock, and as the dying warrior hit the deck, Asal engaged his next foe, pressing forward like a storm assailing a forest of old trees. The trees split and shattered, swayed and fell. Asal dodged them as they toppled, shouting Indravarman's name, once again fighting toward him, the dead and dying in his wake.

Jayavar offered a prayer of gratitude for Asal's delivery. He then tried to reenter the melee, but a line of his own men moved to separate him from the combatants. Swords clanged, smoke drifted, and arrows whistled. Yet Jayavar had eyes only for Asal, because the Cham continued to fight as if he were not one man but five, scattering his enemies, barely pausing when a spear thudded into his battered shield.

The Khmer king pushed his men aside and fought forward to reach his new ally, longing to help him. But in his haste to reach Asal, Jayavar didn't notice the tall Cham with the trident held aloft. The trident was bloody, and held high, pointing at Asal's back.

Jayavar finally spotted the threat. He started to cry out a warning, but something hammered into his side, knocking the breath from his lungs. He gasped, managed to kill his attacker, but his voice was gone.

The threat went unchallenged.

When Asal had first seen Indravarman, all reason had left him. His sole thought was of revenge, not for his own torture, but for the threat against Voisanne. He had fought in a way that he hadn't known was possible, his sword and shield vicious predators that seemed to act on their own volition. Men faced him and died. Others leapt from the boat rather than endure the steel in his hand. Though he had always been a fierce fighter, on this day his fury had made him much more lethal.

Once again Indravarman met him near the center of the boat. The Cham king held a shield in his left hand and the massive war axe in his right. The shield was barely marred, while both sides of the axe were bloodied. Indravarman cursed Asal, boasted that he would have his woman, and then attacked, swinging his axe in a blow that would have felled a horse. Asal blocked the strike, but his shield splintered and his arm went numb. Still, he didn't pause or back away, but chopped down with his sword, surprising Indravarman with his speed and strength. The king managed to knock the blow aside with his own shield. Chams pressed forward to help Indravarman, but Jayavar and a few men engaged them.

Asal threw himself at his larger adversary, his sword striking from unexpected angles, his half-ruined shield managing to keep the big axe at bay. The combatants forced all other men aside. No one wanted to interfere; to engage either man would be to die. Asal and Indravarman fought and raged, both strong and quick, experienced and wise. Not a warrior on either side could have wielded the axe as Indravarman did, for he swung the heavy weapon as if it were a child's toy. His shield in tatters, Asal tried to avoid the axe rather than cast it aside. He spun on his toes, seeming to dance on the bloody deck, twisting to one side or the other as the steel pursued his flesh.

His breath now ragged, his chest heaving, Asal tried to counterattack, but Indravarman was amazingly quick. The two warriors came together, weapons locking. They strained against each other, their heads and shoulders banging, their sweat and blood mingling.

"You betrayed me," Indravarman said through clenched teeth.

"Gladly . . . Lord King."

"Your whore shall—"

"No!" Asal shouted, thrusting himself forward, smashing his forehead into Indravarman's nose. Blood sprayed and the king howled in pain, stepping back. Asal disengaged his blade from the axe and stabbed it forward. His lunge missed, but he continued to press against Indravarman with all of his strength, forcing the king back. Asal struck again and felt his weapon bite into flesh. Indravarman screamed.

Seeing that their king was in mortal danger, other Chams jumped into the fray. Asal countered one sword stroke, heard Jayavar shout a warning, and managed to turn aside Po Rame's trident with a desperate flick of his shield. One of the trident's barbs stuck in the wood, gouging Asal's forearm.

Indravarman regained his balance and smashed the flat of his axe into Asal, who stumbled, his back striking the gunwale. Pinpricks of light danced in his vision. His breath seemed to catch in his throat. He felt himself tipping toward the water.

Po Rame leapt through the air, a dagger in his right hand. Somehow Asal caught his wrist, halting the blow. Yet the assassin's momentum pushed Asal backward, over the gunwale. Both men twisted head over heels and then struck the water.

Asal clutched Po Rame's wrist. But he was deep in the brown water, unable to see or think or breathe.

Po Rame smashed his knee into Asal's belly. Involuntarily, Asal cried out, water entering his lungs. He choked and gagged, thrashing desperately now, the end approaching more quickly than he had imagined.

Though distracted by the battle raging around her, Voisanne managed to maintain a nearly constant supply of arrows for the queen. Ajadevi wasn't a great archer, but she had been pouring a steady barrage of arrows onto a nearby vessel dominated by Chams. The enemy fired back, and arrows thudded into the wood near the two women. When the bolts didn't bite deeply enough into the deck or hull, Voisanne was able to wrench them free and hand them to Ajadevi, who promptly took aim and fired. Since she had so many men to target, her strikes often resulted in curses and screams.

Ajadevi seemed fearless of the arrows that whistled past her, but Voisanne was unnerved by the danger. She had insisted that Chaya remain with the children, who crouched behind a wall of shields. Several of the children had already lost mothers or fathers, and Voisanne was proud of Chaya as she tried to comfort the young.

Whenever she ran to retrieve an arrow, Voisanne glanced at the ship that held Asal. She hadn't seen him yet but couldn't stop looking for him, even when her queen shouted at her to hurry. Ajadevi was also desperate for news of the fight, as Jayavar was in the thick of it. But if she didn't keep the nearby boat at bay with her arrows, its men would board their craft and either cut their throats or ravish them. So Voisanne collected arrows, gave updates on the fighting, and tried not to notice her queen's tears.

Everything changed for Voisanne when she finally glimpsed Asal. She saw his sword rise and fall like a farmer's hoe as he battled Indravarman. The Cham king reeled backward. A smaller man leapt at Asal, and Voisanne cried out when he and this new foe struggled, then fell into the water and disappeared. Without thought, she jumped overboard, an arrow still in her right hand. She swam with all of her strength, frantic with worry. She imagined Asal in pain, in darkness, and the thought of his terror propelled her on, past the limits of her own exhaustion. Though pieces of smoldering wood bobbed on the surface, she kept pushing her way ahead, calling out his name between breaths of air.

She neared the boat. The water in front of her was thrust up as a stranger's head appeared. He gasped for air, then went under again. Voisanne kicked as hard as she could, opening her eyes underwater. Though everything was dim, she saw a flash of steel.

Asal's face appeared next, his mouth open, his teeth bared. She could see more clearly now and realized that the two men were fighting over a knife. Asal was beneath his adversary, pinned deep. Voisanne swam toward the back of the slighter Cham. She neared him, unseen. Holding the shaft of the arrow, she thrust it forward with all of her strength. The steel-tipped point bit deeply into the flesh beneath his right shoulder blade and she heard a muffled shriek. The knife twisted in her direction, but she didn't defend herself from it, continuing to push harder on the arrow, to thrust it deeper into her enemy. Asal lunged for the knife, turning it away from her, changing its direction and plunging it into the man's side. He screamed as the water turned red. He tried to fight, but Asal was stronger, and the blade struck again and again. The Cham shuddered and shrieked, bubbles escaping his mouth. His eyes widened; his movements stilled. He convulsed one last time, then seemed to turn into a statue, sinking down, his pained features frozen and unchanging.

Voisanne pulled Asal after her, kicking hard toward the surface. They broke through, into the light. He coughed, gagged, and was finally able to draw air into his lungs.

She held his face in her hands, told him that he was finished fighting, that he was coming with her. He didn't resist, and she pulled him away from the madness, toward a place where the swells seemed to shimmer.

Though Soriya was no warrior, she could see that the battle was reaching its climax. It seemed that men on both sides fought with renewed fury. Boats collided and capsized, men struggled against one another in the water, and war cries were exchanged. She prayed for the safety of Boran and Vibol, and then saw an arrow slicing through the air, heading directly toward Prak. Instinctively she leaned in front of him and grunted as the arrow slammed into her chest. The pain was ferocious, but she opened her eyes, worried that Prak had also been struck. Yet he hadn't. His skin was unmarred. His face bore no pain.

She slipped to her knees, grunting.

"Mother!" he cried out, dropping down beside her.

A burning agony tore through her, as if someone had poured hot oil down her throat. She wanted to run from the pain, to find a place of shelter, but each breath added to her misery.

"No," Prak muttered, his hands following the arrow to her chest. "No, Mother. It can't be. Please, no."

She heard the terror in his voice, which pulled her from her pain and into his. "It's . . . nothing."

"It's not nothing! You've been hurt! I can feel your blood!"

"My blood . . . your blood."

"What are you talking about? What are you saying?"

"You're . . . my son. My beautiful boy."

"Stop!"

She tried to control her thoughts, her words, but struggled to breathe. A haze seemed to envelop her. She glimpsed the sun, then his face. "It . . . hardly hurts," she lied.

He ripped up a piece of cloth and pressed it near where the arrow emerged from her chest, trying to stop the bleeding. "What should I do?" he asked, desperation in his every word. "Tell me what to do!"

"Just . . . hold me. As I held you."

His mouth moved, but for once she didn't focus on his voice. She knew that her time was short. Whatever she said next would have to matter, would have to last, because he would carry her words for the rest of his days.

And so she thought as the sights grew dim around her. She thought about what to say.

*   *   *

Jayavar had shouted out to Asal in the moment before the tall
Cham had attacked. Though his warning had saved Asal from
the initial strike, it hadn't come soon enough to keep him from
being forced overboard. Jayavar had wanted to rush to his aid,
but Indravarman was badly wounded, his thigh gushing blood.
The Cham king would never be more vulnerable than he was at
that moment.

Raising his sword, Jayavar rushed forward, desperate to attack
Indravarman before his men regrouped around him. The Khmer's
blade whipped down but was cast aside at the last instant by the
shaft of Indravarman's axe. Yet Jayavar had the advantage of surprise, and he reversed his sweep, bringing his sword back, dragging it along Indravarman's side. His blade sliced through the
king's quilted armor and bit deeply into his flesh. Indravarman
roared in pain. He swung wildly with his axe, trying to decapi-
tate Jayavar, but the Khmer king ducked beneath the blow, attacking again, aware that the fate of his kingdom rested on this
moment. He brought the hilt of his sword up, striking the underside of Indravarman's chin. Again the blow was not fatal, but
blood flowed, and Indravarman stumbled backward, trying to
protect himself, to flee from the Khmer's sword.

On another day, against another man, Jayavar might have
asked his adversary to lay down his weapon and surrender. But
not on this day, not against this man. He pressed ahead, swinging and striking. The axe fell from Indravarman's fingers. With
one last, frantic motion, the Cham king smashed his shield into
Jayavar's chest. The blow sent Jayavar stumbling backward, but
even so, he brought his sword down with all of his strength and
focus, its end biting deeply into Indravarman's shoulder.

The Cham fell to the deck, weaponless and defenseless. For a moment it seemed that his men would rush forward to protect him, but the remaining Khmers beat them back with a sudden burst of fury. Sensing the inevitable loss of their king, several Chams, rather than fight to the death, leapt off the side of the boat. Those remaining regrouped and tried to battle toward their king, but Jayavar shouted at his warriors to keep them back. Men fought, screamed, and died. Aware of their looming victory, the Khmers attacked with vast strength and resolve, driving the Chams away. A space cleared around the two kings. For the moment, their confrontation was uninterrupted.

Jayavar stepped toward Indravarman, his sword leveled. "You're no man," he said, his chest heaving. "You put my children to death. And that makes you less than human, less than an animal—a mere thing to be stepped on in the jungle."

Indravarman spat out blood. "Yet I took what was yours . . . and made it mine."

"Like a common thief."

"I'm a king!" Indravarman roared, trying to get up.

Surprised by his enemy's sudden defiance, Jayavar leaned forward, the tip of his sword pressing against Indravarman's neck. "Even now, your men desert you," he replied, motioning toward Chams who were jumping off the boat and swimming away. "Men don't desert true kings."

"You're weak, Jayavar. You shall always be weak."

Jayavar shook his head. "I shall make war on no kingdom that doesn't make war on me. Perhaps that makes me weak. But I care not. My people will be free. Your reign here will be remembered as nothing more than a speck of dust against an infinite sky."

"We're all dust, Jayavar. The Gods blow us from place to place."

"And had you let my children live, I would show you mercy. I would let the Gods blow you where they wish."

"Your children had to die. You know that."

"I know nothing of the kind," Jayavar replied, biting his lip, the faces of his loved ones blossoming before him. "But they've come back to me. I feel them now. I sense them now. Who will you go to, man of dust, once you're dead?"

Jayavar turned to several of his warriors, who were battered and bloody. "Take from him whatever he took from you."

Indravarman shouted as the Khmers fell upon him. He shouted for help that did not come, and later, for mercy that made no appearance. In the end, when he could do nothing but whimper, he was held up to show his countrymen that he was vanquished. Then the warriors threw him from the boat.

Khmers around Jayavar began to cheer, prompting the battle to ebb. A few Cham officers on other boats tried to rally their troops, but with Indravarman gone, no leader had enough authority or respect to take control of the remaining warriors. Chams began to flee the fighting, swimming toward unbroken vessels still captained by their countrymen. The Khmers let these warriors go, continuing to celebrate, shouting triumphantly and holding their banners high. The Cham officers were killed, their pleas silenced.

Jayavar's knees almost buckled. But he forced himself to stand tall as he scanned the horizon for Ajadevi, searching for the one person who would make this victory complete.

The pain in Soriya's chest subsided even as her vision blurred and the world grew dim. The sound of cheering drifted to her, echoes of celebration. Prak held her head on his lap, careful of the arrow still sticking from her chest as he cradled her. He explained that the Chams were retreating. He wept as he spoke, blaming himself for her injury, certain that if he had been able to see he would have warned her of the danger.

"You've seen . . . your whole life," she whispered, holding his hand with her own, her mind clear even as her body shut down.

"But the arrow. It should have hit me. I—"

"A mother . . . should die before her son."

"Why?"

She thought about bringing him into the world, about holding him to her breast and smiling at his hunger. "Because my hopes, my dreams . . . they lie with you."

"We should never have traveled here. Vibol was wrong."

"No. He was right. We're free. And I . . . I'd trade my life for your freedom."

"I wouldn't."

"Someday . . . when you're a father . . . you'll understand. You'd do the same." She shifted on Prak's lap, thinking about how she had held him so many nights, just as he now held her. "I've always been poor, my son," she whispered. "But you've made me feel rich."

His tears fell to her face. "You should save your strength. Father and Vibol will be here soon. They will find us."

"I know. They live. Tell them . . . of my love for them."

"You tell them. Please."

Something seemed to stick in her throat, and she found it hard to bring enough air into her lungs. She reached for his face, tracing his features, recognizing herself and Boran within him. "Death . . . should be sad. But when I see you . . . I'm happy."

"Please don't die, Mother. You can't die."

"My perfect boy. My son. How you make me proud."

He bent down, holding her against him, weeping freely now, his sobs mingling with the distant cheers. "You make me proud," he replied.

She smiled, needing to rest, her breathing more difficult, her thoughts more disconnected. She saw herself as a girl, running through the jungle, chasing someone. How had the years passed so quickly? How had she traveled so very far? Would she now journey to those who had gone before her?

"I'll come back . . . to all of you," she whispered.

"How . . . how will we see you? What should we look for?"

"Listen."

"To what?"

"To whatever sounds . . . you hold most dear. And play your flute. Let me hear you."

He hugged her again, his tears falling on her cheeks.

For a while longer she saw him, but soon he started to fade. She whispered his name, then the names of Vibol and Boran, envisioning each of their faces, reminding herself of their beauty so that she could find her way back to them.

Her journey began.

*C*linging to a wooden plank not far from an undamaged boat, Voisanne and Asal watched in disbelief as the Cham army retreated. On the nearby vessel, Khmers and Siamese warriors celebrated. Some hugged one another while others cast aside their weapons and leapt into the water.

Voisanne didn't trust her own eyes. Surely the battle could not be over. The Chams would soon regroup and attack again. "Where . . . where are they going?" she asked, her forearm touching Asal's atop the plank.

"Home."

"But they will come back. With more men."

He shook his head. "Perhaps someday. But most of my people didn't want this war. Indravarman willed us to come here. With him gone . . . I think the others will stay within our borders."

She reached up to touch a shallow wound on his cheek. "When I saw you fall . . . I saw my world collapse."

"You saved me, my lady."

"No, I only helped."

He put a cupped hand to his lips and drank. "You did more than that. You risked everything for me—your former captor, your former enemy."

Thinking of him fighting against his countrymen, she bit her lower lip. "How can you be so gentle and loving . . . and so ferocious?"

"Because of you."

"Me?"

"All I want is you. But to gain you, I needed ferocity."

"But what about power? Or wealth? Men seek such things."

He smiled. "Not I, my lady. I covet you and you only."

"And daughters. I know you want a daughter."

"Daughters and sons. A family. Why would I need anything else? If the Gods grant me such blessings, I shall be forever grateful."

She leaned forward to kiss him. Their lips touched and the world disappeared. She didn't hear the cheering or feel a cut on her hand. But she imagined things. She saw him as a father, saw herself weaving the stem of a flower into their daughter's hair.

"We won," she whispered, still kissing him. "I don't know how we did it, but we won."

"Yes, my lady. We did. A Khmer and a Cham. We won together."

Two boats approached each other. Both were full of the dead, but also of the living. Covered in blood, bowed but not broken, Ajadevi sat near one craft's bow holding a crude bandage against a woman's forehead. She watched Jayavar's vessel approach. He stood at the bow, both hands wrapped around a staff that supported the banner of Angkor Wat. The banner fluttered in the breeze, unsullied by the battle.

Though Ajadevi tried to hold back her tears, her relief at seeing Jayavar alive was too much for her. She shuddered, quietly weeping, amazed and honored that they both still lived. How he had survived was nothing short of a miracle. Her prayers must have been heeded, her longings heard and fulfilled. The Cham officer was a gift from above, she knew, for she had watched him fight, had seen how his sword had changed the course of the battle. She could live a thousand more lifetimes and still lack the time to fully repay him.

The bows of the two boats touched. Khmers cheered as their king and queen were reunited.

Ajadevi thanked their audience for their sacrifices, meaning each word. Then she stepped forward to embrace her battered husband, holding him tight and not letting go.

By the time Boran and Vibol found Prak on board a heavily damaged boat, the lump on Boran's head had shrunken. His thoughts were again clear, his stance steady. He held on to Vibol with vigor, but when he saw the look on Prak's face, he knew immediately what had happened. He suddenly felt as if he were falling, as if a gaping hole had opened up inside of him. His knees buckled and he dropped to the deck.

Tears rolled down his cheeks. He closed his eyes, trying to find her, to sense her. But all he felt was the terrible emptiness within him.

She was gone.

Twenty-four

Rebirth

A day and a half later, as the air warmed in the mid-morning, Boran, Vibol, and Prak stood on the shoreline of a wide river. A cove provided flat, calm water ideal for lotus flowers, and they grew in abundance, their reflections in the water as graceful and colorful as the flowers themselves. The cove wasn't far from their old home and had been one of Soriya's favorite places. She'd once swum among the flowers, rested on the shore, and watched her sons play in the shallows.

Remembering these moments, Boran studied the lotus flowers, a tear rolling down his cheek. In many ways, this place reminded him of his wife—its simple and understated beauty, its quiet strength. They had also come here as young lovers and spoken eagerly of the days ahead, of their dreams of having a home and family of their own. He hadn't been able to promise her wealth or comfort, but she had not asked for such things. She had wanted only to live a peaceful, contented life.

Turning to where her washed and perfumed body lay atop a

pile of nearby branches, Boran wanted to fall to his knees and weep. But he had to stay strong for his sons, and so he walked, trembling, to her side. She was positioned at waist level, and he reached out, his fingers tracing the contours of her face. He couldn't imagine her face leaving him, vanishing from his life like raindrops on a warm stone. His fingers paused at her lips, and he suddenly wished that he had kissed them more often, that he hadn't wasted so many moments away from her. He'd been a fool.

Though he tried to keep his emotions under control, he wept as he felt her face, the curves of her shoulders, the frailty of her hands. His sons moved to either side of him, but he felt only her, touching her as he wished he could every day for the rest of his life. He found it hard to breathe, to stand.

Leaning forward, he kissed her brow, then adjusted the iris in her hair, his tears falling to her cheeks. He and his sons had scattered flowers over her entire body, offering her one of the few gifts that she had ever given herself.

Boran closed his eyes, praying that she had already started to follow the path to rebirth, that she was headed in his direction.

When he finished praying, Boran turned to Vibol and Prak. "She . . . died for all of us," he said quietly. "So honor her by living your lives as she would want. Let her see your joy."

His sons nodded, their cheeks glistening with tears.

"And she'll be watching," he continued. "She always watched over you. Nothing will change."

The wind stirred, causing the flowers to quiver. He didn't want them to blow away from her, and so he kissed her once more and stepped back. Vibol and Prak said their farewells, their tears as numerous as his. They held her hand and kissed her cheek.

Underneath the pyre was a mound of dried moss. Vibol went to his knees, carefully dropping some hot coals that he had carried in a stone bowl. The coals fell onto the moss, and he blew against them, causing them to redden and ignite. The moss turned brown, smoked, and he stepped back as a small flame caught.

The fire trembled at first, like a new life emerging from the womb. Then it spread, consuming the smaller twigs, then larger branches. Though the heat was soon strong, Boran remained standing close to the flames. He watched her face, aware that he would never touch another woman as he had touched her. She would return to him in some way, and when he felt her presence he would find peace once again.

He reached for his sons' hands. He held them with strength, squeezing hard, watching the flames grow. Finally they were forced to step away from the inferno.

Boran had always expected that he would die first, that she'd be the one left with their sons. He had not prepared himself for this moment, for the years when he would be old, when he would care for his grandchildren while his boys and their wives labored.

"Your mother . . . she taught me well," he whispered, squeezing their hands again. "I watched her with you both. And I'll be there for you both." He cleared his throat, which was dry and seemed filled with soot. "And she'll be there too. I know she will."

Prak turned toward him. "You won't be alone either, Father. I promise."

The flames rose. Prak raised his flute with trembling hands. At first his notes were unsteady, but he managed to play a song that she had favored. As he played, an updraft of wind sent ashes skyward. Some flowers, still untouched by the fire, were lifted from her body. They swirled above the flames, and though most fell back down to be consumed, one small white orchid dropped between the brothers. Vibol reached out with cupped hands and caught it. At first he didn't seem sure what to do with it, merely staring at its trembling petals.

Vibol had hardly spoken since his mother's death, and Boran knew that he blamed himself for her passing. Putting his hand on his child's shoulder, he asked, "Do you see, my son? She is with us."

"No," Vibol replied, weeping.

"She is."

"It's my fault. It's all my fault."

"But you're holding her right now. She wouldn't go to you . . . if she blamed you."

Vibol stared at the flower, reverently touching its petals. He began to shudder, his hands shaking, his chest heaving.

Boran reached for his sons, drawing them against him. They put their arms around him, and he promised them that they would be happy, that somehow the flower gave him hope. He had sensed her presence when he least expected to, when her body was an inferno, when she was being taken from him. Her body was leaving, but she was not. She was within him, within them all.

They wept together, huddled close, seeking and receiving comfort in one another's grasp. Vibol continued to cradle the flower, to hold it near his chest. "Are you sure?" he finally asked, his voice barely audible.

Boran nodded. Though he still ached and wept, he saw the flower as a sign. She was nearby. A part of her lingered.

He knew then that they would build their home right there, right beneath their feet. They would plant flowers where her body had once burned, and one day laughter would return to them, children would splash in the shadows, and life would grow and blossom.

And then, someday, when all was well with his sons, he would follow her. He would feel himself being carried away by the wind as she had been. He would soar up, looking down on his loved ones, savoring each and every memory, cherishing the bond that would forever keep them together.

His sons were free now. They were safe.

Knowing that, she would rest in peace. And someday he would rest beside her.

Later that day, outside the walls of Angkor Wat, thousands of Khmers celebrated King Jayavar's victory. Despite the distant commotion, within the Echo Chamber all was silent. Asal and Voisanne stood beside each other, hands together, backs pressed against the stone. They beat their chests, heard the distant bells, and sent their prayers of thanks upward.

Both smiled.

"I am blessed," Voisanne said, "that so many of Chaya's friends are still alive. She's overjoyed to be with them."

Asal nodded, still disbelieving that everything had led to this moment, that his dreams had come to fruition. He had expected to die, either with Voisanne or without her. Yet now he stood holding her hand, trying to convince himself that all of it wasn't an illusion, that somehow he had emerged from so many horrors and miseries into a place of beauty and contentment.

"As I told you once," he said, speaking quietly, "when I first came here, I looked up at Angkor Wat, and was so . . . so swept up in its majesty and its magic that I knew Khmers must be a good and noble people. To create such towers, such wonders, one would need a pure heart."

"It's true."

"But what I did not know, my lady, what I did not expect, was that I would fall in love with a Khmer, with a woman who would make me feel more alive than I ever had."

504   John Shors

She brought his hand to her lips, kissing it. "And what are we to do now that the war is over?" She kissed his hand again, then gently bit the knuckle of his thumb. "Will you grow bored with me now that you don't have to save me?"

"Perhaps," he teased.

Voisanne laughed, pushing against him. "Is that all you can say?"

"No."

"Why are you suddenly so quiet? Where has my brave Cham gone?"

His heartbeat quickened. He started to speak, stopped, and then smiled. "I'd like to ask you something. A question I've never asked before, nor do I expect ever to ask it again."

"What?"

He took her hands in his own, facing her. "It pleases me to call you 'my lady.' But it would please me much, much more to call you 'my wife.' Will you share your life with me, Voisanne?" He bowed his head to her. "Nothing would make me more contented than if your face was the first and the last thing I saw each day."

She rose to her tiptoes, pulling herself up against him, kissing his lips. "But I'll be the last to close my eyes. I won't want to leave you. Not even to sleep."

"So it's 'yes'?"

"It's 'yes' a thousand times over."

Without another thought, he picked her up so that she still faced him, his arms wrapped around her thighs. She felt so light in his grasp, yet she was the most powerful force in his life. He would die for her, devote the rest of his life to her.

"I want to shout," he said, grinning. "To shout my thanks to the Gods."

"So do. Let them hear you."

He stared into the blackness above, aware of something building within him, a surging joy the likes of which he had never felt or imagined. Its strength was more potent than the rage of battle, the fear of death. It continued to build, gathering within his soul, igniting unknown fires within him. The joy lifted him upward, bringing him closer to the Gods than he had ever been.

And he didn't need to raise his voice, to shout out loud, because the Gods knew what he thought, what he felt.

They rejoiced in the heavens together.

Near the top of Angkor Wat, Jayavar and Ajadevi stood beside each other and stared out at their city. Khmers of all backgrounds and ages had come to the immense grounds outside the temple to celebrate. People feasted, sang, prayed, and banded together to pull down any trace of the Cham occupation. The banners that had accompanied the victors to battle hung from many homes and even the towers of distant temples.

Ajadevi glanced toward the utmost summit of Angkor Wat, which glowed in the setting sun. Her gaze traveled in all directions, taking in the temple's wondrous sights and then falling to the moat, settling on throngs of people who lined its shores or swam in its waters. She sensed the unity of her people, and her pride in them swelled.

She turned to Jayavar, who wore the golden sword of his father and a colorful hip cloth that depicted a variety of flowers set against a green background. Precious jewels dangled from his neck and wrists. He hadn't wanted to dress in such a manner, but she had insisted. To rule as a king, he must look like a king.

The platform that supported them was empty of any other person. Soon they would join in the celebration, but for the moment, they wanted only each other's company. They stood facing the setting sun and holding hands.

"The Chams are gone," Jayavar said, nodding toward the north, remembering how he had led his army back to Angkor, seized the war elephants, and driven the remaining Chams from his land. "Our scouts tell me that the few Chams who survived our attacks have fled in disarray."

"Yet you shall have to prepare for their return."

"Yes, but what do the signs tell you? What do you see in our future?"

She looked toward the sun. Its face wasn't the hue of blood, but a much lighter color, almost the shade of gold. "I see a potent Khmer army. I see strength. I also see peace and prosperity."

"Good," he replied, smiling. "Because we've wasted enough of ourselves on destruction. Now it is time to build."

"Tell me what you will build."

"Roads and hospitals, temples and gardens. I want to feed our hungry, cure our sick. I long for our land to be remembered throughout the ages as one of the noblest that ever existed." He smiled again, laughing at himself. "Simple tasks, I know."

"And you? What do you covet for yourself?"

"What I covet, I already have," he replied, his eyes locked on hers. "All my other desires are for my people—and for you."

She traced the outline of a silk bandage on his forearm. "And your heir?"

"If an heir is born, Nuon shall raise him. But you and I shall teach him. We'll teach him and love him."

Nodding, she repeated his last words to herself, feeling warmth spread within her. "We should go. The people await you. And Bona has asked to take you hunting."

"He makes me happy."

She started to turn, but Jayavar reached for her hand.

"Wait," he said. "Just until the sun sets."

"Why?"

"Because it shall be beautiful. And I want to share all such beauty with you."

A smile graced her lips, and she moved closer to him. The sun touched the horizon, swelling, spreading its colors across rolling hills, upon faraway towers. The colors grew richer, almost as if a divine spirit was painting the landscape.

"Stay with me forever," he said.

"I shall," she replied, reaching for his face, knowing that she would.

Author's Note

While much is unknown about those who inhabited ancient Angkor, this much is true: In 1177, the Cham king, Jaya Indravarman IV, led a surprise attack against the Khmers. Though Jaya Indravarman's victory was resounding, Prince Jayavarman VII and his beloved wife, Jayarajadevi, avoided capture. For the sake of my story, I simplified their names and condensed their time spent in hiding. In reality, it took them four years to gather an army.

After defeating the Chams in an epic battle on the Great Lake, Jayavarman and Jayarajadevi returned to Angkor, where they oversaw an unprecedented revival and ultimate expansion of their empire. Roads, hospitals, and canals were built, as well as Bayon, a marvelous temple dominated by carvings of Hindu Gods and the smiling faces of Buddha.

To this day, Angkor Wat remains majestic and noble, dominating the landscape as if it were the mountains that its builders tried to re-create. From Angkor Wat to Kbal Spean to the Great Lake, one can still walk where Jayavarman and Jayarajadevi walked, exploring the gifts that they left to the world, imagining times long since past but not forgotten.

Acknowledgments

Temple of a Thousand Faces is my sixth novel, and in some ways it was the most difficult to write. Everything about Angkor Wat is epic, and my book needed to reflect those dimensions, to reincarnate a story that was nearly lost in the passage of time. Yet precious little historical record was available, so I had to rely on my wanderings within Angkor and my imagination to create this novel. I hope I've done justice to the people and culture that thrived so long ago.

The opportunity to create *Temple of a Thousand Faces* would not have been possible without the steadfast support of my wife, Allison, and our children, Sophie and Jack. I'm so proud of each of you, and am blessed that you comprise such a large part of my life.

I'd like to express my gratitude toward my agent and friend, Laura Dail, who encouraged me to once again create a piece of historical fiction. Ellen Edwards, my superb editor, worked tirelessly on *Temple of a Thousand Faces*, enhancing the plot and the writing. I'm also grateful to my parents, John and Patsy Shors; my brothers, Tom, Matt, and Luke; as well as Mary and Doug Barakat, Bruce McPherson, Dustin O'Regan, Amy Tan, Sandra Gulland, Pennie Ianniciello, Pheng Pouk, Sery Sok Thea, Darlene Smoliak, Serena Agusto-Cox, Louise Jolly, Dom Testa, Julie

Dugdale, Jon Craine, Brigitte Bednar, Beth Lowe, Shawna Sharp, Bliss Darragh, Diane Saarinen, Chris Doyle of the Adventure Travel Trade Association, and the delightful staff at the gorgeous Heritage Suites Hotel in Siem Reap.

To everyone in Cambodia who made me feel so welcome— thank you.

And finally, please know, dear reader, that I also greatly appreciate your support. In honor of you, and everyone else who has helped me, a portion of the funds generated from *Temple of a Thousand Faces* will be donated to the Jayavarman VII Children's Hospital. This wonderful hospital, only a few minutes' drive from Angkor Wat, provides free treatment to children in need.

Photo by Jim Barbour

John Shors is the bestselling author of *Beneath a Marble Sky*, *Beside a Burning Sea*, *Dragon House*, *The Wishing Trees*, *Cross Currents*, and *Temple of a Thousand Faces*. He has won numerous awards for his writing, and his novels have been translated into twenty-six languages.

John lives in Boulder, Colorado, with his wife and two children, and he encourages reader feedback.

CONNECT ONLINE

www.johnshors.com
facebook.com/johnshors

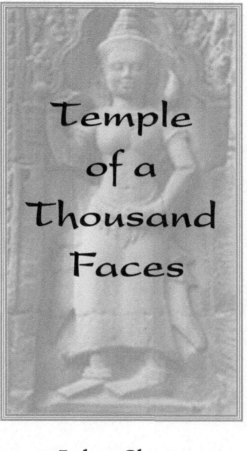

Temple
of a
Thousand
Faces

John Shors

A CONVERSATION WITH JOHN SHORS

Q. Temple of a Thousand Faces *is your sixth novel, and yet it most closely resembles your first book,* Beneath a Marble Sky. *Why did you decide to return to historical fiction?*

A. Many readers asked me to write a sequel to *Beneath a Marble Sky*, my novel about the building of the Taj Mahal. I certainly considered writing such a book, but at the end of the day I decided that I had already brought the Taj Mahal to life, as I had intended to. The story that I had wanted to tell had been told. However, the concept of once again writing about a special place and culture intrigued me. I started exploring possibilities and ultimately learned about the remarkable tale of Jayavarman VII and Jayarajadevi. I knew that I had discovered a story that excited me.

Q. Can you describe your experience at Angkor Wat?

A. Angkor Wat is a magical place. It's located just a few miles from Siem Reap, Cambodia—a small city that has sprung up to accommodate the tourists who travel to Angkor Wat. Siem Reap is less than an hour's flight from Bangkok, and is easily accessible. The landscape around this vibrant city is lush and tropical. One can get from Siem Reap to Angkor Wat in a car or bus, but many tourists opt to ride on a motorcycle taxi of some sort, often behind the driver or in a comfortable cart attached to the back of the motorcycle.

Angkor Wat is extraordinary in so many ways—its sheer size, the vast number of statues, and the intricacy of the carvings are all quite compelling. The temple is in remarkably good condition, a testament to its engineers and builders. Though one is free to wander about without having to worry about rules and regulations (a philosophy that has its drawbacks since not all tourists are respectful), the site does attract a lot of visitors, so in order to deeply understand the spirit of the place, and to imagine my characters there, I explored the temple when most tourists were back at their hotels—mainly during the heat of the day. The hotter it was, the fewer people were there, and the happier I became. A few times it seemed as if I were the only person present. That's when the temple came alive for me. I stood in the Echo Chamber, where the amplification of every sound created the impression that I was listening to my very thoughts. I climbed to the temple's summit and beheld the beautiful landscape spread out below me. And I imagined what I was seeing as it might have been nearly a thousand years ago.

Q. How important is hands-on research to your writing process?

A. I certainly could not have written *Temple of a Thousand Faces* if I hadn't explored the Angkor region on my own. I had read about certain places there—Kbal Spean, for instance—so I had an idea of where I wanted various parts of the novel to occur. But seeing things with my own eyes enlightened me in so many ways. Again, using Kbal Spean as an example, traveling into the Cambodian countryside to visit the site changed my perspective in many ways. I walked through the thick jungle to find Kbal Spean, which was discovered only a few decades ago, and felt as if I were on a movie set. Standing below immense trees and listening to monkeys scurry about the heights, I studied how the small river flowed over the ancient carvings. As time passed, I increasingly appreciated the wonder of the place. I hope that this appreciation can be felt by readers. My goal is always to bring settings to life on the page, to in a sense turn a setting into a character. Studying a place firsthand is an integral part of that process for me.

Q. *The Khmer civilization flourished over centuries. Why did you write about this particular moment in time?*

A. Once I decided to write about Angkor Wat, I read about the Khmer Empire from its origins to its demise. I was looking for what I thought was the most interesting period within that empire's history. I settled on the story of Jayavarman VII and Jayarajadevi for several reasons. First, I was fascinated by how they managed to rebuild an army and retake all that had been stolen from them. Second, I admired their deep reliance on each other. I believe it was the strength of their relationship that allowed them to succeed in reclaiming their kingdom.

Q. *You just discussed two characters who are modeled after real people. Now talk about some of the characters you fabricated.*

A. Well, Asal and Voisanne come to mind first. I created Asal because I wanted to show that Chams weren't necessarily the villains of this story or of this history. Khmers and Chams struggled against each other for many generations. Since I re-created this conflict from the sympathetic point of view of the Khmers, I conceived Asal to add balance to that perspective. Voisanne embodies the characteristics of the women I met in Cambodia—strong, clever, witty, and hospitable.

Q. Why did you decide to tell the story of Boran, Soriya, Prak, and Vibol?

A. Much of *Temple of a Thousand Faces* is centered on the trials and triumphs of powerful people. While I enjoyed bringing these characters to life, I also wanted to tell the stories of typical Khmers. Farmers, weavers, priests, and fishermen were extremely important to Khmer society. I decided to create a family that relied on fishing because it would be reasonable to include them in the battle on the Great Lake, and I wanted to show that everyday Khmers played an essential role in driving the Chams from Angkor.

Q. What was the hardest part about writing Temple of a Thousand Faces?

A. Throughout my career as a novelist, I've researched a variety of ancient cultures. One commonality among these different groups is that people seemed to speak more eloquently than we do today. It doesn't seem to matter if a person lived in sixteenth-century India, medieval England, or twelfth-century Cambodia—the manner in which they addressed their friends and loved ones was often more formal than the language we use today. I wanted to re-create some of this formality without going too far and slowing down the story. Finding the proper balance was a challenge. I hope I've created distinctive voices that readers will enjoy.

Q. It seems that many writers find a subject matter and tend to stick with it, or close to it, book after book. In your case, three of your novels have been works of historical fiction and three have had contemporary settings. Why have you bounced back and forth?

A. I'm not terribly interested in writing the same book over and over. To keep things fresh for me (and I hope for my readers), I try to identify what I think will be a compelling story. If that story occurs seventy years ago in the South Pacific, so be it. If it occurs a few years ago in Thailand, that also works. All my books are set in exotic places and centered on cultures that might not be well-known. I have always enjoyed discovering distant lands through the pages of a memorable novel. That passion has played a large part in what I write and why I write.

Q. Speaking of a passion for writing, what did you like most about the process of writing Temple of a Thousand Faces?

A. Trying to re-create the wonders of Angkor Wat was difficult, but quite gratifying. I wanted to bring the grandeur of the temple back to life and to populate the world around it with characters whom the reader would come to enjoy. Working on the initial draft, while probably the hardest part of the whole process, often left me daydreaming about my characters and the land that they inhabited. As a writer, I enjoy getting swept up in my own story.

Q. What finally happened to the Khmer Empire?

A. According to many historians, the city of Angkor thrived until about the middle of the fourteenth century, when the Khmers seem to have been overwhelmed by their neighbors to the west—the Siamese. The disease known as the "Black Death" may have also played a role in the demise of the Khmer Empire. Scholars debate about whether or not Angkor Wat was abandoned, but in any case, Western civilization wasn't made aware of the temple until centuries later, when European explorers wrote about discovering a temple the likes of which the world had never seen. French explorer Henri Mouhot said about Angkor Wat: "One of these temples—a rival to that of Solomon, and erected by some ancient Michelangelo—might take an honorable place beside our most beautiful buildings. It is grander than anything left to us by Greece or Rome."

Q. At the end of your novel, you mention that some of the funds generated by Temple of a Thousand Faces *will be donated to the Jayavarman VII Children's Hospital. Why does this particular cause appeal to you?*

A. Cambodia is a beautiful country, but a poor one—a fact that often translates into malnourished and vulnerable children. According to a recent United Nations report, the mortality rate of children under five years old in Cambodia is about nine times higher than it is in the United States. Treatable illnesses such as tuberculosis, malaria, and dengue fever take a terrible toll.

The Jayavarman VII Children's Hospital is located in Siem Reap, just a few miles from Angkor Wat. I walked past the hospital many times and was always moved by what I saw. I was also deeply impressed by the local children, who gave me a warm welcome. Supporting them in return is important to me.

Q. Can you tell us about your next novel?

A. I'm in the midst of writing a story set at the Great Wall of China during the sixteenth century. The novel will highlight the Great Wall as well as a remarkable clash of cultures and will be loosely based on a famous Chinese legend.

QUESTIONS
FOR DISCUSSION

1. What was your overall reaction to the novel? What parts did you particularly enjoy?

2. Had you heard of Angkor Wat before reading *Temple of a Thousand Faces*? If so, what were your original impressions of the temple and how did they change, if at all, while reading the book?

3. Clearly John Shors tries to bring Angkor Wat and its surroundings to vivid life. Is he successful? Can you visualize the temple and the people?

4. Discuss how Jayavar and his wife Ajadevi complement each other. What abilities do they each bring to their partnership? What character weaknesses does each possess, and how does the other compensate for them?

5. Several of the major characters are powerfully influenced by their belief in reincarnation. Why do you think the author felt compelled to explore this belief?

6. Who do you think is the strongest character? Who starts out weak and becomes strong? Does anyone start out strong and become weak?

7. Discuss the villains. Do you prefer Indravarman or Po Rame? Who do you find more fearsome? More compelling?

8. If you were Voisanne, what would you do after the death of your family?

9. Do you think that works of historical fiction serve to make the world a smaller and perhaps a better place? Why or why not?

10. If you could write a sequel to *Temple of a Thousand Faces*, what would you have happen to the characters?